THE FACILITY

Book 1, The Breeder Files

About the Author

Eliza Green tried her hand at fashion designing, massage, painting, and even ghost hunting, before finding her love of writing. She often wonders if her desire to change the ending of a particular glittery vampire story steered her in that direction (it did). After earning her degree in marketing, Eliza went on to work in everything but marketing, but swears she uses it in everyday life, or so she tells her bank manager.

Born and raised in Dublin, Ireland, she lives there with her sci-fi loving, evil genius best friend. When not working on her next amazing science fiction adventure, you can find her reading, indulging in new food at an amazing restaurant or simply singing along to something with a half decent beat.

For a list of all available books, check out:

www.elizagreenbooks.com/books

BOOK 1 IN THE BREEDER FILES

THE FACILITY

ELIZA GREEN

Copyright © 2016 Eliza Green
Third edition (Updated from 2016 original)

The moral right of the author has been asserted in accordance with the Copyright, Designs and Patents Act 1988.

All rights reserved. No part of this publication may be reproduced, stored in a retrieval system, or transmitted, in any form or by any means, without the prior written permission of the author, nor be otherwise circulated in any form of binding or cover other than that in which it is published and without a similar condition being imposed on the subsequent purchaser.

All characters in this publication are fictitious and any resemblance to real persons, living or dead, is purely coincidental.

ISBN: 9798425650238

Cover by Deranged Doctor Design
Original Editors: Andrew Lowe and Rachel Small
Third Edition Editor: Nerd Girl Edits

To those who hated it when Panem forced tributes to compete against each other in a game-like scenario. Huh, less of you than I expected...

1

The ends of Carissa's long, white dress trailed on the dirty ground in a space not many other Copies visited. She hesitated by the entrance to the workshop filled with spare bellies, legs and tails attached to steel girders in the roof. A retractable roof, currently closed, dominated the center of the room. Three wolves in shutdown mode stared at her.

An old man in grease-covered overalls bent over the open body of a fully assembled wolf on a work table. The Collective ten called them 'Guardians', but the Inventor's term, 'wolves', was a more accurate description of the part-organic, mostly metal beasts.

The workshop had already turned the hem of her white dress gray. The Collective liked order and cleanliness but the Inventor said clothes were for getting dirty.

A pungent smell of oil and grease filled her nostrils. She pinched the end of her nose, waiting for the Inventor to notice her.

He bent in for a closer look. 'Sorry, boy. This is going to hurt a bit.'

He tweaked something in the wolf's belly. The wolf growled, deep and long.

The Facility

The Inventor patted its head. 'I've got to get you ready. That means connecting your voice box and your pain sensors. Almost done.'

The wolf lunged at the Inventor's arm. Carissa snatched at her throat in shock. With a hiss, the Inventor eased his bloody arm out of the jaws of the wolf.

She had warned him about treating the Guardians like pets; they were dangerous, even while under the Collective's directive: Copies must not be harmed.

Her shoe scuffed against the ground.

The Inventor looked up fast, hand on heart. 'Miss, you gave me a fright. How long have you been standing there?'

'Not long.' Carissa entered the room, keeping her eyes on the alert wolf, whose yellow gaze tracked her movements. 'Is it going to Arcis?'

'Yes. The Collective wants these four to supervise.'

'To keep the teenagers in line?'

The Inventor shrugged. 'I assume so.'

'How, when the teenagers are not,'—she chose her next words carefully—'in their right minds?'

'They'll feel enough to be wary.' The Inventor wiped his hands clean.

The wolf's pink tongue darted out to lick its metal lips. When its gaze fixed on Carissa, she pointed shakily at the beast. 'Has this one received its directive yet?'

'Yes, miss.' The Inventor looked down at the wolf. 'It won't, or can't harm you.'

With more confidence Carissa inched closer to the table. The wolf watched her silently. 'Do you think the rebellion is over now?'

The Inventor kept his gaze on the wolf. 'No.'

'Structure and protection—that's what the

townspeople need now.' The rebels had poisoned them. 'Essention and Arcis will give them that.'

The Inventor visibly stiffened. 'The Collective doesn't get it. A damn Arcis facility in the middle of some fake town will not protect anyone.'

'What will, Inventor? Their own kind tried to kill them.'

'The rebels aren't the problem, miss.' He jerked his hand up. 'This city is. The Collective's only solution is to lock people away.'

She would not have the Inventor speak ill of the Collective. They had been the only ones to rescue the adults from rebellion attacks.

Carissa lifted her chin. 'You should remember where you came from, Inventor.'

He sighed. 'I do, miss. Every day.'

'Should the Collective have left them in their towns to die?'

The Inventor concentrated on the wolf on his table. 'No, miss. But shipping them off to a monitored town like Essention is not the answer.'

The Inventor was an Original human; naturally his loyalties lay with the townspeople, possibly the rebels. But a bout of nerves almost tied her tongue.

She forced out her next question. 'Are you a rebel sympathizer?'

The Inventor flicked his gaze to her. 'Of course not.' He patted the wolf on its head. The wolf snarled at him. 'But forcing the townspeople to live in Essention—'

'—so they can get medical treatment.'

He sighed. 'I knew you wouldn't understand, miss. You're not like—'

'Like you? An Original?' The reminder hurt.

Around the Inventor she felt less like a Copy, more human.

'Well, yes, if you must know.'

She lifted her chin. 'No, Inventor. I'm better than an Original. I am an improved design.'

Quintus, the spokesperson for the Collective, contacted her through her communication disc.

'173-C. Please report to the Great Hall.'

She touched the disc embedded in her skull, just above her ear. 'Understood, Quintus.'

Carissa looked up at the Inventor.

He nodded. 'Tell the Collective the wolves will be ready by morning.'

She climbed the stairs beyond the workshop leading up and out and crossed a small courtyard to the Learning Center.

Her shoes clacked on the white tiles as she entered the Great Hall, a bright, white room with a matching podium set in front of a grid-like screen. She laid her palm flat on the podium and touched a second disc on the side of her head that connected to her brain. She shivered as the day's thoughts and memories passed from her cerebral unit into the podium. The screen shimmered and beeped to mark the transfer of the information.

In one corner of the screen, a shape morphed into a familiar face. The slightly distorted features, representing the Collective's many voices, depicted a dark-skinned male in his thirties.

'173-C. Has the Inventor finished with the four Guardians?'

'Yes, Quintus. He says they'll be ready by morning.'

'Good,' said Quintus.

Carissa felt him search through the upload of her latest memories.

On screen he frowned. 'It seems the Inventor is not as keen on our plans for the teenagers as you.'

'He is an Original, Quintus. He views things differently to us.'

'Will he be a problem?'

'No, Quintus. The Inventor wants to help us.'

'Do you believe he is a rebel sympathizer?'

Carissa answered truthfully. 'No, Quintus.'

'Good. We must ward off any planned attacks on Praesidium. This city must never fall into rebel hands.'

Quintus believed the teenagers who were destined for Arcis would help to uncover the rebels' secrets.

Through her communication disc, Carissa heard other members of the Collective speak: Septimus, Octavius, Unos.

'The teenagers are en route to Essention,' said Unos. 'They will be treated at the hospital first, to alleviate the conditions of the radiation poisoning. They will be allocated accommodation in Essention. Families together. It will help them to adapt.'

'What can we learn from the teenagers that we didn't from the adults before them?' said Octavius.

Septimus spoke. 'The adults were too rigid in their thinking, too loyal to the rebellion. The teenagers are still young enough to shape and mold.'

Carissa wondered how she'd feel if the Collective forced her to leave her home.

'And the rebels? Can they be reasoned with?' said Unos.

Quintus' voice took on a new edge. 'The rebels will kill whomever they must to get to us. We will rise above their attempts. We will protect those they have abandoned.'

'And we all agree we need the teenagers?' said Octavius.

'Yes.' said Quintus. 'They will be instrumental in our survival.'

2

The nine walkways connecting the two towers of Arcis rippled overhead, suspended in individual anti-gravity streams. Their faint purples, greens and yellows reminded Anya Macklin of a rainbow after heavy rainfall. An arboretum complete with fully grown trees stood in the middle of the tall room.

She looked around nervously at the bright, glass-filled atrium that stank of heavy disinfectant. Eleven others stood next to her, a mix of boys and girls who'd also been instructed to attend Arcis that morning. Other teenagers watched their new group quietly, having paused in their mopping the moment her excitable group had entered. Her cheeks reddened at the attention on her. She dipped her head, to hide behind her shoulder-length hair.

Only last week she and her brother had been sick. People from Praesidium had rescued them from their home, brought them to Essention and countered the effects of the poisoning at the hospital in the south of the town. If they hadn't shown up when they did, she and Jason might be dead. At seventeen, she fit the profile for Arcis' program, but Jason, nineteen, was too old. This temporary separation would be good for them. What happened on the outside had shaken them both.

Participants. That's what the wolf—one of four—called them when her group of twelve had shown up in the lobby. Anya had recoiled from the giant beast that came up to her shoulders in height. But her hazy thoughts muted the danger.

A short speech about education, order, cleanliness and obedience had followed.

Inside the atrium with its rippling walkways, eighteen teenagers—she counted—continued to stare at the newcomers. They looked on edge, as if something had just happened. Some of the participants looked disappointed. A boy with olive skin and brown dreadlocks appeared to be angry. Commotion overhead drew her eyes to the first-floor walkway. Several excited teenagers hurried across the unstable looking floor.

She moved farther inside the atrium with no obvious privacy. Later, she'd find a place just for her.

The more experienced dragged the newcomers around the room. The boy with the dreadlocks straightened up when he saw a girl—tall, tanned, pretty—who was part of Anya's group. Her name was Sheila, and she looked exactly like the girls who used to bully Anya at school.

The guy smiled at Sheila.

One of the wolves stalked among them, appraising her and the other new participants with narrowed, yellow eyes. Anya's skin hummed when its gaze lingered on her a moment. She realized her observations had set her apart from the others.

The wolf swept past her and to the back of the atrium. It disappeared behind an open shutter nestled in one wall. The shutter rolled shut, sending high-pitched squeals through the room. Both the olive-skinned boy and

Sheila covered their ears. Nobody else had noticed the wolf leave.

Excitement replaced the muted energy among the new participants. Sheila punched the guy's arm. *So they know each other.*

She heard them talking about something called rotation.

'How often do these rotations happen?' Sheila asked him.

'Every month,' said Dom.

'Without fail? Do they ever skip a month?' Sheila twirled a piece of hair around one finger, but the move had a nervous vibe to it.

'I don't know.'

Anya watched the boy for a moment. When he caught her looking, he whispered something to Sheila and walked over to her.

'Pay attention, I'm not going to repeat myself.' He strode past Anya without stopping.

She followed him over to a wall with several cleaning vestibules, her shoulders rounded, her eyes watching her feet.

He opened one. 'This is where we keep the mops and buckets.' He checked a roster on the wall beside the vestibule. 'Looks like you've been assigned Section Eight.'

He marched over to the other wall.

'This is where the garbage chutes are.' He pointed to the higher walkways. 'Anything that falls from up there should be thrown down here. Your dirty water gets chucked down the chute, too. The wolves like a clean space.'

A holographic grid marked out the different sections

on the floor. Her section of the grid had an orange border.

'Red means dirty. Green, clean. Orange, try harder. Got it?' he said.

Anya sighed and looked around. One wall made of glass looked to the North; she saw a criss-cross pattern of pipes in the distance. The fourth wall held the shutter into which the wolf had disappeared. There was a door to the left of the shutter.

She dragged her gaze back to the boy. 'What's the deal with the wolves?'

'Why?' He looked at her as though she'd just asked him to show her his underwear.

'I mean, what's their purpose?'

He laughed. It was a strange, detached sound. 'They supervise us. That's all.'

'So they just hang around while we, what, mop floors?'

The boy shrugged. 'Yeah, that's pretty much it.'

'Do they say anything?'

He seemed distracted, bored almost. 'They're here to supervise the ground-floor activity, that's all.' He looked over at another group being shown the ropes. 'I've got others to help out.' He turned back to Anya. His eyes lingered on her a moment too long. 'You clear on what you need to do?'

Anya nodded.

Ω

The morning turned into afternoon. Anya mopped her section, until the border changed from orange to green and her section smelled of disinfectant.

The boy with the dreadlocks stood in the section

next to hers. She counted twenty-two dark-brown spirals of snarled, thin-and-thick hair that hung just below his broad shoulders, all bunched together with a white elastic band. The other boys' hair was short and neat. This boy looked more like one of the rebels, scattered far and wide beyond Essention's walls. Her stomach heaved as she remembered snippets of her last moments with her parents.

Anya concentrated on the boy beside her. She thought about asking his name, but she didn't want to invite anyone in yet. Not today, when she felt okay, like what had happened to her parents had been someone else's fault. She would ride that safe feeling until the guilt devoured her again.

An hour later, the four wolves emerged from behind the shutter in the wall. The metallic clacking of nails against the white-tiled atrium floor filled the room. Seeing one was bad enough, but four together put Anya on alert. They stalked closer, eyes on the participants. Their movements were lithe and graceful for beasts covered in a metallic skin. Legs, long and spindly, sat on sharp, narrow nails. Each paw lifted and pressed with precision on the tiled floor.

Anya's alertness gave way to curiosity as she studied their movements. The beasts approached with their heads low; not submissive, but more like predators assessing a threat. Anya had heard rumors that the living machines from Praesidium were germophobes.

After a short while, the four wolves returned to their dark space and the shutter rolled down.

Her hands began to shake; a sign of hunger, and a symptom that had only started after her treatment for radiation poisoning.

She stopped at the outer glass wall and looked up at

the rainbow-colored walkways. Her hunger tugged her back to reality, as thoughts about her last night in Brookfield crept in. A camera was perched on one of the steel girders above the first-floor walkway. She adjusted her position until one of the railings blocked it from view.

Her new safe place.

Anya pulled an apple out of her overalls pocket and ate. Eating helped her to forget. It also reduced the shaking in her hands. A steady calm trickled through her that usually lasted until her next meal.

She startled when the boy with the dreadlocks appeared beside her. Anya shuffled to the side, to put distance between them, annoyed by his presence.

The boy shifted beside her while she ate. Before she could tell him to go away, he spoke.

'Hi, I'm Dom.'

Anya peered up at him. His easy smile didn't reach his deep-brown eyes and she wasn't buying his friendly act.

Dom shifted under her intense scrutiny, causing her to look down at the ground.

He elbowed her. 'This is the point where you tell me yours.'

'Anya.'

'How's your first day going?'

She almost laughed at the casual question. She shrugged and looked up at the camera.

'Did you know this is the only spot in the atrium where the cameras can't see you?'

He laughed as he answered. 'Yeah, actually. I was about to tell you to go somewhere else.'

She looked up at him. 'So why didn't you?'

'Because I saw you needed a moment.'

More than a moment, but it was enough for now.
'Thanks for letting me have it.' She put the rest of her apple away and walked back to her section.

3

The repetitive ground-floor tasks kept Anya's nightmares at bay. It comforted her to know the rebels couldn't breach the force field surrounding Arcis without a special chip, like the one in her wrist. After the rebels had killed most of the adults in their town, and followed up with a radiation attack, Jason had wanted to stay on in Brookfield. But the tainted water and food supply was killing them too fast.

They had both witnessed their parents' murder, several weeks ago. While the event had forced Jason to grow up, Anya had only regressed further into herself.

The rumors that rebel sympathizers were in Essention made Anya nervous. Maybe she should stay permanently in Arcis. The rebels had been looking for her the night her parents were killed. She expected they would come for her again.

The memories of that night punched her in her chest. She squeezed her eyes shut for as long as was bearable.

Seconds.
She counted.
The double-crack of thunder still rang in her ears.
Muffled crying.

Jason's.

She had been oddly silent.

Anya was to blame for her parents' death. The rebels had wanted *her*. That's why her mother had been so angry. She'd messed up.

Two short blasts snapped Anya out of her waking nightmare. She looked around to see the others were putting their mops away and walking fast from the atrium. Some flashed her an odd look as she remained stock still in Section Eight, clutching her mop handle so tight her knuckles had turned milky white.

Anya heaved the nightmare out in one long breath, put her mop away, and followed the others out.

She and Jason had never spoken about that last night. Some days it felt like he sympathized with the rebel cause. He'd told her about rumors that the towns were no longer contaminated, but she had no interest in checking.

She half-walked, half-ran to the female changing rooms, located off from the lobby in Tower A. She peeled off the all-in-one jumpsuit and pulled on her Essention uniform: a coffee-colored tunic and loose black trousers. If she had her choice, she would wear something blood red to match her mood.

The chatty mood in the cramped room tightened her skin. She grabbed her bag and strode out into the lobby. More memories of that last night surfaced. She steadied herself against the white podium near the door, where she had to log on and off using her chip. The wolf had shown them all how that morning. She pressed her wrist to it, but not fast enough, it seemed. Several of the girls flooded out of the changing room and into the lobby, laughing and joking.

'Hey,' said a girl with long, brown hair. 'You're

Anya, right?'

Anya nodded.

'We were just talking about what happened in the towns.' She lowered her voice. 'I mean, the attacks. It was awful, wasn't it?'

'I guess.'

The girl leaned in close. 'What happened to you? Marie said her mother and father were gunned down in the street. Thankfully she was at her friends' house at the time. But someone was looking for her, she said.'

The girl pulled back and Anya saw her pupils were heavily dilated—almost black.

'Everyone's stories in here seem to be the same,' the girl continued. 'But none of us actually saw it happen. Did you? Did you see who did this? Was it the rebels?'

Anya's carefully crafted mask slipped.

She whispered, 'I didn't see anything.'

The girl leaned in again. 'Come on, I'm not going to tell. I heard that you were there when it happened.'

Anya stepped back, her pulse racing. 'No... I didn't see anything.'

'Sure you did.' The girl persisted. She was strangely calm. Anya felt the opposite.

'Please, I need to go...'

The girls surrounded her, bombarded her with questions. Someone grabbed her arm and pulled her out of the group.

'Sorry, ladies,' said Dom, 'but Anya and I have plans to walk home.'

The smiling girls lost interest in Anya. It wasn't the first time today that the girls blushed whenever Dom was around.

He logged out and pulled her through the door

toward the force field that surrounded Arcis. It was 5pm, and an orange slant of light bisected the walkway to the front of the building. She shielded her eyes from the weakening light.

'Stop pulling me.'

They passed through the force field, which left her wrist tingling. Near the base of the Monorail station, he let go. In a haze of anger, she stomped toward the stairs that led to the raised platform. Dom followed her. She stopped abruptly at the start of the steps and turned.

'I don't need a bodyguard, Dom, so stop following me.'

He towered over her by several inches. Anger transformed his face.

'It just so happens that I'm going this way, so stop being a brat and thank me.'

Anya laughed. 'For what?'

'For rescuing you back there. I know what they were asking you about.'

'Yeah? Well I had it under control.' She noticed his eyes weren't as dilated as the girl's. They were brown and rich, and packed with secrets—none of which Anya wanted to know.

'So, why weren't you rotated the last time?'

Dom shrugged. 'I wasn't taking it seriously.'

'How does rotation work? Is everyone rotated eventually?'

'Not everyone gets off the ground floor. Sometimes you need a little... motivation.'

'Like what?'

'Just do what you're told and they'll notice you.'

'What does that mean?'

'It means just what I said.'

Dom's vague answer irritated her.

He continued. 'Well, the wolves have you in their sights now. If nothing else, that should work in your favor.'

'For what?' She pulled out a banana she'd been saving from the dining hall and took a bite.

'For rotation. You want to leave this place, don't you?'

The rebels lived outside Essention's walls. Arcis made her feel safe.

'Not really.'

'Let's see if you'll still be saying that in a few weeks.'

Her anger muted the sweet flavor of the banana; she shoved the rest of it back in her pocket.

She turned back to the stairs and climbed them. The sound of Dom's heavy steps told her he was close behind.

They stood on the platform in silence and waited for the train.

In the distance, the Monorail hovered on clear alloy girders that ran the circumference of the town, crossing at several points. A couple of girls giggled at Dom, making comments about his dreadlocks. He stared ahead and paid them no attention.

Arcis was the beating heart of Essention, its vast double towers and glass atrium surrounded by grass, flowers and foliage. The town was divided into four equal sections: East, South, West, and North. The water purification system stood to the North; she'd seen it from the atrium.

The train slid to a gentle halt, balanced on an anti-gravity stream similar to the walkways in the atrium. One of the nurses from the hospital had told her how the limited tech in the town worked.

Anya and Dom entered the same carriage. The packed conditions forced them to stand close. Dom pulled out a book from his bag and began to read.

Anya ground her teeth and stared out at Arcis.

With its giant mushroom cap and two towers, it loomed over the rest of the town. Tower A, with the lobby and elevators, was a solid structure the same height as the atrium but twice as wide. To the left, the windowless Tower B was even wider.

Anya's eyes lingered on the mushroom cap, which housed the ninth floor. To graduate from the training program the orphans had to reach this floor, carrying with them the lessons of the previous eight. The ninth floor held a mild curiosity for her, but with the rebels still a threat, she was in no hurry to reach it and be released from this safe place.

Anya's stop approached, but Dom didn't move. His gaze was on the book in his hand. His mouth was set in a tight line.

She assessed him—a potential ally.

The door slid open and Anya leaned into him quickly. He looked up at her, surprised.

'Thanks for rescuing me,' she said.

His mouth softened slightly as she alighted from the train.

4

East Essention, where the orphans lived, lacked personality. The neat, gray apartment blocks looked like they'd been created from a mold. Each unit was identifiable by a silver door and one block ran for a kilometer in each direction. The ground-floor units opened out directly into the street. Access to the upper levels was by stairs. The rear of the block was pressed up against the tall, inner perimeter wall. Two feet of space existed between inner and outer, the latter with the guns and sensors.

Anya dropped her backpack on the cold, gray hall floor with a shiver, still not used to the apartment that felt too sterile and functional to be a home. She passed by the black-and-white living room that looked like something lifted straight out of a catalog. Anya preferred the worn, red sofa and warm, wooden floors of their cottage in Brookfield—even if those floors were now covered in blood.

An earthy smell caught her. She followed her nose to the black-and-white kitchen to find Jason standing over a bubbling pot. He looked up when she came in.

'So, how goes the program to teach you... What is it

for again?'

She walked over to him and peered into the pot. Her stomach grumbled. 'To teach life skills, apparently.'

'I'm making soup. And there's a loaf of bread. We're not supposed to take the leftover vegetables, but Max said they were only going to be thrown out. They weren't injected with anti-radiation medication, so they won't affect our dosage.'

Jason had been put to work in one of the food processing factories in Southwest Essention.

He looked at her. His eyes were partially dilated, less than those in Arcis. Anya assumed the degree of dilation depended on the dose of anti-radiation medication in the body. Some probably needed more.

She inhaled the delicious smell. The medicated food in Arcis had a sickly flavor and barely any smell. 'I miss our food from Brookfield. Everything's the same in Arcis...'

'Well, this will make a nice change then.'

'Won't you get into trouble?' Food in Essention was strictly controlled.

'Max says it's okay to take anything marked as defective. He says he'd rather feed the defects to stray dogs than throw good food away. The machines don't tolerate anything less than perfection.'

The wolves—part machine, part organic—came to mind. Were they really germophobes or just perfectionists? Today, they had obsessed over the cleanliness of the floor.

She grinned and ruffled his light-brown hair, which was long enough to fall into his eyes.

He groaned. 'Get off, sis.'

She'd almost forgotten why they were in Essention.

But then the memories came flooding back and took her smile away.

'Just because they aren't here doesn't mean we should stop living,' said Jason, eyeing her.

His eyes were light blue, speckled with darker blue flecks, even with the dilation. The same color as their father's. Anya hated her dark-blue eyes, ringed with lighter blue flecks. Like Grace's.

'We're not the only ones without family here,' said Jason. 'What about the others in Arcis?'

'I'm doing fine on my own.'

He opened the cupboard and took down two bowls. 'Maybe Arcis will help you to control your anxiety.'

Her anger caught her by surprise. Anya turned away and pressed a hand to her chest.

Maybe it was just hunger. She always felt better after eating. Everything made sense with food in her belly.

She was fine. She could cope.

A painful memory slammed into her mind.

A dull thud caught Anya by surprise.

'Who's there?' said Grace, her mother. There was no answer.

Her father took two steps to the door.

A second thud sounded like a jackhammer. She absorbed her parents' fear as if it were her own.

Grace whispered. 'It's them, Evan. They've finally come for her.'

Her father's fingers grazed the door's handle.

'Don't answer it, please.'

'I have to, Grace, love. They'll only keep coming back until I do.'

Grace liked dramatics. But it worried Anya to see

her father worked up. Anya cut her eyes to Jason. His shrug did nothing to soothe her.

'They're here for her.' Grace pointed at Anya. 'She needs to leave, now.'

Her mother's coldness deflated Anya. Grace made no secret that she preferred Jason. And now the rebels were here to take her.

She bit her lip and stood up.

A hand on her shoulder surprised her. She looked up into her father's warm eyes.

'Anya, I need you to hide.'

'Who's coming for me?'

His hand felt too heavy to be comforting. He steered her to her bedroom.

'What about Jason?'

The third knock was heavier, as though it had been made with a fist. Anya's eyes flicked over to the door.

Grace was glaring at her. 'Get rid of her. Now, Evan.'

'Yeah, I'm going,' she shouted at her mother.

Her father grabbed one of the wooden legs on her bed and pulled.

'Help me, Anya.'

She tugged on the other leg. Their combined efforts revealed the bottom half of the wall, clad in strips of varnished pine.

Evan loosened a large section of paneling. There was a small air vent at the bottom, and the gap between the walls was clean and dry.

Thump, thump, thump.

'Open up or we're coming in.'

He pushed down on her shoulders. 'Get in.'

'What about Jason?'

'He can look after himself.'

'So can I, Dad. Please, let me help.'

'Your mother and I need you to do this.'

Anya's stomach flipped at the thought of helping Grace. But she trusted her father.

She squeezed into the wall space she remembered being bigger when she was younger. Evan replaced the panel, and she lay down with her face near the air gap as he moved the bed back into position.

He dashed out of the room but left the door open. Through the gap she could see the base of the front door and her mother's stockinged feet.

Her father opened the door. Two sets of male feet entered and lingered near the sofa. The men wore black trousers and black leather shoes. Sturdy, practical.

'I'm so sorry. We didn't hear—'

'Where is she?' said one of the men.

Grace forced a laugh. 'Who?'

'The girl.'

'Oh,' her father said, as if surprised. 'She's not here.'

'Hand her over and you get to live today,' said the second man. He idled near the door, by the sideboard with a collection of framed photos, including a family group shot featuring Anya.

'It's the right house,' said the second man.

The first man pushed past Grace.

'I told you she's not here.'

Grace blocked the path of the second man. He pushed her to the side causing her to stumble. The man moved farther into the room, out of Anya's view.

'You can't take her,' said Grace. 'She's matched and useless.'

Useless. That one word punched the air out of Anya's lungs.

A sudden shriek sounded, followed by a loud thud. Grace slumped to the floor. A scream bubbled in Anya's throat. She clamped a hand over her mouth.

Her father rushed to Grace's side. Anya remained as still as possible. Her body flooded with cold, shivering fear.

One of the men grabbed her father and pulled him up.

'Please,' he said. 'We're telling you the truth.'

A dull *clunk* followed and her father dropped to his knees.

'Stop it! Don't hurt them,' said Jason.

Anya couldn't see her brother.

Anya pushed against the paneling. Evan flashed her a warning look not to move.

The first stranger hovered over her stricken parents. 'I won't ask again.'

'She... left with her friends this morning,' said Evan.

'Which friends?'

'I don't know. From school.'

'You're lying.'

'Please. We're begging you. She's matched.' Matching her with another boy was all Grace talked about these days and something Anya refused to accept.

Anya pushed against the false wall again, but the bed was wedged up against it. Jason's voice became muffled. She stopped pushing and held her breath. Two pairs of feet, one resisting, blocked her view of the living room. The second man searched her bedroom with Jason in tow, before moving back to the living room.

'No!' said her father. 'Please. Leave the boy alone. I

can explain...'

'You're wasting our time.'

A double-crack sounded. Anya blinked and her parents slumped forward. She blinked again and the two men left. Ruby-red blood snaked along the worn wooden floor toward her room.

She blinked a third time. Jason was on his knees, shaking Grace, and then their father. He lifted his hands that now glistened red.

Anya's throat tightened. The ringing in her ears persisted as she pushed against the panel. She crawled out of the wall space and stumbled to the edge of the sofa.

Both her parents lay motionless on the floor.

Shock froze her to the spot.

'Are they okay?' she whispered.

Jason shot her a hard look. 'It's your fault.' His bloodshot eyes matched the color of his hands.

More gunfire outside. The ringing in her ears muffled the cries of their next victims.

Salty tears tightened the skin on her face. Tiny drops of blood slithered down her arm from where she had dug her fingernails into the skin.

Anya coughed when some of the soup went down the wrong way. She didn't remember sitting down.

Across the dinner table, Jason gave her a familiar scolding look. After that night, both traits of their parents had emerged in him: the strong, kind energy of their father; the nervous, overcritical energy of their mother.

When she finished, she said, 'Thanks for the soup and the bread.'

He shrugged and raked his fingers through his hair. 'It was nothing special.'

The word 'special' caught her attention. She cupped her mouth as she realized. 'It's your birthday.'

Jason stood up quickly. 'It doesn't matter.' He picked up the bowls and carried them to the sink.

'Happy birthday,' she said softly.

'Birthdays aren't important anymore. We're safe. That's all that matters.'

Without a glance at her he left the room. She retrieved her backpack, and substituted a wedge of Jason's bread for her mostly uneaten lunch sandwich, which she tossed on the table. She wasn't supposed to bring outside food into Arcis, but what the cameras couldn't see...

Tomorrow, she would look for something special in the dining hall. A small gift for Jason to mark the birthday he was keen to forget.

5

Happy birthday. He laughed. For Jason, getting older meant the start of something scary.

He'd just turned twenty, but he was no adult, and Anya was too young to go it alone. He realized now that Grace had been hard on her for a reason. The world was dangerous, the rebellion even more so. Grace had been trying to toughen her up.

But his mother's reasons for matching Anya with a boy confused him. When he'd asked his father about the archaic practice, Evan had said it was to keep the young off the radar of some very bad people. The rebels, Jason assumed.

He hoped Arcis would help Anya acclimate to her new orphan status. At least one of them would get something out of it. His eyes grazed the large gate in the distance—the only way out of Essention.

This town was not new. Months before the radiation attack on their town, Essention had appeared overnight. In the beginning, Praesidium had used it to showcase new technology to the townspeople. Jason had tried to get in, but only adults had been allowed inside.

He adjusted the strap on his backpack, containing a

portion of soup he'd made last night, and a wedge of bread. His fingers touched the smooth concrete wall that divided the town into quadrants. His sensible black shoes padded along the gray-bricked street leading to the Monorail. Teenagers rushed past him, dressed in similar brown tunics and black trousers to his.

While he walked, he ate the rest of the sandwich that Anya had left on the table. He hated the sweetness of medicated food, but it was heaven compared to the sickness after a blast of radiation contaminated Brookfield. He thought he'd never get his appetite back.

His lips puckered as he finished the rest of the over-medicated sandwich. The drug muddied his thoughts too much. Max had been keeping back some non-medicated rations for him to eat.

Jason climbed the stairs to the train platform. The Monorail approached and Jason jostled for space on board the packed train. It stopped at Arcis first, before running north over the water purification plants.

The train pitched to the right and headed south where plastic-covered vertical farms and the hospital was. Scanners and orbs were the most active in this area. Patients with sunken eyes stood with their hands and faces pressed up against the hospital windows. The train passed overhead. Their pleading stares of help sent a chill through him. New patients had the worst skin lesions. Not that long ago he'd stood at that very wall.

Jason got off at Southwest and followed the inner perimeter wall to Essention's two food factories. The paved road carried on past the buildings to a residential area with rows of bungalows. In contrast to the new builds where he and Anya lived, the bungalows here had been part of a town once. There were even gardens and footpaths. Essention had been built around whatever town had existed in this region.

Scanners were perched on high wires above him. He walked through the blue light of their scan and his wrist tingled. His chip differed to Anya's; for one, he couldn't get inside Arcis.

Two factories came into view. He entered the second factory through a rear door. Co-workers were pulling on royal-blue overalls and hygiene gloves. Jason stored his backpack in one of the lockers and got to work.

The food from the vertical farms arrived in bright, shiny metal boxes packed in a germ-free protective atmosphere. The workers spent the morning unpacking the products that were ready to feed into the machines.

A man in his forties with a buzz cut entered the floor, followed by a second, older man. Max Roberts, manager, and his father, Charlie.

The pair spoke in hushed tones as they watched over the four giant machines from a raised platform. Jason found himself drawn to their secrecy. Broad-shouldered and slightly taller than Jason at five foot eleven, Max was imposing, even in his factory overalls.

Jason concentrated on the meat labeled 'chicken'. He picked up the slimy block—about a foot long by a foot wide—and released it into the back of one of the machines. This prompted the machine to add the clear liquid medication. Jason added flour substitute and liquid stock to the mix, designed to make the meat go further. He stocked individually sized containers at the other end of the machine. The machine pulverized the meat and squeezed it out into little pots, intended for Arcis.

In another section, workers unpacked fresh fruit. A team of workers manually injected each piece with the anti-radiation drug. Essention's orders.

The room was quiet enough that Jason could hear whispering. He looked over at Charlie and Max. Max stood straight with his arms folded and a deep frown on his face. Charlie, with graying hair and bright-blue eyes, stood beside him, sporting a similar look of concern.

Lunchtime came around, and Jason sat in the room next to the factory floor. Max surprised him by sitting down at his table.

Jason offered him what remained of the soup. Max shook his head and folded his arms on the table.

'You're from Brookfield, right?'

Jason nodded.

'Have you given any thought to your old town?'

'Every day. But there's nothing to go home to right now.'

Max leaned forward. 'What if I told you I've seen evidence of crop revival?'

'I thought that was just a rumor. And you must have been on the outside.'

'Not me, but friends have seen it.'

The rebels came to mind. 'There's nobody out there, except—'

Max looked around him. 'Stay back after work. Charlie and I have something to propose to you.'

He glanced at the apple in Jason's hand.

'You've been taking your rations from the food in the back?'

'Yeah, never from the floor.'

'Good. It tastes better, anyway.' Max stood up. 'After work.'

Ω

Jason changed and waited by the lockers for Max after his shift. His stomach fluttered as he hoisted his backpack over his shoulder.

Surely a month wasn't long enough for radiation to dissipate and crops to grow again. And why was he the only one being asked to stay back?

The door to the factory floor opened. Max swept past Jason as if he wasn't there. He removed a flat black screen from a cradle on the wall. It hissed and crackled as Max slapped his finger on its flat front. The screen, donated from Praesidium, was glitchy wires, processors and chips. The kids from the towns referred to the old tech as 'the white city's hand-me-downs'. Jason understood Praesidium had tech far more advanced than what the towns saw.

Max hit the screen a few more times, then appeared to give up. He put it back into its recharging holder.

'Come with me.'

Jason followed him outside. 'Where are we going?'

Max took long strides toward the bungalows. 'I'm taking you home.'

Half a kilometer away, four neat rows of bungalows followed the curve of Essention's perimeter wall. The rest of Essention was occupied by adults—too old for Arcis—who had managed to evade the rebel attack, or had already been in the town it was created from.

Jason followed Max to a gray-bricked bungalow with a black roof, four windows to the front and a faded-green door. Max unlocked the door and Jason followed him inside.

Before he could ask what was going on, Max removed a smooth metal pipe with three small holes from his coat pocket. He waved the device over Jason's wrist. A faint-blue light lit up his skin.

'Why are you scanning me?'

'I'm temporarily disrupting your location. You're not supposed to be here.' He gestured to the next room.

Jason entered a living room with a green sofa and two matching chairs. A bright green-and-red rug covered the wooden floor. The walls were painted in warm ochre with wood paneling on the bottom half. Charlie Roberts sat hunched over in one of the chairs, shining a torch at something in his hand. Family photos adorned one wall. Neither Max nor Charlie was in any of them.

'I'm glad you decided to come, Jason.' Charlie gestured to the sofa. 'Please sit.'

Jason did, dried his sweaty palms on his trousers.

'Why am I here?'

Max sat down beside him. 'We've been watching you for a while. You know your way around electronics.'

'Yeah, it was my skill at school.'

With a sigh, Charlie removed his glasses. 'We believe the towns are no longer contaminated, and we want volunteers to help verify that. We need experts like you to help us improve our equipment—soil sample analyses, Geiger counters to measure radiation levels, whatever we need. So we can keep a better eye on what's going on out there.'

Jason flicked his gaze between Charlie and Max. 'Have you asked those who run Essention about it?'

'Absolutely not,' Max snapped.

'I'm sure they'd let us leave to check. They only want what's best for us.'

Charlie stood up and paced the room. 'Come on, Max, he's not ready.'

Jason looked between the pair. 'Not ready for what?'

'He will be. Give me a minute with him, Dad,' said Max.

Charlie stopped pacing and sat down.

Max turned to Jason. 'The machines in this town are part organic. They're afraid of two things: the rebels and contamination getting inside the town. If we ask to leave, they will freak out. We just want to take a quick look around and be back before we're missed.'

It sounded reasonable, but was out there better than Essention?

'What about the rebels? Are they still operating out there?' Jason asked.

'Their numbers are small, and there's no sign of them in the towns. They won't expect us to go back there. And before you ask, no, we're not working with them.'

'You've wondered about the outside, haven't you?' said Charlie. His smile was faint, like he'd lived a thousand lives, dealt with a thousand problems and was done with it all. 'Most scientifically minded people have. It's a problem with you intellects. You always need something to solve.'

'Yeah, sure, I've wondered. I still don't understand why we can't tell the operators of Essention.'

Charlie grabbed the torch next to him and stood up. Before Jason could move he was shining a light into his eyes. He flicked the light away. 'He's still under their influence. See how quickly he sides with them? We need to counteract the effects permanently. Talking won't work.'

Jason frowned. '*Influence?* What are you talking about?'

Max left the room and returned with a syringe and a vial. He sat next to him and stuck the needle into the vial.

Jason drew back. 'What's that for?'

The syringe filled with orange liquid. Max grabbed Jason's arm. Jason tried to twist out of his grip, but he was too strong.

'What are you doing?'

'Please stay calm. It's an antidote.'

'To what?'

'To the drug they put in the food and water supply. The smallest amount can stay in the body for several days. Every time you eat you're simply topping it up.'

Jason didn't understand. 'It's just anti-radiation medicine. You said so yourself.'

'It's much more serious than that,' said Charlie. 'It puts you in a trance. You believe everything you're being told. Without question.'

Jason shrank back as Max came at him with the needle. But Max, stronger than him, jabbed the needle into his upper arm. He pushed the plunger.

Jason's head swam. His body swayed. 'What did you give me?'

'Essention is drugging us,' said Max. 'We call it "Compliance". It calms your most active thoughts and nerves. It also suppresses anger. Your willingness to believe everything you're told about this place is also one of the side effects. We've given you something to make you immune to its effects. It should kick in soon. What you'll feel is a concentration of everything you've had suppressed.'

A tingle started in Jason's hands. The heavy veil clouding his mind lifted. It unleashed a surprising anger.

'What did you give me?' He stood up too fast, an

action that caused his heart to pound. Through clenched teeth he said, 'Why do I want to punch something really hard?'

Max jumped up and steadied him with his hand. Jason tried to focus, but the room refused to slow down.

'Take a deep breath. The drug fogs up your emotions. You don't notice their absence until the fog has lifted. The anger will dissipate soon and you should feel like your old self in a few hours. You'll also see things a lot clearer.'

The rage bubbled and boiled. Jason made two fists.

'Is that why you told us to take our rations from the back?'

Charlie nodded. 'Even with the clean food the drug stays in the system. Your hands shake. Your eyes remain dilated. But over time, and with a controlled diet, the effects can be weakened. The antidote works instantly, but I've only been able to get my hands on a few vials. We've had to be selective about who gets the treatment. Compliance should no longer affect you, even if you accidentally eat contaminated food or drink. And don't panic if you notice your eyes are still a little dilated. The antidote is designed to fool those who run Essention.'

The room still spun, but slower than before.

'Is that why I'm here? To be cured?'

'Partly,' said Max. 'There's something in the basement I want to show you, after you've calmed down.'

'I'm calm.' He drew in a shaky breath, feeling far from it. 'You'd better tell me something *damn* specific, Max, or I swear I'm out of here.'

'We're digging a tunnel,' Max said quickly. 'It's how we're going to escape Essention.'

6

Nearly a month had passed since Anya entered Arcis and she still stared at the same rainbow-colored walkways, trying to block out the bad thoughts.

Her hands shook; it had been a couple of hours since she'd eaten something. Now, the bad thoughts were returning with a vengeance. She couldn't explain why, but the anti-radiation medication kept everything at bay for longer.

A door slammed overhead, cutting into her waking nightmare. Her thoughts dissipated like wisps of smoke. A young man ran across the first-floor walkway. She'd been trying to figure out the reason for the faster tempo one floor up, so different from the leisurely pace on the ground floor when the wolves weren't around.

The young man disappeared and the smoke reformed.

Anya sucked in a lungful of atrium air and squeezed her eyes shut. She gripped the mop handle harder.

A thunderous bell signaled lunchtime. She hurried to the dining room, located to the left of the wolves' den. Anya picked up a tray and selected a sandwich, a banana and a bottle of water. Four weeks ago, she'd left a piece of cheese for Jason on the kitchen table, to mark his birthday. She'd barely seen him since then. Late nights at the factory.

Anya recorded her food selection on her chip, then sat in one of the rows of white tables and benches. Sheila, the tall, tanned friend of Dom's, passed by her table with her food, laughing loudly at something a girl in her group had said. The sound of Sheila's fake laughter made Anya want to vomit.

Dom slid into the seat opposite Anya. He'd been joining her for lunch on and off, never talking, just eating. Anya unwrapped her sandwich and took a bite.

She eyed the mysterious boy with the dreadlocks who appeared to be searching for something inside the dining hall.

'How long have you been in Arcis?'

Her question dragged his eyes away from his search. 'Nearly eight weeks.'

'How long did it take for your dreadlocks to grow?'

'Hmm?'

'Your hair. How long?' It wasn't that she cared, but idle conversation kept her mind off other things.

His eyes finally settled on hers. They were a nice shade of brown: warm and kind of mysterious.

'A year. Why?'

This time last year the rebels weren't a threat and everyone lived peacefully in the towns. Six months later Essention had appeared. Six weeks ago, the rebels had killed her parents.

She shrugged. 'The other boys all have the same short cut. Why don't you?'

'I don't like to be a sheep.'

'Forget it. I was just making conversation.' She

stared at her sandwich.

Dom sighed. '*Fine*, what town are you from?'

His gaze was softer, curious.

'Brookfield. You?'

'A place called Foxrush.'

'Were your parents killed by the rebels?' she whispered.

He looked away briefly. 'No. Yours?'

'Yes.'

'That must have been a shock.'

'I was hiding.'

Dom brushed his fingers over the tops of her hands. Startled, she pulled them back.

He retracted his hand and his mask went back up. 'You need to rotate. You should prepare now.'

'I don't want to rotate.'

Dom slammed his bottle down. 'This isn't a game, Anya.'

'I understand what rotation means. I'm not ready to move on.'

He sneered and took a bite from his sandwich.

'What's so funny?'

He put his food down and moved closer. She examined his eyes that were never quite as black as the other participants' after they'd eaten. 'The rest of them, they act like a bunch of kids and blindly follow orders. But not you.'

She frowned. She thought that was exactly what she did.

Dom continued. 'You watch the wolves, study them. You seem interested in what they're about. But then you pretend like this place is a joke, like you don't care about progressing.' He leaned back and ate some more.

'It's not a joke and I do care. It's just... not the right time.'

'You're happy to stay where you are, and that's dangerous.'

Dom stood up and jerked his tray off the table. He stalked off before she could reply. Anya watched as he dropped his tray back at the food counter on the way out.

Their fight had drawn the attention of the other participants. Anya gripped her sandwich so tightly, her fingers touched through the thin slices of bread.

A couple of girls giggled.

Her face burned with the attention on her.

Sheila called over. 'Hey, Anya. What the hell did you say to him?'

Anya ignored her. Sheila huffed and followed him out.

She made a fist under the table and tried to focus on something else. But what she really needed was air.

Outside, the sun warmed her pale skin and soothed her anger. She dropped onto the grass, closed her eyes and tilted her head up. Before she knew it, the siren sounded for the end of lunch.

Back in the atrium, her step slowed. Waiting for them were the four wolves. Dom was alert, standing in an almost military-like pose, his hands behind his back.

Anya slipped into line with the other participants. The mood was light and jovial among those who'd started with her. She couldn't muster up the same enthusiasm.

The lead wolf scraped the floor with its nails. The sound rattled her teeth, but it worked to kill the chatter.

'Participants, rotation is imminent,' the lead wolf said in a synthetic voice.

A frazzled looking girl and boy appeared on the

first-floor walkway. A different voice boomed through the atrium's communication system.

'All participants on the walkways please report to your supervisors immediately.'

The excited pair ran to Tower A, their ill-fitting shoes slapping against the walkway.

Sheila stood beside Dom.

Anya looked at the others caught up in a mix of emotions: from excitement to anxiety, from apathy to curiosity. A boy with shaking hands smiled.

'Jack, Emily, Fiona, Sheila and Dom,' the wolf called out. Another seven names followed. 'You twelve will be rotated to the first floor. Please follow me immediately.'

Dom released a long, quiet breath. Sheila squealed and threw her arms around him. She looked at Anya and, almost as an afterthought, buried her face in his neck. The others who were rotating hugged each other. Not everyone looked happy.

She wanted to walk over to congratulate Dom, but her legs wouldn't work.

The wolf moved toward the lobby.

Dom unzipped the top half of his gray jumpsuit and pulled his arms out of the sleeves. Underneath, he wore a white T-shirt that showed off his lean, muscular contours. The other girls giggled at Dom's show of defiance, but Anya stared at him for a different reason. Dom looked too old for the program.

The announcement left her feeling conflicted. Her only friend was leaving, but so was the annoying Sheila.

She picked up her mop, hoping the hard work would dull the pain in her chest.

Several minutes later, new laughter and excitement

echoed through the atrium, as participants on the floors above adjusted to their new schedules. She watched the first floor, anxious to catch a glimpse of Dom one last time, to say goodbye. Three girls and two boys appeared on the walkway. They wore blouses, shirts, skirts and trousers, none of which fit them. They crossed to Tower B.

Then Anya spotted Dom. He hastily fixed a clip-on tie around the neck of his too-big shirt as he walked. His dreadlocked hair hung loose around his shoulders. He looked down at her; Anya's heart soared. Would she see him again? Not if she didn't rotate. The idea of rejoining society terrified her. But losing her only friend in this place scared her more.

Dom pushed his snarled hair off his face and secured it with an elastic band.

'Keep moving forward, Anya.'

A small skirmish sounded above her. Dom visibly tensed. She looked up.

What she saw sent a sharp chill through her.

7

The laughter died away.

Several screams bounced around the atrium as a dark-haired object hit the floor with a sickening thud.

Anya's scream came out as a frightened squeak. Her gaze shot to Dom. She caught the quick glance he traded with Sheila, before he pulled her off the walkway and into Tower B. A second body hit the floor. The sound of bones breaking yanked Anya back to the present.

She screamed for real.

Some of the experienced participants ran to cleaning vestibules to get mops. A girl of about eighteen approached a frozen Anya.

'Here.' She handed Anya a pan and mop. 'You'll need this to clean up.'

Clean up? Anya's gut stirred. She turned and vomited on the floor.

'You'll get used to it. Trust me,' said the girl.

Anya wiped her mouth on her sleeve. Why would she want to get used to this?

The girl pointed down at her lunch. 'Deal with your mess first, then get to work.'

'Wh... what happened?'

'The upper walkways sway more than the lower ones, or something. One wrong move and you're over the edge.'

The two dead bodies teased the edge of her vision. Anya swallowed back another round of discomfort, got to her knees and cleaned up her lunch. She delayed her walk back to her section, hoping someone else had already dealt with it.

Other shocked participants swished red-stained mops close to where the bodies had fallen. Breathing sharply, she flicked her gaze over to where the bodies lay. One was a boy around seventeen; the other a girl whose age she couldn't pinpoint because of her caved-in face.

The boy had hit her section. The flat, warm air flushed her cheeks. She sank to her knees beside his broken body, as if her legs no longer worked.

The shutter rolled up and a single wolf emerged. A second wolf followed pushing an anti-gravity stretcher with its nose and aimed it for one of the bodies.

'Pick up the body and carry it to the stretcher,' said the first wolf.

Anya got to her feet; two other participants helped her to pick up the girl. As she pulled upwards, the girl's head rolled back.

A scream bubbled in her throat. Anya turned her face away as she and the pair carried her to the stretcher. Another stretcher waited, close to where the second body had fallen.

Her blood-covered hands reminded Anya of Jason's, when he'd cradled their dead parents in his arms. She worked through blurred vision to clean the floor fast. When she was done, all traces of blood were gone, except from her hands.

She scrubbed them in the bathroom sink until they were flushed and raw, and rinsed the knees of her uniform underneath the water. No amount of soap in the world could erase the memory of today.

Ω

On autopilot, Anya changed into her brown tunic and black trousers. She placed her bloodstained uniform in her backpack, folded in a way so the stains didn't touch the inside of her bag.

She logged out and saw Dom up ahead, making his way toward the Monorail. Sheila was with him. Dom's cool reaction to the suicides still bothered her.

She climbed the stairs to the platform, keeping away from the pair. The train pulled up. Anya climbed on a different carriage. The train glided above rooftops, moving toward the perimeter. When it reached her stop at East Essention Anya stayed on board.

Only three stops remained in East. When the last one neared, she worked her way to the door, ready to alight. She spotted Sheila on the platform, but not Dom. Anya frowned and stepped back into the carriage.

The train passed through the southern part of Essention, near the hospital and the vertical food farms. She kept watch for Dom but he didn't get off.

When the train reached Southwest she finally saw him, his backpack slung over his shoulder, his dreadlocks hanging loose around his face. Anya followed at a safe distance, head up, pretending she belonged in this part of the city.

Dom moved fast from the platform to street level, forcing Anya to jog to keep up. He slipped through a crowd of people who'd gathered at the base of the stairs.

Dom passed the food processing factories on the right, heading for the residential area at the end of the road. Anya looked up at Arcis' scanners, perched high on wires which criss-crossed the city. They scanned at certain times of the day. She'd make sure to return to East before the next scheduled scan, two hours from now.

Beneath the stilts of the Monorail a train hummed overhead. Anya kept to the shadows.

Dom slipped between two bungalows, one with a faded-green door.

She followed him and heard voices to the rear of the house. When she heard a door slam shut and the voices vanish, she crept to the back of the house. A single light from the kitchen brightened the garden. Gentle laughter drifted through the wooden door.

Bushes as tall as her camouflaged the back of the house. She noted the tree stump at foot height with an empty can in the center, and an upturned plastic chair and table.

She crouched beneath the worn and peeling window frame. Her pulse pounded, but it was too late to turn back now. Dom and his odd behaviour had forced her to do this. The laughter inside gave way to murmurs. She lifted her head up. Slowly. Dom and an older man with gray hair were in the kitchen.

Dom was sitting in a chair. The man pulled a pair of scissors out a drawer.

'You have to go deeper. You need to blend in more.'

Dom sighed. 'I know.'

Her fingers gripped the worn edge of the window.

The man held the scissors up to the light. 'You

could have done this yourself.'

Dom laughed. 'No I couldn't.'

'Are you sure about this?'

He nodded. 'You're the only one I trust to do it right.'

The man pulled out one of Dom's twisted locks and cut it off at the base, then handed it to him. Anya squeaked, then covered her mouth. The next dreadlock fell to the floor, and the next, until all of them had been cut off.

Dom grimaced when he looked in the mirror. 'It'll take some getting used to this.'

Why would Dom grow dreadlocks for a year only to cut them off?

Her foot knocked against the tree stump, rattling the tin can. Anya cursed and groped for it, then cursed again when it clattered to the ground.

'Stay here,' the man hissed.

She stumbled in her hasty efforts to flee. She shouldn't have come.

But she had no choice.

She raced through the narrow gap between the houses, down the street, along the edge of the inner wall, past the food processing plants, past the closest Monorail station. She turned right when the inner wall opened up. Her lungs burned as she hid in a dark corner. She saw no sign of the older man or Dom.

She staggered, breathless, to the next Monorail station.

Blend in, go deeper. What did that mean? Were there really rebels in Essention?

Ω

The sound of running water greeted her when she opened the door. She found Jason in the bathroom with the tap on and his hands—bloody and dirty—in the sink.

'What happened?'

He looked up sharply. 'Crap, where did you come from?'

'I just got home.' Anya stayed by the door.

Jason tried to hide his hands from her, but then gave up and continued to wash them. His knuckles were scratched and raw.

'Have you been fighting?'

'It's nothing. There was... an accident at work. I scraped my hands trying to help him.'

She pointed to his fingernails caked with dirt. 'There's dirt on the factory floor now?'

'Max, uh, asked me to help out in the food farm after. Didn't have time to wash my hands.' When Jason finally looked at her, it felt like an afterthought.

'What's going on? You can talk to me.'

'It's nothing, Anya. Just leave it.'

She glared at the boy who'd become secretive over the last four weeks.

'Are you in trouble?'

'No.'

He continued to wash his hands.

She was in no mood for a fight. Her eyes drooped from exhaustion. Her muscles ached from lifting strangers onto stretchers.

Jason lifted his brows. 'Was there something else? I need to get on with this.'

Her lips thinned. 'No.'

'I've left some of my rations on the table. Take

them with you tomorrow.'

'I don't need the food, Jason. Arcis feeds me.'

'I know, but please take the food. And when you can, swap it for the rations they give you.' When she didn't respond Jason said, 'Just do what I ask, Anya.' He placed one wet hand on the door.

'Fine.'

'Good.'

Jason flicked the door closed.

Anya pressed her ear to the door for a moment, then went to her room.

She plopped down onto the bed and stared up at the ceiling. Memories of her family on their last night together slipped in and threatened her fragile peace.

Maybe I should have died that night. Then everyone would be safe.

She was a loose end. The rebels could still come for her.

To keep Jason safe she had to play it smart.

Her hunger trickled back, making her hands shake. A mix of emotions flooded through her.

A part of her wanted to let go, to scream as loud as possible, but something else sapped her energy to try.

She turned on her side and cried herself to sleep.

The Facility

8

Anya didn't see Jason the next morning. Not that she'd been looking for him.

In the changing room in Arcis she hung up her backpack, bulging with food rations Jason had brought home. She took out a banana and ate it. It didn't taste overly sweet like the food from Arcis did. Nor did it mute her lingering feelings of anger. She jammed an apple from yesterday's lunch into her pocket. Anya took a deep breath and walked into the atrium.

The ground floor buzzed with excitement—ten new participants had just joined the existing eighteen. The newbies stood nervously in their own groups, waiting for instructions. It was a different space without Dom. She hated the idea of starting over.

The suicides should have been front and center in her mind, but Dom's visit with the old man dominated her thoughts. That and Jason's strange cuts on his hands.

She watched the newbies for a while, their eyes full of wonder and curiosity. She wanted to feel like that again. Not scared or numb. Just curious.

Sweat rolled down her back as she took a hesitant step forward.

Two groups of five had gathered, one louder than the other. Anya walked over to the group of quieter participants who gave off an easier, less-manic vibe.

'Hi,' she said. Four of the five in the group turned toward her. One boy was looking elsewhere.

'I'm Anya.'

A girl with a delicate face and fine, golden shoulder-length hair smiled at her.

'I'm June.' She pointed to the others. 'That's Tahlia, Frank, Jerome and Warren at the end.'

Anya nodded to each of them. Their smiling faces relaxed her. Tahlia was shorter than she was, and dark-skinned, but not as dark as Jerome. Her hair was dotted with streaks of fake pink. Frank bounced on his feet. His high energy matched his messy hairstyle.

Warren was taller than Anya, but not as tall as Dom. He had light-blue eyes and strawberry-blond hair, and was quieter than the others. When Anya caught his eye he looked away. His shyness made her blush.

June pointed at her knees.

'Is that blood?'

'Where?' Anya looked down. She'd forgotten about the faller's blood that had turned a reddish-brown.

'Oh, nothing. Just scraped my knee, that's all.'

June looked relieved. 'Good. I don't like blood.'

Frank, Jerome and Tahlia didn't react. Warren just watched her. Should she tell them about what had happened after rotation? No. Hopefully it was a one-off.

While other participants took care of the remaining five recruits, Anya marshalled her five and showed them the ropes. Someone had already turned on the floor grid to illuminate the numbered sections. She showed them the arboretum, their assigned sections and explained their job.

June had been given Dom's old section.

Last, Anya nodded to the metal shutter.

'Just ignore them when they come out.'

June and Tahlia frowned at her. 'When who come out?'

'Our supervisors.'

A bored Jerome and Frank roughhoused with each other. Warren watched the pair. Anya couldn't get a read on him. Perhaps not shy as she'd first thought, but just not interested in the play.

A sharp clanging noise rattled Anya's eardrums. June and Tahlia jumped. The metal door rolled up and the first of the wolves walked out. Jerome, Frank and Warren smiled when they saw the half-machine, half-animal contraption.

'Wow,' said Jerome.

Frank grinned and slapped Jerome hard on the back. 'I'm right with you, man.'

Everyone lined up.

The remaining three wolves followed, examining each participant with bright yellow stares. The lead wolf's eyes looked more orange than yellow.

'New recruits, welcome to Arcis,' said the lead wolf. 'Your role here is simple: work hard and you will be rewarded. The floors are designed to challenge you, so you will leave this place with the necessary skills to be productive human beings. You will begin your work immediately.'

It was the same speech Anya had been given a month earlier by the same wolf, but in the lobby.

As the busy day commenced the last of her thoughts about rotation faded, thanks in part to her new friends. She caught herself giggling at Jerome and Frank's antics. Jason was far too serious these days. Their fight last night still tied her stomach up in knots.

Mid-morning, Anya pulled out the apple from her pocket, took a few quick bites and put it away. She looked up at the first floor. The giddiness of the participants from yesterday had been replaced by anxiety. One stressed looking girl crossed the walkway from Tower A to Tower B, with a file tucked under her arm.

Then she saw Dom Pavesi.

Her breath caught in her throat. Last night, Dom's dreadlocks had been snipped off just below his scalp. But this morning, his hair was short, tight to his crown. He now looked the age she guessed he was.

Donning a serious look, he walked on. Then he stopped, looked down at Anya.

Her heart almost stopped. Did he know she'd followed him?

Of course he didn't.

He nodded at her, his body tense.

Anya pointed. 'I like the new look.'

Dom smiled crookedly. 'More practical this way.'

When he walked on her fear tripled, but her thoughts remained clear.

She had no desire to stay on the ground floor.

She didn't want to see another dead body.

And the longer she stayed put, the farther away she got from the only person who possibly understood her.

9

Anya hardly saw Dom for the next two weeks, but her new friends kept her occupied. Tahlia, June, Frank, Jerome and Warren became her new lunch companions.

'I was looking at how you clean your section, June,' said Tahlia. 'You really should use long, broad strokes across the entire section. You only waste energy by tucking the mop in to your body.'

'I'll keep it in mind.'

'I'm only saying. Before I learned how to draw, I painted walls. It's the same principle. Think of the mop as a brush and your section as a canvas.'

June rolled her eyes. Tahlia liked to boss people around.

'So what was Oakenfield like, Tahlia?' said Anya, hoping to lighten the mood.

'Boring, like all the other towns.' Her eyes lit up. 'Did you know Praesidium has a really good art program? I learned a lot there.'

Apparently, Tahlia had lived with her parents in Praesidium for a year before returning to her town.

It was customary for all teens to choose a skill in school, something to master above all else. For Anya, it had been sport.

She pressed her fingers into her ribs, feeling her emotions slip again. June was watching her carefully.

Anya forced a smile for her. 'What did you do in Goldenvale?'

June returned the smile, but her eyes remained wary.

'Needlepoint. My mother said it would come in useful if the factories ever needed small hands to do delicate work. How did you get into sport, of all things?' said June.

'My father encouraged me.'

'What about your brother... Jason, right?' said Tahlia. 'Did he do sport, too?'

Anya smiled. 'No, Jason's more intellectual.'

June was a delicate flower: fine hair; small oval face and light-blue eyes, which were partially dilated; petite frame. Yet, she was the hardest worker among the participants on the ground floor.

Tahlia was the opposite of June in appearance: shoulder-length brown hair with pink streaks; stocky frame; round face with brown eyes darker than her mocha skin. She was a foot shorter than both June and Anya.

She looked farther down the table to where Jerome, Frank and Warren sat. They were playing a game involving dinner knives. Jerome had his hand splayed out in front of him while Warren stabbed the table with his knife, barely missing Jerome's fingers. Jerome looked terrified but Warren was grinning.

'What about them? What's their story?' Anya asked.

'Frank and Jerome are from Goldenvale, like me,' said June.

'Yeah, Warren came from Oakenfield,' said Tahlia.

June went on. 'Frank and Jerome are inseparable.

The Facility

Jerome came to live with Frank and his uncle when Frank found him stealing food from their garbage.'

'What happened?'

'Dunno. His parents died years ago. He was a walking skeleton when Frank found him.' June leaned in closer. 'Frank never knew his mother and his father died of radiation sickness.'

Anya glanced at the boys again. 'Did Warren lose his parents, too?'

Tahlia's expression hardened. 'His parents abandoned him to join the rebels.'

'What? That's awful.'

'Don't feel sorry for him. He's such a competitive freak.' Tahlia leaned forward. 'I remember after school we used to race each other, you know, for a bit of fun. But one girl started to overtake him. Well, you should have seen his face. He flicked his foot out to the side...'

'What happened?'

'She fell and broke her nose. He apologized after, but you could tell he wasn't sorry he'd done it.'

'But he seems so nice.'

'Yeah.' Tahlia didn't sound convinced. 'I don't really talk to him much. What about your parents, how did, you know... it happen?'

Guilt tightened Anya's chest. 'Same story as everyone.' She stood up, desperate for air. 'See you back in there.'

She hurried outside, trying to calm her breathing. She passed by a group of boys sitting on the grass playing poker. Dom and Sheila were huddled together in another area.

Anya strode past hoping they wouldn't see her.

Sheila stood up suddenly, twisting her golden hair

around her finger. 'Hey, skinny girl. It's Anya, right?'

Anya stopped and gave her a fake smile. 'Sheila. *So* nice to see you again.'

'Sorry you can't sit with Dom anymore. You obviously weren't good enough to make it to the first floor.'

Anya glanced at Dom who was busy staring at his hands. Anger bubbled inside her.

She glared at Sheila. Her eyes were set a perfect distance apart and her nose was small enough not to overshadow her face. She was tall like Dom and had more curves than Anya did.

Sheila laughed as she inspected her.

'You know you only got into this program because your parents are dead.'

'Sheila, that's enough,' muttered Dom.

Anya made two fists and ground them into the sides of her legs.

'Your parents were killed and you're here because they had nowhere else to put the ugly kids. There's a reason you're still on the ground floor. It's because you're not good enough to do *anything*. They feel sorry for you because you're such a loser.'

Dom said nothing. Anya pictured him wearing a collar, being led around by Sheila. She stifled a laugh but it came out as a full-blown, unattractive snort.

'What's so funny, loser?'

'Nothing, I was just picturing you taking your pet for a walk, that's all.' She glanced at Dom. His curious, dark-brown eyes were on her. Was that a smile?

She forced her attention back to Sheila, who had taken a step forward.

The medication had mellowed her, but now her

anger egged her on.

Sheila poked her finger hard into Anya's chest. Anya stepped out of her space, but she came at her again.

'You can't talk to me like that, *loser*. You're just jealous that Dom doesn't want to hang around with you anymore. And that's all it is. *Hanging around.* He would never want to be with someone as childish as you.'

Sheila jabbed at Anya again, this time finding her left breast. Anya flinched and protected herself with her hand.

Anger slipped over her like a second skin. She grabbed Sheila's elongated finger and twisted her arm out to the side. Sheila screamed as Anya pulled her arm behind her back.

'Get off me.'

Anya yanked Sheila's arm up her back, far enough for it to hurt but not enough to break it. Standing behind her, she resisted the temptation to pull her hair.

Instead, she lifted her foot and jammed it into the back of Sheila's knees. Sheila dropped to the grass with a thud.

Still gripping Sheila's arm, Anya eased her forward until she lay face down.

Then she let her go.

She raised both eyebrows at Dom. His lips twitched with the hint of a smile. His eyes danced with mischief.

Walk away, Anya. She needed to be the victor.

June, Tahlia, Warren, Frank and Jerome stood at the corner, jaw slack and eyes wide.

Anya stomped back inside, her hands shaking from anger. The boys slapped her back as she passed.

Frank grinned. 'Anya, I didn't think you had it in you.'

June and Tahlia followed her. June looked concerned, but not Tahlia.

'Girls like that deserve everything they get,' she said smirking. 'Where did you learn those moves?'

June shook her head. 'You've just made things worse for yourself.'

Worse how?

'Sheila and I don't work on the same floor,' said Anya.

And if we ever do, I'll deal with the fallout then.

The siren signaled the end of lunch break. Anya's stomach rumbled. Her hands shook. She pulled her sandwich from her pocket, unwrapped it and took a few bites.

Dom entered the lobby, his eyes downcast and his arm draped around Sheila. She was cradling her stomach while leaning into him for support. Anya shook her head; she hadn't touched her stomach.

Dom avoided Anya's gaze as he passed, but Sheila shot her a look that caused her breath to hitch.

They climbed on the elevator. The drama fizzled out when the door closed.

But her frayed nerves warned Anya it wasn't over.

Anger and indifference battled inside her.

Food in her belly softened the edges of the former.

Anya walked unsteadily back to the atrium. Her insides, coiled into a tight uncomfortable knot, began to unravel. By the time she'd finished eating the knot had vanished.

She felt calm again.

10

Her bag weighed more than usual. Anya pulled out an apple from Jason's rations. The sharp, tangy fruit popped as she took her first bite.

Thick wires overhead carried static cameras. Near the water supply, hospital and Essention's entrance, silver orbs roamed freely. Jason had told her the orbs contained cameras. Why would cameras be necessary in a place like Essention? Only the guns threatened the peace, but they pointed out from the wall, not in. Apart from Sheila, everyone was so polite and well mannered.

The shaking hands that preceded each meal were gone. She'd been eating more of Jason's leftovers, which tasted far better than Arcis' food. In the evening light, she assessed the place with a clear mind.

She froze mid-turn when she saw Dom and Sheila walking through the force field. Dom was supporting Sheila while she hugged the arm Anya had almost broken to her body.

Anya stumbled and hid behind a Monorail stilt. In the deep shadows, her heart hammered. She wasn't ready to face Sheila. New emotions stirred deep within, urging her to start something.

Through a flurry of breaths she watched them pass.

Dom put his lips to Sheila's ear and whispered something. Sheila let out a whiney laugh.

Anya followed them to the platform and boarded the train, staying past her stop. Just like last time, Sheila disembarked at the last stop for East. When Dom got off at Southwest again Anya followed. The fading light gave her plenty of deep shadows to hide in.

Dom headed for the bungalow with the faded-green door. She waited until she was certain he was inside, then crept around the back.

Muffled voiced reached the garden. She assessed the garden. A large leafy bush could act as camouflage if there wasn't time to run. The tin can. Move it? They'd know she'd been there. Leave it.

A second voice she recognized as the older man's reached her. She kept her head below the window.

'How long before you're locked in?'

'Soon. They brought me in today to tell me. They said they "require the participants to remain on-site to prove their commitment to the program".'

She pictured Dom air-quoting Arcis' message.

'Participants.' The man grunted. 'Is that what they're calling you?'

'Well, we *are* participating in a skills program, so the name fits, Charlie.'

Anya imagined Dom shrugging his shoulders.

'So, what are we talking about—a couple of weeks before we lose contact?'

'Something like that. I might be able to stretch it out to the next rotation. I'll try to stay on the outside as long as possible, but at some point they're going to insist.'

There was a pause. Anya heard someone pacing.

'If the team can configure the communication signal to pass through the force field,' said Dom, 'I should be able to get a message out. I just need to figure out a few things, like timing.'

The pacing stopped. 'Skills program.' Charlie grunted a second time. 'What a joke. We both know it's more than that.'

'And I promised to find out what. But things have become complicated. There's someone I need to keep safe.'

Anya craned her neck to hear better.

'A girl?'

Dom didn't answer. Anya ground her teeth at the thought of him saving Sheila.

'Does she know what's going on with you?'

'No. It's not the right time to tell her. I want to give her the antidote. Can Max get me a shot?'

Charlie paused. 'Will she be of help to you when the time comes?'

'I can't be sure.'

Sheila? Helping?

Anya almost laughed but the word 'antidote' threw her.

'Not until you're sure,' said Charlie. 'She's better off half-caring than caring too much if she can't help. You understand?'

'Yeah. But I'll need people on my side while I'm in there.'

Another pause. 'I'll see what I can do.'

Anya readjusted her foot; it brushed against something solid. The tin can rocked. She held her breath and steadied the object with her hand. The conversation fell quiet. She considered diving into the bush. Instead, she ran.

Anya didn't go far, just back to the street that ran alongside the factories.

Dom emerged from the narrow gap between the houses. He jogged toward her. She hid behind one of the Monorail stilts. He took a sharp left toward one of the food factories.

A new clarity of thought hit her, told her to stop playing it safe.

She saw Dom enter one of the factories by a side door and followed. When her courage caught up to her actions, she opened the door and stepped inside.

A series of thudding sounds came from an adjoining room. Faint yellow light slipped underneath the slightly open door. She walked toward it and peered through at the factory floor.

Dom had his back to her and was facing a blue padded bag suspended from a chain in the ceiling. He wore a black T-shirt and black cargo pants, and a set of red boxing gloves. His brown tunic top was in a heap on the floor beside him. Anya held her breath while he punched, worried about disturbing the air around her.

Dom grunted as his fist found the bag. He continued to punch the bag, oblivious to her presence. She stood frozen and stiff by the door, just watching.

Finally, he stopped punching. Sweat stained his T-shirt and dripped off his neck. He stood facing the bag, and ran a palm over his short hair.

'Are you going to stand there all night or are you coming in?"

11

Anya froze in the doorway. She coaxed the door open a little wider.

Dom turned, his skin glistening from the physical exertion. His T-shirt clung to his contours. Her eyes took in the body that was more man than boy.

A smile tugged at the edges of Dom's mouth. 'What, you've never seen someone punch a bag before?'

Her shock melted away and she entered the room.

Too many questions filled her head; none that she'd expected to ask that night.

'How did you know I was here?'

The laces on Dom's gloves were undone, and he used the crooks of his arms to pull the gloves off. He let them drop to the floor.

'I've been waiting for you to come and find me this past week. Couldn't have made it easier.'

Anya frowned. 'I don't understand.'

Dom folded his arms. 'How long are you going to pretend this is the first time you've followed me?'

She pressed her clammy hands to her burning cheeks.

'Fine! I followed you. Once.'

Dom's smile faded. 'Calm down, Anya. I'm not angry with you.'

His words only made her face burn hotter. 'Why would you be angry with me? I don't answer to you. I can go where I like.'

He snatched his clothes up from the ground. Underneath were a couple of bottles of water, which he also picked up.

'What are those for?'

'Come with me.' He strode out the door and to the exit.

She followed him, more curious than angry.

'Why were you expecting me, then?'

"You are very predictable.'

'Predictable?' Anya ran to catch up. 'How?'

'You're here, aren't you?'

She snorted. 'A week late, according to you.'

'Well, I had to do something to make sure you would show.'

She stopped. 'What did you do?'

Dom didn't slow. 'I saw the way you handled Sheila today. You've had training.'

She stared at him. 'You set that up?'

'I had to be sure.'

'You stupid, selfish—'

Dom glanced over his shoulder. 'Hurry up.'

She stumbled after him. 'Where are we going?'

They passed the bungalows with the eyes, past the one with the pale-green door. She glanced at it but there were no lights on.

They reached the end of the street by the dividing wall for West. A laneway sat between the last house and the wall. The space opened up a little and Anya saw a steel gate.

'We can access the land at back of the houses in West,' said Dom.

Anya saw a lock on the gate. 'Are we breaking in?'

He produced a key from his pocket and opened the gate. She followed Dom through, wondering how he got the key.

But her curiosity gave way to excitement when she saw the smooth running track ahead. Her body shuddered with excitement at the thought of running properly again.

Dom dropped his stuff on the ground.

'Just leave your stuff here, it'll be safe.'

He handed her a water bottle.

'Where did you get the key from?' Anya dropped her bag and placed the bottle on top of it.

'Come on. Last one to the end is a loser.' Dom jogged backward taunting her.

She took it easy at first, but when Dom turned and sprinted ahead, she picked up her pace.

Tall walls and foliage to their right marked the boundaries of the bungalows in West. The evening was still and warm. Anya concentrated on the rhythmic suck and release of air.

After the first kilometer her breaths shortened. Dom also breathed hard, but not as hard as her.

'Not far to go now.'

She wheezed. 'Where?'

'There's a park up ahead.'

He sprinted ahead. She jog-walked to the end.

The track stopped at another gate. An out of breath Dom drank from his water bottle. Then she remembered her own, still on top of her bag.

Dom used the same key to open the new gate. They

entered a children's playground, complete with swing set, slide and miniature climbing wall. The place was deserted.

'Are we supposed to be here?'

'It's fine.' He shut the gate with a gentle click.

Dom walked on. Anya spotted a steel structure off to one side and ran to it. She pressed the button and a stream of water appeared. Her mouth was inches from its glistening stream when Dom yanked her away.

'Don't drink that.'

'Why not?'

'It's contaminated.' He shook his bottle at her.

She grabbed it from him and chugged the water.

He walked over to one of the swings and sat down. Anya did the same, grateful for the chance to rest.

'How often do you come out here?'

'As much as possible. But it's getting harder to be consistent.'

'Why, because of the first floor?'

He didn't answer her.

Anya recalled the conversation between Dom and the older man. 'What's the first floor like?'

'It's okay.'

'But what do you do there?'

Dom hesitated. 'You'll find out soon enough.'

'It would be easier if you just told me.'

Dom looked at his feet. 'Let's just say it's all about timing.'

Timing?

The moonlight provided the only light in the playground. Dom looked at her sideways.

'Are we friends, Anya?'

She held his gaze for a moment before looking away.

'I don't know. Maybe.' She swallowed. 'Truth is... I don't know if I can trust you.'

Dom laughed gently. 'I was thinking the same thing about you.'

Even though she'd said it first, his uncertainty cut her like a knife.

'This part of Essention used to belong to a town called Annavale. The cameras don't cover this section. I thought that maybe I could teach you how to defend yourself.'

Anya snorted.

Dom gave her a look. 'What's so funny?'

'You saw how I handled Sheila today. Do you think I need lessons?'

'Defense is about preventing an attack, not initiating one. It can't hurt to be ready for the danger.'

'Are you talking about the wolves?' She couldn't think of another danger.

'The program is designed to test us. I just want you to be ready.'

The two deaths on the ground floor had been enough of a test.

'What if I try to leave?'

'You can't.'

Dom grabbed her wrist and ran his finger along the spot where the hospital had implanted her chip. Her breath caught in her throat. He released her. 'Our chips are hardwired into us. If we leave, it will sever the connection between body and mind. It will kill us.'

'How do you know that?'

'I just do.'

She looked around. 'But we're out here now and nothing's happening.'

He pointed at Essention's high perimeter wall. 'We can't venture past those walls while we are in the program.'

'I don't understand. Why are we being locked in?'

'The program is important to Arcis. All I know is it has something to do with what's on the ninth floor. We're special enough that they've chipped us.'

Dom's brown eyes looked almost black in the moonlight. 'Right now, you're not in any danger. It's safer to stick with the program and do as you're told.'

She snorted. 'You sound like my brother. Sometimes I think he cares more about what the rebels are doing than starting over.'

'You don't trust the rebels?'

'No.' A knot tied up her stomach. 'They killed my parents. I saw them.'

'You don't think it might have been someone else?'

'Like who?' She wasn't ready to consider an alternative.

He looked away. 'Nothing. Forget it.'

She drank some water. After, she said, 'Can I ask you something?'

Dom looked back and shrugged.

'How old are you?'

'Seventeen.'

She snorted. 'Bull crap.'

The moonlight glinted in his eyes. 'You think I'm lying?'

'Yeah.'

Dom didn't correct her.

'I'm right?'

He stood up and faced her.

'Time to learn something new.' He held out his

hand. 'You game?'

She dropped the water bottle and took his hand. It felt rough and warm. His gaze was on her. Her heart thrummed as loud as it did when she ran.

He let go and turned her so he stood behind her.

'Okay, say I sneak up behind you. What do you do?'

She made two fists and went to turn. Before she could, Dom had grabbed both wrists, spun her to face him and pinned her arms above her head. Anya wriggled beneath his strong grip. He released her.

'Let's try that again, and think about what else you can use against me.'

This time she stepped forward before she turned. Dom grabbed her wrists too easily and spun her to face him again.

With his hands on hers, his body was open and vulnerable. She attacked him with her knee. He jumped out of the way before she made contact.

Dom let go of her wrists. 'Better. But not all attacks will be the same. Want to try another?'

She smiled and nodded.

'Turn around as before.'

One step and he was behind her again. He worked his arms around hers, pinning them to her side. Her body buzzed with anticipation. His soft breath tickled the side of her face.

Anya tried to turn, but Dom gave her no room to move. She kicked out behind her, hitting only air. Dom pressed on the back of her knee with his foot. She dropped to the grass and he straddled her.

'Again.' He straightened up, offering her his hand. Anya waved off his help and scrambled to her feet, brushing the grass off her trousers.

She heaved out a breath before turning back around.

He was close again, but a new hesitation slowed down his moves. And when he pinned her arms down by her sides, he wasn't as close as before.

She wriggled like a wildcat, but her actions only caused Dom to tighten his grip. The space between them vanished.

'Let me go,' she whispered. He did.

'Maybe we should talk through the move first,' he said. 'When someone grabs you from behind you have about a second to react. You need to straighten your arms, and push them out.'

She followed his instructions.

'Then, grab my hands, while stamping your foot on mine. When the attacker's hands are open, pull one arm from his body, turn and drive your elbow into his chest.'

Anya did.

'Now, let's do that again without the tutorial.'

They repeated the move, faster this time.

Dom stepped back from her elbow jab. 'Then you run, or stay and fight. Your choice.'

She buzzed from the session. 'That was fantastic.'

His eyes danced with a new lightness—or possibly relief. 'See? All it takes is a little practice.' He looked at his watch. 'Come on, it's getting late. We should get back before the scanners do their thing.'

They walked back to where they'd left their bags. Dom dropped the key off at Charlie's house. She wanted to know who Charlie was.

They rode the Monorail together in a comfortable silence. But when Dom prepared to get off at Sheila's stop, her heart sank. Was he going to see her now, to laugh about their evening together? Their friendship troubled her. She didn't trust Sheila.

'Come by tomorrow. We'll pick up where we left off.'

Anya nodded, her mouth tight. 'Sure. Thanks.'

She wanted to meet him again.

By the time she reached her stop she'd talked herself out of it.

12

For the first time since the suicides Anya felt good about things to come. She still buzzed from last night's session with Dom. She grinned and jerked her mop at each new private thought.

Tahlia and June slowed their own work efforts. The frown on Tahlia's face sent Anya into a fit of giggles.

'What is with you today?' said Tahlia.

'What?'

'You look like the cat that's got the cream.'

She didn't want to say, but leaving them hanging wasn't an option, either.

'I went for a run last night.'

'Aaand?' said June.

'And nothing. I used to do sport before I came to Essention, remember? I miss it. That's all.'

This was true. But it wasn't why she felt the way she did. Last night she'd convinced herself not to meet Dom again, but that morning she'd changed her mind.

June leaned on the top of the mop handle. 'Are you sure there's nothing else?'

Anya looked down at the floor. 'Of course. What else would there be?'

'I don't know. A certain tall, dark, handsome someone who's on the first floor? Don't think we haven't noticed how you two look at each other.'

She looked up. 'No!' Her shriek attracted Warren's attention. Blood pooled in her cheeks. 'No,' she repeated, softer this time. 'There's nothing going on. He's with Sheila.'

June shuffled in closer. 'I heard they broke up.'

'Who told you that?'

'*They* did. I saw them getting into the elevator this morning and she looked angry with him. He was looking anywhere but at her.'

Anya's stomach flipped at the thought *she* might be the reason they'd broken up.

'What does that have to do with me?'

June rolled her eyes. 'Now he's free and you can go for it.'

'I'm sure he'll find someone else in no time.'

Anya pushed her mop across the floor. June groaned.

Her feelings for Dom were new, but what did they have in common? Dom was moody most of the time and they fought way too much.

But what if he and Sheila really had broken up?

Anya looked up to see Warren staring at her. As soon as their eyes met, he looked away.

Ω

After her shift ended, Anya headed for the factory in Southwest. The side door was locked. She waited around for a while, then headed to the running track to find the gate also locked. Looking through the iron railing, she saw none of Dom's things on the ground.

Disappointed, she walked back. The retreating day had given way to a dark and shadow-filled night. She saw a figure stood underneath the Monorail and she smiled. Dom? She was about to jog over to him when the figure stepped out.

Her smile faded.

'What are you doing here, Warren?'

'I'm just out for a walk.' He frowned, hands in his pockets. 'You look like you were expecting someone else.'

'Nope. I'm doing the same.'

He wore the uniform of brown tunic and black trousers. His black shoes were scuffed around the edges. It was her first time to speak with the shy Warren. So far, Tahlia's depiction of him as wily and competitive didn't ring true.

'Mind if we walk together? I want company.'

Anya could understand that. 'Sure.'

They walked around Southwest for a while. Anya hoped Dom might see her with Warren and regret standing her up. But soon, she felt the eyes of Southwest close in on her.

'Let's go back to East,' she said.

Warren looked disappointed. 'Okay. We can take the Monorail if you'd like?'

'No, I mean we could walk the long way around. I don't feel like going home yet, either.'

Warren's shoulders relaxed.

As they walked in the direction of Arcis, Warren kicked a stone with the side of his shoe. 'Your brother works around here, doesn't he?'

'Yeah,' Anya said. 'In the food factory.' She glanced at him. 'Um, Tahlia told me your parents joined the rebellion.'

Warren concentrated on the stone. 'I didn't know Tahlia was so interested in my life.'

Anya flinched at his cool reply. 'I don't think she meant anything.'

'She could do with minding her own business.'

'It's not her fault. I asked.'

'Yeah?' He looked up at her, his eyes hard. 'What else did she say?'

Anya said nothing.

He stared at her. 'That's what I thought. Some crap about me in school, no doubt.'

She changed the subject. 'Um, Jerome and Frank are nice.'

Warren shrugged. 'I think sometimes they'd rather I wasn't around.'

'Why?'

'It's a guy thing. I'm not into fighting as much as they are, despite what *certain* people say.'

'Well, that shouldn't matter. You're part of the group. Tahlia and June like you.'

'June, maybe. Tahlia's never been my number one fan.'

'Why?'

'She seems to think I'm a dick who goes around beating people up.'

'Because of the girl and the race?'

Warren sneered. 'So she told you about that? It was one time. *Jesus*, she doesn't forget anything. She's labeled me this over-competitive freak.' He stopped walking. 'I'm just trying to survive like everyone else.'

Tahlia had a sharp tongue. Perhaps she'd exaggerated the truth. 'Well, I like you.'

Warren lifted his eyebrows. 'Yeah?'

She quickly qualified. 'As a friend.'

'Good enough, I suppose.'

He pushed his hands deeper into his pockets.

A silence lingered between them that didn't feel as natural as her silence with Dom. She felt the need to break it.

'How are you finding the skills program at Arcis?'

He shrugged. 'Okay, I suppose.'

They passed by Arcis. The street lights flickered briefly. Warren looked up at the monstrous building with its black towers and glass heart. The lighting enhanced his strawberry-blond hair. His face was dotted with freckles and his eyes were a pale blue.

'It's a bit boring. I just want to finish and get out. What do you want to do when it's all over?'

Anya pulled her bottom lip through her teeth. 'Something in Praesidium, I guess.'

'Yeah, that's where I want to end up, too. Not in some pokey town fighting for resources. I hear Praesidium has endless opportunities. You can do whatever you want there.'

Anya hugged herself at the mention of the capital. 'Doesn't it bother you that it's controlled by so many machines?'

Warren laughed. He stopped walking and pulled his hands out of his pockets. 'You lost your parents to the rebels, right?' Anya hesitated. 'I might not say much, but I listen a lot.'

She nodded.

'So we both have something in common. The machines in Praesidium can protect us from the rebels' lies.' Warren rested his hands on Anya's shoulders. He leaned in so close she worried he might kiss her. But he stopped at her ear.

'We need to stick together, Anya. Make it through the program. Get on with our lives. We can't let the rebels steal our basic rights from us. There are people in Arcis who shouldn't be trusted. Like that Dom Pavesi you hang around with.'

Anya's pulse thumped in her ears. She pulled back from him. 'What's wrong with Dom?'

'Nothing. Something. I don't know. He's unfriendly.'

'Do you know him?'

Warren shook his head. 'I know his type. Tall, good-looking, arrogant. They were all over my school in Oakenfield.' He changed the subject. 'I'm looking forward to rotation. Have you been through it before? What happens exactly?'

Her thoughts shot to the dead girl. She still felt the wet and sticky feel of her blood, even after endless washing. 'No, and I'm not looking forward to it.'

'Why?' He buried his hands back in his pockets and walked on. 'Rotation is a good thing. It means we're closer to getting out of Arcis.'

'I just mean it doesn't end well for everyone.'

Warren stopped walking and frowned at her. She caved and told him about the boy and the girl without faces. She didn't mention her vomiting, or how clinical the others had been about the whole thing.

He let out a low whistle, as if impressed.

Anya felt sick all of a sudden. 'Do you mind if we get the train back now?'

'Sure.'

They boarded the half-full train.

Warren dropped into the seat beside her. His leg brushed against hers and she made herself smaller. She wanted to be alone, to think about a plan for rotation and moving on.

'Maybe we should stick together,' said Warren. 'Make it to the first floor? We could watch each other's backs.'

The train pulled off. 'I'd just hold you back.' She hadn't considered forming alliances in Arcis.

'Frank and Jerome are inseparable. June and Tahlia have each other. So that just leaves you and me. I saw how you handled Sheila. That was impressive.'

Anya wished she could agree; Sheila didn't seem like the type to forgive and forget.

Warren readjusted himself in his seat while Anya squirmed in hers.

'Come on. Just you and me.'

'This isn't a game, Warren. We're not here to pair off. This is real life.' Her tone was sharper than she'd intended. 'I can't be responsible for anyone's success or failure in there. I just can't.'

Warren rested his arm on the back of her seat, causing her to shift forward slightly.

'I'm suggesting you think about it.' He sounded hurt. 'I can be a good person to ally with. And I don't need babysitting.'

'I'm sorry, Warren. I'm just sick of everyone telling me what I should do.'

He moved his arm and rested his hands on his legs. 'Just think about it, please. We'll need alliances at some stage and it would be better if we guaranteed each other an early exit from Arcis.'

'I will.'

The Facility

For the remainder of the short journey, Warren bit his fingernails while Anya gazed out the window. When her stop approached she headed for the door.

'Thanks for the company tonight, Warren.' She smiled back at him. 'I will think about it, I promise.'

'Sure. See you tomorrow.'

Anya jogged down the stairs to street level and ran all the way home.

13

Over the next two weeks, Warren became Anya's new companion at lunch and tried to include her in Jerome-and-Frank-fueled conversations. Despite Tahlia's wary glances —and, more recently, June's—she liked him. An alliance could be advantageous.

She'd returned to the factory twice more since that night she'd bumped into Warren, but there was still no sign of Dom. She tried to get on with her work, to stop searching for him on the first floor. Then one day she saw him, weak, pale and limping. Her heart had dropped into her sturdy shoes when he didn't look for her.

At least once a day she replayed his conversation with Charlie in her head.

So, what are we talking about? A couple of weeks before we lose contact?

There's someone I need to keep safe.

Last night, Jason was a no show for dinner again. And on the nights he did show up, it was only to wash away the evidence of his fighting. But at least he'd stopped talking about leaving.

Peace and quiet she liked, but last night in the apartment had felt different. She'd thought about things she didn't want to remember, sounds she never wanted to hear again, faces she hoped she'd see again. Tears had stained her flushed cheeks as she ate. The sweet food always tasted worse after Jason's rations. She'd spat her food out and gone to bed.

Anya arrived at Arcis that morning to an announcement of rotation.

Twenty-six people chatted and laughed around her. Frank and Jerome teased June and Tahlia. She looked Warren's way and he nodded at her. She moved next to him, realizing one thing: no matter how much she delayed, the rebels would always come for her. And when they did, she needed to be ready.

The shutter rattled and squealed. One by one the wolves appeared from their dark cave.

Her heart fluttered. She had to leave this floor. She refused to look up. *Please, no more bodies.*

The wolves moved like restless wild animals, shifting forward, then back, then forward again. The wait was torture. She dried her clammy hands on her uniform.

The lead wolf called out a bunch of names, five in total. She opened her eyes and focused on the empty walkways overhead. Not hers.

Then the wolf spoke again. 'June, Tahlia, Frank, Jerome, Warren and Anya. You eleven will rotate to the first floor.'

She swayed with relief. Was this how Dom had felt during last rotation?

She turned to see Tahlia hugging June. Then Tahlia high fived her. Jerome and Frank both grinned and punched each other's arms. Anya hugged Warren briefly.

'See?' Warren elbowed her. 'You were worrying for nothing.'

Three of the wolves returned to their shelter while another led the way to the lobby.

'Rotated personnel, please follow me.'

Anya took one last look at Section Eight, at the spot where the dead girl had been.

'Get your belongings from the changing rooms.' The wolf stood by the elevator.

They ran inside and grabbed their things. June was smiling so hard Anya thought she might explode. But Anya felt something else: relief.

They emerged to see the elevator door wide open and the wolf waiting.

'Your new supervisor will greet you on the first floor.'

All eleven piled into the elevator that could hold twenty people. As the door closed, the wolf flashed an incisor at them.

One floor up the doors opened. A chubby man with thinning hair and a ruddy complexion waited. He was dressed in an all-black tunic, except for a ring of gold fabric stitched to his collar. The buttons on his coat strained against his waist. Anya recognized him from when she and Jason had first arrived at Essention. He'd injected location chips into their wrists while they were both patients at the hospital.

'I'm Supervisor One,' he said. 'Work hard and do not ask impertinent questions. Everything you do on this floor is set to challenge you. Your time on the ground floor was to teach you about structure, balance, patience. You must bring those lessons with you as you continue on with the program—'

One of the girls Anya didn't know put her hand up.

The supervisor turned to her. 'Yes?'

'What will we be doing on this floor?'

The supervisor glared at her. 'Impertinent question.'

He stepped back and waved them inside the square-shaped changing room. The walls were painted a slightly cheerier gray than the walls in Anya's prison block. Steel benches ran the circumference of the room, split by a single white door. Above the benches Anya counted thirty hooks. Clothes hung on eleven of them.

The supervisor pointed to the clothes. 'Change into your new uniform. Please drop your overalls in the bin marked 'Recycle'. When you've dressed, you can follow me.' He walked toward the white door.

'Where's the female changing room?' said June.

'You're standing in it,' said the supervisor. He exited through the door.

The girls stood on one side while the boys took the other.

'How about we all agree to turn our backs?' said Frank.

'Fine by me,' said Tahlia. 'I don't think I could bear the sight of your chicken legs, anyway.'

The room exploded with laughter. Anya took the opportunity to undress while she felt okay.

Holograms of their names shimmered above the hooks. She grabbed the skirt and blouse from her hook.

The clothes hung loosely on her frame. Either she was too skinny, or the person who wore them before was a bigger size than her.

Anya slipped her bare feet into a pair of black, low-heeled shoes. They rubbed a little against her foot.

Everyone turned around on an agreed signal. The boys were dressed in shirts and trousers. Some had clipped on neckties.

Through the door, they entered a larger room with rows of filing cabinets stretching upwards about fifteen feet, to the height of the ceiling. Wheeled ladders clung to the front of each row. Frazzled first-floor workers climbed to the highest parts and pushed themselves along. The strange metallic echoes made the space sound larger than it appeared.

Supervisor One was leaning against one of the rows. 'The purpose of this floor is to accustom you to working conditions. We wish to observe your ability to work under pressure. The clothes you wear, the environment you're in, has been closely matched to that of a twenty-first-century office.' He turned and walked toward a set of white double doors with '1A' marked on them.

'Follow me, please.'

Anya fell into line with the others. The supervisor opened one side of the doors to reveal the shimmering rainbow-like walkway she'd so often stared at from the ground floor. She hesitated at the start of the walkway suspended in an anti-gravity stream that looked far too dangerous to cross.

The supervisor pointed to a set of doors on the opposite side. 'Your training begins in Tower B.' He marched across the bridge.

The others followed, clutching the floating handrail. Anya's foot wavered at the start of the anti-gravity platform, which held together millions of temporarily solidified particles. Her head swam as she experienced a new fear: heights.

A first-floor worker rushed through the door behind her and nearly knocked her onto the walkway. She grabbed the handrail. It bent then adjusted itself, as the worker galloped past her.

The Facility

Okay, now she was nervous.

Supervisor One stepped forward.

'Get on the walkway, now. Or you forfeit your rotation.'

The thought of returning to the ground floor pushed her forward in one jerky motion. The walkway wobbled and shook, but corrected itself for her weight. She grabbed the handrail at hip height.

She reached the other side. The others had gone on ahead. Warren waited for her.

He held the door open. 'Are you sure you don't want a buddy in here?'

'Maybe,' said Anya, catching the door and closing it behind her.

Tower B matched the size of the records room. But she saw, where the ceiling extended further than the plain walls, it was a room within a room.

Two-dozen rows of single-user terminals contained screens but no chairs. The supervisor leaned against one of the terminals.

The room buzzed with first-floor workers hastily scanning transparent A4 files. Their tired and stressed faces didn't put Anya's mind at ease.

She searched the faces in the room, her pulse racing at the expectation of seeing Dom.

There was no sign of him. But there was no Sheila, either.

She could live with that.

'The rules are simple,' Supervisor One said. 'The terminals will request specific file numbers. You must retrieve those files from the records room in Tower A. You will scan the barcode on the front of the file using this.' He held up a black, gun-shaped object and pressed a trigger on the side. A cross-hatched red pattern decorated the side of the gray desk. 'The scanner will record the time of entry. Then you must deposit the file in this black box.'

The box fitted to the side of the table and connected to the floor. The slot looked wide enough to accept the A4-sized files.

There were two doors at the back of the room, one labeled as the dining room. The supervisor touched his wrist to a control panel and exited through the second door. What lay beyond their room? Why were they confined to a small section of a larger space?

Anya pressed forward onto her toes and felt a slight spring in the floor. She hunkered down and touched the spongy material. A flicker of red on one of the screens drew her attention and she stood up. Each terminal screen flashed with a different file number. A red clock started to count backward from ten minutes.

She claimed the closest terminal and memorized the file number on screen before exiting the room. She faltered at the walkway that felt as solid as air. Then the walkway firmed up beneath her. She closed her eyes, but the walkway's motion jerked her eyes open. She kept her steps even, not wanting to fall like the girl and boy had.

In the records room, each wooden cabinet was labeled with a specific range of holographic numbers. She searched for the set that her file—8351—fell into. The others charged through the doors—new workers and experienced alike—all fighting for the ladders. She panicked and climbed on the nearest one in the row with her file. But the ladder she needed was one over. Others shoved and jostled for prime positions.

She felt an extra weight on her ladder as she started to climb down. A girl about eighteen with wiry blonde hair was on her way up.

'Get off the ladder if you're not using it.'

'I... I'm trying to. I need a different ladder, anyway.'

The girl grunted at her. Anya placed her foot on the lower rung, but the wiry blonde climbed over her slamming her into the frame. Anya made it down, a little shaken, and rubbed the pain from her ribs.

Warren held the next ladder, and pointed up. 'There, Anya. The file you need.' A boy was trying to use it, but Warren kept pushing him away with his hand.

She jumped on the ladder and muttered her thanks. The boy cursed and shook it from below. Warren searched for his own file on a different ladder.

It took her a moment to find the row starting with the number 83 and even longer to find 8351. She grabbed a transparent file with a barcode stuck to the front and climbed down fast. The boy elbowed her hard as she passed.

Warren was already gone. Tahlia and Frank each gave a quiet *yes* under their breaths when they found their files.

Anya hesitated on the walkway again. A dark shape plummeted past her, swirling the air around her. She snatched at air and closed her eyes, hearing the sound of bones cracking on tiles.

Gasps filled the atrium below. She opened her eyes and peered over the side, seeing what she didn't want to: another girl and boy.

Swallowing back bile, she rushed back to the terminal room and scanned the barcode using the gun. The first-floor workers were already there. The countdown clock stopped with three minutes remaining. Anya deposited the transparent file in the box attached to the side of the table. Her pulse raced, her stomach heaved.

The wiry-haired blonde stood beside her screen with her arms folded, glaring at her.

Warren was grinning. She returned the smile, relieved he hadn't seen what had just happened outside.

Tahlia rushed into the room second-last and scanned her file.

'What happens if the clock runs out?' Anya asked Warren.

He shrugged. 'No idea.'

Anya didn't want to know. This job was easy, compared to the ground-floor work.

Dom had called her curious. Would that help or hinder her progress?

Would she ever see Dom again?

She shook her head and the thoughts flittered away. She was here to learn how to protect herself against the rebels.

The last boy scanned his file within the allotted time. A new number popped up on the screen and the clock reset itself. She prepared to begin again. This time she wouldn't hesitate to push the wiry blonde out of her way.

As Anya geared up to learn how to work under pressure, she tried to forget the deaths on the ground floor and everything Dom had taught her.

14

'Timing is everything.'

That's what Dom had said when she'd asked him about the first floor. After almost three days of running laps between the two towers she had to agree. But long, repetitive work didn't bother her. She'd spent many hours training alone for competitions she would never enter.

As soon as the last person scanned his or her transparent file, the timer reset itself. Then they started over, and over, and over again. The supervisor was nowhere to be seen during their file-fetching.

At the end of the first day, she'd arrived in the changing room to see thin cards under each hook.

Access card for the first floor.

She'd tucked hers into the front of her bag.

She had stopped eating Jason's food from the factory. Jason would be gone soon. Last night's conversation with him only cemented her decision to go it alone. Her heart still hurt from his news.

'I'm leaving.'

He'd been standing by the door to the bathroom where Anya had been washing her sweat-stained uniform.

Anya crushed the soapy fabric between her fingers.

'What? Why?'

'There's real talk of crop revival in the towns. A few of us are going out to check.'

'How?'

'We dug a tunnel that will take us past the guns.'

His admission hit her like a slow-moving train. The fresh cuts on his hands; the dirt under his fingernails—he'd been preparing to leave for some time.

'When are you going?'

'I don't know. Soon.'

Tears pricked her eyes. She let them fall.

'And I can't talk you out of it?'

Jason shook his head. 'You'll be safe in Arcis. I'll be back in a couple of days. Probably sooner.'

Dom had said the chip prevented people from leaving the town.

'How will you leave? The chip will kill you.'

'I know people. They have tech from Praesidium. They can disguise the chip's signature. Make the controllers think we're still here.'

Anya plunged her hands into the soapy water. More tears fell.

'Jason...'

He stepped closer. 'I know.'

'Be careful.'

Her worry about Jason leaving tightened her chest too much. She longed for the outside, but all first floor workers had to stay on-site during lunch. A new rule.

Lunch was a quiet affair. Nobody talked much—everyone was too exhausted from the hectic schedule. Tahlia slept on her hand.

The space closed in on her. With minutes left before

the bell, Anya stole out to the walkway to find it empty.

She looked up at the second-floor walkway, and the third, and the fourth, in staggered positions all the way up to the ninth.

The door above her swung open and her hand flew to her throat.

She hadn't seen Dom for over two weeks. He wore a white boiler suit over his clothes, fitted so tight to his broad chest that she could see the outline of his T-shirt. His limp was gone, but his eyes were hollow and vacant, like Tahlia's. When he didn't see her she called out to him.

He stopped and looked down, putting a hand on the railing to steady himself.

'Anya,' he said softly, with a smile that didn't reach his eyes. 'I'm glad to see you took my advice to move forward.'

A brief sparkle to his gaze brought a smile to her face. But it disappeared too fast.

'Are you okay? You don't look so good.'

'Nothing a decent night's sleep won't fix. How are you finding the first floor?'

'A little boring, if I'm being honest.'

His tired gaze sharpened. 'But you're not the slowest?'

Her skin prickled. 'No. Why?'

'Just remember what I told you. Timing is everything.' His finger fluttered by his ear, and he walked on.

'I've got to go. It's good to see you, Anya.'

She believed him. But seeing him walk away twisted her heart horribly.

She wasn't ready for him to disappear again.

'You told me that already. Tell me something new

about this floor.'

Her heart lifted when he stopped.

'I can't tell you much, I'm sorry. Pay attention to the timer. The first floor is not just about pressure.' Then he disappeared through the door for Tower A.

Anya stared at the door hoping he might come back, but he didn't. He was gone again.

For another two weeks?

Forever?

Anya returned to the terminal room and waited for the afternoon shift to begin. A round, gray clock on the wall ticked more loudly with the passing of each second. The others chatted by the terminals. Warren looked as if he was processing a strategy in his head. The clock's monotonous ticking drowned out all thoughts. Except for one.

Pay attention to the timer.

She stared at the clock's third hand—the one counting down the seconds—as it moved toward the hour. Her terminal whirred into life and a file number flashed up on the screen: 1671. On day one, she'd written numbers on her hand until she ran out of space. Then she'd started memorizing them. But today she wanted to see how long it took for her to get the file from the records room. She'd stolen Jason's spare wristwatch with a timer.

Her screen flashed danger-red. She stared at the timer and the allocated six minutes—four fewer than before lunch.

Anya blinked away her distraction. The others had already left. Her eyes flashed to the screen and the ten seconds she'd already wasted. She started the stopwatch in mid-dash from the room and ran onto the walkway without pausing.

The files were listed in order. She'd be fine.

But the frantic activity in the records room jolted her to a stop.

'Everything's been moved around,' said Frank. 'I can't find my file!'

Panic spread through her. The original first-floor workers were the only ones keeping it together.

Anya jumped onto the first free ladder, and tried to work out the new order of the files.

Pay attention to the timer. Timing is everything.

She moved to three more ladders before locating her file—1671—among the eight hundreds. She snatched the transparent folder but it slipped from her sweaty grasp and landed on the floor. She moved down two rungs at a time. Tahlia had found her own file and was running out the door.

On the last rung, her foot caught and her ankle snapped to the side. She bit back a scream. Then she hobbled as fast as she could with a sprained ankle and second-hand shoes. June and Frank still searched. Warren was nowhere in sight.

Silence greeted her in the terminal room as the others who'd already scanned their files waited. All eyes were on her, Frank and June as they smashed through the double doors. Warren clamped his thumb between his teeth. Anya grabbed the scanner. She shook with fear.

What happened when the timer ran out? Why did it matter?

She pressed the button on the scanner and the red hatch illuminated the front of the file.

Her eyes flashed to the screen. The timer still counted back.

Seven seconds, six, five...

She stared at the file in her hand and gasped, flipping it over when she realized the barcode was on the other side. She pressed the trigger once, twice, three times. The cross-hatch appeared. The timer had reached zero. She kept her eyes on the screen.

A low rumble started from inside the terminal. It changed to a higher pitch, increasing with fervor as the air supercharged statically around her.

She felt it in her hands first. Sparks of potent light sprang from the terminal to her fingertips, using the scanner as a conduit. She choked on a breath and tried to release the device, but it had become part of her hand.

The electricity pitched and rolled in waves, pulsing through her, searching for a way out. A searing pain streaked through her like hot needles, puncturing her skin at every imaginable point. And still she couldn't move. She smelled burning skin.

The strands of light keeping her frozen dimmed suddenly, and she flopped to the cushioned floor. The fire scorched and blazed in her fingertips, her nerves, her feet. She still couldn't move. Her arms and legs had become jelly.

She saw a moaning Frank and a drooling June on the floor beside her. Anya knew now why the floor was cushioned.

The pain marginally released its grip and she tried to move, but her limbs wouldn't cooperate. A concerned Warren appeared at her side and tried to help her sit up.

She caught new movement at the double doors. The supervisor entered, surrounded by several attendants dressed in white boiler suits. Then she saw Dom. He carried a green box with a white cross on the front.

Dom pushed Warren out of the way and knelt down

The Facility

beside Anya; the others tended to June and Frank. She tried to lift her head, but a pain ripped through her skull.

'Lie still,' he said quietly. He pinched her wrist with his fingers and checked her pulse. 'The first time is the worst. But it's not enough to kill you.'

He coaxed her mouth open and shone a light down her throat.

'Your throat is swollen, but I have something for that.'

He helped her sit up, and slotted something in his ears. He pressed a metal circle to her skin. Anya flinched at its coolness.

'The electricity alters your cardiac rhythm.'

He stared blankly at Anya's chest as he listened to her heartbeat. He put away the stethoscope and took out a syringe from his medical box.

'This will help to counteract the effects and reduce the swelling in your throat.'

He jabbed her upper arm and pushed the liquid. She didn't ask what was in it. She trusted him.

Others worked on Frank and June, who were sitting up and seemed fine. June tensed up when the medic came at her with a needle. He didn't explain anything the way Dom had for her.

'It's okay,' said Anya. 'It will help.'

Dom had turned to June at the exact same time. She nodded at both of them.

Warren sat on the edge of a desk staring at Dom.

When the shock had eased a little, several spots on her hands and feet began to throb. Dom took out a tube of paste from the box. He removed her shoes and applied some paste to the burned areas where the electricity had entered and exited.

'The skin salve will clear those wounds right up.'

His touch should have tickled her feet, but an intense burning preceded cool relief.

'I thought the floor...'

'Rubberised?' Dom flashed a crooked smile. 'That would make more sense. No. It's just to cushion your fall. In about ten minutes, you'll be up and about like none of this happened.'

She stared at him, seeing the dark circles under his eyes. She also saw a bright ring of gold along the outer edges of his partially dilated pupils.

'You look w-worse than I feel.' Anya stumbled over the words, the effects of her electric shock still present.

Dom didn't respond straight away. He packed away his things. 'Work smart. Timing is everything.'

'How often... f-for you?' Her tongue didn't feel like her own.

'Too often.' He shone a light into her eyes, leaning forward until his lips were at her neck. She almost didn't hear what he said next.

'You're going to feel different in a while. I need you to keep how different you feel to yourself. Do you understand?'

Anya shook her head.

'Promise me that whatever you feel you'll maintain a cool head. Just keep going.'

She held up her scorched hand. 'Is this... why you... didn't tell me?'

He pulled back from her. 'Just rest, Anya. No more questions.'

Supervisor One appeared and Dom helped Anya to her feet. She turned to ask Dom something else, but he was already walking away.

The Facility

The supervisor dominated her vision.

'After your shift, you three will remain on-site for the next couple of days. For observation.'

Anya hesitated. 'I... I need to let my brother know.'

'That's an order. You have just been hit by a bolt of electricity. We will inform your next of kin.'

Next of kin? She wasn't dead.

'What—why did this happen?'

Supervisor One gripped her arm. 'Are you motivated? Do you want to progress?'

Anya nodded.

'Then you must accept what Arcis asks of you.'

She boldly asked her next question. 'And what is Arcis asking of me?'

'You're here to help others learn from your mistakes.' The supervisor let go and walked on. 'Work smart. Timing is everything.'

15

The supervisors ordered Anya, June and Frank to keep working, despite their heart palpitations. Her hands shook; from anxiety or the after-effects of the electricity, she wasn't sure. Anger, rage, frustration consumed her in unequal measures.

Dom had said that whatever she felt, she should maintain a cool head and keep going. But what she really wanted to do was jump off the walkway and run out of Arcis.

Warren liked the new, angry Anya.

Sometime in the afternoon the timer reset to ten minutes. The shorter period had served her anger well—made her responses smarter, sharper and more aggressive. But as the anger retreated, so too did the layer of fog that was keeping her in a hazy, unclear state of denial.

Her hands no longer shook when she felt hungry. When she looked in a mirror, her pupils were the least dilated they'd been since arriving in Essention. She was that girl in Brookfield again, but older, wiser and stronger.

Anya worked out her timings with military precision. She noted how long it took to get to the records room and find the right row. She factored in extra time in case others got in her way, or if the files were out of order. She would never be the slowest worker again. The others sped up too, and for the rest of the day everyone avoided electric shocks.

That evening, Anya entered the infirmary room on 2B wearing a borrowed pajama set and clutching a towel and soap to her chest. Her hair was still damp from the shower the supervisor had ordered her to take. A dozen or so beds occupied the antiseptic-smelling, white-walled space. White curtains hid some of the beds.

June and Frank sat on a bed each, their hair also damp. June was alert. Frank was staring at his hands. Anya's backpack sat by the bed between them.

Workers dressed in boiler suits buzzed around expensive-looking hospital equipment. Frank got up and snapped the curtain closed across the front of their beds, leaving the partitions open. The flurry of activity from the infirmary workers died down, replaced by the occasional soft padding of shoes on the gray floor.

The front curtain snapped open. A girl of around sixteen appeared. She was holding a screen. The girl looked at all three of them, made a note on the screen, then snapped the curtain closed. Anya heard her doing the same to the other curtains.

She wanted to tell the girl she felt fine. In fact, she'd felt okay about ten minutes after Dom's injection. Her hands and feet had already healed.

The soft padding drifted further away.

$$\Omega$$

A gentle sobbing sound woke Anya. She sat up slowly and looked around the pitch black space. She groped for the lamp on her bedside locker. Flicking it on, she checked on June, but she was snoring gently. Frank had his back to her, his shoulders moving in time with the sobs.

'Are you okay? Are you hurt?' His crying surprised her. This wasn't the usual bright, bubbly Frank. 'Should I get someone?'

He sniffed. 'I'm fine, Anya. I do this every night. I don't need your help.'

Anya pulled the covers up to her chin.

'Want to talk about it?' she whispered.

'No.' Frank got up, yanked the partition curtain closed and continued to sob.

On the other side, June stirred. Her hands were nestled, prayer-like, against her cheek. 'He misses his father.'

Frank shouted over. 'Shut up, June.'

'We all miss someone in here,' she said louder, for his benefit.

'Who have you lost?' said Anya.

June looked away. 'I don't want to talk about it.'

Frank called over from the other side of the curtain. 'Oh, but you want to talk about *my* family.'

'Go to sleep!' June turned her back to Anya.

Anya switched off the light.

Her mind sparkled with insight, with clarity, and with more sorrow than she could handle. She had slipped up, allowed the pressure of Arcis to get to her. She had been stupid. All three of them had. The electric shock was a reminder to pay attention. To learn. To survive.

And she would begin her healing by forming an alliance with Warren.

On the third day, the supervisor released Anya, Frank and June from the second floor ward. She left Arcis behind, eager to sleep in her own bed again. The sun felt good on her pasty-white skin. She closed her eyes and breathed in the fresh, clean air. The train pulled up to the platform and she climbed on board.

At her stop she got off. Groups of girls in street clothes passed her, but made none of their usual small talk. Workers dressed in the royal-blue uniforms of the factories walked without a word uttered between them. Anya never remembered activity being this quiet before.

Dom had given her something. She believed it to be the case.

He'd warned she would feel different. That evening, she was seeing the town in a new light.

A chill at the thought sped up her walk home. She tried to forget that rebel sympathizers might be in Essention.

Anya hesitated at the front door before opening it. The second she stepped inside a force hit her.

Jason gripped her.

'Where the hell have you been? I've been worried about you. I thought—'

'Thought what?' Anya put down her bag.

Crap. Arcis must not have told him what had happened.

He pulled back. 'I thought you were dead. There was a huge power-dip at work, and Max said it was because something happened at Arcis. Then when you didn't show...'

His worried gaze forced her to step back from him. 'It was nothing. I got an electric shock and had to stay in the infirmary for a couple of nights. I'm fine.' She walked into the kitchen and he followed her.

She spotted a loaf of stale bread on the counter and

found a tin of beans in the cupboard.

Jason watched her from the doorway while she grabbed a can opener from one of the drawers.

Her spine stiffened under his intense gaze. She felt different to *before*, less able to deflect Jason's concern without feeling angry.

'I said I'm okay. Stop staring at me.'

'Are you sure? Electricity can have lingering effects.'

She faced him, one hand gripping the can opener.

'They injected me with something. I feel fine.'

He looked skeptical. 'So they have a way to ease the after-effects of electric shocks now?'

'Apparently.' She twisted the side until the lid popped free. 'And I'd say it's a good thing, because otherwise I might not be here right now.'

Jason said nothing while Anya emptied the can of beans into a pot. She turned on the heat.

His silence unnerved her.

'I'm leaving tonight.'

Her throat tightened. She watched the beans.

'Where are you going?'

'To a town called Foxrush. It's the closest.'

Before, she might have accepted his plan to leave. But now, nothing felt right.

'And how will you get past the guns? You can't scale the wall. It's too high.' She stirred the beans with a jerk.

'There are no perimeter alarms under the wall. The tunnel will take us far enough outside of the guns' range.'

'Why do *you* have to go?' Her voice quivered as she met his gaze.

'Because I was picked for this job, Anya. I've

already told you this.'

She looked away from him.

His tone softened. 'I'm sorry, but I have to do this. I'll be back before you know I'm gone.'

She stared into the pot. 'And if you're not?'

'Then finish your program at Arcis. We're the only generation to survive the cull in Brookfield. Let's make our time here count for something.'

Tears formed in her eyes. 'What can I say to change your mind?'

'Nothing.'

'Then don't tell me what to do. I don't need protection, least of all from Arcis.'

Jason banged his fist on the door, startling Anya. 'Why are you being like this? You were okay with it before.'

Anya glared at him. 'And now I'm not.'

'Fine. Then I guess there's nothing more to say. I'll see you when I get back.' He picked up a bag from the floor, turned and left. A moment later the front door slammed shut.

Anya dropped the spoon and slipped down to the floor. She pulled her knees up to her chest. They'd argued many times before. But this was the first time Jason had left.

The beans burned in the pot above her. She didn't care. Her appetite was gone anyway. The rebels were still active on the outside. Maybe Jason needed to see that for himself.

16

With a change of clothes and some food, Jason traveled by foot to Max and Charlie Roberts' place. He inspected the cuts on his hands. The tunnel in Max's basement was complete. He and a few others had taken turns to dig it out in the evenings. It was possible that Max and Charlie were wrong about and the crop growth in the towns and their efforts could be for nothing.

Jason's own emotions had returned to normal. For several hours after inoculation, he had yelled, screamed, punched things—he'd even left a hole in Max's wall. Max had said the dominant reaction to return was different in everyone, but for the orphans, it was mostly anger.

Jason's mind raced to keep up with the changes in his life. Everything was happening so fast: the antidote, the news of crop growth, the possibility of facing a horde of angry rebels on the outside. The guns that sat on top of Essention's perimeter wall would make their first steps outside difficult, but if there was a chance the towns were livable, he had to know.

He was doing this for Anya, too.

The lights were off in the bungalow with the pale-green door. He slipped around the back and shoved a key

The Facility

into the lock that Charlie had given him.

It was dark inside, but noise rumbled from below. He tensed when he caught movement in the living room. A boy around fourteen years of age jumped up from where he'd been sitting on the sofa.

'Who's there?' he asked, shining a light on Jason's face.

Jason shielded his eyes. 'It's just me.'

The boy stood in the doorway between the living room and hall.

'Don't tell Max I wasn't watching the door. I was just resting my eyes for a moment.'

Jason pushed the boy's arm down until the light lit up the floor.

'No sleeping while you're up here, okay?'

The boy nodded.

Chatting and murmurs, but no laughter hit Jason when he opened the basement door.

Eight sets of eyes watched him descend the stairs. Max Roberts stood in front of a map pinned to the wall. Gathered round him were eight volunteers, young men and women too old for Arcis' skills program.

Excavated earth had been piled high in a section of the basement. The plan was to get back before anyone else noticed they'd gone.

A trestle table in one corner of the room had several items laid out on it. Max turned around.

'Good, you're here,' he said to Jason. 'I was just about to go through the plan.'

He pointed to a red 'X' on the map. 'This is Foxrush, where we've received news of the crop revival. It was the first town the rebels attacked. If the land is clean there, we can expect the other towns to follow suit within a matter of days or weeks. We will leave Essention under the cover of night, but don't underestimate the range of the disintegration guns or heat sensors on the wall. They operate in all conditions. Our aim is to emerge far enough outside of their range so we won't be detected.'

He pointed to the little green clusters on the map.

'You're heading for this forest area. When you're out of the tunnel, make a run for it. Keep running east until you reach a clearing on the other side. Wait for me there and we'll make the journey together.'

Max handed out three compasses from the trestle table. Jason took one.

'Those who have compasses, stand to one side.' Max divided the remaining people into the compass-led groups. 'Everything will look the same in the dark so stay in your groups. Don't wait for the others or me. Just reach the clearing.'

Another problem came to Jason's mind. 'How are we going to mask our location?'

Max picked up a small, black box on the trestle table and opened it. He held up what looked like a pearl-colored disc. 'These magnetic discs will attach to the ones under your skin by use of polarity. It will delay the signal between the chip marking your location and sending the info to Arcis. The disc will give Charlie time to intercept the signal and replace it with a false location before it reaches Arcis. If everything works as it should, all nine of you should show as being in Essention.'

'What about the rebels?' one of the boys asked.

Jason wondered that too. They were venturing into rebel territory. Who knew how many of them still operated? Their motives for the attack were still unclear. Some people believed their targets had been the orbs that roamed the landscape between Essention and the towns. Others, including Jason, believed the rebels had contaminated the towns' food and water supplies so the residents would be forced to follow them.

'They haven't been seen for a few weeks. The towns are clear. That's all I know. If we travel at night, we should be fine.' Max pointed to a box of food under the trestle table. 'Take as much as you can carry.'

Jason's group included a girl and boy, both about nineteen. He stuffed as much food as he could carry into his backpack.

They gathered behind Max at the entrance to the tunnel, bulging backpacks slung over shoulders. The tunnel's narrow width and low height forced everyone to crawl. He twisted his backpack around so it rested on his front. It weighed him down, causing him to breathe harder.

His hands pressed into cold earth. There was no light to guide them, just the sounds the person made ahead of him.

His skin tingled from the cold. His muscles strained when the tunnel veered upwards toward the opening. Ahead, he heard someone exit and run for the forest.

Jason groped for the surface and pulled himself out. He glanced down at the chip in his wrist. His pulse matched his fast breaths. They'd tested the range of the disintegration guns on Essention's walls, but not their heat sensors. Keeping his eyes on the black forest, he ran.

The guns didn't fire.

He made it to the edge of the forest, out of breath and his heart pounding.

From his backpack, he pulled out a torch and the compass and checked for east. Others ran past. His group came together, and he used his torch to shine a way forward through the cluster of trees.

Jason's lungs burned. He rested against a tree for a moment, but a rustling in the trees overheard moved him and his group on.

They arrived at the target clearing on the far side of the forest. Everyone gathered together. Max looked nervous.

Something brighter flashed ahead of him: a set of lights turning on and off. The sound of wheels approaching froze him to the spot.

The rebels.

A truck appeared suddenly and skidded to a halt a short distance away. The headlights dazzled him into submission, cutting off his one chance at escape. Max raised his hands in surrender.

The driver and passenger dressed in green military fatigues got out of the truck. The driver pointed at gun at the group.

'Stop right there!'

A blue light shone out from the front of the truck. It reached them.

Jason didn't dare move.

'They're clear.'

The driver kept the gun on them.

'Don't try anything.'

Max lowered his hands a little. 'Easy. We're not going anywhere.'

The driver gestured with the gun. 'Get on the truck.'

Jason looked at Max, who was already walking to the rear. He waited by the back door while the others climbed on.

The Facility

Jason squeezed himself into a spot on one of the benches. Max climbed in last, looking too tense to relieve his own worries. The driver closed the door. The sound of a lock or a bolt being drawn followed. He looked down at his hands caked in mud. His knees and boots weren't much better.

The truck bumped over uneven land, forcing Jason to grip the underside of the bench to keep steady.

'Where are they taking us?'

'Shhh,' said Max.

Jason concentrated on the bumps and divots in the road. The truck stopped a short distance later and the man with the gun ushered them out.

He recognized the stop as Foxrush. Sheets of corrugated iron attached to steel fences protected the town from prying eyes. Cameras were attached to the tops of the fences. A shallow trench had been dug around the property. Dirt was piled up across the entrance and around the perimeter, like an over-ground moat.

Jason exited the truck slowly, anxious not to rattle the man with the gun. The truck stayed outside the main gates while their group was brought to a smaller side entrance. Jason's pulse thrummed in his ears. The rebels could not be negotiated with. He'd seen that first hand.

A gate opened. He swallowed hard and entered the camp.

Abandoned houses lined the entrance to the town. The main road widened as their group moved away from the perimeter. In the distance, the torn plastic covering the vertical farm billowed in the wind.

People in green military garb swarmed everywhere.

A young woman dressed in green fatigues and black boots approached them, gun in hand. The barrel was pointed off to the side. The driver whispered something to her and walked away.

'I knew this was a bad idea,' someone said.

'Quiet,' hissed Max. He followed the woman holding the gun.

Jason and the others trailed after Max through the center of town. Temporary lights positioned on the roofs of houses brightened their route in the dark. A short distance ahead, a large white tent came into view surrounded by several smaller pitches. Jason saw some of the smaller tents were being used as gun and ammo stores. Another held supplies such as ropes, small and large knives, binoculars and camouflage gear.

The young woman pointed inside the large tent. Max entered first and they followed. The woman stayed outside.

Jason looked around the space with a foldout table in the middle of the room and three chairs. Max perched on the edge of the table.

Something about this felt off. His skin prickled as Max stared at the ground. Why weren't they in a prison cell?

'Max, what's going on?' said Jason. 'What is this place?'

Their leader looked up at him. 'It's a rebel camp.'

'I guessed that, but something's not right.'

'It was the only way to get you here.'

Max stood up and began to pace. The crunching sound his heavy boots made on the dirt floor only escalated Jason's fears.

He stumbled back toward the exit. The woman with the gun appeared and blocked his escape.

Jason glared at Max.

'Who the hell are you?'

Max stopped pacing.

'My name is Colonel Roberts. I'm the leader of the rebellion. I brought you here because Praesidium has been feeding you a pack of lies.'

17

Carissa approached the white podium in front of the screen in the Great Hall. She laid her palm flat on it and waited for her thoughts and memories to pass into the unit. Nothing happened.

Faces flashed and disappeared on small squares of a larger black screen in front of her. A conversation she appeared to have interrupted carried on.

'There are fresh reports of rebel activity in an area to the south of Praesidium. How long before they reach the town of Pottersfield?'

'Soon.'

'We should act quickly, to stem their power.'

'Not until we're sure we can control them. Killing them will only incite the rebellion in others.'

'Then we must build another Essention in the south of the region.'

The Collective preferred to speak in a unified way, but on occasion, individual minds would express their opinions.

The familiar hum of a connection reached her. Her arm tingled as her memories started their download for the Collective.

In one corner of the screen the distorted image of Quintus appeared.

'173-C, your experiences yesterday were varied. I notice you enjoy many things, unlike the other Copies.'

'I like to learn. Watching the humans helps me learn faster.'

'But you are no longer interested in what Praesidium has to offer.' It was more of a statement than a question.

Not since my Original died.

Carissa would erase that thought from tomorrow's offering.

'I'm a child, Quintus. Curiosity and boredom are natural for someone of my age.'

Quintus' distorted mouth turned up into a smile. '173-C, the Collective has found your experiences to be the most interesting. Continue to watch the participants, as before.'

'Thank you, Quintus.'

The Collective, made up of ten masters presiding over Praesidium, continued their conversation without her.

Her arm had stopped tingling. She waited for someone to dismiss her. Faces flashed up on the multiple screens that never held one face for too long.

'We have a week at best,' Unos said.

'They're shielding their location from us,' said Septimus. 'We cannot pinpoint their location on the outside.'

'Are they in the towns?' said Quintus.

'Some of them. We believe others are already in Essention.'

A brief silence, then, 'The rebels must not divert us from our mission. The young are too important. We must protect them, keep them from the false truths. The participants are the only ones who can set us free.'

A second face—a white female the same age as Quintus—appeared to his left. The image started out blurry then became clearer.

'173-C,' said Octavius. 'Talk to the Inventor. Tell him to prepare the machines. We must build another Essention and Arcis at its core, then relocate the young as before, so we may control the message they receive.'

New faces flashed onto the screen—Septimus, Unos, Quatrius—and disappeared just as quickly. The Ten's voices sounded like hushed murmurs in the room, but Carissa heard them clearly through her cerebral unit.

'All that matters is we continue with the Arcis program. Praesidium must be ready to act in this war.'

'What about the rebels?' Carissa asked.

Quintus' face shifted; his mouth settled into a deformed smile. 'Patience, 173-C. With time, we will flush them out.' His almond-shaped eyes sharpened. 'Now hurry, speak to the Inventor. We shall begin building the new Essention tonight.'

Carissa nodded.

She disconnected from the podium and hurried from the room. The muted clacking of her heels followed her back to the glass lobby and entrance to the Learning Center.

She exited the building; a glare assaulted her and she shielded her eyes. She hurried across the courtyard and entered the dark stairwell in the long building opposite.

The darkness gave her relief from the pain of her new human eyes. But a short, sharp stabbing in her chest slowed her descent. She stopped midway and tried to catch her breath.

The Facility

The pain subsided enough for her to reach the bottom step. The short walk from there to the Inventor's workshop left her out of breath.

She found the Inventor in the far corner as usual, working on a Guardian that was set on its side, the exoskeleton held open with a strong winch. More wolves stood off to the side, eerily still and in shutdown mode. If it weren't for the beasts, Carissa would probably visit more.

The Inventor looked up as she approached; his face was smeared with grease. His glasses were on the end of his nose.

'They want to build another Essention,' she breathed out.

The Inventor nodded and removed his glasses. 'Where?'

'Close to Pottersfield.' Carissa gripped the counter for support. 'How fast can you make it happen? They want to keep the young safe.'

The Inventor shuddered, then pointed at the two large digging machines, each with a flatbed.

'As soon as you need them.' He looked up at the retractable roof. 'How many are we expecting the town to hold?'

'Upwards of five thousand.'

He removed his glasses and cleaned them with an oil-stained cloth. 'We'll need a week to make the Essention big enough.'

'Can you do it in three days?'

The Inventor frowned, putting his glasses back on. 'Yes.'

'I'll let the others know.' Carissa tapped a second circular disc, just above her ear. It allowed her to connect to the network and get a message to Quintus. The Inventor watched, waiting for her to finish.

She nodded at the wolves. 'Have them ready to go in an hour.'

The Inventor turned back to the beast on his operating table. But when Carissa didn't leave, he frowned at her.

'Was there something else?'

Carissa pressed a fist into her chest. 'There's something wrong with me. My heart feels strange, stressed.'

He gestured to a second table and cleaned his hands with some gel. 'Take off your dress, Carissa, and lie down.'

She yanked her dress over her head. Underneath, she wore a white camisole and white leggings. She slipped the camisole strap off one shoulder and lay down.

The Inventor pulled on a pair of latex gloves and made a cut in her skin, then pulled back the flap to reveal a metal cage.

'Your pulmonary artery is faulty.' He flicked the dented tube with his finger.

Her breaths shortened while the Inventor worked fast. She felt every tug, every new connection, in her chest. Then he closed the cage and lasered the skin-flap closed.

Carissa sat up and checked her pulse. 'That's better. Thank you.' Sometimes her part-organic heart was more trouble than it was worth.

'My pleasure, Carissa.'

She stared at him for a moment. 'Inventor, why do you call me that?'

'It's your name.'

'My name is 173-C. *I* chose Carissa.'

The Facility

The Inventor smiled. 'Carissa is a name, miss. 173-C is a designation.'

'Why do you stay here, in Praesidium?'

'Because I'm too valuable to the Collective.' The Inventor flashed a smile at her and steered her out. 'Tell the others I'll be ready on time.'

Carissa climbed the stairs with less effort than before.

The bright sunlight pinched her human eyes once more.

She spotted two women, identical in appearance, walking on different paths. One wore white, the other a purple dress. One served the Collective, the other, a human like the Inventor, worked as a librarian. The librarian, or Vanessa, hurried along with several books under her arm. Originals were confined to places like the business plaza, the school for Originals and the library. The Copies worked in any primary zone that served the Collective ten.

Originals and Copies rarely interacted with each other because the Collective saw no value to it. But Carissa was noticing differences overlooked by the ten minds, differences she hid daily from them.

On her walk, she nodded to other white-clad Copies. Their interaction was polite or functional. The Originals smiled, laughed, talked too fast and too often.

Her communication disc pinged. She checked the message. Quintus was calling her back to the Great Hall.

Carissa smoothed down her white dress. There was much to do, and it didn't involve watching footage of the participants in Arcis.

Watching the teenagers had become the highlight of her day.

Their lives—their drama—excited her.

Because like Carissa, they were one of a kind.

18

The temperature outside the tent had plummeted to single-digit figures. Inside, Jason shivered in his thin tunic and trouser ensemble, but his chill had nothing to do with the cool air.

Before him, Max perched on the edge of the trestle table, brows drawn forward. He had his arms folded and was watching them. The woman with the gun remained by the door. Max's declaration had stunned everyone into silence.

Max and Charlie had tricked him.

But had he been tricked? Jason had been off Compliance when he'd entered the tunnel. Nobody had forced him to leave.

Max stood up and spoke. His voice sounded louder and more confident than Jason remembered. He could tell that Max was someone important around Foxrush. Anyone with the title 'colonel' had to be.

At first, his speech was just a jumble of words. Then Jason heard the words 'infiltrate' and 'enemy' and 'Arcis' and his mind sharpened.

'Wait...What?'

Max flicked his eyes to him, and then away.

'Charlie and I targeted each of you because you have the skills we need. Runners, mechanics, electronics experts, gun operators. All of these skills will help us to infiltrate the one place we've tried to get inside for months.' He looked at each of them in turn. 'Your parents helped us to get you ready.'

Foxrush, the town supposed to be showing signs of crop recovery, was crawling with dirty rebels. The vertical farms were in tatters. Jason guessed that nobody was checking the radiation levels in the soil.

He pushed his hair out of his eyes.

Infiltrate Arcis? Why? He mouthed both questions.

Max continued. 'We have tried to access their systems from inside Essention, but their force field and tech-dampening equipment has made that next to impossible. We need to attack Arcis from out here. The Copies don't venture beyond the perimeter because they're safer inside than out. And Compliance controls the residents' actions, so they are not a danger to them.'

'Back up a second.' Jason finally found his voice. 'Why are you looking to infiltrate Arcis?'

'Because the place is dangerous.'

Jason's throat tightened, making it hard to breathe. Anya was in there. 'What's wrong with it? '

Others began making similar demands.

'I thought you understood—'

'Are you telling me... My sister is in danger?' He backed away as far as the edge of the tent.

Max sat on the edge of the trestle table again. 'Your sisters and brothers are tied into Arcis' program. They're safe, for now.'

But Jason needed more than the reassurances of a rebel leader. 'You've done nothing but lie to us since

Essention, Max. I've seen first-hand what happens when people disobey your rules.' His parents had died to protect him and Anya.

Max worked his jaw, as if the subject matter unsettled him. 'You'll hear many things about the rebels. Some will be true, others are lies, made up by those who hold greater power than us. But what we have done, and continue to do, is in the best interest of the people.'

'And that includes lying to us?' said another boy. 'Killing the people we care about? Why not tell us from the start who you were?'

Max glared at the boy. 'Would you have come with me if you knew who I was? You believe the rebels killed your parents. It wasn't us, it was Copies from Praesidium.'

More lies.

Jason gritted his teeth. 'Praesidium has been good to us. So have the controllers of Essention.'

'Up to a point, yes.'

'And the radiation?'

Max nodded. 'That was us.'

'Why?'

'Our target was the Copies and the machines that are part organic. The towns were an inevitable casualty. We had planned to pull you out of the towns and treat you for the sickness, but Praesidium beat us to it.'

'Why wait until now? Why not trust us from the beginning?' Jason shook his head. 'And what the hell are *Copies*?'

Max turned his hard blue eyes on him. 'What would you have done if I'd told you? Would you have listened to me or blabbed to the first person in Essention so they could deal with us?'

Probably the latter.

'To answer your other question, Copies are the machines that look human. They're part AI, part organic, built to look like us so we can relate to them easier.' Max frowned at the stunned faces. 'They're all over Arcis. I thought you knew. They came to get you from the towns? They treated you at the hospital in Essention?'

Heads shook around him. Jason remembered a man and woman at the hospital dressed in black tunics with gold neckbands. They had injected him and Anya with their location chips. But there hadn't been anything odd about the pair.

Max rubbed his chin. 'I suppose it makes sense. Why ruin a good illusion? The Copies from Praesidium are far easier to relate to in Arcis than the wolves are.'

'Wolves? In Arcis?' His mind raced.

Max stood up straight. His broad shoulders and height gave him a sense of command.

'I know you have questions, but things will be clearer after a good night's rest. We can pick this up in the morning. Thomas will show you to your dorms.'

A slim boy had appeared at the entrance and was standing beside the woman with the gun. He was about nineteen, with short brown hair and dressed in green fatigues. He didn't look much like a soldier.

'We can talk more later,' said Max. 'Please give all your food to the kitchen.'

The sky brightened as night turned into early morning. Jason and the others followed Thomas through Foxrush. Jason considered making a run for it, but gun-toting rebels lining the perimeter changed his mind. Beyond the main tent pitched in the center of town was a large farmhouse made of flat, gray stone, with an adjoining building. Thomas showed them into the kitchen in the farmhouse, where a numb Jason emptied his bag of food.

By the time Thomas reached the adjoining building the adrenaline had depleted, leaving Jason bone tired. Dozens of 'beds'—green material stretched across horizontal poles—were laid out neatly in the large square room. He caught the faint smell of grain in a space that may have once operated as a barn.

'Just pick a free one,' said Thomas. 'We don't have any favorites around here.'

Jason dropped his empty bag on the floor. He lay down in his mud-caked clothes and closed his eyes. But his mind refused to settle.

$$\Omega$$

A few hours later, nothing had changed. They were still prisoners and Jason had left Anya in a place the rebels were trying to infiltrate.

He had assured his sister she would be safe in Essention.

Could he trust Max? Or Charlie?

If he was really a prisoner in Foxrush, he didn't feel like one. No shackles, no rough treatment. But Jason wasn't ready to hand his trust over to Colonel Roberts just yet.

Anya was his priority. He would do as Max asked as long as it helped her. If Arcis was dangerous, he needed to know how much.

Jason whipped the blanket off him. His boots, hands, tunic and trousers were covered in dried tunnel mud.

He found the bathroom down a small corridor that was just a sink and a toilet. He pulled off his tunic and washed his face, neck and hands in cold water, then dressed in his dirty clothes again. Next, he hit the kitchen and ate a modest meal of chicken substitute, apple slices and a wedge of bread—all food they'd brought from Essention.

With food in his belly he was ready to ask more questions.

Jason returned to the main tent, half-expecting an armed soldier to shadow him, but no one followed. He found the tent empty. In one of the smaller ones, a rebel soldier was testing one of the weapons. He jerked to a stop when the soldier cocked it.

'Colonel Roberts has gone out,' said the soldier without looking up. He aimed the gun at the tent wall and fired with a small click.

Jason watched him slide back the empty chamber. Anya had shown him how to fire a gun once. He'd hated it then, but now, maybe he should learn properly. An array of guns was spread out on the table. He stepped closer to them. Would the soldier notice if one went missing?

The soldier gave him an odd look and Jason left the tent empty-handed. He spent the next hour wandering around Foxrush, looking for an alternative way out. In addition to the armed rebels protecting the perimeter, the corrugated steel surrounding the town was too high and too slippery for him to climb.

More houses near the steel fence had been gutted and blackened from fire.

Had the rebels done that?

His school, run by Praesidium, had warned of the rebellion. The rebels were marauders who gutted and burned any property they looted, and killed whoever got in their way.

But something bothered Jason about this particular rebel camp. He felt too comfortable here.

An hour later, Max and several others came through the main entrance, holding what looked like a cache of weapons. Max handed his haul over to a twenty-something soldier.

'We found them in the next town over,' he said to the young man. 'They were just lying there. I've sent Louise and Kelvin to monitor things. It's closer to Essention than Foxrush.'

Jason's stomach turned. Brookfield was close to Essention. Were they talking about his old hometown? Why had they found guns there?

Max strode over to him. Jason stood his ground, his fists tight by his side.

'You look like you're ready to talk some more.' Max nodded at the main tent. 'I promised you answers. Come on. I'll tell you whatever you want to know.'

As Jason followed, he saw the others from his group exploring Foxrush. Were they ready to believe Max?

In the tent, Max pulled forward a couple of chairs and sat in one. He gestured for Jason to take the other.

'I'd prefer to stand.' Jason folded his arms. 'When are we going back to Essention?'

'Soon.'

'But not as soon as you led us to believe?'

Max shook his head.

'What about my sister? If Anya's in danger like you say, I could have brought her here.'

Max leaned forward and rested his arms on his legs. 'She has a different chip in her wrist. It will kill her if she tries to leave Essention. All the Arcis participants have them.'

Jason remembered Charlie's tech was masking their location. 'But not our chips?'

'Charlie wasn't sure but he didn't want to take that risk. All we know is the chip will only release its hold on her when she completes the program. Anya is safe as long as she believes she is.'

Had Jason been too sick to notice the Copies in the hospital, or that they'd given Anya a different chip to him? His stomach twisted with guilt.

Max was watching him. 'Don't give in to the guilt, Jason. You couldn't have done anything to change Anya's outcome.'

Perhaps not, but Jason wanted to know something else. He dropped into the chair.

Max eyed him. 'You want to know if we came by this town peacefully.'

'It had crossed my mind.'

'There was nobody here when we took over. The towns closest to Essention were all cleared out. Their residents are living in Essention now.'

'Let's say I believed you and what you said about the Copies from Praesidium. Why did they kill our parents?'

'They wanted to separate the teenagers from the adults. Would your parents have let them take your sister if they were still alive?'

Jason shook his head. 'Praesidium was saving us from you. From your attacks.'

'Yes, we were responsible for the radiation attacks. But it was to halt Praesidium's control over the towns.'

'Control of what?'

Max sighed and straightened up. 'We don't know why they want the teenagers, or why you and I are too old for their program. But whatever they want, it has to do with the ninth floor.'

'What proof do you have that there's anything going on?'

'A huge power surge occurs there when rotation happens. Nobody's ever completed the nine floors and come out of there to explain why.'

Jason frowned. 'What, they just disappear?'

'Yes. Never to be seen again.'

Jason glared at Max, searching for signs of his deceit. Nothing.

'Why do you and Charlie care so much about what happens in Arcis, anyway?'

Max shifted in his chair. 'Several months ago, when Essention was first built, I lost my wife to that place. At the time they passed Arcis off as a place to learn how to use the latest Praesidium technology.'

Jason remembered. He'd been refused entry into Essention at the time.

'There was no program then, just the promise of work,' said Max. 'The former idea came later to motivate the teenagers it was so desperate to attract.'

'And she never came out?'

Max shook his head. 'The very same thing will happen to your sister and hundreds of others if we don't figure out the purpose of Arcis. We don't know what's on each of the floors, but we do know that the participants must complete the program without fail.' He leaned forward, his gaze wary. 'I'm sorry for lying to you, but we need to make things right. We took too long to act before.'

Yet Foxrush took them away from the problem. 'Why did we leave Essention?'

'We operate freely inside Essention but our equipment doesn't. Arcis emits a jamming signal that renders any non-Essention equipment useless. We've been trying to monitor what happens during their power surges. Our equipment appears to work better the farther we are from their signal. Less interference.'

The chips, the scanners, the shiny orbs. Jason had seen plenty of visible tech that could be disrupting their attempts to monitor Arcis.

He wasn't sure if he could trust Max, but if it meant helping Anya, he would play along. He touched the pearl-colored disc attached magnetically to the chip beneath his skin.

'How long before the disc stops working? Before they know we're not still in Essention?'

'A few days, a week, indefinitely. I don't know. Friends in Praesidium smuggled this tech out of the city, so it should be powerful enough to fool them. Charlie will keep intercepting the signal and updating your location for as long as he can.'

'So your plan is to keep us here until we agree to fight with you?'

'Actually, I was hoping you'd help us to figure out the rotation pattern.'

'Pattern?'

'The length of time that passes between each rotation cycle. They use a lot of power during rotation, enough for the energy levels to spike and dip. The power surges weaken their defenses. We need to manipulate weak spots in Arcis rather than challenge the whole system. I was hoping you'd help us if you saw what we have so far.'

Jason leaned forward. 'And if I want to return to Essention now?'

'That's not possible. Getting out of Essention is easy. Going back will take careful timing.'

He leaned back. 'We can use the tunnel.'

Max shook his head. 'The tunnel is gone. Charlie will have seen to that. We can't risk the orbs finding it.'

Jason dragged a hand through his hair.

'You don't think the Copies are smart enough to know the rebels are out here?'

'Oh, they know we're out here. But they don't run the show. They are workers, drones. We're hoping the controllers have yet to figure out our numbers or what we want.'

'Essention isn't that big a place. You could probably take it.'

'There's more than one Essention with an Arcis at its core, but if we take down one of them we might weaken the network.'

'You mean Praesidium's network?'

Max nodded. 'Something happens inside Arcis that draws power from the town's supply. It disrupts the power to the guns and sensors on the perimeter wall, and, I'm guessing, the force field around Arcis itself. We have people monitoring the power levels and how often they drop, but we need to learn more about the cycle, predict it. That's where you come in. With your analytical mind, you might see new markers that will give us an early detection. You understand electricity, right?'

Jason shrugged. 'I don't know much about Praesidium technology.'

Max stood. 'It will be enough. Whatever Arcis is doing, it needs a hell of a lot of power to do it. It's where we'll strike when the time's right. Until then, we must plan our way back in to Essention.'

19

Anya had learned a simple way to avoid the worst of the shocks: drop the scanner. The electricity still caught her, but at least she could function after.

Maintain a cool head and keep going. That's what Dom had said to her.

She wanted to ask him why her thoughts were clearer than before, why her hands no longer shook. Why she could see the blue of her eyes.

He'd given something to her.

But for the last three weeks, Dom had been like a ghost on her floor, only showing up when someone got shocked. He never talked to her, nor did he reassure her everything would be fine. Anya did the only thing she could: she watched what Dom did to treat her. A head start for when she rotated to the second floor.

Jason's departure had picked open a wound of loss that had not yet healed. The morning after, she'd woken to find her brother gone. It prompted her to pack a bag and do the same.

The first-floor dormitory was her new home now. It wasn't long after her arrival that Warren, June, Tahlia, Frank and Jerome did the same. She looked around the coed space with plain beds on either side, covered in blankets matching the cold gray color of the walls and floors. Some participants had stuck pictures on the wall behind their beds. A reminder of what they had left behind. The space above Anya's bed was bare.

Girls on one side, boys on the other.

Since arriving on the first floor, Warren hadn't mentioned the alliance. Anya wondered if he'd changed his mind about needing her.

No matter. With her mind clearer than before, she could do this alone.

For nearly three weeks, she'd sprinted between the rooms, sometimes not fast enough. Tahlia's shorter height was working to her disadvantage. It was taking her twice as long to get her files as the others. Most days, everyone received a shock from their machines. Anya had carried Tahlia's file once, and received a double-shock as punishment.

All last week, the timer had held steady at eight minutes. But when a clean run and no shocks cost them two minutes, Anya finally got the most important rule on the first floor: speed. To pass their test everyone had to be slower than the clock. If she and the others beat the timer, the time decreased. If anyone was late, the time remained a constant, but the straggler received a shock. With rotation around the corner, all timers were holding steady at five minutes.

Anya was on one ladder when a wailing siren signaled the end of shift. She slotted the file back into the hanging folder with a quiet sigh and dropped down to the floor.

With a yawn, she shuffled to the dining room, where she queued behind Tahlia for one ration of scrambled eggs and toast.

The first-floor participants sat at tables; most of them had avoided shocks. Their proficiency had cost them some time. But at least Tahlia's clunky efforts had kept the clock steady.

The tension in the room made her skin hum. The shocks and sleepless nights had put everyone on edge. Even best friends Jerome and Frank could barely look at each other. Anya dropped into a seat between them.

June played with her food, yawning between little bites. Tahlia's pink strands had almost grown out, replaced by dark brown hair that matched the color of her skin.

At least they'd made it this far.

'Do you know what we need?' she said.

Nobody looked at her, except for Warren. He held a fork loosely in one hand, as if bored.

'We need to do something to blow off some steam.' She turned to the other groups in the room.

The girl with the wiry blonde hair looked over. Anya had since learned her name: Yasmin. 'What did you have in mind?'

Anya hadn't really thought that far.

'What floors do we have access to?'

Her heart fluttered when she thought about sneaking up to the second floor to see Dom.

'This one,' said Frank. 'We work, eat and crap on this floor.'

June wrinkled her nose. 'Why do you have to be so disgusting?'

'Because I'm a guy and that's what guys do,' said Frank, half-joking, half-ready to throw something at the wall behind June's head.

An idea came to Anya. She looked down at her food and scooped some scrambled eggs into her hand. She flung them at June. June gasped, her mouth hanging open in shock. Anya blushed hard. She was about to apologize when June flung a bread roll at her nose.

'Ow.'

June's grin made her laugh.

Someone giggled at the next table over. Frank scooped some meat out of a pot and... aimed for her. She jerked out of the way in time. The meat landed on Jerome's face.

Frank stuck out his tongue at Jerome. 'I've wanted to do that all week.'

Anya slid under the table. The room exploded into fits of laughter. She heard slapping sounds above her as food landed on tables, on people—on anything other than the plates.

A hand groped for her. It was Tahlia. 'Where do you think you're going? You started this. You need to finish it.' Mischief flashed in her eyes as she pulled Anya out from safety.

Anya wriggled out of her grasp and ran over to the food counter. A splodge of food missed her face but caught her skirt. She pulled her blouse out from her waistband and made it into a bowl, then scooped whatever soft food she could find—more scrambled eggs, stew, bread rolls—into her blouse. Others copied her idea, and she flung food at whoever wandered too close. Yasmin smashed soft banana into her face. Anya clawed the worst of it away so she could see.

The Facility

The slimy food made the floor slippery. The benches and tables disappeared under a layer of gunk.

Anya crept up on Yasmin while she was distracted. She scooped up her remaining food stash, pulled out the back of Yasmin's blouse and dropped it down her back.

Yasmin yelped and spun around.

'That's for being rude to me on my first day.'

Yasmin stared at her for a moment, then let the food drop from her blouse into her hand. She dashed over to one of the boys and pressed it into his neck.

Anya smiled at the faces around her, bright and jovial. This was one of her better ideas.

After the fight, some of the boys shook their heads like dogs while the girls carefully combed food out of their hair with squeals of disgust. They cleaned the dining hall as best as they could, laughing while they worked. Anya ate whatever wasn't on the floor.

She entered the girls' bathroom that was close to the dorms in Tower A. June and Tahlia stripped out of their uniforms.

'That was great fun,' said June, smiling. 'I didn't realize how much I needed it.'

'Me too,' said Anya.

Tahlia and June both hummed tunes as they elbowed each other for space at the sink. Anya soaked her blouse and skirt in a basin of water and changed into her Essention tunic and trousers.

If rotation occurred every month, that left a week on the first floor. She could handle seven more days.

Anya squeezed out the excess water from her blouse and skirt and carried her clothes to the door.

'See you back in the dorm,' she said to the pair, who were still scrubbing their clothes.

Anya walked down a corridor that took her past a couple of doors to empty rooms. One of the doors flew open suddenly. Anya jerked to a stop.

'Hey, Anya. Can you come here for a minute?'

Yasmin stood at the half-opened door.

Anya frowned as she entered the small room.

The experienced first-floor workers were inside, but one familiar face drew her attention. Anya stared at a clearly nervous Warren.

Her pulse thrummed against her throat. 'What's wrong?'

'Anya, we notice you've been quick in getting your files,' said Yasmin.

She nodded slowly.

'And we've noticed there are a few in your group who haven't been so fast.'

She bit her lip.

'Well, you've probably figured out that the time decreases if we all make it back on time, but it stays the same if one of us is late.'

Anya cut her eyes to Warren. He was chewing on his thumb and staring at the wall.

She flicked her eyes away. 'So what?'

Yasmin stepped forward. The move made Anya nervous. 'We've been here one rotation more than you. We can't miss another.' Yasmin nodded at Warren. 'And he says you two have formed an alliance to progress.'

Anya glared at Warren. He glanced at her before looking away.

Yasmin continued. 'Warren overheard two supervisors say that they will rotate everyone if someone is consistently last.'

She hadn't seen the first-floor supervisor around lately. 'When? Where?'

She was looking at Warren, but Yasmin answered her.

'Just now.'

'Where?' she repeated.

'There were two of them in the elevator room,' said Warren. 'The male said the dining hall had been trashed. He said the Collective wanted to move us on because we were causing too much trouble.'

Something about this didn't feel right.

She focused on Yasmin. 'And why am I here?'

Yasmin's wet hair glistened. She was close enough that Anya could smell banana on her skin.

'The supervisors said that without a consistent last-place finisher, the Collective will take an average count of all our performances. Any of us could be left behind. Possibly more than one.'

Anya swallowed down a hard lump as she realized what Yasmin was asking. 'You want someone to volunteer for last position?'

Yasmin nodded. A look of desperation flashed in her pale-green eyes.

'We want you to make sure someone finishes last,' she said. 'And you know who that someone is.'

Anya shook her head. 'Tahlia is my friend. I can't do that to her.'

'Come on, Anya,' said Warren. 'We're in competition with each other. She's not your friend. She and June talk about you behind your back. She'd do the same to leave this floor.'

'No, she wouldn't.'

Warren huffed. 'Jerome and Frank have each other. Tahlia and June have paired up. We need to do the same.'

Anya stared at Warren, Yasmin and the others. When had life become so cheap and friendships so disposable?

'If you don't do it and we're left behind,' said Warren, 'I'll make you regret that decision.'

All eyes were on her. Anya stepped back, needing out of the room.

'Can I think about it?'

'Don't take too long,' said Warren. 'We may not have a lot of time left before rotation.'

Outside, she released a shaky breath. She returned to the dorm to find Tahlia and June sitting on their beds. Looking secretive.

'Where did you get to?' said June. Tahlia lay down and closed her eyes.

Anya looked at the ground. 'I was talking to Yasmin.'

'What about?'

She looked up. 'Nothing. Just about the food fight.'

June smiled and lay down. 'Yeah, it was good fun, wasn't it?'

Warren entered the room and watched Anya all the way to his bed. Then, he flicked his eyes away and joined Frank and Jerome, who were playing cards.

'Is something up?' June glanced at Warren then looked at Anya. 'What's going on with you and Warren?'

'Nothing. I'm just tired, that's all.'

June propped herself up on one elbow and whispered, 'Don't trust him, Anya.'

Tahlia was snoring.

Anya leaned in closer. 'Did Tahlia tell you that? You know she hates him, right?'

'Yeah, but it turns out I can make my own mind up about people. Don't be so quick to trust him.'

Anya smiled. 'Like you and Tahlia? You two have been whispering behind my back since the day I met you.'

'Not about you.'

'I don't care. I'm tired. I want to go to sleep.'

June lay down again. 'Just think about what I said. Okay?'

Anya ground her teeth so hard her jaw hurt. 'Okay.'

What the hell was she supposed to do now? She could see the logic in Yasmin's plan. It wasn't cruel; Tahlia would rotate eventually.

Guilt pinched at her heart. Could she do that to Tahlia? Could Warren?

Tahlia's snores got louder until Anya's skin crawled at the sound.

Her friend would get over it. She was strong-willed. All would be forgotten by the time she and Anya met up on one of the upper floors.

If it made so much sense, why wasn't Anya saying yes to the plan?

20

That night, Anya got no sleep. Yasmin and Warren's plan caused her to toss and turn all night. When the morning siren jolted her awake, she shook off the lethargy, dressed and tied up her hair.

A new day. A new gauntlet run.

At 9am, Anya's screen flashed up the file number: 6112.

The timer began to count back from five minutes, the lowest it had been all week.

She ran barefoot to the records room to get there faster. But while her start felt strong, seeing Tahlia on her heels shocked her enough to speed up.

Anya burst into the records room and skidded to a halt. Her eyes scanned the holographic displays which illuminated a small section on the wooden cabinet. She bristled when Tahlia came to stand right at her shoulder. When the others arrived, Anya lunged for one of the ladders. The ladder jerked when someone else climbed on.

'I'm 6330,' said Tahlia from below. 'I saw your screen. My file is near yours. I won't have time to get mine. You have to grab both.'

The Facility

They had discussed this strategy among their group: to help each other out if they were close to another's file. But after Yasmin's talk yesterday, Anya had to make a choice.

Tahlia's weight on the ladder slowed her search.

Should she waste her lead by looking for Tahlia's file? Her decision could risk Tahlia being last again. But if what Yasmin had said about rotation being a lottery was true, Anya could be the loser no matter how well she performed.

But Tahlia was her friend.

'Get off the ladder first,' said Anya. 'I can't move it with you on the end.'

But her friend didn't budge.

She hesitated over a bunch of files, knowing Tahlia's was in there and that she could grab it in seconds.

'Come on, Anya. It's right there.'

Irritation streaked through her. She grabbed her own file and started to climb down.

'I don't have time. The sooner you get off the ladder, the faster you can get it yourself.'

Her friend hesitated, but saw sense and moved.

Anya's bare feet hit the walkway, but her guilt soon slowed her down. By the time she reached the other side, she'd convinced herself that Tahlia would have done the same thing if she'd been in her position.

The thought flittered from her mind as she crashed through the double doors. All that mattered now was beating the clock. The terminal, with thirty seconds remaining, brought her to a sudden halt.

Anya scanned the file, certain she'd made the right decision to look after herself. Her timer stopped and she released a breath. The others had made it back safe, all except one.

The timer on Tahlia's screen continued to count backward, puncturing the silence with its mechanical *tick, tick, tick*. A blur of brown and pink flew past Anya. Tahlia slammed into her terminal and fumbled with the scanner. Anya wanted to be sick.

She took a step closer, but Warren flashed her a warning look and she stopped.

A breathless Tahlia pressed the scanner over the barcode. Anya's own chest rose and fell too fast.

The mechanical ticking stopped. She couldn't see her screen. Before or after the clock ran out?

BEFORE OR AFTER?

The terminal whirred, rumbled, and screeched. Still holding on to the scanner, Tahlia stared blankly at the screen,

'Drop the scanner!' Anya shouted at her.

Yasmin shot her a look.

Anya ignored her. 'Drop it, now.'

Tahlia looked up at her, confused, and then down at her own hand. A jolt hit her and her eyes rolled back into her head. She stood frozen to the floor while a current leaped from the terminal to her hand. Anya felt the shudder through the cushioned floor, so violent that it looked like it might break Tahlia's bones.

Anya muffled her cries with her hand.

The shock was bad. Very bad. The current never lasted more than a few seconds, but this one continued to pulsate through a connected Tahlia.

Her friend shuddered as wave after tiny wave ran through her. Bright strands of light jumped from the scanner to her hand. Her pink hair danced as if alive.

Anya glanced at the door, expecting to see the first-aiders. But they were alone, watching their friend die. And it was all because of her.

'Tahlia!'

She looked at June, Jerome and Frank, willing them to do something. Frank stepped forward, but changed his mind and stepped back. Even Warren and Yasmin looked shocked.

Anya searched the room for something. She spotted a sweeping brush in one corner, grabbed it and ran over to Tahlia. Through blurred vision she extended the brush, inching the top of the handle toward Tahlia's chest.

She anchored her stance and jabbed the top of the handle sharply.

Tahlia stumbled backward, releasing the scanner. The sparks died the instant the connection broke. Warren and Jerome reacted fast and broke her fall. They lowered her to the floor.

She wasn't moving.

All the terminals powered off. The electricity from Tahlia's machine dissipated into a gentle hum.

Warren was staring at Tahlia. Jerome was chewing on his thumb.

June looked at Anya, eyes bright with tears. 'What do we do? I don't know how to help her. I'm not trained for this.'

Anya shook her head to clear her thoughts. She tried to remember what Dom had done. This time was different: none of them had been rendered unconscious before. Was it a malfunction, or punishment? Was Warren telling the truth about the supervisors? Had they known that Tahlia was the slowest? Had they targeted her on purpose?

Anya shook her head again. *Focus.*

She knelt beside Tahlia and checked her pulse. It was weak. She checked her airway and breathing. The shock had swollen Tahlia's throat a little, but it was enough that she might not be getting sufficient air. She tilted Tahlia's head back gently and pinched her nose, then breathed into her mouth. Her chest rose and fell. Anya checked her pulse again to find it stronger. But her heart rhythm felt uneven.

She steadied her own breathing.

Everyone was staring at her, waiting for her to fix this. She wasn't trained for this either. She didn't know what else to do.

She continued to blow air into an unconscious Tahlia's mouth, then checked her pulse again. If she lost the pulse, she would need to do compressions. Dom had said once that the first few minutes were crucial to saving a person's life.

Anya was blowing new air into Tahlia's mouth when someone in a boiler suit knelt down beside her.

She caught the look of shock on Dom's face. But he wiped his expression clean. He carried a bigger box this time; a black one. He pulled out a light and an oxygen mask from the case.

'I'm sorry, Anya. I was held up. How long was she connected to the scanner for?'

He shone the light down Tahlia's throat, then placed a mask connected to a small oxygen tank over her nose and mouth. He held up the syringe that was designed to counter the effects of shock.

'I... I don't know.'

'Three seconds—Five? What?'

'Longer.'

His dark eyes flashed with anger as he gave Tahlia an injection in her upper arm and checked her pulse. He inspected the wounds on her hands and feet. Circles of red and black marked the soles of Tahlia's bare feet where the electricity had grounded itself. Dom turned Tahlia's hands over and applied salve to her wounds. He used the stethoscope to check her heart.

Two first-aiders arrived, lifted Tahlia onto a floating stretcher and carried her toward the exit.

Dom packed away his things, hesitating for a moment. He squeezed Anya's arm.

'You might just have saved her life.'

'Will she be okay?'

'I don't know.' Dom's eyes were deep and familiar pools of warmth. He flashed a smile that didn't last long enough to calm her. 'But you've given her a decent chance.'

Anya held his gaze until he broke away. She watched him leave after the stretcher.

Whirring and pinging noises broke the silence. The terminals were rebooting.

Anya snapped out of her trance. The others watched their terminals. The lingering electricity—and maybe a sense of dread—had transformed the air around her, making it feel thicker.

'Whatever happens,' said Yasmin. 'Don't hold on to the scanner.'

New file numbers appeared. The timer remained static at five minutes.

Tahlia didn't realize it, but she'd given them all the gift of time.

Anya, on the other hand, had tripped her up and stomped over her to get it. Her stomach churned with a mix of adrenaline and regret.

Rotation week was coming. She had to get off the first floor.

21

Three days had passed and there was still no news about Tahlia.

As Anya entered what she hoped was the final week before rotation, many feelings consumed her: guilt, desperation, sadness. Hope.

It could have been her. She had to do it.

You could have said no to Yasmin.

She hated herself.

Despite the somber atmosphere created by Tahlia's absence, Anya pushed on with her busy schedule. The timer didn't care about the fallen or the weak or the sad.

Yasmin continued to avoid her. But Warren had the nerve to console her.

'Don't beat yourself up, Anya,' he said an hour after Tahlia had been taken away. 'It could have been any one of us. Tahlia's strong. She'll make it. You did it so the rest of us would have a chance.'

But the blame wasn't hers to shoulder alone. It had been a group decision to target Tahlia.

When had Arcis turned Warren so cold?

The slowest had been taken out of the equation. Yet, here they still were, still running between the rooms.

She was in the records room, one foot on the ladder, another on the floor, when Supervisor One walked in. She spotted him through the gaps between the shelves, the collar of his black tunic tight against his thick neck.

'The timer has been paused. Come down, please.'

Anya stepped off the ladder without her file. The supervisor spoke to the group.

'I have news about your fellow worker, Tahlia Odare.'

Anya's heart thumped. *Odare.* She didn't even know Tahlia's last name.

'She's been in a coma for a few days now. I'm afraid the medics can't do anything more for her. As of ten minutes ago, they turned off her life support. She passed away.'

A coma? But she was supposed to be recovering in the infirmary.

Anya's searched the room, for a way out perhaps.

Supervisor One walked past them to the elevator room. He paused at the door.

'One more thing. Rotation is scheduled for tomorrow. In light of... recent events.'

He left, and the guilt slipped into her heart like a knife.

Tahlia was dead?

What about the things Warren had overheard? That they'd *all* rotate if someone was consistently last. Had this all been for nothing?

Anya hadn't meant for Tahlia to die.

What kind of monster did that make her?

She collected her file and ran.

Ω

The mood in the dormitory that evening barely elevated above flat and quiet. Yasmin and her friends either slept or read. There was a noticeable shift in the group dynamic. The remaining ground-floor participants had joined Yasmin's group. Yasmin must have spoken to them, too.

Anya lay on her bed facing the wall. The knife of guilt slipped deep, making her chest hurt. The springs on her bed creaked. Someone moved her feet, causing her to turn sharply.

'Make room,' said June, squashing her back against the wall. She pulled her feet up close to her chest.

Anya sat up. Frank, Jerome and Warren sat down on the bed opposite. Warren had tears in his eyes. At least he looked remorseful.

'I didn't expect her to die,' said June.

Warren shook his head. 'I don't think anyone did.'

June hugged her legs. 'I don't like this place. There's nothing educational about it. They're pitting us against each other.'

Like a test.

The boys sat still, but their eyes refused to settle.

'What happens if we aren't picked for rotation?' said June. 'I don't think I can go through another month of electric-shock therapy.'

'Okay, we know they administer first aid on the second floor,' said Frank. 'I can do that. But what's above that, and above that?'

'Well, Franklin,' said Jerome, 'since we've only ever interacted with those from the second floor, that will probably remain a mystery.' He looked at Anya. 'You'll be a natural at first aid. You were amazing with Tahlia.'

Heat pooled in her cheeks. She stared at the wall.

They sat in silence. It was easier than talking about it.

Eventually, June spoke. 'What Dom does seems easy enough. Maybe the first floor won't be that bad.'

'For the people who survive,' said Anya.

The pain returned. June crossed her arms over her chest. Anya fiddled with the stitching on her pajamas.

'Anya, you know Dom best out of all of us,' said Frank. Her cheeks flushed again. 'Any chance he could give us a heads-up on what's above him?'

June stared at Frank. 'Why do you care what's on the third floor? We haven't even got to the second floor yet.'

'Child,' Frank said in a mocking voice, 'boys look ahead. Girls are just happy to be busy.'

Anya threw her pillow at Frank. He caught it and clutched it to his chest. Frank reminded her of Jason, before their lives had changed. Her heart twanged with the pain of not knowing if her brother was okay.

An announcement played over the intercom.

'Participants on the first floor. Please gather in the records room at 8.30am sharp. Rotation is imminent. Bring your personal belongings with you.'

Warren smiled down at his legs.

'Are we likely to get any sleep tonight?' said June.

'Nah, I'm too wired,' said Warren. 'Let's play a game.' He pulled out a pack of cards from his pocket.

They played poker for about twenty minutes, then blackjack. An hour later, after the boys had won almost every hand, they all climbed into their beds. Frank tossed Anya's pillow back over.

She fell asleep, but woke in the middle of the night, shaking with a grief that would not go away.

22

Anya leaned against the wall of the records room and dropped her backpack by her feet.

June was to her left, Warren to her right. She gripped both their hands. Seeing Warren cut up about Tahlia's death had softened her feelings toward him.

The mood around her had a strange, anticipatory feel to it. She stared at the filing cabinets that she hoped never to see again.

Supervisor One entered the room, clutching a small screen in one hand. Anya swallowed hard.

This was it. She had to rotate. She hadn't gone along with Yasmin's plan for nothing.

She released her friends' hands and dried her own on her black skirt.

'The following people are being rotated: Jerome, Yasmin, Warren, Lisa, Terrence, Damian, June.'

That was almost everyone from Yasmin's group. None of the original ground-floor workers' names had been called.

The shock almost floored her. Warren got it wrong. They weren't all rotating. Tahlia's sacrifice had been for nothing.

Jerome stared at Frank. June released a quiet breath, seemingly unaware that two members of their group were missing from the list.

'The seven of you please show me your cards.'

They each took turns, and the supervisor ran their elevator cards through a black plastic unit attached to his screen, then handed them back. 'Your card will take you to the second floor. Please wait for me in there.' He gestured to the changing room.

'The rest of you, back to work.'

That was it—she wasn't rotating?

You don't deserve it.

She turned to go, but the supervisor said, 'Anya, please wait a moment.'

She stopped.

Jerome refused to leave Frank. 'What the hell, man? Why aren't you coming with us?'

'Don't worry. Anya and I will see you soon.' Frank's voice broke on the last word as he returned to the terminal room with the others.

Warren gave Anya's shoulder a squeeze; June's gaze lingered on her for a moment before she left.

The room emptied until it was just Anya and Supervisor One. Fresh tears threatened to fall.

'Anya Macklin, the ninth floor has remarked on your efforts to save Tahlia Odare. They've decided you aren't suited for the second floor.'

She gulped back a rising sob. 'Please, I'll work harder than anyone else on the second floor. Give me a chance. *I can't—*'

'Silence. You've already shown them what they need to see. They want to rotate you to the third floor.'

Anya shook her head. 'What? How?'

'Follow me, please.' He walked away.

'I don't understand.'

The supervisor didn't wait for her. She picked up her bag and stumbled after him.

The third floor? She'd cheated to get there.

The others were already gone by the time they reached the elevator.

'Give me your card,' said the supervisor. He upgraded it and handed it back to her. 'This will give you access to the third floor only.'

The elevator door opened and he gestured her inside. 'Get in.'

Anya stepped inside the all-steel elevator and presented the access card to a brushed silver panel. She kept her back turned to Supervisor One. If she didn't look at him he couldn't change his mind.

The elevator closed and opened again. Anya turned around.

She exited the elevator and stared at the large railing with clothes in the center of the room. There was a sign attached to the rail.

Wear what you want.

She ran her fingers along the different-colored clothes, then looked down at the skirt and blouse she hated more than anything.

Anya stripped down to her underwear and dropped the sweat-stained blouse, skirt and shoes into the recycle chute. She found a fitted pair of black trousers and a white long-sleeved top. She grabbed a gray hoodie and zipped it right up to her neck. She pulled on a pair of socks—oh, how she had missed socks—and slotted her feet into a pair of gray and white trainers.

A high-pitched whistle came from the elevator shaft. Then a whirring sound. Her left foot bounced as she sat down.

Who would she be working with? What would she be doing?

The elevator doors opened and Dom appeared first. His tight hair had grown back and was coming in dark and thick. She hadn't noticed it before but his hair had a natural curl to it. His dark-brown eyes were framed by even darker circles. He looked the palest she'd seen him.

Four others appeared, including a girl and boy younger than Anya. She did a double take when she saw a smiling Frank with them.

Then Sheila appeared, and Anya's breath caught in her throat. She focused on Frank.

'I just left you...'

'I know,' said Frank with a smile. 'Supervisor One came to get me when you left. He sent me to the second floor. Jerome nearly had a heart attack. But then Supervisor Two sent me to this floor. And here I am.'

At first, she ignored the attention Dom gave her and Frank. Then, her eyes flickered to his and she saw surprise there. It was a surprise to her, too.

Dom made quick introductions all round. The younger boy was Lucas and the girl was Lilly.

'And you already know Sheila...'

'Um, yes,' said Anya. Sheila ignored her and looked around the room. Then she gave Anya a what-the-hell-are-you-doing-here look. Anya's cheeks blazed.

She pointed to the rail with the assortment of clothes. 'We can wear what we like, apparently.'

The Facility

'Thank God for that,' Sheila said, and stripped down to her underwear. She didn't seem bothered by the three males in the room.

Anya looked away as the others pulled off their boiler suits and dropped them into the recycle chute. She stole a glance at Dom. He wore a black tee, which he chose to keep on.

Anya peeked at Sheila next, hoping to see a horn growing out of her back. But to her disappointment, all she saw was smooth, golden skin. Frank and Lucas—even Lilly—stopped to admire her.

Soon, everyone was dressed in either hoodies or plain sweatshirts. Dom had chosen a bottle-green hoodie.

Frank shrugged. 'What do we do now? There should be a supervisor here.'

Dom yawned into his fist. 'I need sleep before I fall down.'

He strode past Anya toward the exit. She followed as did the others. The next room—directly two floors above the first-floor records room—was empty. The walls were painted a muted gray. Anya's trainers squeaked on the wooden floor.

Dom opened a set of doors marked '3A'. A new walkway, much higher up, beckoned.

'Come on.' Dom didn't slow down. 'Maybe the supervisor's waiting for us on the other side and we can get this over with.'

Anya stepped onto the third-floor walkway. It felt more stable than the one two floors below, but her nerves gave her pause. The trick was not to over think it. Or look down. She moved fast, keeping her focus on the door. A twinge of guilt hit her and she paused.

On the walkway below June, Jerome and Warren emerged. They were following a thin female supervisor. They wore the white boiler suits of the first-aiders.

Then they were gone. She caught up to the others and entered a space marked '3B'.

Anya couldn't see much in the dark room. Her eyes adjusted slowly to the weak and muted light, enough to see more detail. A wall lay ahead of her with three openings, each one marked by three separate colors. The contained space spanned several hundred meters in length. Three sconces lit up each plain entrance point.

There was no supervisor.

A flickering light on the wall behind Anya caught her eye. She turned to see a small screen that appeared to show a rough map of the room.

'Hey, there's a map here,' said Sheila, pushing her out of the way.

Anya gritted her teeth.

Dom stepped in and examined the map.

'Seems to be some kind of maze beyond these walls.' He ran a finger over the smooth, thin screen, following the lines of the puzzle.

'There are three sections, apparently.' He looked back at the wall. 'We didn't need a map to know that.'

Anya studied the wall with its three color-coded openings: black, dark-green and royal-blue. She turned back to see Sheila resting a hand on Dom's shoulder. A flare of jealousy hit her and she snatched her gaze away.

'According to the map, there are corridors beyond these entrances,' said Sheila, tucking a piece of hair behind her ear. 'It's listing the blue section as the dormitories. The green area is a communal space with a kitchen. The black area isn't listed at all.'

Dom's mood brightened. 'Well, I know where I'll be. Whoever's not sleeping, come wake me if someone shows up.'

Sheila followed Dom.

Seeing her again had knocked loose feelings she thought she'd suppressed. Jealousy. Anger. Hate? Such a strong word. Maybe 'dislike' was a better fit. Sheila didn't deserve her strongest emotions.

But maybe seeing her every day for the next month might change her mind.

How long could she take Sheila's taunting? How soon before she vomited at the sight of Dom and Sheila making eyes at each other?

Anya caught herself. *Remember why you're here. You killed Tahlia.*

There were worse people in this world than Sheila.

23

The lack of urgency in Foxrush was getting on Jason's last nerve. It had been three weeks. Shouldn't they be leaving for Essention to rescue those caught up in Arcis?

At least he hadn't been idle. He'd worked with Thomas to figure out the rotation pattern, but all they had so far was basic information about Arcis' power dips. If Max had a strategy to get back inside the town, he wasn't sharing it. Jason was sick of waiting. It was time to get Anya out.

He'd come to know the soldiers in Foxrush. He even called some of them his friends now. People like Thomas, the inventor of the group. Or maybe even Preston, the communications expert—when he wasn't being a narcissistic control freak. Jason's job was to help with electronics. But Preston refused to let him do anything.

That morning, Preston hit another wall with a new modification and had called him to help. But Jason couldn't do much with the signal-booster if Preston wouldn't let him touch it.

'If you just let me in at the machine properly, I might—'

'What's wrong, you can't figure it out from there?' Preston taunted.

Jason ground his teeth. 'Yeah, I can. But we've been at this for weeks and clearly you don't want my help.'

Preston banged his fist on the table. 'I can do this on my own.'

'Fine. Call me when you *really* want my help.'

Jason walked away, but didn't go far. He leaned against the house gable, hoping that Preston might change his mind.

Gunfire sounded nearby. He followed the noise to a practice area behind the accommodation block, where six of his group from Essention were being shown how to handle weapons. Jason wondered if he'd trained in the wrong skill.

An assortment of guns was laid out on three trestle tables. Some were made of grayish metal and smooth. Others were boxy and matt-black. Some shot electricity, others fired projectiles. The generic-looking guns took standard bullets. He'd seen the soldiers practicing with all of the weapons on the tables at one time or another. The group looked eager to learn.

The soldier cocked his gun. Six paper targets rustled in the distance, pinned to the front of one of the gutted houses.

'To help you get used to holding a weapon you'll be practicing with real bullets.' He bent his elbow at a ninety-degree angle, and trained the gun on one of the targets. He steadied his shot by supporting his wrist with his other hand. 'Bullets are fine if you want to hurt people, but they're no good against force fields and machines. We use other weapons for that.'

He breathed in, then pressed the trigger. The gun recoiled and Jason searched the paper target. From this distance he couldn't tell if the shot had found the center.

An acrid smell lingered in the air. The six trainees tried to mimic with live weapons what the soldier had done. They popped off a couple of shaky shots.

Jason considered looking for Max and asking him if he needed help, but Max was usually out doing supply runs to the other abandoned towns. They had uncovered caches of weapons buried under floorboards in most towns. Had his parents ever stored weapons in their house in Brookfield?

Recently, Max had been returning empty-handed.

Jason walked away from the gun range, wishing he could help more.

A skinny boy of about fourteen bounded up to him.

'Preston says you need to come with me.'

'I'm going to get lunch. Can it wait?'

The boy shook his head.

'Does he actually *need* me for something?'

The boy said, 'You have to come now.'

Curious, Jason followed. He returned to the house nearest the entrance to Foxrush. Soldiers sat with guns and binoculars on a flat roof, to the front of the house. Jason climbed the stairs to the second floor while the boy ran ahead.

'He's coming,' he heard the boy say to Preston.

'About time.'

Jason idled by the doorframe and looked inside the room. The kitchen table had been dragged into the living room and shoved against the window leading out to the flat roof.

Preston sat at the table hunched over the signal-booster, which was wired up to a broken but operational screen.

'Come over here,' he snapped, not bothering to look up. 'I'm out of ideas.'

Jason pulled over a chair and scooted closer to the box. He waited for Preston to move away.

Preston conceded with an irritated sigh. 'I've tried everything to boost this damn signal, but it still won't penetrate the force field.'

Jason peered inside the small rectangular box with a thick antenna on the side. The amplifier for the booster appeared to be connected properly. He examined the main signal box.

'What about the external antenna? Have you tried repositioning it?'

Preston stood up and paced behind him. 'Of course I have. It doesn't make any difference. The signal won't carry the distance we need. It won't go any further than Arcis. Something's blocking it.'

'What about Charlie?'

'Clear as I'm talking to you. The problem isn't Essention.'

'How did you get through to Arcis the last time?'

'Just luck, I guess. That, and the power fluctuations weakened the force field. We've been using the exact same methods to communicate from inside Essention. There have been no issues, until recently. I thought it was the distance. I assured Max that Foxrush wouldn't be a problem.'

Jason frowned as he disconnected the booster box from the screen Preston had propped up against some other equipment. He hooked up the main signal box.

'I've already tried that. All the figures look right. There's no reason why the booster can't push it the distance we need.'

Data streamed and scrolled down the screen. Jason checked the numbers. 'There's nothing wrong with the booster. It has the range to reach beyond Arcis, possibly further than the other side of Essention.'

'So, why can't we get inside?'

Jason scrolled the data down with his finger. A series of smaller numbers appeared, one after another, all different, all containing sixteen digits. The numerals were gibberish, encrypted.

'Are you reconfiguring the signal to match the force field's frequency?'

Preston leaned over him. 'The *what*?'

Jason pointed to the encrypted numbers. 'Here. The frequency code for Arcis. It seems to change several times a day.'

Preston sat back down and pulled the screen toward him. 'Shit. Since when?'

'If they're changing the frequency we need to match it. When the field is weaker the signal makes it through, no issues. But the frequency code will get you in any time you want. Reconfigure the box and booster to match and we have our way in.'

Preston rubbed a hand over his hair and swore again. 'I only have one. I didn't know they would start randomizing it. How are we going to get the rest of them?'

Jason looked up at Preston.

'Your soldiers in Arcis will have to find them.'

24

The black area intrigued Anya the most, but her rumbling stomach had other ideas.

She entered the green section and followed a straight corridor to the communal area and kitchen. Maybe a little food in her stomach would help to ease her guilt over Tahlia.

Dom had barely said two words to her. Did he know about what she'd done?

The kitchen area was large with a separate room off to the left. There was a sink, a wall unit with five cupboards, a silver refrigerator and a white kitchen table with eight plastic chairs. Anya looked up to where the gray ceiling met the walls. She thought she heard snoring.

To her relief the cupboards were fully stocked, mostly with small pots of meat and canned beans. A bowl on the table had bread rolls in it. Another held apples and bananas. She opened the fridge and lifted her brow in quiet amusement. Before her were cartons of milk and orange juice, alongside several bottles of water.

Anya ate a roll and some meat. She finished it off with a glass of milk. This was too much food for just six people. There had to be other participants joining them. And where was the supervisor?

She walked into the second room. Giant beanbags in various colors, sizes and patterns dotted the floor. The fabric was worn. The items looked like they'd come from the towns.

On one wall was a dartboard pricked with hundreds of tiny holes. She grinned at the opposite wall and the dozen sets of varied headphones. A screen next to them showed a playlist of titles and artists. It had been so long since she'd heard music.

She slipped on a set of headphones and picked something upbeat. She sat on a beanbag and closed her eyes, allowing the music to carry her somewhere else.

Images flashed through her mind: Tahlia, helpless on the floor; the blue color of her ice-cold lips.

She pictured Dom and Sheila in the next room discussing the killer in this one.

She imagined eyes on her, watching her from a monitor...

Her eyes flew open and she snatched the headphones off her ears. She stood and scanned the space for cameras, but couldn't find any. Still, the space sent a chill down her spine. Anya replaced the headphones on their hook and returned to the map room.

The mysterious black section beckoned. Maybe what they needed to do was in there.

Sconces provided light to the entrance, but not much inside. The first corridor ran straight, then split into three. She chose the right channel, but got turned around at a dead end. Except for a weak glow brightening the tops of the partitions, she navigated the route almost entirely in the dark. Anya doubled back and tried the middle route. It carried on for a while before splitting, this time into four. She tried the first split on the left; it split again, into two. To simplify any backtracking, she stuck to only left turns.

A shiny black door appeared against what she assumed was the outer wall of the maze.

Could the third-floor test be that simple? Just open a door and leave? Weak illumination leaked over the top of the partition, indicating that the ceiling carried on further. She tried the handle but the door was locked.

Doubling back, she tried the right side of the two-way split. It led her to another door so glossy, it almost looked wet. She tested the handle. The door opened to reveal a brick wall.

Okay, these two splits don't lead anywhere...

She backtracked to the split of four and explored each route. But when the corridors split further again, it only confused her more. At the end of each split she found either a door that wouldn't open or opened onto nothing, or a dead end.

Anya worked her way back to the start. When she thought she was almost there, a new wall forced her in a new direction. It took her ten minutes to make it back to the map room.

'That was a waste.'

She thought about waking the others. But what more could they tell her about this place? Where the hell was the supervisor?

She tested the door leading back to the walkway. It was locked. No way out. The thought made her shudder and the large food supply suddenly made sense. They would be here for a while. Craving company suddenly, even Sheila's, she entered the royal-blue section.

A straight corridor led to a room with three doors. 'WC' was printed on the first door. The second had a picture of a sprinkler; she checked inside to see a row of showers. The third had no picture.

She opened it, not seeing much at first. Gentle and not-so-gentle snoring reached her ears. She tasted sweat, old and new, in the air. As her eyes adjusted, ten beds appeared in the dark; five on either side. She noticed Sheila and Dom on opposite sides of the room.

Anya returned to the communal area. She dropped into a beanbag, closed her eyes and drifted off to sleep.

A hand rocking her shoulder startled her awake. She blinked and sat up straight. The mass of beans readjusted, shifting her lower to the floor.

'Wakey, wakey.' Dom looked alert and brighter than she felt.

She rubbed sleep from her eyes. The others were there: Frank, Lucas, Lilly and Sheila, who stood with her arms folded. Her skin tightened. She'd been hoping Sheila had forgotten how Anya had humiliated her. It *was* a few weeks ago.

But the look on Sheila's face said otherwise.

She crawled forward and climbed to her feet, waving away Dom's help.

'How long have I been asleep?'

'A few hours. Not sure. There aren't any clocks in here.' Dom looked around. 'Did the supervisor come?'

Lucas was chewing on a bread roll. Frank had gravitated toward the dartboard.

She shook her head. 'I can't figure out what we're supposed to be doing here.'

Dom smiled.

She blushed. 'What?'

He reached out and adjusted a piece of her hair. Her fingers fumbled blindly over her scalp. After a lot more blushing, she coaxed the unruly piece back in place again.

Lucas was too busy eating to notice or care. Lilly tried to reach one of the cans in the kitchen and Frank was helping her.

But Sheila's smirk was all Anya saw.

'So, are we still pretending, Dom, or can I drop the charade now?' Sheila stood more confidently than Anya remembered: her arms folded, one foot out to the side. She was also quite a distance from Dom.

'Not now,' Dom muttered.

Sheila planted her hands on her hips. 'Because I thought the plan was to get her this far. And now here she is.'

'I *said*, not now.'

Anya looked from one to the other.

'What are you two talking about?'

'Nothing,' said Dom. 'Just Sheila shooting her mouth off.'

He glared at Sheila; she held up her hands.

'Oh—kay. You're the boss.'

Dom avoided Anya's gaze.

When he finally looked at her, his eyes were liquid, soft.

'I, uh, I'm sorry about Tahlia.'

'Thanks.' Anya dropped her head to hide behind her hair.

'So what did you find out while we were all horizontal?'

'There's—' Anya coughed to disguise the wobble in her voice. 'There's nothing in this part, other than the kitchen and communal area. I can't figure out what the black section is for.'

Sheila, Frank, Lucas and Lilly were all listening now.

'It appears to be a series of corridors that split out into further paths. Some have doors at the end, but they're either locked or lead nowhere.'

'What do you mean, "lead nowhere"?' Frank said. 'Doors have to lead somewhere.'

'I mean, there's no way to go through them. I found brick walls behind some.'

'That doesn't make any sense,' said Lucas. 'What's the purpose of the black maze, then?'

Anya shrugged.

'Come on, there must be something there,' said Sheila, walking away. 'I mean, why would they put us in this giant room with nothing to do?'

Frank followed her. 'I'm on for that plan. We need to explore every last part.'

Anya smiled at Frank, glad to see him back to his old, happy self.

They gathered in the map room and stood at the entrance to the black section.

Anya led the way to the first set of corridors that split out into three. Lilly stayed close to her.

'There's nothing down this one.' Anya pointed to the split on the right. 'It's a dead end.'

'Let's split up,' said Dom, turning. 'We can cover more ground that way. We should double-check where you've been, just to be sure we've covered the entire section. Let's meet back here once we run out of options.'

Anya didn't remember electing Dom as boss, but they agreed.

Frank and Lucas followed the middle route. Dom and Sheila took the corridor on the left. Lilly and Anya started for the dead-end corridor.

'There's no point checking this one,' Anya muttered. Lilly held on to her arm. She felt like a dead weight.

They walked along the corridor that started out straight then curved back on itself to a dead end.

Anya was about to tell Lilly they were done when she noticed a glossy black door beyond the curve. It hadn't been there before, and its position seemed to suggest it connected to the middle corridor. She pulled her arm out of Lilly's and tested the handle. The door opened.

'I thought you said this was a dead end?' said Lilly.

Lilly looked like June: fine blonde hair and thin frame. But Lilly was weaker-minded than June. Would she survive a place like this?

Tahlia had been strong, and she'd died. Anya couldn't figure Arcis out.

'It was, the last time I checked.'

Anya stepped through into another corridor, half-expecting to bump into Frank and Lucas. She examined the smooth gray ceiling with no markers to use as a guide.

Further on the corridor twisted, then doubled back. They arrived back at the three-way split where they had begun. They hadn't emerged from the middle corridor as she had expected, but from the corridor they had started with.

'I don't understand,' said Anya, turning around.

Lilly shrugged and wrapped her arms around her birdlike frame.

Lucas and Frank appeared, then Dom and Sheila.

'There's nothing down there,' said Dom. 'It runs on for a while and comes to a dead end.'

'The middle corridor splits off into four,' said Lucas, beckoning for them to follow.

At the four-way split, they each took a corridor. Lilly insisted on staying with Anya while Frank and Lucas stayed together. This time, Dom and Sheila separated, taking one path each.

The corridors started to look the same. Again, a new door appeared at the end of Anya's split that she didn't remember being there the last time. She tried the handle but it wouldn't open. They doubled back.

The others emerged from their corridors. Only one of them had anything worthwhile to report.

'Mine seems to run to the end of the maze,' said Sheila to Dom. 'It may be a way out.'

They all followed Sheila back down her corridor, which ran closest to the outer wall. Doors stood out as before, shiny and glossy against the matt-black of the walls. The lack of light gave Anya a headache.

They tried each of the doors as they passed. Some had a brick façade behind them. Others didn't open.

The corridor widened slightly and they emerged into a larger space; not quite room sized, but big enough that they could all fit into it.

Anya looked at the gold-colored door with a sign that read: *Danger. Do not open.*

'There's nothing here,' said Anya, turning to leave. 'Come on. Let's go back and see if there's a way to communicate with someone inside Arcis.'

But the boys stayed put.

'Why is this door a different color to the others?' said Lucas.

'Yeah,' said Frank, 'and why is it the only one with a warning sign?'

'I think we should open it,' said Lucas.

Anya shuddered at a recent memory: a sharp, white light massaging her heart; pain pulsing through every nerve in her body; that same light searching for a way out.

This was a bad idea.

'No,' she said. 'Has everyone forgotten the first floor?'

Lucas scoffed. 'This is hardly the same.'

'I agree with Lucas,' said Dom. 'This isn't the first floor, but it could be a test.'

'What kind of test?' said Anya. 'If we open the door, are we right or wrong?' She couldn't bear the thought of anyone else getting hurt.

Sheila arched a mocking brow at Anya.

'We agree to open the door together or not at all,' said Dom. 'Let's have a show of hands.'

They were tied. Lilly and Anya were against opening it, Lucas and Frank were for. Sheila was also for. Dom had the deciding vote.

'I'm with Anya and Lilly for now,' said Dom. 'We need to know more before we open it. Let's go back to the communal area. Do something else for a while. I'm sick of strategizing.'

Lucas, Frank and Sheila looked disappointed. Anya battled both relief and confusion. She'd pegged Sheila as the run-away-from-danger type.

The farther away they got from the gold door the more she relaxed.

25

In the communal area they set up a darts tournament. They played six games before the novelty wore off.

'I need to get out of here,' said Sheila, shaking out her hands. 'I can't stand how this place closes in on me.'

'The exit door is locked,' said Anya.

'I'll come with you, see if I can figure out the screen with the map,' said Frank. 'Maybe we should try communicating with someone. The screen is the only thing here that might carry a signal.'

Lucas seemed up for it, but not Lilly. She settled into a beanbag at the front of the room and put on a pair of headphones.

Sheila smiled sweetly at Dom. 'While I'm gone, don't do anything I wouldn't do.'

Dom glared at her.

With the others gone, Anya's stomach fluttered. It had been too long since she and Dom had spoken properly. She didn't know where to begin.

She sat in one of the beanbags at the back of the room. Lilly looked ahead and bobbed her head in time to the music. Dom pulled up a beanbag beside Anya's and sat on it.

He fiddled with the drawstrings on his hoodie. The friendship dynamic had changed between them. Ever since Dom had injected her with something, her thoughts were no longer muddled.

'So,' she said, staring down at her lap. 'What was life like on the second floor?'

Dom gave a short laugh. 'Exhausting.'

She studied his paler-than-normal complexion.

He stared at a spot on the floor. 'We were on call day *and* night. Things were busy on the higher floors. Sometimes I didn't sleep at all.' He flashed a familiar grin that made her heart flutter.

The tension eased. Anya settled into the beanbag.

'What were the upper floors like?'

'We weren't allowed to see them. I guess they didn't want us gaining any advantage. So we had to treat people in private rooms.'

Anya frowned.

'There are these medical prefabs on the fourth floor in Tower A. None of us had been on the floor before, so the supervisors brought the injured to us there.'

'But you visited the first floor...'

'The first floor was different. We'd all seen it. We all knew what was going on.' He paused and looked around the room. 'I never treated anyone on third.'

'Maybe there's no need for first-aiders here.'

'Maybe.'

His eyes pressed into every corner of the room before settling on Anya. He watched her quietly before his gaze drifted to her mouth, staying there a moment too long. She followed the hard movement in his throat.

'You're different,' he said.

'Yeah, so are you.'

He hesitated, like he wanted to ask her something. She stared at her lap, dreading the inevitable question.

'How are you... you know, after Tahlia?'

Anya chewed on her lip, tasting blood. 'I'm still shaking.'

'I'm sorry I couldn't see you after, you know, when she died. I asked, but they wouldn't let me.' He chuckled and folded his arms across his broad chest. 'I even tried to pretend it was part of some routine check-up.'

Dom had tried to see her? Why?

'It was probably better you didn't. I was in a foul mood.'

He nudged her foot with his. 'No different to normal, then?'

This was the Dom she remembered; the one from the playground. The one without Sheila or secrets. Then she recalled the older man in Southwest Essention and new questions began to pile up.

They both fell quiet. Anya stared at her hands. Dom's gaze was on her.

'There was something else I wanted to ask you,' he said.

A thousand hummingbirds beat their wings against her chest.

'Why did you tend to Tahlia after she was shocked? Why not any of the others?'

She shrugged. 'I was the closest, I guess.'

'That's not what I heard.'

Her face bloomed with heat. 'What did you hear?'

'That the power didn't cut, so you had to break the contact manually.'

'I had to. Tahlia needed me. You don't understand...'

'It was dangerous, Anya. You could have been killed.'

'I can handle myself.'

'You need to be careful in here.' He touched her hand. '*I* need you to be careful.'

His sympathy tipped her over the edge.

She snapped her hand away and looked at him through damp eyes. 'It was my fault, okay? Is that what you want me to say? I killed Tahlia. It was my fault.' He reached for her again, but she shifted away. 'I felt guilty. That's why I helped.' Her chest rose and fell, too fast. 'And where were you? If you'd gotten there quicker, then maybe she'd still...'

Dom said nothing. His own chest heaved with anger, or possibly regret, at ever having known someone like her. She covered her face with her hands, wishing she could become invisible. But when Dom slipped his fingers between hers, she sat upright.

Anya blinked, prepared for his next lecture. Her ragged and uneven breaths sounded just like his.

His pity—or whatever this was—tore new holes into her already damaged heart. She tried to tug her hand away, but Dom wouldn't let go.

'It's not our fault that she died. It's theirs. *They* ran the electricity for longer than normal.'

'It was my fault,' she whispered.

Dom stared at her. 'How?'

She dropped her gaze. 'I delayed her. She asked me to get her file. She was late because of me.'

Dom released her hand and lifted her chin, forcing her to look at him.

'Listen to me. The same thing happened when I was on the first. There was a girl. Brianna. We were told the slowest had to be sacrificed for the rest of us to progress. We thought it meant get left behind, not killed.'

She stared at him through tears. 'Was it you?'

He looked away. 'It was all of us. We were set up.' He looked back. 'It wasn't your fault and it wasn't ours. And I'm guessing you didn't come up with the idea all on your own.'

Anya shook her head. She dried her tears with one hand.

'I went back the next night, after the self-defense classes. But you weren't there.'

His lips parted as his gaze drifted to her mouth, her throat, and then back to her wet eyes. He swiped a thumb through her tears. The hummingbirds returned in force, fueled by his touch.

'Arcis forced me to stay after my first shock. Then Sheila was shocked the next day.'

Sheila. She'd forgotten about her.

She snatched her hand out of Dom's.

'I don't know what's going on with you two, but I don't want to get in the middle of something.' She swiped at her cheek, to erase the feel of Dom's fingers there.

'Yeah, I wanted to explain about that...'

They heard voices, and Anya stood up, almost to attention. Their moment was over. She needed to concentrate on leaving Arcis.

The others appeared just as Dom climbed to his feet.

'Anything?' he asked Sheila.

Sheila looked from Dom to Anya, then back to Dom. She rolled her eyes at him.

'So, Frank here tried to bypass the screen by taking it off the wall. He managed to get the back off, but it shut

The Facility

down as soon as he did. Looks like we're stuck here for now.'

This new brazen Sheila drew Anya's attention. She had tied her long, golden hair up in a ponytail, which showed off her equally golden skin and perfect bone structure. She wore a white sweatshirt. The Sheila she'd known on the ground floor had been too girly for sweats.

Sheila folded her arms and lifted her perfect brows at Anya.

'What?' said Anya.

'Why were you and Frank bumped from the first to the third floor?' she said.

'I don't know. They said I'd done enough to impress the ninth floor.'

Frank grinned. 'And I was just lucky, I guess.'

Sheila ignored him. 'Like what, exactly? What did you do to impress?'

More than she should have. Not enough.

Anya dropped her gaze.

'Sheila, leave it,' said Dom.

'All I'm saying is... If she's best buddies with the ninth floor, maybe she can tell us what the hell's going on here.'

She looked up. 'I know as much as you.'

The weak lighting flickered off and plunged the communal area into darkness, before spluttering back into life. Both Dom and Sheila stared up at the ceiling.

His eyes cut to Anya. 'What Sheila means is that everyone has to experience all the floors. It's what we were told when we joined. No skipping.'

'Well, I didn't *ask* them to bump me,' said Anya. 'They just did.'

'Maybe they changed the rules,' said Frank.

Dom and Sheila both glanced at each other.
'Maybe,' said Dom.

26

They decided as a group not to touch the gold door. The decision allowed Anya to relax for the first time that day. As the evening rolled around, there was still no sign of the supervisor.

She yanked a pair of headphones off her head. The music she'd found so comforting in the beginning now irritated her. No siren marked the start and end of the workday. There was no official start or end to anything on this floor.

The others had gone back to the dorm. Dom was making something to eat.

Anya got up and stretched. 'I'm so sick of sitting around. I wish I could go for a run.'

'Me, too,' Dom called from the kitchen.

She smiled. Her hands and feet twitched with the memory: the delicious strain on her lungs, the slow burn in her muscles. Her mind returned to the one place in Essention Dom had shared with her. Running was their therapy.

'Night, Dom.'
'Pleasant dreams.'

She returned to the dorm to grab a bar of soap and a toothbrush from her bag and headed to the bathroom. Dressed in a red T-shirt and pajama bottoms, she stared at her reflection in the mirror. Her hair had grown a few inches since she'd started in Arcis and now hung past her shoulders. She tucked it behind her ears and washed her face.

The door flew open suddenly. Anya jumped back from an agitated Dom. He pushed past her, diving for the nearest sink. A large, brown stain on the front of his white T-shirt accompanied the smell of coffee. He turned on the tap and splashed cold water his skin.

'I'm such an idiot. I wasn't paying attention.'

Dom pulled his T-shirt up to expose his flat stomach. He splashed more cold water on the parts of his skin that were noticeably red.

'What happened?'

'Spilled scalding coffee on myself...' He glanced at her. 'Sorry for barging in like this.'

'No, it's fine. I'll leave you.'

'Please stay. I'm almost done.'

He sighed and pulled up his T-shirt higher. The move exposed more of his back. Anya drew in a tight breath at what she saw.

A large C-shaped scar ran underneath his armpit to just below his ribs.

Dom turned and caught her looking. 'Ah, I shouldn't have... Stupid...' He yanked his tee down so fast he almost ripped it.

Before she could ask him about the scar he was gone.

She blinked once, twice, then the door opened and Sheila walked in. She carried a small bag under her arm. Anya tensed up.

Sheila eyed her and walked to the sink that Dom had used.

'What did you say to him? He ran out like his pants were on fire.'

'Nothing,' said Anya. 'He burned himself.'

Sheila arched a manicured eyebrow at her. How did she manage to look so perfect all the time?

'There's only one thing that freaks him out.' She looked in the mirror and brushed her finger over her brow and under her eye. 'He has other scars, you know. He's secretive about it.'

More scars? 'What happened to him?'

'He was very sick as a child. He had a lot of operations.'

'For what?'

Sheila turned and flashed an amused look at her. Her finger hovered over her brow. 'Ask him about it. If he wants you to know, he'll tell you.'

Anya caught her pale-faced reflection in the mirror. Next to the tall, tanned, and curvy Sheila she felt horribly plain.

'And don't think I've forgotten what you did.'

'You provoked me.'

'Yeah, I guess I did.' Sheila smiled sweetly. 'But humiliate me like that again, and I'll make you pay.'

Had this been a month ago Anya would have replied with something smart. But here on this floor Sheila seemed different, less confrontational than before.

Or maybe Anya had changed, thanks to Dom's injection.

'Don't worry. I'm done with that.'

The bittersweet smell of coffee lingered in the corridor. Back in the dorm, the lights were off and Dom was already in bed. His soiled T-shirt was a crumpled mess on the floor. She glanced at him as she passed. His eyes were closed.

Anya folded her day clothes neatly and placed them on the floor. She climbed into bed and tried to sleep.

But the lingering smell of coffee reminded her that Dom had secrets. His private chats with Charlie and his veiled warnings on the first floor were just the tip of the iceberg. Then there were his scars...

Anya had no idea who Dom was.

Ω

Movement in the dorm woke Anya. She looked around for the source of the commotion. Frank was cursing. She squinted at him. When she saw he was fully dressed and pulling on a pair of trainers, her heart hammered against her ribs.

Then he slipped out the door.

The others slept on. Anya sat up, dressed quietly and followed him.

There was no noise in the corridor outside the dorm. She checked the bathroom and showers but heard no activity. Maybe Frank just went to get a snack. She buried her hands in the pockets of her hoodie as she walked to the start of the blue dorm. She was about to enter the middle section when she heard noises coming from the black section.

'Damn it, Frank...'

The Facility

Anya half ran through the twisting and turning corridors of the black section. Frank's muffled curses up ahead reached her as he struggled to find his way. But he never doubled back, which meant he'd found the route to the bright gold door, the one they'd agreed not to open yet.

'Frank, don't do this!' Anya called out, but he didn't answer. She wasn't sure if he could hear her.

She picked up the pace and narrowed his short lead.

'Frank, talk to me,' she said, pulling in breaths of air. Whatever fitness she'd had was almost gone because of her sedentary lifestyle.

'Go back to bed, Anya.'

She rounded the corner to find him standing in front of the gold door.

'What are you doing here, Frank?' She already knew the answer.

'I can't stand it any longer. I have to know.'

'We agreed to vote again on opening the door. We haven't done that yet.'

She stepped closer to Frank. He was taller than she was, but she was strong. If necessary she'd fight him.

He turned to face her. 'Look, Anya. There's nothing else on this floor except a gold door that they're telling us not to open. Don't you see? That's our invitation to open it. It might end the game.'

The game? Anya almost laughed. The farther she ventured into Arcis the less game-like the floors felt. The controllers were preparing them for something. She just didn't know what.

Maybe he had a point though. If they opened the door, it might conclude their time on this floor. But something about the door unnerved her. What if it was set up to shock anyone who touched it?

She stepped closer to it, examining the exterior: glossy, like liquid gold. She glanced back at Frank, who egged her on with a smile.

'We have no idea what this door is even connected to.'

She extended her hand, keeping it several inches from the door's surface. She knew what electricity felt like: hundreds of tiny wasp stings on her skin. She jerked back at the memory, then inched her palm closer. She detected no similar energy from it.

Anya brushed her fingers over the door's surface. It felt how it looked: cold. No heat source, no fire waited for them.

She stepped back and released a breath. 'I can't be sure if it's connected to anything. But we should wait until morning so we can all take a look.'

Anya turned to go, but movement spun her back around. Frank lunged for the door.

She caught his wrist before his fingers touched the handle. 'Don't! I'll break your wrist if I have to.'

Anya tried to twist it to disable him, but he'd locked his arm so she couldn't move it. He pushed her away too easily. She slipped, lost her grip on him and fell to the floor.

'Sorry,' he muttered as he went for the handle again.

From the floor, she reached out for him in vain. 'Please. Don't—'

He hesitated, his fingers inches from it. 'You don't understand, I *need* to make amends. The rebels shot my father and I did nothing to help. That haunts me every day.'

Anya's lower lip trembled. 'Me too. Please, Frank. Wait until the morning.'

The Facility

He stared at her. 'Really? You seem so together.'

Anya looked away. 'I'm messed up, just like everyone else.'

Frank turned back to the handle. 'What if this door is the way out of here? What if I can do something that's worth a damn in this world?'

'Think about what you're doing. Think of the risks.'

Frank gave a short, bitter laugh. 'Risks are what get me out of bed in the morning. Risks make me feel alive after feeling dead for so long.'

He grabbed the handle and pressed down.

'*Don't!*'

A noise—a grating, sliding sound—stopped her cold. The metal handle softened and curled back on itself, ensnaring Frank in its steely grip. He tried to pull his right hand free from the circle of steel.

'I can't move...'

Anya scrambled to her feet and worked her fingers underneath, where the handle had doubled back on itself. Metal had melded with metal; she couldn't find where it began and ended.

'There's nothing to grab.'

He tugged and strained against the wrist clamp. 'Really stupid move, Frank.'

'I'll get the others.'

'No, don't leave me!' Frank jerked and pulled, one foot behind the other.

A new sound filled the air—a grinding, high-pitched squealing noise. A large, metal disc extended out from the wall to the left of the door. The blade spun like a circular saw. It was lined up with Frank's neck, and was moving toward him.

'What the hell is that?' Frank pulled again. 'Oh, God, I'm an idiot.' He shouted, 'I'm sorry,' at the ceiling, as if speaking to the controllers of Arcis.

Anya wrapped her arms around a wriggling Frank's waist and pulled. The blade drew closer. Its spinning disturbed the air, blowing strands of hair into Anya's face.

'Pull me loose, Anya!'

'I can't...'

A smaller blade extended out beneath the larger one, rotating at the same speed. This one was coming at waist level.

The vibrations in her hands increased the closer the blades got. She kept tugging at Frank's waist.

A force drew her wrist to the door, like a magnet. Frank's too, as his free hand slammed into the glossy gold door. He screamed and she thought she heard the bones in his wrist break.

A deep shudder ran though hers upon contact. The smaller blade, moving faster than the larger one now, made her nervous.

Her trainers gave her no grip on the smooth floor. Her chip had glued her to the door. The smaller blade nicked her once, twice on her arm. Anya gritted her teeth and smacked her limb to shift it down and out of the blade's line.

But Frank couldn't move. He squeezed his eyes shut. 'Oh God, Anya. Please, do something.'

She wrapped her free arm around Frank's legs and pulled again, her chest heaving with the effort.

The blades continued to spin overhead, seconds away from reaching Frank. He leaned back from the door.

Not far enough.

The blades ground into something solid.

Warm and wet rained down on her face. She tasted copper and iron.

Something heavy dropped to the floor. She heard gurgling.

Finally, her wrist broke free.

She opened her eyes to see Frank on the floor. She slid over to him. The larger blade had sliced into his neck. He was bleeding heavily from a large gash. She yanked off her bloodstained hoodie and pressed it to the side of his neck. That's when she noticed he was missing a hand.

She swallowed back bile. 'Frank, stay with me. Hold on. Help's coming.'

Anya checked his pulse and pressed harder on his neck.

But the gurgling in Frank's throat had already faded. He stared at nothing, his eyes glassy and lifeless.

'*Frank...*' She pulled the hoodie away, refolding it and pressing it to his wound once more.

The blades had disappeared inside the wall. Frank's right hand still gripped the handle. The smaller blade had cut through his wrist with surgical precision.

There was blood everywhere. Bile rose in her throat at the smell. If she closed her eyes, maybe she'd wake up from this bad dream.

Someone lifted her to her feet. Her eyes shot open to see Dom there. Her foot slipped in the blood and she steadied herself against him.

Dom's eyes blazed. 'What the hell happened here?'

His anger fueled her outrage, and she jerked away from him.

'I followed Frank. I tried to stop him from opening the door.'

Sheila appeared, skidding to a halt when she saw the horror. Anya waited for the screams and her insistence that Dom protect her. But she didn't even flinch.

'What happened?'

'Frank was trying to open the door,' he said, in a softer tone that only fueled Anya's anger.

Sheila glared at her. 'And you were *helping* him?'

'No! What's wrong with you people? I tried to stop him.'

Dom took Anya's elbow, but she snatched it away.

'I don't need your help.'

She stumbled away without a backward glance. The shock kept her numb.

She made it only halfway through the black section of the maze when an ear-piercing siren rattled her bones and brought her to a sudden stop.

Anya covered her ears. The walls on either side dropped down. The siren stopped.

She removed her hands. The exit to the walkway opened and a slightly thinner version of Supervisor One walked in.

'Congratulations,' he said in a flat tone. 'One of you disobeyed our sign and opened the door. Twenty-four hours. It's a new record. You're all being rotated to the next floor. Grab your things and meet me by the elevator.' He turned and left without a glance at Anya covered in blood or Frank, dead.

The beanbags in the kitchen and recreation room looked pathetically small without walls to give the space context. Their dorm room was equally exposed. Both Lilly and Lucas were standing by their beds.

Anya looked behind her. Sheila was still by Frank's body, but Dom had started to follow. She stepped over the retracted walls, her movement slowed by her shock.

Lilly screamed when she saw her approach.

By the time Anya grabbed her backpack Dom had caught up to her.

'You need to sit down. You're going into shock.'

He didn't try to touch her.

She saw the concern in his eyes, but it must have been for someone else, because this wasn't happening to her. She wasn't covered in Frank's blood. It was just a bad dream. One she would wake up from soon.

Somehow she made it to the elevator.

Supervisor One was waiting by the rail of clothing. He gave Anya's appearance the once over. Then he pointed at her arm and spoke to Dom.

'You'll need to sort *that* before she crosses the fourth-floor walkway.'

Anya turned to see she'd left a trail of blood behind her. She lifted her arm and examined where the blade had caught her, twice.

Anya had no energy to change. The fourth floor could take her as they found her.

Dom grabbed a T-shirt off the rail and ripped it into one long piece of material. He tied it like a tourniquet around Anya's left arm to stem the bleeding.

She felt nothing. Because this was a dream.

27

Jason was the talk of Foxrush. His discovery—that Arcis had been altering the frequency of its force field—had sent Preston into overdrive. Jason had offered his help, but when Preston worked he worked alone.

They were getting closer to leaving Foxrush and saving Anya. Jason could feel it. He thought about going it alone, but Max and a rescue group had already tried the front-door approach. According to Max, those who had successfully made it inside Arcis that day were never seen again.

But if Jason and Thomas could figure out the pattern of rotation, it might give them an edge the rescue group hadn't had. Max's wife was still missing. Jason would help him find her as long as it meant getting Anya out of Arcis.

He found Thomas sitting cross-legged on a patch of grass behind one of the smaller tents. Ten sheets of paper surrounded him, each scrawled with numbers and data. He and Jason had been trying to work out when and why the power fluctuated, so they could predict Arcis' schedule.

Thomas was two years older than Jason, but his studious eyes and soft, boyish looks made him look younger than the battle-scarred soldiers of the same age. He looked up when Jason approached.

'Max gave me the paper. I find it easier to visualize something when I see it planned out.'

Jason folded himself on the ground beside Thomas, his eyes skimming over the pages that charted the sequence of events: how long the participants in Arcis spent on each floor before they were rotated, and when their soldiers had reported dips in the lights.

'There's not much to go on,' said Jason with a sigh.

The lack of information about the inner workings of Arcis continued to frustrate him.

They'd been able to get only snippets from the soldiers inside Arcis, when the force field was weak enough to receive a strong, masked signal. But if they could maintain a steady connection through the fully operational force field...

'Max said the pattern was much more predictable in the beginning.' Thomas scooted closer to the papers. He pointed to the first page with his pencil.

'According to our people, rotation on the ground floor occurred in twenty-eight days.' He pointed to the second page, which showed movements from the first floor. 'Here, they rotated in exactly thirty days.'

The third page had details about the second floor. 'Twenty-five days here.'

Thomas tapped his finger on the fourth page, leaving behind a smudge of graphite.

'This is where things changed. They rotated in twenty-four hours on the third floor. Preston said they just called it in.' He paused, his eyebrows drawn forward. 'He also said that some participants skipped certain floors. Why?'

'Too predictable?' It was meant as a private thought, but the look on Thomas' face forced Jason upright. 'What did I say?'

Thomas tapped the first four pages consecutively with his pencil. 'Twenty-eight days, thirty days, twenty-five days, twenty-four hours.' He lifted his brows at Jason.

'They know we're trying to get in?' said Jason. When Thomas didn't react, he added, 'I'm wrong.'

Thomas flashed him a smile. 'I never said that.'

He tapped the fifth page, which related to the fourth floor.

'What happens here will tell us a lot. Maybe the twenty-four-hours thing was just a fluke. We'll know more when they rotate again. Our insider says the lights always flicker right before rotation. But that's too late—we can't use this flicker as a marker because the force field returns to full strength almost straight away. We need something else to get us inside.'

Predicting the energy pattern was their best shot of getting into Arcis undetected. But they needed more data if he and Thomas were to pinpoint exactly when the force field was at its weakest. If Preston could get the frequency codes for the force field, he could modify the signal-booster. It was up to the rebel soldiers in Arcis to get them more.

Thomas fell quiet as he studied the pages.

'How did you end up here?' Jason asked. 'How did Preston?'

Thomas looked up at him. 'I'm originally from Foxrush. When teams of men showed up and killed most of the adults, I hid in the cellar for days without food. Then a rebel group showed up, led by Charlie and Max. Preston was with them. When new teams from Praesidium came to take the survivors away, both Charlie and Max pretended to be sick. The rest of us waited in the cellar.'

'They wanted to be captured?'

Thomas nodded.

'And the people didn't tell on them?'

'Everyone was too sick to care, or notice.'

'What's Max's story?'

'What do you mean?'

Jason shifted position. 'How did his wife end up in Arcis? How long ago was it?'

'Uh, about six months, I think. When Essention was first built they put out a notice, said they were looking for people to test their new technology.'

'What were they showcasing exactly?'

Thomas shrugged. 'Probably nothing. His wife and others had been going to Arcis secretly. Some confidentiality clause, Max thinks. One evening, when they didn't return home, Max and a group tracked them to Essention. Two Copies found them loitering outside Arcis, asked them if they wanted to see the latest Praesidium tech. The others entered the town, but Max declined.'

'So what did he do?'

'He headed home. By morning his group still hadn't returned. He went back to find guns lining Essention's perimeter wall and the gates shut.'

Jason shuddered. Why had he been so quick to believe that a place needing disintegration guns could be peaceful?

'Have you ever seen a Copy? I mean, up close?'

Thomas nodded and gave a little shiver. 'In Praesidium. They are copied in the human image, but they're different, colder in attitude. They give me the creeps. The Copies call the humans who live in Praesidium

"Originals". The machines use Copies in an attempt to relate to us, or some other bull.' He lowered his voice to an almost-whisper. 'You've heard of matching, right?'

Jason nodded as a chill crept up his spine.

'That's a thing the towns made up to keep Praesidium off their backs, you know.'

'What about it?'

'It has something to do with the Copies. I don't know what.'

His mother had nearly driven Anya away with constant talk of matching. What did Praesidium have to do with it?

He needed time to think. 'I've got to go. I'll talk to you later.' Jason stood up and Thomas went back to studying the pages.

As he walked away, Jason wondered what his parents would have made of Foxrush. This place was filled with the rebels they had fought hard to protect him and Anya from.

He entered the house closest to the perimeter fence and climbed the stairs to the first floor. Three boys huddled around Preston's collection of communication equipment.

Through the open window he saw a couple of gun-toting spotters on the roof. To their left was a homemade satellite dish made from a wheel hub and a long antenna Preston was using to boost his signal. The dish was as close to Essention as it could get. They couldn't risk its discovery by positioning it beyond Foxrush.

Jason entered the room, but Preston didn't look up.

One of the boys pointed to an open transistor box. 'What if you try that there, or this here?'

Preston sat with his head in his hands. 'I've already tried that. It doesn't work.'

Jason cleared his throat. Preston looked up.

'Anything?'

'I relayed the message about the changing frequency codes when one of the soldiers called in about rotation.' He shook his head. 'I didn't get a reply. I'm not even sure if he got the message. We'll have to wait and see.'

Jason nodded, disappointed it wasn't more. 'It's a start.'

When Preston started to argue with one of the boys, Jason left.

He needed to do something, anything. He came across the tent with the camouflage gear and found no soldiers manning it. A pile of knotted ropes lay on the ground. Jason unknotted it and coiled it neatly, so it would be useful again.

Max walked past, and did a double take.

'When I asked you to help, this wasn't exactly what I had in mind. Anything new on the energy fluctuations?'

Jason shook his head. 'Preston thinks he got the message through about the frequency though.'

'That's good.' Max hooked a finger at him. 'Follow me.'

Jason dropped the rope on the ground. He followed Max inside the main tent.

'Preston is the best comms guy we have, and with your help we'll get there. We need to take it slow. I don't want to tip our hand to Arcis that we have people on the inside.'

A comms radio crackled on the table. Max perched on the edge of the table and picked it up.

'We've seen an object flying near the edge of the forest,' the voice said. 'Could just be a bird.'

'Keep an eye on it. Let me know if it gets closer.' Max pressed a button and the crackling stopped.

Keeping hold of the radio, he folded his arms across his broad chest. 'You seem anxious about something.'

Jason copied Max's stance. 'How many floors must Anya complete before we move on Arcis?'

'As many as it takes to figure out the energy pattern.'

'And what if we never figure it out?'

Max's gaze turned cold. 'Then we have a problem. I won't send anyone in blind. Not again.'

'Thomas told me what happened with your wife. If Anya and the others are in danger, we can't wait.'

Max clenched his jaw and muttered, 'That boy talks too much.' He glared at Jason. 'We'll go when I say and not before. I need you to help Preston and Thomas, get as much information as we can before we move. And if you're thinking of going it alone, don't. I'll shoot you before I let you ruin our efforts.'

The thought had crossed Jason's mind. But if Charlie had collapsed the tunnel, he didn't fancy going through the main gate with Essention's guns tracking him.

'I wasn't.'

Max sighed. 'Thomas told me about your theory, about the unpredictable timings and the possibility they're not flukes.'

Jason wished he had more. 'Less than a theory. More like a wild guess.'

'Still, predictability and parameters is what machines do well.' He pointed a finger at him. 'I want you and Thomas to look at how the machines might be using the change in schedule to their advantage.'

He stood up and plucked a rolled-up map from a box on the ground. He opened it out on the table. Jason stood beside Max and saw it was a map of Essention and Arcis. Arcis was sketched out as far as the third floor. The rest of the floors were blank.

'Thomas drew this up for me. Our people in Arcis have been feeding back details about the layout. That's as much as we have so far. How long they spend on the fourth floor will determine if the twenty-four-hour rotation was a fluke, or part of a more strategic move.'

He tapped on the schematics of Essention, a town divided into eight equal sections.

'Approximately three thousand people live here, all from the border towns. Some are orphans, most are not. But they all have something in common: they can't leave. Not voluntarily, anyway. What we are doing is for all of them, not just your sister.'

Anya was all Jason had left.

He stared at the map. 'So how do we go back?'

'Getting back inside Essention will be the hardest part. We can't carry weapons. The scanners would pick them up as soon as they came back online. Once we're back inside, we need to get in here.' He stabbed a finger at Arcis' ground floor. 'This is where all the participants start. There are walkways connecting the two towers. And this elevator connects the nine floors.'

Max pointed to the second tower. 'The majority of the program operates out of here.' He pointed to the empty dome at the top. 'And this is the ninth floor. This is where the most energy is consumed. Whatever they have running there needs a lot of power.'

Jason focused on the incomplete drawing of the ninth floor. 'How do we get past the force field?'

'First we get back inside Essention, then we'll work it out.'

'Do you think Arcis knows what we're planning?'

'Possibly. But if we make our own movements unpredictable, they won't know how to respond. I think the twenty-four-hour rotation was their way of upping the ante.'

One of the soldiers came rushing in, out of breath. 'Sir, you need to come now. They've sent one of their scouts. They're looking for us.'

'This is all we need...' Max bolted for the door. The soldier followed and Jason ran to catch up.

'Scouts?' said Jason.

'Small, quick orbs,' said the soldier. 'Impossible to take down. If it gets close enough, it will be able to scan us and send our location to Arcis.'

Jason searched the sky for the orb as he ran. He finally spotted it a short distance away: a shiny object hovering in the air. It was similar to the orbs that monitored the hospital in South and the water purification system in North.

In the distance, Max yelled, 'Shoot it down!'

28

The elevator doors opened. Somehow, Anya's feet carried her into the fourth-floor changing room. Her mouth was dry and her throat was sore from yelling at Frank. His blood, dried in parts, clung to her clothes and hair. She felt pressure on her left arm where Dom had wrapped the T-shirt too tight.

A woman was waiting, dressed in black trousers, and a long black tunic with a band of gold around the collar. Anya squinted at her. She looked exactly like the woman from the hospital who'd chipped them when she and Jason had first arrived in Essention.

'I'm Supervisor Two,' said the woman. 'Welcome to the fourth floor.'

Anya's eyelids felt heavy. With grief or shock she couldn't tell anymore. The supervisor's ice-blue eyes drew Anya in and held her there.

Dom gripped her elbow, breaking the spell she was under. She looked anywhere but at him.

Supervisor Two turned to Dom. 'You, medic. Take her to the infirmary and get her cleaned up.'

The supervisor then called the elevator and left.

Anya resisted when Dom tried to move her, but a bout of dizziness caught her off guard, forcing her to lean into his side. He shuffled her forward.

The adjoining room, just before the walkway, contained three gray prefabricated cubicles. Dom guided Anya inside the first one.

The smell of antiseptic burned her nose. The prefab appeared to be a self-contained infirmary, with a medical bed, two chairs and a cabinet containing medicines, syringes and bandages. Dozens of green boxes with printed white crosses were stacked on the floor.

Dom sat Anya down on the bed. She focused on a door on the back wall as Dom untied the torn piece of fabric around her injured arm. He rotated her arm and a new pain—previously hidden by the shock—tore through her.

She screamed and yanked her arm away.

'Anya, please.' Dom held her arm more firmly. 'I need to check how far the cut goes. I'm going to have to disinfect it.'

She nodded, staring at her lap.

A fresh sting ripped through her and she pulled air through her teeth.

Dom released a shaky sigh. 'It's not as deep as I thought.'

He opened a brown bottle. Anya's nose twitched when he doused a piece of cotton wool in some strong smelling liquid.

'Hold on to my arm. This is going to sting.'

When Anya didn't move, he guided her left hand and laid it over his forearm. She concentrated on his light-blue T-shirt.

Something wet touched the cut and she hissed. Tiny pinpricks of pain tore at her resolve. She sucked in air and curled her fingers inwards.

'Almost there,' he said, through clenched teeth.

The pain eased; Anya loosened her grip on Dom. She looked down at her left arm to see a long, angry welt. Tears pricked her eyes. She looked away.

Oh, Frank. I'm so sorry.

Dom dressed the wound with gauze and linen.

She lifted her eyes to meet his. He looked exhausted, but his focus was completely on her. He was watching her as though he expected her to break.

Then something did. Her hands shook. Her body trembled.

Dom pulled her into his arms. Sobs, thick and fast, hurt her chest. He stroked her back. The sound of his heart beating too fast didn't settle her.

Remembering Dom's reaction to finding her with Frank yanked her back to reality. She pushed him away.

Her hair, matted with Frank's blood, felt heavy on her head.

'Maybe you should shower,' said Dom.

She nodded, giving his appearance the once over. 'You, too.' Slashes of red covered his arms and T-shirt, from when he'd pulled her away from the gold door.

'You first. Just keep the dressing dry.'

He turned and tidied away the antiseptic, the bandages. The throbbing in her arm reminded her of how close she'd come to dying.

Ω

The hot water helped to clear her head. She used soap from a special dispenser to scrub her hair and skin, but it was awkward with one hand. She kept the other arm, wrapped in gauze, on the outside of the shower curtain. The soap smelled like lemons and lavender. Deep-red water circled around the drain.

She found two sets of clothes on the sink. One had a pair of flat, cream leather sandals sitting on top. The other set had men's shoes, along with some essentials.

She brushed her hair and then shook out the folded fabric and groaned. At least the sand-colored dress came to her knees. She shaved her legs and dressed, feeling better to be in something clean.

Anya slipped on the sandals and returned to the infirmary. She flashed Dom a shy smile.

His eyes trailed over her.

'Better,' he said.

She waited for him to shower. He soon emerged dressed in a sand-colored top and trousers. He folded his T-shirt and combats and packed them in his backpack.

'How long do we have in here?' said Anya, perching on the edge of the bed again.

Dom leaned against the counter, facing her. 'As long as you need.'

She stared down at her hands.

'Had you known Frank for long?' said Dom.

His question startled her. She'd forgotten that Dom and Frank had never met before the third floor. Dom had already been rotated by the time Frank started.

'Long enough.'

'I'm so sorry. Can I get you anything?'

She clamped her bottom lip between her teeth, to stop it from wobbling. What she really wanted was to go home. Even a gray block in Essention was better than here. She searched the room.

'There are no cameras here,' said Dom, following her gaze. 'I checked the first time I used this place.'

She shook her head. 'I want to go home, Dom. To Brookfield. I don't want to do this anymore.'

'We can't leave.' He pointed to his wrist. 'Remember?'

His words fueled her anger. 'I wasn't trying to open the door.'

'I saw you there and I just—'

'Jumped to conclusions about me?'

Dom lowered his gaze. 'I'm sorry.'

'I was trying to stop Frank.'

'I'm sorry,' he said again, this time looking at her. 'I didn't handle that well. I'm not good at this.'

'Good at what?'

She glared at him until he turned away.

He had his back to her, his hands resting on the counter, head dipped low. He drew in a hard, shaky breath and released it.

'Sheila says I'm too impulsive. That I make snap decisions.'

He turned back around, holding her gaze for a split second before looking away.

Her heart slammed against her ribcage.

'No more lies, Dom.'

He nodded not looking at her.

'What did you inject me with after that first shock? You said I would feel different.'

He met her gaze. 'An antidote to Compliance.'

'To *what*?'

'The drug the controllers of Essention have been putting in our food and water to keep us... compliant.'

'How long have you known? How long have they been—'

'From the beginning.'

'Why?'

'We're easier to control.'

Anya dug her fingers into the soft mattress. She admitted to feeling different since Dom's injection. For one, her hands no longer shook. And her eyes were only a little dilated.

'One of your impulsive decisions?' she said.

'I don't regret that one.'

'Why give it to me?'

Dom sighed. 'I needed your help. I still do.'

'For what?'

'I need to make it to the ninth floor alive. You're strong minded, but you're stronger when you're off Compliance.'

She stared at Dom, his deep-brown eyes full of remorse, concern, worry. He folded his arms across his chest.

'What's going on with you and Sheila?'

'Nothing.'

'Don't lie. You've got this weird love-hate thing going on.'

'There's nothing between us, Anya. There never was.' He dragged a hand down his mouth and chin. 'It was all an act.'

She widened her eyes. 'For what?'

'For you, so you'd keep moving forward. You were so content with staying on the ground floor that I needed to do something drastic. Sheila and I pretended to be together. It seemed to ignite something inside you.'

Sheila hadn't been the catalyst for her progression. It was that night in the playground, when she and Dom had been honest with each other.

Anya jumped off the bed. 'You lied to me. You thought I'd opened the door. You thought I was so weak willed that Sheila would get under my skin.'

Dom's jaw flexed. 'I lied to you for a good reason and I didn't really think you'd tried to open the door. When I saw you there covered in blood... I don't know.' His voice wobbled. 'I thought I'd lost you. And the thing with Sheila was *her* idea, not mine. She said it would be only a matter of time before you became obsessed with her and that you'd do what you could to see her fail.'

Anya blushed. She hadn't been obsessed with her, but she admitted to being drawn in by Sheila's games.

She wanted to slap Dom in the face, but opted for biting her lip instead.

'Well, I don't know what *secret* you feel the need to hide from me, but that's your business. And, Sheila?' She smiled. 'Yeah, dangle a bitchy girl in front of me and I'll take the bait. But the last twenty-four hours were different. She's different. You, on the other hand—'

Dom's eyes grew large. 'No, *you're* different. It bothered me how you used to watch the wolves. I never saw the point of it. But you taught me to look at things from a different perspective. And that made me curious about you. '

Dom's warm and soft gaze reassured her that he was telling the truth.

'Why are you curious about *me*?'

She tried to stuff the words back in her mouth.

'I don't know. Sometimes I wish I weren't.'

'Why?'

He stepped close enough that she smelled lemon soap on his skin.

'Because I'm terrified that when you discover my secret, you'll feel different about me.'

She searched his face. 'I've watched my parents die, and two strangers. I helped to kill Tahlia and I couldn't save Frank. I think I can handle a little more truth from you.'

Anya leaned against the bed, trying to ignore the ache in her arm. 'I want to go home. You tell me I can't. The game on the third floor finished when Frank tried to open the gold door. How long would we have been there if none of us had opened it? This place feels less like a place to teach us and more like a testing facility. I'm asking you to give me a better reason to keep going. Because if you don't, I'll find a way out of this place alone.'

Dom pressed his lips together. 'Sheila and I work together, on the outside.'

'Work where?'

He lifted his eyebrows as though it were obvious. She gasped and touched her fingers to her lips.

'You're part of the rebellion?'

He nodded, his expression cautious. 'We both are. Six months ago my mother stepped inside this building. I haven't seen her since. Sheila and I are trying to expose this place for what it is.'

'What?'

'I don't know. That's why Sheila and I are both here.'

The Facility

Anya shook her head. 'This program is for sixteen- to eighteen-year-olds. Why would your mother be part of it?'

'It didn't start out as a program. In the beginning, Praesidium invited certain adults to enter Essention, and ultimately, Arcis. They never left.'

'Is that why you're in here? How old are you? How long have you been a rebel fighter?'

'Yes, to find my mother. Nineteen. Since her disappearance.'

The answers flowed a little easier from him now. He looked at her, waiting for what she couldn't give him yet: her approval. She had questions. Who was the man who cut Dom's hair? Had Dom killed anyone? Did the rebels really kill her parents?

She searched his face for deceit, but only found a friend who had taught her how to defend herself, who had explained how to treat electric shocks, and who had treated her cut. But he was part of the rebellion movement.

'My parents were killed by the rebels,' said Anya. 'Do you know who did it?'

'It was people from Praesidium,' he said. 'Our fight is with them, not the townspeople.'

She wanted to believe him. It would make Jason's venture to the rebel-infested outside easier to cope with.

He shifted closer. 'How do you feel?'

Her stomach danced at his proximity. 'About what?'

'About what I've told you. I already know how you feel about the rebels.' His voice had worn thin. 'Tell me what you're thinking. Do you hate me?'

She laughed at the absurdity of the question. But it also caught her off guard. The last thing she felt for Dom was hatred.

'I feel a lot of things right now, Dom Pavesi, and I should be angry at you for keeping this from me. But I understand why you did.'

'You didn't answer my question.'

Anya stared up at him, at his slender nose and his slightly parted lips.

She touched his arm.

'No, I don't hate you. I never could. You're my...'

Her friend? More?

She wasn't sure what they were. She'd resisted her feelings for so long.

'Your what?' he said softly.

An inch of space was all that separated them. Anya concentrated on his tight breaths and the rapid movement of his chest. A new dizziness caught her that had nothing to do with the pain in her arm.

'You're my friend.'

Dom stepped back. The intensity in his eyes startled her.

'I need you to say you forgive me. I've been sick with worry over telling you.'

'I do, but...'

He jerked a hand over his short, curly hair.

'I'm an idiot. I never should have let Sheila talk me into it.'

Anya placed a hand on his chest. Dom stared at her, in expectation.

'I was going to say no more secrets.'

A slow smile spread across his face.

'Never again. I promise. Friends. I can live with that.'

His smile faded and a small blush stained his cheeks. When he didn't move, Anya pressed up to her toes and brushed her lips against his. He gasped and closed his eyes. The sound caused her own breathing to hitch.

Dom cupped her neck, drawing her near. Their lips touched again, but for longer this time. Sharp jolts of electricity pulsed through her. Instead of draining her energy this mild shock fueled her, gave her strength. Dom kissed her so hard and hungrily, she had to lean against the bed for support.

She twisted her good hand into his hair. Dom tasted sweet and hot. He smelled of lemon soap and his natural musk.

His hair felt soft beneath her fingers. She pulled on it hard when he tasted her again.

This was like no other kiss she'd had before. They'd all been awkward and rushed experiences, with a side of expectation that she hadn't known how to deal with. This... non-friendship with Dom felt natural, easy, safe. Passionate.

He moved her hand down to his chest while his lips trailed along her jaw, her neck. His soft breaths tickled her neck. A strong heart beat drummed out a rhythm against her open palm.

Dom pushed her up against the edge of the bed. His hand trailed down her back to her outer thigh and back up. She shivered as her dress rode up a little and his fingers brushed against her bare skin.

'Screw friendship,' he whispered, against her throat. 'We weren't that close, anyway.'

He pulled her tight against him. His kisses switched between relaxed and impatient. She wanted more, to feel his skin against hers. Anya worked her good hand under the hem of his tunic and ran her fingers along the raised skin of his scar.

Dom jerked away from her.

'I think we should stop.' He was breathing hard. 'Being alone here with you is too... tempting.'

Anya blushed, trying to calm her racing heart. 'Yeah.'

He took her hand and kissed the top of it.

'I've wanted to kiss you ever since I saw you take down Sheila in the courtyard. No, probably before that.' He laughed. 'She was so pissed with you after.'

Anya cringed. 'Yeah, that.'

'But I wasn't sure if you liked me in the same way.'

'I wasn't sure either. Maybe Sheila did have something to do with it. She has a way of getting under my skin.'

'She's good at that.' Dom smiled and lifted a brow. 'But you came back after that night.'

'Yeah, I really enjoyed the running.'

'Nothing else?'

Anya pretended to think about it. 'I wanted to learn some more self-defense. I remember us getting pretty close at one point. You must show me that move again.'

Dom pulled her close and kissed her again, whispering against her lips. 'Anytime...'

He pulled away, but kept hold of her hand.

'There's so much more I want to say to you,' said Dom, 'but I think we should go.'

She nodded, happy to wait.

'Are you ready for the fourth floor?'

Her sorrow hit her again. 'Someone's going to have to tell Jerome about Frank.'

'I will. First chance I get.'

'No. It should be me.'

Her bloodstained clothes were still on the bathroom floor where she'd left them. She retrieved her favorite red T-shirt, which was only lightly soiled, and stuffed it into her backpack. Dom carried both packs.

On their way out, Anya pulled Dom back from the door. She needed to ask something else.

He looked from her arm to her face. 'What is it? Are you still in pain?'

Anya shook her head. 'I need to know if Jason is okay. He was going to the towns before I came here. Is he with the rebels?'

Dom nodded. 'He's with Max. Max is a good guy. I trust him with my life. I've been communicating with the outside since I got locked up in this place.'

'How?'

He showed her a small S-shaped scar behind his left ear. 'I can hear them when the power is down, and I can relay messages through a series of taps.'

'Like a special signal?'

Dom nodded. 'I sent the last message when the game ended and the supervisor showed up. The reply almost didn't make it through before the window closed. I wasn't expecting us to be rotated so soon.'

'Does that change things for your people on the outside?' It felt weird talking about the rebels like they were friends, but Dom, a rebel, had saved her life more than once.

He opened the door a crack. 'Possibly. If we reach the ninth floor in one piece, we'll need backup. I need to find a way for them to get inside Arcis. The force field at full strength is too strong.'

They arrived at 4B, a dimly lit space that appeared to be separated into three sections: one with clear glass, one with frosted glass, and an empty space in between. A giant screen was positioned over three doors at the back of the space that Anya guessed must be the dining room and two separate bathrooms. She looked around the quiet space. Again, no sign of the supervisor.

She saw the girls were together behind the clear-glass section on the left. In an extension of that space, with its own entrance, were tables, chairs and old typewriters. She couldn't tell who was behind the frosted-glass front with a single door, but she guessed it was the boys. Her mood fell at having to be separated from Dom so soon.

Movement in the female dorm caught her eye. Sheila jumped up from her bed and walked toward them. She wore the same style of tunic dress as Anya, but it looked so much better on her. Anya wondered if she and Dom had ever been an item.

Sheila skidded to a halt in front of them. 'No time to explain. The sexes are separated on this floor. Dom, you need to go that way.' She pointed to the frosted-glass section with brightly lit panels.

Dom hesitated.

'I'll be fine,' Anya said smiling.

He handed over her backpack and she followed Sheila. Dom went the other way.

'You two made up, I see?' said Sheila.

Anya blushed, but to her relief Sheila wasn't looking at her.

'Did he tell you anything specific?' She looked back at her and Anya nodded.

'Well since you're still talking to each other, I'll take that as a good sign.'

The clear-glass section had twelve beds facing out, a few bedside lockers and not much else. Anya shivered in her dress, wondering if the boys had a similar view.

'There's not much privacy for the girls here,' said Sheila, as if she'd read Anya's thoughts. 'I think that's the point of this floor.'

Anya counted eight occupied beds. Lilly's blonde hair spilled over one pillow, and someone with brown hair was in the bed at the end. She took one of the spares, next to Sheila.

'There's not much left of the night, but you might as well get some rest. How's the arm?'

'Okay,' said Anya. 'I didn't try to open the door, you know.'

Sheila shrugged. 'Why do you care what I think?'

'I don't.'

Sheila sat down on her bed and slipped her slender legs under the covers. 'Look, don't feel too bad. I come from a long line of mind manipulators.' Anya frowned at her. 'Psychologists? I assume Dom told you it was my idea to mess with your mind. He didn't want to do it, but he couldn't resist me, you see.' She winked.

Anya's blood heated. She hid under the covers.

All she saw was Sheila close enough to see all of Dom's scars. The same ones he'd tried to hide from her.

29

Jason stood back when a soldier pushed past to get to the window and gain access to the flat roof. Preston cursed at the soldier who stepped on his capacitors without so much as an apology.

Jason followed the soldier out to the roof. He picked up a spare pair of binoculars and kept to the rear of the activity. More soldiers climbed up the side of the house, carrying guns of various shapes and sizes. The space could hold ten people, but with the satellite dish taking up valuable space and more guns than the supply tents, it was a little crowded.

The roof offered the best unobstructed view across the landscape. Foxrush was about ten kilometers from Essention's walls but a thick forest in between protected them from Essention's prying eyes. Sending orbs to spy on them made sense. It was the only way to watch the towns.

A small object zigzagged in the open space between the forest and the town. Max perched a rifle on his shoulder and looked through the scope. Preston climbed out and passed Jason with a monitoring device in hand, swiping at the screen.

'Nothing yet,' he said to Max.

The Facility

Jason guessed he was trying to hack the orb's software.

Max lowered his rifle and cursed. 'I can't get a clear shot. It's moving too fast.' He turned to one of the younger soldiers. 'Get Thomas. Tell him to bring the Disruptor. Now.'

The soldier nodded and used the drainpipe to slide down the side of the house fast. Jason pressed the binoculars to his eyes. He could see the scout clearly now: a bright metal orb zigzagging horizontally, but definitely heading for Foxrush.

Max directed the soldiers with guns. 'Unless you have a clear shot don't take it. That thing's recording everything we do.'

They set their aim but nobody fired.

Thomas climbed out the window a few minutes later, out of breath. He handed Max a strange-looking gun —the Disruptor, Jason presumed—boxier than the sleek and smooth weapons carried by the soldiers.

'He'll need a clear line of sight for it to work,' said Thomas.

Max nodded and handed the gun to Preston. A short fat barrel had been soldered to the front of the homemade weapon. Jason frowned at the exchange. Surely the soldiers were better trained to fire it?

Thomas stood beside Jason, gnawing on his thumb. 'This had better work.'

They both watched as Preston flicked a switch on the side of the boxy gun, as if he'd done it a thousand times before. Bright floodlights, normally used to illuminate the town's main street, were temporarily arranged around the roof, angled outwards to give Preston a clearer view.

Jason stared at the strange weapon. 'What's he going to do?'

Thomas glanced at him. 'The Disruptor displaces energy, momentarily disrupts the orb's signal. Stuns it. The orbs can change direction fast. We need to disable it before it transmits our location back to Arcis. Bullets are too slow. The orb can compensate easily for the speed.' He flicked his finger at Preston. 'Watch.'

Jason turned just as Preston pointed the barrel and pulled the trigger.

The gun released a burst of shimmering air. The nearby orb drew toward the disturbance. It pitched and rolled to an almost-stop, as though it had hit a body of water. Preston pulled the trigger again and the gun shuddered in his hand, as if reabsorbing the shot.

'We need the orb intact,' said Thomas, 'so Preston's disabling it by sucking out its power. It's one of my designs. As well as displacing energy, it absorbs it too. Basically, it steals energy from the machines.'

The orb dropped from the sky about a hundred feet from the gate. Max climbed down from the roof and Jason and Thomas followed. Three soldiers stepped outside the defense perimeter and returned a moment later, carrying the fallen scout.

They handed the shiny silver object to Max. It looked as smooth as glass. Jason stared at it. He'd seen the orbs before, in Essention, but never this close up.

'Both of you,' Max said, holding it out. 'I want to know what this is made of and how we can attack it.'

Thomas took the orb, and Jason followed him to a room attached to the rear of the accommodation block. In the area where Thomas worked was a trestle table and an assortment of tiny screwdrivers, wires, molds, sketchpads and rough drawings. Around the edges of the room consoles had been dismantled, and the parts divided into neat piles.

Jason stood by the table while Thomas set the orb down and picked up a small, black box that fit neatly into his palm. It emitted a blue scan, which he ran over the orb —the same blue that the scanners in Essention emitted.

The orb beeped erratically at first but then the energy signal faded.

'What's the scan for?'

'It looks for machine parts. It's the same one that scanned you when you came into Foxrush.'

'Why?'

'Some people carry Praesidium tech inside them. Tech they were given when they were young.'

'Tech? Like what, exactly?'

Thomas shrugged. 'All I know is the scanner picks it up.' He checked a display monitor that he'd rigged up to the scanner. 'There's a faint energy signature, but I don't think it had time to transmit anything before we disorientated it.' He grinned at Jason. 'You wanna see what's inside?'

Jason nodded and moved to the other side of the table just as Thomas stepped back.

'Go ahead. See if you can open it.'

Jason ran his fingers over the orb's surface, not feeling any divots or deviation in its smooth outer casing. He picked it up and turned it over, looking for a tiny hairline crack that might accommodate a flathead screwdriver. There was nothing.

Thomas stood with his arms folded. 'Think of the outer casing in an organic way. It might help if you close your eyes.'

Jason did and gently pressed at the sides of the orb. His thumb sank in farther than the casing should have allowed. He opened his eyes to see the soft depression.

Thomas smiled. 'Go ahead. Push it all the way in.'

Jason did and heard a click as the top half separated from the bottom. He placed one hemisphere on the table, and examined the middle of the other half, where a dull-gray ball sat in the center of a cluster of white gel. He noticed the tiny lever that had kept the covers closed.

Thomas supported Jason's hand and carefully removed the sphere from the gel.

'This is both recorder and transmitter. It's far more elaborate than the tech we use.' He placed the ball in a small ceramic bowl. Judging by the flat sound it made, the object was solid, dense.

Jason had never seen any tech like this from Praesidium.

'What's the gel around it?'

'It probably provides some kind of protection for the sphere, but it may also store energy that keeps the orb active.'

'Like a battery.'

Thomas nodded.

Jason looked at the half-shell in his hand. 'Can they still transmit the data without the gel?'

'I'm guessing no, not once the sphere has been removed. But I'll keep an eye on it.'

Thomas took a seat at the table and read some data from the monitor. Jason pulled up a chair beside him.

'If we can figure out how it works, we should be able to design a weapon to harm it. Let's start with this casing, then we'll move on to figuring out what the gel is made of.'

The Facility

Ω

For the next couple of hours, Jason and Thomas ran all sorts of tests on the hard casing to try to break it down. They used chemicals, acids of different strengths, alkaline solutions, but to no effect.

Some soldiers were practicing at the range when Jason and Thomas brought one half of the orb shell, with a sample of the gel, to the firing range. One of the soldiers close to Jason's age, who had a deep scar on his cheek, stopped firing when Thomas tapped him on the shoulder.

'I need you to fire at this.'

Jason wondered who or what the soldier had fought to gain such a nasty injury.

Thomas held out the casing to the soldier. 'Don't bother with bullets. They don't make a dent in it. Try these two.' He pointed to two medium-sized guns finished in slick black.

The soldier picked up the first.

Thomas stepped back and said to Jason, 'He's using an Electro gun. It emits a highly concentrated burst of electricity.'

The soldier pointed the gun and fired. A sharp crackle sent a rattling shock wave through Jason's eardrums.

Thomas had his fingers in his ears. 'Sorry. I should have warned you.'

The outer casing liquefied momentarily, then re-hardened into its original shape. The gel remained unaffected.

'I have something else I want to try.' Thomas ran back to the accommodation block.

Max stood silently beside Jason, staring at something off in the distance. Jason wanted to ask him about the tech that Thomas had said some people carried inside them. But Thomas returned too soon, carrying a weapon that was cruder in design than the homemade Disruptor.

'Try this.' Thomas passed it to the soldier. Jason lifted his brows at the silver box with two sticks fashioned as handles.

The soldier frowned. 'Another Disruptor?'

'No. I call it the Atomizer.'

Jason tried not to laugh. The soldier, not as polite, rocked with laughter.

Thomas huffed. 'The name is a work in progress, alright?'

He stepped back beside Jason while the soldier readied himself. 'It can break down pure elements. In a lump of copper, there are trillions of copper atoms,' he said. 'You can apply heat and change the copper to a liquid, gaseous or different hardened state, but the atoms will still exist. Elements cannot be divided into smaller units without large amounts of energy. Normally you'd use a nuclear reaction to destroy or change the atoms, but we're not dealing with something as simple as copper in the orb's outer casing. They use this very same material to make the exoskeletons for those giant wolves.'

'What powers it?'

Thomas wiggled his eyebrows. 'A little antimatter.'

Jason backed away from the highly volatile substance. 'What?'

Thomas laughed. 'Don't worry. It's perfectly safe. It has its own containment field. They use it in Praesidium tech quite safely. That's where I came across it. In a piece of their tech.'

'Okay, so how does it break down the atoms?'

'It doesn't. It inserts minuscule amounts of antimatter into the atom and breaks the bonds of the protons and neutrons. It forces space between them to create a paper-like fragility.'

Jason cut his eyes to the soldier, who had steadied the gun against his chest. He aimed and fired.

The single blast caused a ripple in the casing. The soldier bent down and pushed his finger through it.

Thomas slapped Jason on the back. 'Told you it would work.'

It was a start, but when would they storm Arcis? He turned to ask Max but he'd already left.

A boy from Preston's team ran up to Jason. 'Preston needs you.'

Jason followed him, happy for the distraction. If they could get the communication sorted, that would bring them one step closer to leaving for Essention and getting Anya out.

30

A bell sounded in the girls' dormitory, so loud it threatened to shatter Anya's eardrums. Harsh lighting illuminated their sleeping quarters. Anya groaned and draped her good arm over her eyes. She couldn't shake the tiredness that ran bone deep. Her arm throbbed. At least the cut was superficial.

She peeked out from under her arm and saw Sheila sitting up in bed. Her long, wavy hair cascaded around her shoulders. Sheila caught her staring and cast a long, cool look her way. Anya held eye contact until Sheila laughed and looked away.

She looked across the space to the boys' section and caught shadows moving across the frosted glass. Anya pulled back the covers. She still wore her tunic dress. Changing in an exposed sleeping area hadn't appealed to her. She stood up and the dress fell neatly around her body.

Anya slipped her feet into her sandals and glanced at the giant inky-black screen in the void between the dormitories that was easier to see in the harsh illumination. The smell of fresh coffee, toast and bacon reached her and made her stomach rumble.

She looked around her. Yasmin, the wiry blonde from the first floor who had convinced her to go against Tahlia, had made it. The hole in her fragile heart let in a fresh wave of guilt.

A second blonde stirred in the bed next to Sheila. June. Had Frank not just died she'd have been thrilled to see her.

Lilly hovered like a bird at the end of Anya's bed. In contrast to Lilly, June got up and moved with a confidence Anya had only seen glimmers of before.

Three unknown girls brought their total to eight. After quick introductions, Anya followed her nose to the third door underneath the screen, next to the his-and-hers bathrooms.

Lilly hung on to Anya's good arm. But the extra weight irritated her, and she eased Lilly off. Anya slipped to the back and pulled June along with her.

She told her what had happened to Frank. They hugged. 'Poor Jerome,' said June. 'Who's going to tell him?'

'I will. I was the last one to see him alive.'

They entered the dining hall. A range of smells hit Anya all at once: strong, bitter, sweet, sugary, hot, buttered. Her mouth moistened. Sheila and Yasmin arrived first at the counter. The food, normally presented in an open cabinet, had been separated into portions behind glass covers. The boys, dressed in tunic separates, were already there and carrying trays.

Anya's fingers fluttered against her neck when she saw Jerome. His jaw was clenched, his head hung low. At least he had skipped the horror of the third floor.

When Dom turned, her heart raced for a different reason. He nodded at her arm. She smiled and mouthed,

'Better,' even though it still ached. Dom gave a quick nod in Jerome's direction.

He'd told him. Her grip tightened on her tray.

She wanted to be the one to explain to Jerome what had happened. But would he even hear her out? She'd allowed the boy who'd been like a brother to him to die.

Warren, who was just ahead, left the queue to stand beside Anya.

She gave him a brief hug.

He frowned at her arm. 'What happened?'

'An accident. I cut myself.'

The line moved forward, and Anya noticed the boys were using the chips in their wrists to open the food coverings. Some were marked with labels: one point for standard servings, half a point for lesser portions. Her stomach rumbled to the point of distraction.

'Well, you seem to be flying through the floors,' said Warren, smiling. 'Maybe I'll stick with you.'

Anya avoided his gaze. She hadn't mentioned their pact to finish the floors together to anyone. She was starting to rethink their alliance.

'Maybe. How was the second floor?'

Warren rolled his eyes. 'Brief. Didn't get to do much. What was on the third floor?'

Dom turned slightly, as if he were listening.

'Nothing. It was some sort of maze.'

'A maze?'

'It was less interesting than it sounds, believe me.' Her eyes flickered to Jerome. He was turned away from her, but she caught the tension in his shoulders. She wanted to tell Warren the whole story, but not with so many people around and Jerome listening.

The queue of boys moved on. Warren turned back.

'I'd better go before I lose my place.'

'Okay. See you.'

He slipped back into line and used his chip to open a portion of scrambled eggs, bacon and a slice of buttered toast. He selected a coffee from the machine at the end.

Sheila stopped at the bacon. She touched her wrist to the box, but it wouldn't open. She tried it again; the cover stayed in place. She tried a different box, then slid her slender fingers under the lip and pulled. But the lid wouldn't budge. Anya and Yasmin tried their chips next. It was the same for them.

Anya walked over to the coffee machine. The smell made her stomach hurt. She tried it. Nothing happened. 'Why aren't the boxes opening for us?'

The boys watched from their table. June glanced at Sheila. Lilly started to cry.

Dom jumped up and walked over to them. 'Probably just a mistake. Let me use my chip to open them.'

One of the older boys with blond hair stood up. 'I wouldn't do that if I were you.'

'Why not, Ash?' said Dom. 'Their chips aren't working. What does it matter if I open a few?'

'You're not supposed to help them,' Ash said.

'They need to eat.'

Dom ignored him and used his chip to open several boxes, but then it stopped working. He glared at Ash. 'Why can't I open more?'

The boy sat back down. 'Because you've used up your rations for the day. It won't work again until tomorrow morning.'

'So what are *their* rations? Surely everybody can spare a box?'

Jerome glanced at Warren, who stared at the table, fork in hand. The ones who had rotated from a lower floor looked like they might help.

Ash looked down at his food—food Anya wished she were eating.

'The more you help them outside of the game, the worse you score. Trust me. I've been here one rotation too long.'

The lower-floor boys dropped their gazes to the table.

'I'm not letting them starve,' said Dom.

Ash laughed bitterly. 'You'll change your mind, trust me. Besides, there are more "official" ways they can earn food.'

Anya's ears perked up. Earn food?

'I'm sorry I couldn't do more,' said Dom, and rejoined his table.

Anya helped collect the plates from the boxes that Dom had opened. The girls shared the food out between the eight of them. There wasn't much to go around, and Anya's stomach still grumbled when she had finished her portion.

After breakfast, everyone converged in the main room in front of the giant screen; the girls stood on one side, near their section, the boys on the other side. Ash patted his stomach and grinned, attracting hateful glares from both Sheila and Yasmin.

The giant screen flickered to life and listed everyone's names. The girls were in one column, the boys in the other.

The layout of this floor made sense to Anya. The sexes were separated.

The Facility

Numbers beside each name confirmed this was indeed a game, as Ash had said. The girls all had a score of minus one. In the boy's column, only Dom had minus one. The rest had been credited with plus one.

She still didn't understand the reason for being denied food.

The scores disappeared and a face appeared on the screen. It was the female supervisor who'd brought them to the floor.

'Welcome, participants. You may have noticed some differences in the dining hall and between the male and female dormitories. The Collective is curious about the differences between the sexes. The females will sleep in basic accommodation, use ancient technology and must earn food whatever way they can. The males will sleep in the best accommodation, use the latest technology and eat whatever they want.

'But don't be fooled. There is no easy way off this floor. There are disadvantages to having everything or nothing. The girls need the boys to survive and the boys need the girls to progress. The Collective wishes to observe how much you'll sacrifice to get what you need. The greater the sacrifice, the more the points you'll earn. You may choose to pair up with the boys or go it alone. Good luck.'

The screen went blank and Anya looked at Dom. His jaw was tight.

'Come on, let's play some more games,' one of the boys said gleefully. The boys disappeared inside the frosted room and closed the door.

Sheila snorted. 'Seems like they have all the advantages if you ask me.' She walked toward the room with the typewriters. 'Come on, there must be some instructions around here.'

The others entered the room while Anya lingered in the doorway. The outer wall was made of glass, like the dormitories. The other three were plain gray partitions. Ten worn, wooden desks sat inside the room, just like the ones from Anya's school. Each had a typewriter, unlike the desks in her school, a bundle of paper and a hand-sized screen. Hard-backed chairs, similar to the ones at school, were pushed against the tables.

A larger screen covering one wall featured instructions for how to play the game. Sheila read them aloud.

'Participants must earn thirty points or more to trigger rotation. Points can be picked up in multiple ways. There is a typewriter and screen on each desk. You can collect points by typing what you see on the screen. For every forty pages typed legibly, you will earn half a point. At any time you can trade your points for food.

'If you interact with the males on this floor, your chances to earn more points increase. There are several ways to improve your earning potential, not least servitude. If you choose to serve the males, you will secure your rotation faster. The males cannot force you into servitude. You must decide for yourself. But once you do, you cannot change your mind.

'If you choose not to serve, you will collect points steadily, but you risk starvation. Choose wisely. Good luck.'

Anya reread the instructions to herself. Lilly stood beside her.

'What do they mean by *servitude*?'

'It means the boys can do whatever they want,' said Yasmin.

'Anything?' Lilly's pale blue eyes were wide.

Yasmin snapped her icy gaze on Lilly. 'Yes, *anything*, little flower. Careful or they'll end up trampling on you.'

Lilly moved closer to Anya's arm. She wasn't sure when Lilly had decided she was her go-to person, but she wished she would leave her alone.

A determined June stood nearby. Gone was the girl from the ground floor who had squealed when she'd seen blood on Anya's uniform. Everyone was changing before Anya's eyes. For the first time she wondered who else had been inoculated against Compliance.

June said, 'So what do we do first?'

Sheila sat down and scooted closer to the typewriter. 'They can go to hell if they think I'm serving one of those losers.'

They all agreed, and with that the mood lightened.

'Does anyone know how to use this thing?' said June.

Anya grabbed a couple of sheets of paper and walked over to her. Her grandmother had a machine exactly like it. Anya used to make up stories and type them up.

'You need to feed the paper into the top like this...'

The others gathered round. Anya allowed the roller to catch the paper, then turned the dial at the side.

'Position it at the start of the page, but make sure the end is caught under this bar thingy to keep it in place.'

She pressed a lever and slid the roller across to the right so the printing blocks were poised at the left.

'When you come to the end of the page, just slide the roller back to the start. To remove the page, pull.' Anya tugged the paper and rotated the dial at the side. She repeated the instructions once more, then sat down at her own desk.

The room filled with the sound of typing all around her: slow at first, then slightly faster, followed by lots of cursing.

Anya's work began well. Hours of practice on her grandmother's machine had given her the ability to type fast. She never thought she'd get to use it in a place like this.

Soon she was watching the screen as her fingers glided over the keys.

Anya noticed the room had gone silent. She looked up. The others were staring at her.

'What?'

'How do you work the machine so fast?' said June.

Anya shrugged. 'Practice, I guess.'

'Well, I know who's doing the typing for us,' said Sheila.

Everyone laughed, except for Anya.

$$\Omega$$

By the end of the morning and despite her early speed, Anya had barely managed twenty pages. Her hunger had sapped her strength. The last job was to feed the pages into the letterbox slot under the instructional screen and scan her chip on a smaller screen next to it. She flexed her fingers and cracked her neck. She would have to work right through the afternoon to complete the forty for her first half-point. She'd already decided to spend it on food.

Anya looked around the room. At least the others were getting the hang of it. Lilly, though, had managed only two pages.

'Are you okay?' said Anya.

Lilly looked up, her pale eyes round and glassy. She thrust her work at Anya. 'Check these two pages. Please.'

Anya took them. They were full of spelling mistakes and half of the words were incoherent. 'These won't count. You'll need to do them again.' She handed them back to Lilly.

Lilly sobbed. 'I did the best I could. I copied the words exactly as they appeared on the screen.'

The others glanced up from their typing, but didn't stop.

Anya frowned at her. 'Lilly, can you read?'

She shook her head. Her shoulders heaved as she sobbed harder. 'Or write. It took me the whole morning to match up the letters with the words.'

The girl's illiteracy shocked Anya. She'd heard that some towns favored practical jobs over academic learning. At least Brookfield favored the latter.

Lilly rested her head on the table.

'What am I going to do? I can't serve the boys. I just can't.'

Anya bit her lip and looked around at the others. 'We can all help if we each do a little extra.'

Lilly lifted her head and sniffed.

Sheila laughed. 'Count me out. I'm barely getting ten pages done as it is.'

'Me, too,' said June. 'You're the fastest, Anya. You need to help her.'

Forty pages a day? No problem. But eighty? She couldn't see how to help Lilly earn her first half-point.

Ω

By late afternoon Anya had done her forty pages plus an extra fifteen for Lilly, before the pain in her injured forearm became unbearable.

The rest of the group had met their quota.

But Lilly wasn't happy. 'It's not enough. You should have done more.'

Anger rippled through Anya. 'Well, why don't you do it yourself next time?'

'You know I can't.' Lilly started to cry.

Anya sighed and nursed her sore arm.

The scoreboard in the main hall showed their current scores. Anya glanced up at it as she shuffled to the dining hall. The girls were all on minus half a point. Lilly was still on minus one. The boys were all on three and Dom had cleared his negative score and was on two.

What the hell? It had taken her all day just to earn a half-point.

In the dining hall, Anya scanned her chip over one of the boxes labeled a half-portion. She chose wisely: a carbohydrate-packed pasta dish with a tomato sauce. But there wasn't much in a half-portion. Lilly looked eagerly at the dish.

'Half of that's mine, right? I worked for some of it.'

Anya struggled to see the logic, but she nodded. It wasn't Lilly's fault she couldn't read or write.

The girls sat down with their half-portions at a table far away from the boys. Dom was the only one without food in front of him; Ash had said his chip had a working limit. But some of the others slipped food onto his empty plate.

The Facility

The gnawing ache in her stomach grew loud as she shared her pasta with Lilly. Sheila and June each donated a forkful of food to the plate.

'Thanks,' she said, fighting back tears.

The girls ate quietly, while the boys joked around. After dinner all the participants returned to their dorms, but the boys seemed wired for fun.

Anya and the others fell into bed. The lights remained on outside their dorm, giving them no relief from the brightness. Anya heard laughter coming from the frosted section. She considered that the control for the lights was in the boys' section.

The supervisor had said the Collective wanted to understand the differences between the sexes.

She yanked the covers over her head. Boys were selfish and girls were more adaptable. What else was there to know?

But something more than the lights prevented Anya from falling asleep. If it was so easy for the boys to earn points, why did they need the girls?

And who the hell was the Collective?

31

The early morning bell rang, and Anya and the other girls headed straight to the typewriting room. She'd thought about doing the work late at night, but the screens only appeared to activate between certain hours. Anya focused on her typing not her stomach. The boys emerged from their section, looking hung over and sleepy. The sooner she completed the forty pages, the sooner she could eat. Lilly had her head on the desk and was snoring lightly.

She kicked Lilly as she fed a page into the typewriter. Lilly bolted upright, and rubbed her eyes.

'What?'

'You need to help me. I can't do this on my own.'

'I can probably manage an extra ten pages if I don't look at the keys,' said June.

Lilly glanced from June to Anya with hopeful eyes. 'I'm no good. You saw me yesterday. I'll only mess it up.'

'So you're going to sit there all day and do nothing?'

Sheila and Yasmin both watched, amused.

Lilly shuffled in her seat. 'No, not nothing.' She looked around. 'I can help feed paper into the typewriter.'

The Facility

What else could she do without the skills to read or write?

Anya sighed. 'Fine.'

Ω

The morning and afternoon passed quickly. June kept her promise and added a few extra pages to the pile, but Lilly soon became bored of her only job. Anya's final tally was five fewer pages than the day before, even with June's help. Her hunger kept her from being efficient.

At dinner, they spent their half-points and devoured their half-portions.

Later that evening, Anya sat with the others on their beds as they discussed their dire situation. Typing alone would not secure rotation or a proper meal.

June studied her fingers. 'I'm not sure I can keep this up. No matter how fast I type, I can't do more than the forty pages.'

Sheila sat cross-legged on her bed. 'So, you want to serve those losers?'

'What other choice do we have?' said Yasmin.

'Is there nothing else we can do besides typing?' said June.

One of the other girls pointed. 'Yeah, it's waiting for us behind the frosted glass.'

Anya studied the boys' section. 'What do they have that we don't?'

Sheila shrugged. 'I don't want to find out.'

'Come on, Sheila. Why not try new things?' teased Yasmin.

'Shut your mouth, Yas, or I'll shut it for you.'

Yasmin snorted before looking away.

Anya leaned forward to look at the communal scoreboard. The boys were all on six, except for Dom, who trailed by two. They had no choice.

'One of us needs to go over there,' Anya said. 'We can't keep living hand to mouth. If there's an easier way to earn points, it's over with the boys. You heard the supervisor. They can't rotate without us, and we can't rotate without them.'

'*Easier*. I like the sound of that,' said a suddenly cheery Lilly. But not everyone was happy.

Sheila stared at her hands. 'Well, I'm not going over there.'

Anya shrugged. 'What else can we do? I can't stay here, starving.'

June stood up. 'I'll go,' she said. Sheila looked relieved.

'No,' said Anya. 'Please. It was my suggestion.'

'I really don't mind.'

Had June always been this confident? Or had Compliance clouded Anya's judgment of everyone?

Anya got to her feet. 'It was my idea. I'll go.'

'Okay, but call out if you need us to come over.'

She felt all eyes on her as she crossed the divide. Her cream sandals squeaked on the plain gray floor. She hesitated somewhere in the middle and almost retreated to the female dorm. But she kept walking. They needed to eat.

That and she'd made a promise to herself last night to help Dom and Sheila get off the fourth floor. Dom needed to find his mother. That trumped any stupid Collective-run tests.

She raised her fist, ready to knock, when the door opened. Ash wore a lopsided grin, as if he'd been expecting her.

'I knew one of you would come sooner or later,' the boy with the sandy hair said.

Anya stepped inside, but froze when she saw how clear the boys' view was into the female dorm.

In comparison to the girls' modestly sized sleeping area, the boys' room was large, bright and divided into sections by frosted-glass screens. A bed peeked out from behind one of the partitions in a row at the back of the room.

She caught the smell of alcohol in the air. Brown bottles littered the floor. In one section, two boys sat melded into chairs. They both wore headsets that covered their eyes and screamed at something on the blank screen as they swigged from their bottles.

The soft carpet-pile brushed against the uncovered parts of her feet. Ash's gaze on her stiffened her spine.

'How old are you?' said Ash.

'Seventeen. Why?'

He flashed his straight, white teeth. 'You look older.'

It wasn't a nice smile.

'Yeah, well, this place will put years on you.'

She'd meant it as a joke, but Ash didn't laugh. The smile disappeared from his face.

'So, you're here to serve us?' He tried to steer her to a cluster of sofas.

Anya squirmed away from his touch. 'No. I've come to negotiate with you.'

They stood by the sofa, Anya refusing to sit until Ash did. His politeness felt too forced, his movements too stiff to relax her.

She looked around the open-plan room, not seeing Dom anywhere. Warren, she saw, was one of the boys shouting at the screen, trapped inside some sort of virtual reality.

Ash whistled, loud and sharp.

'Gather round. Someone's here to *negotiate*.'

Dom appeared from behind one of the partitions. He rubbed his eyes. They widened as soon as he saw Anya.

'What the hell are you doing here?' he barked at her.

She stiffened at his greeting and readied a snappy retort. But the boys closing in unsettled her. Their curious gazes drifted from her face to her body to her bare legs.

'Says she's here to do a deal,' said Ash.

Dom stood at the back, arms folded, his mouth straight and tense. Warren had unhooked himself from the chair and was watching the show from the back of the group. He smiled at Anya. Her pact with Warren had been made before Dom's antidote to Compliance opened her eyes. Now, his ambitious gaze unsettled her.

She took a deep breath. 'We can't rotate off this floor and eat. It seems to be one choice or the other. We understand we will earn more points if we help you.'

She was careful not to say 'serve'.

Ash gestured to the sofa and she sat down, placing her hands on her knees to pin her dress in place. He sat beside her. The rest of the boys stayed standing. Some looked excited, others nervous.

'We knew the girls would cave,' said Ash. He stroked Anya's hair.

She jerked away. 'Don't touch me.'

Most of the other boys sniggered. Dom just glared at her. Warren also looked angry.

Her heart pounded in her ears. This felt like a trap.

'Explain how we can help you.' She tried to hide the tremor in her voice.

Ash stood and gestured at a board where their instructions were written out. She got up and followed him over to it. Ash waved his hand over them.

'As you can see, we earn points for doing practically nothing.'

He was telling the truth. The boys earned three points simply by trying out the VR equipment. It didn't matter how long they spent on a particular task; their daily points were capped if they carried out the task with another boy. If they avoided the girls completely, they would lose the points they'd worked up. But to earn points with the opposite sex, the girls had to make the first move.

Below was a list of the activities requiring participation from both sexes, and an explanation of how the girls could benefit from the shared-points scheme. Some of them were harmless, like joining one of the boys in the virtual world. Other tasks were more menial, like tidying up after a boy you had pledged to for the whole day.

Anya's cheeks flushed when she read the last item —it drew the most points and guaranteed rotation for both parties.

Ash smiled at her. 'Of course you're free to choose whatever you like. My personal favorite is the last one.' His fingers brushed her neck causing her to shiver.

She glanced at Dom. His left leg bounced, like he was a second away from pouncing on Ash.

No, no, no!

She wouldn't ruin Dom's chance to rotate.

She grabbed Ash's hand and twisted it behind his back.

'I haven't agreed to anything yet, so no touching. Okay?' Her words sounded confident, but she was a quivering mess inside. She had to get out of there.

Ash laughed through the pain that he seemed to be enjoying. 'Okay, okay. Being restrained by a beautiful girl is a turn-on, by the way.'

Anya let go of his arm.

He rubbed his wrist. 'Talk it over with the others if you must, but you'll be back.'

Through the frosted window, Anya saw the girls waiting for her to return.

She left the room, not daring to look back.

Sheila was leaning against the door of the female dorm, arms folded. 'So?'

'They can see us through the glass.'

Sheila unfolded her arms and straightened up.

Anya hooked a finger and stalked past her to the female bathroom, where they all gathered.

She spoke quietly while Yasmin kept watch at the bathroom door. She told them everything they needed to do to earn points.

Lilly looked to be the most scared. June seemed oddly pragmatic.

'So,' said June, 'we have to... you know, have sex with one of them to guarantee rotation?'

Anya nodded. 'There are other ways to earn points, just not as fast. But not all of the boys look like they want to go that far.'

'But some of them do?'

Anya nodded. 'I'd say about half, but some might have been exaggerating for the other boys.'

'But we can get by with the less-demeaning tasks?' said Yasmin.

Anya shrugged. 'Maybe. But the last item guarantees rotation.' She glanced at Sheila, who dropped her gaze. Anya frowned at her odd behavior.

They talked for a while longer, until there was nothing left to say.

The others left, but Anya pulled Sheila back.

She glared at Anya's hand on her arm. 'What?'

'I want to talk to you in private.'

Sheila loomed over her. At five feet ten, she was the same height as Dom; four inches taller than Anya, and much more Dom's type than Anya was.

She removed her hand. 'If you decide to go down that road, I want you and Dom to do it.'

Sheila smirked. 'What makes you think I'm going straight for the main prize?'

'Because you and Dom are here for a reason and I won't get in the way.'

Her expression softened. 'I know. It had occurred to me too. Better to do it with someone familiar, I suppose.' Anya's heart twisted at her words. 'Thanks. I'll talk to Dom about it.'

Sheila left Anya in the bathroom alone. She tried to get the picture of their beautiful bodies entwined together out of her head.

Ten minutes later, she returned to the dorm. The others were already in bed and the lights were off. Sheila was snoring gently in the next bed when Anya slid under her own covers. She was about to nod off when a warm hand clamped over her mouth. Panic filled her. She tried to cry out. Pressure on her shoulders kept her pinned to the bed. But then Dom's face appeared in her line of sight. She breathed out through her nose and relaxed under his gentle weight. He released her and hooked a finger for her to follow.

She followed him to the girl's bathroom. There, an anxious looking Dom paced the length of the stalls.

He turned to her, his eyes blazing. 'What the hell were you thinking going in there alone?'

'I was doing it for the others.'

'It's all they've been talking about since they first read the instructions, and since you left. I had a plan.'

Anya glanced around the room.

Dom shook his head. 'No cameras in the bathrooms. The showers and the infirmaries, too. I guess they don't want to hear or see certain things.'

'Who? The supervisors?'

'Or the Collective. They ordered this place to be built. It wouldn't surprise me if someone from Praesidium was watching us.'

Anya didn't mention she'd seen the cameras track her on occasion.

'What was your plan?' she asked.

'I had arranged with some of the boys to pick the other girls. Then I was going to pick you, so we could work up the points in a safer way. But now a few of them have dibs on you, and I have to choose last because of my weak standing.'

Her legs turned to jelly. She gripped the sink for support. The thought of Ash 'choosing' her sickened her. But she would not go back on her promise to Sheila.

'You and Sheila came here together. You need to leave together. I can't have you risking your progress for me.'

Dom's expression softened. 'I can't leave you behind. I knew that early on.'

He took a step toward her, forcing her to take one back. Her body reacted to him too much. She had to keep her nerve.

'Do you think we'll rotate soon?' she said.

Dom shrugged and looked around. 'Something's different here. They rushed us on the last floor. Here, they seem happy to let things pan out. They must have strengthened their defenses around this place.' He looked at her. 'I wish there was some way to predict rotation. We know the lights flicker before it happens, but that doesn't give much warning to the others. The four of us should discuss strategies sometime.'

'Four of us?'

Dom smiled weakly and scratched his neck. 'Yeah, there's another like Sheila and me, on this floor.'

'Who?'

'I can't say.'

Anya shook her head. It didn't matter. 'You need to forget about me. I was never part of your plan. Don't worry. I'll make it through. I've got a clear head now and I've got—'

'Warren?'

'Yeah. We sort of made a pact on the outside, to progress together... Wait. How did you know?'

'Please don't trust him. He's not one of us. I don't want to see you fail.'

'I don't plan to, but I also don't get to choose who I end up with.'

Dom huffed out a breath. He stalked to the end of the bathroom before turning sharply. 'If either Ash or Warren lays a finger on you, I swear I'll—'

'I can look after myself. Remember why you're here. You came to find your mother.'

His fingers twitched at his side. His eyes were liquid, pleading.

'Anya, promise me you'll be careful.'

'I promise.' She smiled to reassure him. 'Remember those self-defense lessons? Now I can put them to good use.'

In three strides, he bridged the distance between them. 'If anything happened to you, I don't know...' He closed his eyes for a second. 'I only just got you, and I'm not letting you go. Do you hear me?'

He stroked her face with his thumb. His feathery kiss left her skin tingling. Without thinking she leaned into him.

But Dom was too impulsive. If she wasn't careful, he'd blow up his original plan to find his mother. She had to put a stop to this. Dom would strategize better if she wasn't a distraction.

It took all her strength to pull away from him and walk out.

She crawled into bed and hid her face under the covers. Her quiet sobs left her feeling raw and empty inside. What if Dom and Sheila rotated to the fifth floor and she was left behind?

She heard Dom leave the bathroom and stop outside her room.

'Anya,' he whispered.

She fought against the urge to look at him one last time, and buried herself deeper. She got here alone, and she would make it to the next floor without him.

He sighed and left. The door to the boy's dorm opened and closed.

Despite Dom's warnings about Warren, he was looking like her only prospect. His hunger and ambition could serve her well. Together they would rotate. And if the third rebel wasn't Warren, who was it?

A mild tremor rattled the bed and stopped her tears cold. It disappeared as fast as it had arrived.

Anya checked Jason's wristwatch and made a mental note of the time.

32

After a sleepless night battling her hunger pains Anya felt weary. The other girls had fared better with sleep, but it was clear they needed to do something drastic. The boys were their ticket off the fourth floor.

They pooled their rations and picked carb-loaded foods. But it wasn't enough. While the boys ate and laughed, Anya and the others returned to their dorm to discuss strategies.

Anya's stomach trembled. She looked down at the cut on her arm, once a painful diversion but no longer enough to distract her. The slash was still raised and red, but the skin had begun to heal. She'd stopped wearing the bandage.

Laughter filled the void between the two dorms as the boys left the dining hall. Ash led the way. A couple of smiling boys flicked their gazes between the typewriting room and the girls.

Anya watched them go back inside their dorm. Once the last boy was inside Yasmin stood up.

'Come on. Let's get this over with.'

The Facility

Anya smoothed down her dress. The others prepared to leave. A clearly nervous Sheila got up and followed Yasmin. Anya had never seen her so rattled.

Yasmin knocked on the door.

Ash answered. 'Welcome to *mi casa*, ladies.'

He stood back and, with great drama, gestured for them to enter.

The boys hovered by the sofas. Anya's skin tightened at the thought of what was to come. Ash nodded to the sofas and the girls sat down. Yasmin, June and Sheila wore hard expressions. Lilly and the other girls looked terrified. Anya controlled her breathing and pretended she was anywhere but here.

Ash smacked his hands together, startling Anya. 'Okay, let's see who gets to choose one of these lovely ladies first.' He stood by the scoreboard with the boys' names listed.

The whole charade reminded Anya of her first school dance.

Boys on one side, girls on the other. Awkward staring. Shifting gazes and feet. The pressure to be picked, and liked.

Grace had not been a fan of dances. It went against her idea of matching. Anya had only ever gone to one, and that was only after her father had insisted.

Grace had said, 'She needs to settle down, before they come for her.'

Her father had replied. 'Let her have fun while she can.'

Anya had pushed against pairing off with a boy then. But fast forward two years and here she was, in the exact same position.

Ash ran his finger along the first name on the scoreboard: his own.

He looked each of the girls over. Anya's heart hammered.

'I want to pick you.' He pointed lazily at Sheila. Anya hid her shock. This wasn't the plan. 'But you scare the hell out of me. So I pick... you.'

He pointed at Lilly, who sat quivering beside Anya. She stood up slowly, her sniffling loud in a room filled with silence. Anya was sure Ash would pick her.

'Don't worry, Lilly,' he said softly. 'We'll start out with something... easy.'

The next name on the list was Jerome. Anya stared at the floor.

Yasmin jabbed her in the ribs. 'It's you.'

Anya looked up to see Jerome pointing at her. She stood and caught Dom's eye. He nodded at her, his mouth tight. Had he made a deal with Jerome?

Warren was glaring at Dom.

The other boys, the ones Anya didn't know, picked Yasmin and three others. Warren was next and picked June. That pleased Anya. Warren would help June to rotate.

It surprised her that Sheila was passed over until Dom's turn. She got up and stood beside him. He cupped her neck and leaned in to whisper something in her ear. Sheila's face softened and she nodded. He smiled at her in a reassuring way.

The intimate moment caught Anya off guard. Her jealousy, confusion—or whatever she felt—forced her to look away.

Jerome's tap on her shoulder snapped her out of it. She pulled him to a quieter section, away from Dom and Sheila.

'So what do you want to do first?' he said.

Anya gave him a weak smile. 'Eat.'

Jerome nodded. 'I think we can arrange that.'

'Jerome, I'm so—'

His eyes hardened. 'Please, Anya. Let's just get you some food, okay?'

She nodded and followed him out of the dorm. At least Sheila and Dom were together.

Not surprising, the other girls also asked for food. The boys obliged, but Anya feared that some like Ash would ask for more in return. While Jerome wasn't one of the hostile ones, he had a new edge to him since learning about Frank.

After breakfast he showed her around the boys' dorm. 'We can play VR, or there are some board games if you prefer intellectual stimulation.'

Anya shrugged. She didn't care, as long as she could earn points fast.

'What's the next highest-scoring task after... you know?'

Jerome rubbed the back of his neck. 'Slave for the day. You have to do anything I want. Get me drinks, make my bed, clean my clothes, that sort of thing.'

Anya bit her lip. 'Okay, let's start there.' Just like looking after Jason.

It didn't take long for her to feel like an idiot, following Jerome around like he was her master. And worse, he enjoyed the attention a little bit too much.

Ash was making Lilly do the same. She didn't like the way Ash looked at her.

Dom and Sheila weren't around. Anya tried not to think about how they might be earning their points. By the end of the day, her own score wasn't far off twenty points.

After dinner, Anya and Jerome idled outside the boys' dorm.

'You can sleep here if you want,' said Jerome without looking at her. Frank as a topic was off limits, but she needed to say something.

'Jerome. I want to explain. I—'

'Or you can go back to your own dorm.'

She sighed. 'That's probably a good idea.'

Some of the girls decided to stay in the nicer accommodation, but Anya wanted a place where she still had control. June and Yasmin obviously felt the same because they returned to the female dorm too. Sheila was notably absent.

That evening, they sat on their beds and discussed the day.

'Warren's a little creepy,' said Yasmin to June. She pushed her straw-blonde hair back off her face and tied it up.

'He's okay,' said June. 'He's better than Ash.'

They all agreed.

'How's Jerome doing?' June asked Anya.

Anya took her hair down. 'He won't talk to me. I don't know.'

'That's stupid,' said June. 'You tried to stop Frank from opening the door.'

'I'm not sure he sees it that way.' Anya shrugged. 'We're doing the slave thing again tomorrow. We both should have more than thirty points by the end of the day.'

The Facility

Yasmin lay down on the bed. 'The slave thing doesn't really work for me. Maybe I'll just have sex once, you know, to guarantee rotation.'

'Just make sure you don't regret your choice,' said June.

Yasmin looked away. The boy who'd picked Yasmin was tall like her, and slightly muscular. But Anya could tell that she had no interest in him.

'And Jerome?' said June. 'Is he pressuring you to have sex?'

Anya shook her head. 'I think he's too scared to ask. He got embarrassed when I agreed to do the slave thing. Besides, I don't want to upset him. I'll do whatever he wants—within reason.'

'Be careful. Give them a little power and they want more.'

June. Always the cautious one.

'What about Warren?'

June pursed her lips. 'Not so far. But I can handle him.'

Anya smiled. She didn't doubt that.

While Yasmin and June settled under their covers Anya headed for the bathroom, her soap and towel nestled under her good arm. She paused outside the door as another vibration ran through her bare feet, similar to the one she'd felt the night before. She rested her hand on the wall, and it was there too, stronger than the last one.

She looked up. Where was it coming from?

The empty bathroom gave her a moment to think. But not for long. The door swung open and someone entered, causing her to spin round.

She pressed her towel to her clothed body. 'Warren! You can't be in here.'

'I needed to talk to you, in private.' He scratched the back of his neck. 'I was hoping to pick you, but Dom screwed that up.' He took careful, measured steps toward her.

Had anyone seen him come in? June or Yasmin? She wished there were cameras in the room.

His curious gaze flitted over her. 'I wanted to ask what your strategy is with Jerome.'

Anya relaxed and placed the towel on the sink beside her. 'Slave for the day, but don't worry. June wants to progress as much as you do. She's a stronger ally to have right now.' Anya held up her injured arm.

'Well, I don't think so.'

Warren sounded odd, almost nervous.

'Of course June wants to move on. Why wouldn't she?'

'She's deliberately choosing the easier tasks, the ones worth ten points or less, and eating as much as she can so she spends them. That doesn't seem like a good ally to me.'

Warren took another step forward. Anya saw tension in his eyes.

'I can talk to her if you'd like?'

Another step in her direction. 'I wanted her to do the slave thing, but she wouldn't even consider it. And it makes me angry to see you paired up with Jerome. That could have been us.'

'Jerome just lost Frank. We all did. Show a little sympathy.'

Warren shook his head. 'Of course, I'm sorry he died. But I didn't really know him that well.'

His voice sounded soft, distant, but his eyes were still too alert, too focused.

The Facility

'You and I promised to progress together. But now, I'm second-last in points and I need to change that.'

She gripped the edge of the counter. 'What are you talking about?'

'I wouldn't have asked you to do the first task on the list if we were paired up, but June is hurting my chances. Now, I don't have a choice.'

'I'm sure you and June will figure it out.'

His eyes were hard like marbles. 'That's just it. There's only one way to guarantee rotation.'

Her pulse thrummed.

'It's always been just you and me, and now I need your help.'

Warren reached for her and she jerked away. Her soap fell from the sink to the floor.

'Anya, I *need* this. I won't rotate otherwise.'

'It's only been a day. You haven't given it a chance. Talk to June tomorrow—'

'I can't.'

His anger surprised her. She searched his eyes for signs of regret. What she found were tears yet to fall.

Warren grabbed at clumps of his strawberry-blond hair and squeezed his eyes shut. Anya backed away, deeper into the bathroom, making escape harder with every step.

He moved toward her, pale eyes blazing with something darker than desire: desperation, ambition. He grabbed her left arm suddenly and pressed his fingers into her cut. She yelped with surprise and pain.

He glanced down and loosened his grip. 'Sorry.'

But when she tried to free her arm, his grip tightened.

Warren moved in closer. The freckles on his face blurred when he pressed his body against hers. She turned her face away from his hot, fast breath.

'I promise I won't hurt you, Anya. And I'll make it fast. There's no other choice. Please trust me. This will guarantee we both make it off this floor.'

Anya shook her head. Was he really asking her to do this?

She tried to bring up her knee, but her dress restricted her movement. The cold of the wall seeped through the fabric and chilled her.

Warren ran his equally cold hand up the side of her leg, lifting the fabric. She tried to push him away, but he only pressed his fingers harder into her wound. She gasped when he twisted the skin.

No, no.

Warren's weight pinned her against the wall. He kissed her neck roughly. The light-colored stubble on his face felt like sandpaper. Her stomach heaved. She struggled to draw air.

'Yasm—!' He cut off her cry with a rough kiss. She squeezed her lips and eyes shut and tried to forget he was touching her.

He pulled up her dress. With one hand keeping her in place, his other fumbled with his waistband.

Anya grasped at her memories from her time with Dom in the playground. She settled on one. It was hardly the same scenario, but the defensive move could work.

With Warren distracted and his body open, she drove up her right knee and found his stomach. He staggered away in shock. She stepped toward him, fists up, ready to punch him if he came at her again.

He did, and she struck him hard on his jawbone. Pain shuddered through her hand. She bit her lip to keep from screaming and kept her fists raised. She watched every tiny move he made.

'I guess I forgot to tell you I'm good at sports,' she said through a flurry of breaths.

Warren stared at her; shocked, furious. He cradled his jaw with his hand, but he didn't come at her again.

'I need to get out of Arcis, Anya. This is a mistake.'

He staggered to the door.

'Not like this,' said Anya.

He checked the mobility of his jaw one more time, and left the bathroom.

When he was gone Anya crumpled to the floor. Tears ran down her cheeks. The door opened again and she scrambled to her feet. But when June appeared, she dropped back down. Yasmin was behind her, keeping a look out.

June slid down beside her.

'What happened?'

Her lips were thin and white as she held up Anya's arm. Anya glanced down to see her cut had started to bleed again.

'Did Warren do this?' said June.

Anya nodded.

'Psycho bastard. I'll make sure he doesn't get enough points now.'

Anya recoiled from this new and angry June, who pulled her to her feet.

'He's not worth it, June,' said Yasmin. 'Don't sabotage your own chances.'

June looked up at Yasmin. 'Give us a minute?'

Yasmin glared at her for a moment, then shrugged and left.

June turned to Anya. 'Dom asked me to halt Warren's progression. He doesn't want Warren reaching the ninth floor at the same time as him and Sheila. I'll be okay. I can rotate the next time.'

'Why would Dom ask... Are you...?' She stared at her. 'Are *you*?'

June shushed her. 'You can't tell anyone.'

'But I thought—'

'I was a delicate flower?' June smiled and examined her hands. 'It turns out my nimble fingers are pretty good at assembling weapons faster than the boys.'

'Does that mean—'

'Yeah, my parents were rebel sympathizers. They're dead. My uncle trained me.'

'And Frank, Tahlia, Jerome?'

June shook her head. 'Sorry I was so distant on the ground floor. I had to keep up the pretense.'

Anya leaned against the counter. June supported her with one hand while she ran the edge of Anya's towel under the water. She dabbed at the wound, causing Anya to wince.

'You can't stay here for another rotation,' said Anya. 'I need you to move on. I can handle Warren.' Her words came out clipped and fast, but with June there, she felt her control return.

June said nothing as she cleaned the wound.

'Promise me.'

'You don't know him. He killed Tahlia.'

Anya swallowed loudly. 'No. I did.'

'*No*,' she said. 'Yasmin told me it was his idea to target Tahlia.'

The Facility

'But Warren said he'd overheard Supervisor One and Two saying they'd rotate us all if someone was consistently last. It was Yasmin who suggested Tahlia.'

'Warren told her the last part would sound more convincing coming from her.'

'And you believe her?'

'Warren just attacked you. Who are you going to believe? Her group already had a plan to rotate. They didn't need Warren's scheming or Tahlia to do it.'

Anya looked away. 'We were all equally to blame. Nobody put a gun to our heads.' She looked back at June. 'I'm begging you, please don't risk rotation for Warren. Besides Dom you're my only friend in here.'

June seemed to consider this. Then she rolled her eyes.

'Fine. But I was really enjoying messing up Warren's chances.'

33

The camp, including Jason, packed up and moved the operation to Glenvale, a town with the same thick forest covering as Foxrush but closer to Ession. Jason and Preston had exhausted all attempts to maintain a stable corridor to communicate with those inside Arcis. The snippets of information relayed back just weren't enough. With the new move Jason hoped he and Preston might have better luck.

Jason had worked on a Plan B, but getting the random frequency codes remained everyone's best shot at getting inside Arcis.

As their trucks rolled up to the entrance, Jason saw the first group was already setting up. Soldiers pitched tents and counted out food supplies on tables outside a large red-bricked building.

When the truck came to a stop inside the gates, Jason got out and looked around. Ession, a few kilometers away, was visible through a narrow clearing in the forest. Similar to Foxrush, several flat-roofed buildings sat nearest the gates to Glenvale.

Max was already on one of the buildings, looking through a pair of binoculars. A set of pre-positioned crates had been staggered like giant steps against the wall. Jason used them to get to the roof, and stood beside him.

'Can I see?'

Max handed him a second set of binoculars. 'There's no movement.'

'This town is closer than Foxrush. Surely they can see us here. I mean, it's a pretty obvious place to check for rebels.'

Max nodded. 'The orbs' signatures are all over this place. But they're faint now, which means they've been and gone. Thomas picked up a stronger signal heading west, away from here. The sensors on the walls are different from the independent orbs. They rely on power from Arcis to work. But since a lot of power is being prioritized for something inside Arcis, the sensors might not be as powerful as we first thought.'

Jason pressed the binoculars to his eyes and adjusted the range. He saw the high wall surrounding Essention and the guns perched on top, with sensors attached to their sides.

He snatched the binoculars away. 'I should have known there was something wrong with Essention. Those high walls are a dead giveaway.'

The more time he spent with the rebels, the fewer excuses he had to maintain his prejudice.

'You'd have to be a mind reader to know what they had planned. They've been clever. Don't beat yourself up about it.'

'But it's my fault. I can see that now.' Jason snatched at breaths. The binoculars dangled from his hand. 'My parents were preparing us for this.'

Max gripped Jason's shoulder. 'And now you have a chance to do something about it. You can start by helping Preston solve this communication problem of ours.'

Jason and Preston had combined Thomas' energy-displacer technology with the satellite booster. Their plan? To create a corridor for a message to pass through while distorting the force field around Arcis long enough to sustain the connection. Glenvale was the final, unobstructed test to see if it would work.

Jason looked down to see Preston and Thomas coming through the gates. They carried boxes of electronic equipment from the trucks, as well as the homemade satellite dish. Preston waved at him to come down.

Jason helped them to carry more equipment inside. They set everything up in the room just off from the flat roof. Preston fired up the machine that Jason hoped would be good enough to maintain a steady signal through Arcis' force field.

The screen reported the force field's energy was almost at full strength. Their plan to maintain a steady connection to Arcis hadn't worked up until now. But the addition of Thomas' energy-displacer tech would hopefully show an improvement.

Preston spoke into the microphone. 'Testing, testing... Pavesi, Kouris, if either of you can hear me, tap on your communication cards.'

Jason hovered behind him, while Thomas gnawed on his thumb. Preston tried again, but the machine received no definitive signal back.

'We know the lights dip just before rotation,' said Thomas. 'Ask them to report back any other patterns that might indicate a draw in the power.'

Preston glared at him. 'I can't ask them until I hear back from them.'

The Facility

Thomas rolled his eyes. 'Keep trying. They might not be able to answer.'

Preston turned back around. 'Dominic, Sheila. Tap on your communication cards if you can hear me.'

Jason heard something. It was faint, but unmistakable. A series of taps. He looked at Thomas, who translated with a smile. 'I can hear you.'

The tapping stopped.

'I lost it.' Preston huffed. He pulled Jason and Thomas down to sit either side of him. Jason scooted closer as Preston pointed at a box on the table.

'What are you both waiting for? We've got a signal to stabilize.'

34

Carissa turned from the screen, confused. Warren had just left the girls' bathroom. Then Anya had come out with June, looking upset. Something had happened and Carissa was dying to know what.

What had Warren done? Her curiosity had never felt stronger.

She would erase that feeling from her memory banks.

Carissa paced the footage room in the Learning Center, at the heart of Praesidium. Dozens of screens filled one wall, showing stolen moments of time in Arcis.

Different groups. Different screens covering the separate floors.

The cameras didn't capture everything. The Collective said their purpose wasn't to see all, but learn enough from the participants' behavior.

She faced the screen again and folded her arms. She searched for the one person who'd meant something to her Original.

June.

Tears moistened the corners of her human eyes. A small inconvenience for the privilege of having them, the

Inventor had said. Carissa touched her finger to the wetness first, then tasted it.

Salty.

She'd seen the Originals cry in Praesidium before. But her tears didn't carry the weight of their emotions; the sobbing, the wailing, the screaming. The demands to be released.

Emotions weren't part of Carissa's design. Yet, she was shedding tears over someone her Original used to know. But the moment felt too contrived.

Another thought to erase before her download for the Collective ten.

She left the room. Outside, Carissa sat under a tree and removed an orb from her pocket. She tossed it into the air. It hovered beside her like a pet.

She had seen too much, felt too much that day. Her thoughts could prove difficult to erase before tomorrow. Right now, she needed to do something safe, something *expected*. If she erased too many experiences Quintus would get suspicious. He might accuse her of showing sympathy for the human experiments.

The low sun glistened off the metal orb and caused fresh tears to fall. She left that experience intact for the Collective. A little variety was good.

In the distance, Originals headed home for the evening. The electrical force field surrounding Praesidium prevented them from leaving. From the Arcis footage on the first floor Carissa had seen how the right voltage could bring the humans down.

She circled the tree while the orb chased her. She darted one way, then another, laughing lightly at first. But when the humming orb fell into a predictable pattern,

Carissa slowed, allowing it to catch her. She commanded it back into her pocket and sat on the grass.

Her pocket bulged with the obedient orb as she watched Original Vanessa, the librarian, walk back to the library. She wore a primrose yellow dress that complemented her dark skin and her figure, which was rounder than that of her Copy. The Originals wore colorful clothing, while the Copies wore a color that reflected their purity. The forty-six-year-old woman, whose eyes smiled when she did, had a warmer temperament than her Copy.

She stood up and followed her to the library. Interaction between Originals and Copies was limited due to Quintus' fear the Originals might form an attachment. But Carissa expected it was the Copies he worried about.

She still had the memories of her Original, but her limited experiences had frozen Carissa in time. Now, she wanted to move forward. Originals continued to experience and learn. Carissa wanted to do the same.

Vanessa stopped halfway to the library and sat down on a bench. Carissa's part-organic heart skipped a beat, making her reconsider her plan to interact.

While she was certain Vanessa would be punished for the interaction, not her, the idea did not sit well with her. It had upset her to see Anya receive electric shocks, or to see how the supervisor on the second floor had left Tahlia to die alone. The Arcis program had been designed to get the best and worst out of the participants, so the Collective could learn from them. So all the Copies could.

But how could they do that if the teenagers were dead?

Carissa walked back to the Learning Center. She would seek the Collective's permission to speak with Vanessa.

The Facility

Inside the Great Hall, the Collective ten were quieter than usual. Carissa kept her hand pressed to the central podium. Only a handful of voices permeated through her cerebral unit. Then Quintus' voice came through.

'You are here to ask a question,' Quintus said, his voice loud in her head. His face didn't appear on screen.

'Yes.'

'About the Originals.'

Carissa swallowed. 'Yes.'

'What is it?'

'I wish to learn more. I wish to prepare for the others' arrival.'

'There is no reason for you to interact with an Original, 173-C,' Quintus said.

'I understand that. As you know, I've been watching the participants in Arcis...'

She dared not call them by their first names.

'While the experience has been very useful, I feel I would learn more if I spoke to the librarian.'

'You have no use for the librarian's knowledge.' Quintus sounded amused. 'She is here to assist our efforts in preparing the Copies for life beyond Praesidium.'

'Will she help the others when they get here?'

'Of course.'

'Then, I would like to understand how she will do that. And why the Originals are so fascinated with books.' Carissa paused. 'Why do we keep their printed materials?'

'Because books are important to them, so they must be of equal importance to us if we are to be like them. I will check with the others.'

Quintus' voice grew quiet while he consulted with the other nine. Carissa held on to her hope. At least it wasn't an outright no.

Quintus returned. 'We have discussed it. The ten agrees it would be useful to experience what you do. Permission granted.'

Carissa nodded at the screen, even though there were no faces showing.

She kept her thoughts neutral as she left the Great Hall; Quintus would no doubt examine them tomorrow. Outside, she played with the orb for a while to add to her footage for the next day.

Then, when her patience ran out, she headed for the glass and wood building.

Carissa approached the south-facing entrance covered in wooden paneling that protected the books from sun damage. She hesitated before opening the door and walking inside.

Bookcases covered every inch of the glass walls, all stuffed with books. More books lay on the floor, ready to be cataloged; recent finds from some of the towns.

The library was split over two floors. There was a large open space on the ground floor, and the first floor, set farther back, was accessible by a set of glass stairs. Two Originals worked in the upper area, cataloging books. Vanessa was on the ground floor, sorting through a new delivery. She wore a pair of eye glasses.

Carissa hesitated again, not sure what to say.

The Originals stopped to stare at her. It wasn't uncommon for Copies to use the library, but they usually used the terminal by the door where they could access the full collection of books.

Carissa unstuck herself and walked over to the terminal. She pressed her palm to the sensor and the library of books became available to her. She downloaded the entire collection to her cerebral unit, overwriting the previous file. The smell of musty books on the shelves nearest her drew her attention. She disconnected and walked over to them, running her fingers along the spines.

'We're closing up soon.'

Carissa jumped at the sound of Vanessa's voice.

'Okay,' she replied mechanically, the way she did when an Original initiated conversation. The Inventor was the exception to her rule.

'Can I help you with something?'

Vanessa's dark-brown eyes were as warm as her smile. Carissa stared at the librarian. This moment that the Collective would see tomorrow felt too long.

She looked away. 'No, thank you.'

Vanessa returned to her stack of books on the floor.

The Collective would be expecting some interaction. 'Wait, please.'

Vanessa turned. 'Yes?'

'I wanted to ask you a question about these books.'

'Sure. What do you want to know?'

'Why do you keep them when you can just download everything from here?' She touched the terminal with her finger.

Vanessa laughed softly. She tapped the side of her head, at the point where Carissa's cerebral connection disc was installed. Vanessa had only one disc, above her ear, for general communication.

'We don't have an extra connection, like you. We can't simply download what we want.'

'If you can't download, what do you do?'

'We read.'

Carissa frowned at her. 'Why?'

Vanessa placed a hand on Carissa's back; she flinched at the move. If Vanessa was bothered by her reaction, she didn't show it.

'You're about thirteen, right? Let me show you some of the books I used to read when I was your age.'

Carissa permitted the Original to lead her to the pile of books on the floor. The librarian rummaged through it and showed her several titles: *The Adventures of Christina Popple, Reporter*; *Breaking the Rules*; *My First Kiss*.

Vanessa hid a fourth book behind her back. 'This was my favorite. It's not in the system yet, and you look like you know how to be discreet.'

She slipped her the book, then showed her a couple more. Just for show, Carissa realized.

Without looking at the book, Carissa pulled up her dress enough to slip the contraband in the waistband of her leggings.

Several more Copies entered the library. Vanessa hovered close by in case they had questions.

One of the Copies asked to see a book: *The Evolution of Man*. The Collective ten wanted the physical copy, he said. While Vanessa searched the database and located it upstairs, Carissa slipped out of the library with her gift.

She spent the rest of the evening playing with her orb. The book dug into her side. Everything she did today must be carefully planned to hide the gaps in her upload tomorrow. And she really wanted to keep the book a secret.

Carissa finally gave in to the temptation. She found a quiet spot on the other side of the city in Zone C, near the medical facility. She removed the book from her waistband and read the title: *The Curious Child with the Peculiar Eyes*.

She opened it and began to read. Words she could process, but understanding the text required extra concentration.

Carissa slammed the book closed and tucked it into her waistband again. She would find a safe hiding place for it later.

Watching the screens required less effort. But everyone of interest was probably asleep in Arcis now.

Her impatience built as she sat on the grass and tossed her orb into the air. It landed perfectly on her palm each time. She demanded the orb show her pictures of the rest of Essention—dull in comparison to the feed from Arcis. The Collective used the orbs offsite. Hers had just returned home from a stint in Essention.

The orb replayed tedious footage from the water purification area. Carissa switched to imagery from the hospital in South Essention. Through the glass exterior, the orb had observed adults, and children around her age, lining up to receive their daily injections. She fast-forwarded by a day and watched the same adults and the same children receive injections to make them better.

Except, they looked sicker than they had the day before.

35

Anya didn't think the last three months could get worse. But what had happened with Warren in the bathroom several hours ago had trumped that.

Her arm throbbed as she lay in bed. Warren had come close to getting what he wanted.

She rolled onto her side and tucked the covers tight under her chin. June had wanted to wrap her wound in gauze, but Anya had refused. She wanted the angry red strip to serve as a reminder to Warren of what he had done.

The lights came on and she heard movement in the frosted section. Her skin crawled at the thought of the boys laughing over Warren's failed attempt with her.

'Can't we just stay here?' Yasmin groaned from her bed.

Anya pushed the covers off her and glanced at her arm.

Screw Warren.

'I'd rather get the hell off this floor.' A new drive forced her out of bed. An uneven tremor, like a mini shock wave, sprang up through her feet.

'Did you feel that?' she said to Yasmin.

Yasmin still had her feet off the floor. 'Feel what?'

The Facility

She touched the wall behind her.

June did the same. 'What did it feel like?'

'A tiny earthquake.' She shook her head. 'I'm probably imagining it. I don't feel it now.'

The lights dipped suddenly before returning to full brightness.

Rotation.

The giant screen in the void flickered and set her heart to race. She slipped her sandals on and stumbled outside, catching herself before she fell.

'What is it?' Yasmin asked. 'What's going on?'

Anya didn't answer her. She checked the time on her watch. It was 1am.

She looked up at the screen. The scores were all there. Yesterday evening she'd been on twenty. She searched for her name and found it. She covered her mouth in shock.

She'd lost ten points. Warren had, too. Yasmin and June were on ten as well. Most of the others were on twenty. Just four people had hit thirty: Ash, Lilly, Dom and Sheila.

She swallowed back a rising sob. She hadn't made rotation.

A short siren sounded. She was still staring up at the screen when the rest of the girls gathered next to her. The screen changed and Supervisor Two's thin, stern face filled the screen.

'Please gather for an announcement.'

She glanced at the others. Ash seemed nervous. Lilly was quieter than usual. Warren kept his distance from Anya. To her pleasure, she noticed a purple bruise beginning to form where she'd hit him.

Sheila and Dom stood not far from her. Dom looked up at the board and his jaw tightened.

Jerome stood next to her. He was still on twenty points. Her rejection of Warren had cost her ten points. Only four of them had earned enough points to rotate. But that meant she'd be left with Warren.

The supervisor stared down at them.

'There has been a change of rules.'

Anya swallowed hard.

'We have a swelling of numbers on the lower floors and we need to make room for the next team. Everyone on ten points or more will rotate.'

She released a breath and her gaze found June. The petite rebel shrugged.

'Please collect your belongings and wait by the elevator,' said the supervisor.

Lilly brushed past her. Anya reached out and grabbed her arm.

She spun round and stared at her. She had the look of a trapped animal.

'Are you okay?'

'I'm fine,' Lilly snapped. She reclaimed her arm and kept walking.

Lilly and Ash had ended up on maximum points. That could only mean one thing.

Supervisor Two was waiting by the elevator when they arrived with their bags. Anya did a head count. Not all of them had made it.

She climbed into the elevator, standing as far away from Warren as possible. June and Yasmin entered next, glaring at Warren. Dom and Sheila were last in, followed by a despondent Jerome. Dom's head hung low, as if he were deep in thought. Anya expected Lilly to stand next to her, but she pushed herself into a corner and hugged her thin frame.

The biggest surprise to Anya was a quiet and miserable-looking Ash. He stood in the opposite corner, arms folded, staring down at his feet.

The fifth floor awaited.

36

Their efforts to merge the energy-displacer tech and the signal-booster amounted to nothing. Max called for Jason, Thomas and Preston to stop.

'We've tweaked and tested our equipment all we can out here,' he said. 'We need to go back to Essention.'

The news excited Jason. Anya had just rotated to the fifth floor. Soon she would reach the ninth. He had to rescue her before that happened.

It was raining hard. A group had gathered inside the main tent. Max explained his plan to hardened soldiers, and young men and women with valuable skill sets.

'I want people who'll be valuable in there,' said Max. With his first and second in command, he stood in front of a table laid out with soldiers' vests, helmets and long boots that looked like fishing waders.

'The soldiers will wait here for a few days to make sure more orbs don't come. Then, they'll enter Essention in a second and third approach. The first wave will be a select group only—we need to test the town's defenses.' Some of the soldiers shouted their disapproval. 'I know that sounds like a job for the more experienced soldiers among you, but once we're safely back inside Essention, we'll need people with the right skills to send messages to Pavesi and Kouris straight away.'

Max picked up a pile of vests and thrust them at Jason, Preston and a few younger soldiers. 'Put these on. They'll disguise your heat and motion so the sensors can't pick up on your location. The fabric repels heat and vibrates in time with the sensors' frequency, rendering you temporarily invisible. You will be able to move forward without triggering the sensors.'

'How?' said Jason.

'You will appear motionless to the sensors. One moment, you will be far away, the next you will be closer. The vibration knocks you slightly off course, pushes you in the direction you need to go. You will move in a zigzag pattern while the sensors are active.' Max pressed a button on the vest in Jason's hand and the entire suit began to vibrate up his arm. He flicked it off and the vibration dissipated.

'The zigzag pattern is only manageable for short distances. It's going to feel like your head's being knocked about the place. You'll need to concentrate harder while you run.'

$$\Omega$$

The rain had stopped by the time the small team of Max, Jason, Preston and support soldiers stood on the edge of the forest between Glenvale and Essention. Under the cover of night, Jason readjusted the top half of his suit. The too-small vest pinched him, but the waders were thin and comfortable. His helmet lay beside a tree. They had made the journey on foot; truck wheels squelching in wet grass would have been too loud.

Preston carried a mobile version of the satellite dish in his pocket. Thomas had modified the silver orb to carry a signal booster.

According to Thomas rotation was imminent, which meant the guns would be rendered inactive for a short time. Jason's gear weighed him down as they waited for things to kick off. Preston climbed the nearest tree to get a vantage point that would set him parallel to the top of Essention's wall. Jason stayed on the ground with Max and the soldiers. None of them carried real weapons that would be picked up by the sensors. But Thomas had packed the non-metallic Disruptor and Atomizer in Max's bag.

'Good job I like heights,' said Preston to no one. His breathing sounded fast and flurried from his perch. He gripped the thickest part of the tree trunk.

Jason examined Essention a short distance away. The disintegration guns on the wall were tracking something slowly. Then, the gun fired at something invisible in the grass. He shuddered.

Max was looking through a similar pair of binoculars. 'Don't worry, we're far enough out. The sensors can't pick us up.'

'How much longer?' He wasn't quite ready to test the suits.

'Essention runs off a single power grid. Everything feeds from that grid: light, heat, security. Whatever needs power, essentially, but Arcis needs the most power of all. So when there's a dip there, it affects anything else that runs on power. Including the guns.'

Five jittery soldiers accompanied them.

'Are you sure there's enough of us?'

Max nodded. 'Any more will raise suspicions. The next wave will enter when rotation comes around again.' He packed the binoculars away. 'When Preston gets confirmation from Pavesi or Kouris and you see me move, you'd better be on my heels.'

'Preston can already track the power dips from his screen. Why do we need a signal from the soldiers inside?'

'Because rotation is the only guarantee the guns have been knocked offline.'

He looked up to see a frowning Preston.

'I don't know which dip is the big one,' he said from his perch. 'There's one happening right now. Several dips usually occur the day before rotation. But the dip that occurs an hour before is biggest. It's as if something is being reset, or calibrated, or changed.'

Jason looked at Essention; the guns were still rotating.

Preston pulled the orb from his pocket and waved it about. 'Can you hear me? Tap once to acknowledge.'

He went still. 'Once for yes, two for no. Are you close to rotation?'

A double-tap.

'What does that mean?' said Jason.

Preston shushed him. 'Has rotation already happened?'

A single tap came through clearly.

'Tap once if we should go.'

A single tap.

Jason looked at the wall to see the guns were powering down.

Max nodded sharply. 'The window is closing. We have about a minute.'

He followed Max to the edge of the scanners' range.

'We need to stop here for a second,' said Max. 'We're almost inside their range. The scanners will be back up soon, and those guns will disintegrate you in a matter of seconds.'

Jason focused on only one thing: the entrance to Essention.

No secret tunnels. Their way back inside would be through the main gates.

Max addressed the group. 'When I run you follow. Got it?'

Jason nodded. His heartbeat pounded in his ears. He glanced down at the suit he hoped would turn him invisible.

Preston checked his monitor. 'The guns are down. Thirty seconds left.'

Max pressed the button on his own vest and melded with the night. Jason did the same and ran as hard as he could. A few of the soldiers were ahead, others nipped at his heels.

They entered the guns' range.

Jason's lungs burned so bad he wanted to stop. The guns that could shred him into tiny pieces were pointing downwards.

He ran harder, battling against the vibrating suit that snapped him left, then right, then left again. His muscles ached every time he attempted to correct his course.

Movement on the wall caught his eye. One of the guns began to stir. One of the boy soldiers ahead of him stumbled and fell to the grass.

Jason hesitated, then looked up at the guns. They had rebooted and were starting their lazy search of the area beyond the prison-like walls. He pulled the younger boy to his feet.

'Sorry,' said the soldier.

'Move,' said Max.

Jason found new energy from somewhere and pushed on. The guns were rotating faster now. His suit yanked him even farther out of line as they focused on his general position and that of the others.

Jason ran hard through the suit's constant corrections. The boy soldier kept up with him but the fall had put a dent in his progress.

Preston and Max made it to the gate and slipped inside.

The other soldiers were close, but Jason and the boy were still two hundred meters away.

The guns swiveled faster now, detecting the tiny changes in movement. One of them fired close by, as if trying to guess their location. Jason glanced back at the boy soldier, who was still trailing, and ran harder.

He dragged new air through his teeth. His lungs blazed. He had to trust his suit would keep him hidden.

The guns swiveled again. The four he could see were all pointed at him and the boy. Jason glanced up at the barrels but didn't stop. The nearest gun hadn't fixed on anything yet, but it was searching for them. He turned to see the boy had dropped back. The other soldiers had now made it to the gate.

He couldn't wait for the soldier. He had to keep going.

His breaths deepened when the nearest gun's position altered sharply. His suit pulled him into a more violent pattern. He and the boy must be registering as heat and motion.

The gun on the opposite wall turned sharply, its barrel pointed at Jason first, then at the boy. Jason concentrated on not falling and ran harder.

He heard the sound of a laser zap, and an impact somewhere behind him. Jason dropped flat to the ground, just short of the gate. The gun stopped firing. He looked back.

The gun had begun searching again.

The boy soldier was lying flat on his back. All the flesh had been burned off his bones.

Jason gagged and crawled to the gate, but didn't enter. He turned back to where the boy lay, knowing he couldn't leave him.

The guns were online. His suit jerked him toward the remains of the boy. A gun swiveled as it tried to find him. Jason dragged his body back to the gate. His suit rendered him and the boy's remnants invisible. At the gate, he separated what remained of the vest, waders and helmet from the boy's body and carried them inside.

He couldn't allow the machines to find their specialized equipment. The boy he'd left behind? A tragedy.

Charlie was waiting. 'Roll up your sleeve.'

Jason stuck his arm out and Charlie waved a blue light over his arm. He then removed the pearl-colored magnetic disc from Jason's wrist.

'It will temporarily disrupt your location in the system. Just a precaution while their system updates your whereabouts. You can't wear the discs in here. The scanners would detect them.'

He closed his eyes, trying to forget how close he'd come to dying. Someone tugged on his arm and he opened his eyes.

'We're not safe yet,' said Max. 'We need to get everyone off the streets.'

Jason and the others followed Max and Charlie down a path between the outer wall and Essention. Before he knew it they were back in Southwest, at Charlie's bungalow, where their journey had begun.

They slipped inside and gathered in the living room.

Max turned around, and nodded at Jason's extra burden: the suit of the boy soldier.

'That was quick thinking. We can't risk them finding it.'

Jason dropped the suit to the floor and peeled off his own, wanting out of it.

Soldiers collapsed into the sofa and chairs, others folded onto the floor. Preston and the soldiers each sported a new incision on the inside of their left wrists. Charlie had probably given them a chip so they could blend in.

Charlie disappeared into the kitchen then reappeared with a jug of water, several glasses and some fruit, pots of meat and bread. They all drank deeply, and the others ate as if they hadn't tasted food in a week. Except for Jason, who hardly touched his food.

Charlie cast a critical eye over each of them. 'Is this everyone?'

'Except for Noah.'

Charlie closed his eyes briefly. 'How did you get on?'

'Preston and Jason have been able to boost the signal. But we need more time to communicate with Pavesi and Kouris. This would go a hell of a lot quicker if we had the frequency code for the force field.'

Charlie nodded and collected the suits. He gestured for them all to stand up and pulled back the rug. He opened a trapdoor in the floor and stashed the suits in a hidden storage space.

'We'll get these back to Glenvale as soon as possible.'

'When do we make our move on Arcis?' said Jason.

Max turned his tired gaze on him. 'Getting inside Essention was the easy part. If we can't get the frequency code, we'll need to find another way inside. Talking to Pavesi and Kouris is our best bet. We expect the place to be heavily guarded, so we'll need as much detail about the layout as possible. It won't be easy.'

Jason's enthusiasm dropped. He didn't want to wait. He was ready to go now. A boy called Noah had died for their efforts.

Preston occupied himself with his screen. Charlie disappeared for a second time and returned with a screen of his own. Preston sat up straight.

'We've been doing some monitoring of our own,' said Charlie, sitting on the armrest beside Preston. 'I'm sure with your comms experts here we can do more to work out the rotation pattern.'

Charlie looked up at Max. 'You probably haven't heard, but there have been a few casualties since you left. How many here still have immediate family in Arcis?'

'I do,' said Jason, his voice cracking. He was the only one. The rest of the team who'd originally escaped through the tunnel was still back in Glenvale.

'Anya, isn't it?'

'Yeah, is she—' He sucked in air.

'Dom says she's safe. Please don't worry.'

Jason released a breath.

Safe. But for how much longer?

37

Everyone from the previous floor had made it, except for two girls and two boys. Two rails of clothing sat in the fifth-floor changing room; one for the boys and one for the girls. Supervisor Two had instructed them to dress fast.

Anya thumbed through the girls' clothes that included T-shirts and combat trousers. She shrank back when the girls hovered around her, picking sizes and pulling off their dresses. With Warren only a few feet away, she shivered at the thought of changing here. From across the room Dom watched her, his eyes flicking from her face to her arm. She covered her injury, which only seemed to harden his gaze.

Biting back tears, she grabbed a T-shirt. The memory of Warren's touch, his body pressed up against hers, made her want to vomit. He was supposed to be her friend. His entitlement, the pressure of his insistent kiss... Her anger made her grip the fabric too hard.

At least Dom and Sheila had made it. She didn't want to think about how they'd earned their points.

Sheila, Yasmin and June were already half-dressed. A quiet Lilly dressed slowly. Anya snatched a pair of trousers off the railing. She pulled each leg up with the dress still on her.

Dressed in trousers and a T-shirt, she felt less vulnerable.

The elevator buzzed and the doors opened. Three new people piled into the room.

Warren stood too close for her to ignore. She glared at him until he looked away. He would not intimidate her again. Dom was looking between them both, trying to figure out what he'd missed.

She gave Supervisor One her full attention. Dressed in an all-black tunic, this was a thinner version of the man who'd supervised the first floor.

'Welcome to the fifth floor.'

He sounded different, too, less warm.

'The fourth floor was designed to keep you apart and test the responses of both sexes. Here, males and females are back on even terms.'

Anya glanced at Warren.

'This is the games floor. We conduct combat to test your reflexes and instincts.'

Anya hoped for live ammo. Nothing life-threatening, just enough so Warren would feel an enormous amount of pain.

Supervisor One looked the group over. 'Get changed quickly and follow me. We need to begin straight away.'

Anya moved to the next room. June stayed close to her. Once, it would have been Tahlia who kept the rebel company.

The supervisor led them to a weapons room. At the center was a large black unit with inbuilt recesses. Each compartment carried a black gun with blue veins running through it. The unit looked to be a recharging station, and these were Electro Guns, with a metal casing and insulated core. She'd practiced with them while learning how to shoot clay discs out of the sky. 'Clay pigeon shooting', they had called it. Except in the old days, they'd used shotguns and real bullets.

Sheila, Dom and June looked at ease with handling firearms. Jerome examined several weapons.

'Doesn't matter which one you take,' Anya said to him. 'They're all the same.'

Supervisor One waited by the door. Lilly gripped her gun with both hands, its handle nestled in her stomach.

They followed the supervisor onto the walkway. Anya gripped the railing.

A flash of movement beside her caught her attention. She looked up to see Lilly—her expression flat, her eyes blank—lifting the gun and pointing it at Ash.

'Lilly, no!' said Anya.

'I have to. I can't live like this—'

Lilly fired once, twice, three times at Ash. The shots sent a deep shudder through his body, but somehow he remained upright. She stared at Ash, blank-faced and open-mouthed. He looked exactly like Tahlia had after her shock. Then he began to sway, creating a ripple effect in the walkway. Anya grabbed the railing tighter, crouching low when it felt like the walkway might buckle.

The supervisor reached the other side.

Anya gasped when Ash's left leg slid out from under him. But then he righted himself. Lilly took a step toward him. The walkway shifted again; his body leaned too far one way. Then, he disappeared over the side.

Lilly froze, gasping for air, tears falling, still gripping the gun to her stomach.

Sheila inched toward her and reached out her hand. She spoke softly.

'Give me the gun, Lilly.'

Lilly pressed the gun into Sheila's hand, who handed it to Dom, and then turned her attention back to Lilly.

The walkway still swayed too much, causing Anya's stomach to lurch.

Jerome called out 'No!' Anya looked up. Lilly's pale-blonde hair danced around her paler skin. One leg was already over the railing. She kicked over the other, and fell, like Ash.

The next sound was Lilly, hitting the ground floor, and then June, screaming into her hand.

Anya stood and looked over the edge, to see the quiet, mousy girl lying on her back, arms splayed, left leg curled beneath her. Ash had landed in a spot far away from her, near Anya's old cleaning section. She snatched her gaze away. Lilly had needed Anya's protection, and Anya had pushed her away.

The suicides came from this floor. That was Anya's only thought as she walked on, in a daze.

'Unfortunate,' said Supervisor One. He held open one side of a double door with '5B' stamped on it.

Nobody spoke as they followed him inside.

Death and Arcis appeared to go hand in hand. Maybe Dom and Sheila, with their contacts on the outside, could help. The thought carried her forward, gun in hand.

The supervisor's voice snapped her mind into focus.

'The rules are simple. There are fourteen discs scattered throughout the maze.'

The mention of a maze sent a new chill through her. At least the room looked nothing like the one on the third floor. It was twice the size for a start. The room spanned as far as the eye could see in both directions, close to what she believed to be the full floor size of Tower B. A white-walled unit dominated the space, made of the same frosted glass as the boy's dorm: white, bright and thin. Several entry points led inside the maze. Anya checked for signs of a gold door.

'Enter the maze through any of the points along the four edges. Shoot each disc to claim points. You can decide to find them separately, or work together as a team. The game is timed and the person to shoot the most discs earns the most points. The cutoff is undecided as of yet, but those who rank high at the end of the game will rotate.'

He pointed to a square white box attached to the wall behind them.

'Everyone must tag on to join the game. If your Electro Gun runs out of juice, tag off and recharge in the room across the walkway. But for your points to be counted, you will have to tag on again before rejoining.'

Coming and going from the maze could make it easier to learn the layout.

'There's one catch. As soon as you become familiar with the layout, the maze will change.'

But it might prove impossible to find all the discs before the maze changed.

'The game starts now.'

'Wait,' said Anya. 'How lethal are the shots?'

'The worst you'll get is a medium shock. Not life-threatening.'

They dropped their backpacks by the exit. Anya was the fifth person to press her wrist to the box and tag on. She ran for the maze. Thumping music kicked in. It rattled her insides and made it harder to think straight. A giant screen above the maze showed a live scoreboard.

Yasmin, June, Sheila and Dom had already bolted for the four openings to the front. Anya headed for the side, where there were four more. She ran as far as the corridor would allow and almost immediately found a floating hologram of a black disc. She shot it with her Electro Gun. Her name hovered in the air for a few seconds, then vanished. Others fired off their first shots close by. The first one in any game was always the easiest. Anya followed the serpentine corridor, but got turned back by dead ends. Someone took their second shot in the corridor next to hers and she cursed.

She followed the corridor, aiming for the center of the room. A straight run brought her to another black disc. She fired at it and claimed her second hit. Another shot rang out, but the music was so loud, she couldn't tell if it was the shooter's second or third disc. Knowing Warren was one of her rivals made her work smarter.

Anya took the next left, checking the east part of the maze before heading right. Someone fired a shot close by. She followed the sound and ran straight into Jerome. His eyes widened in surprise. But then his expression hardened.

Anya couldn't stand this strain between them any longer.

She noticed he'd been crying. She flung her arms around him. Jerome rested his head on her neck and grabbed fistfuls of her T-shirt, sobbing silently.

Then he pushed her away and ran off.

Anya wiped away her own tears and focused on finding the next disc. The beat of the music cut through her concentration. Pushing through, she rounded the corner, where she found another disc. She shot it.

Three down, eleven to go.

A wall in front forced her back the way she had come, but she was turned around again in seconds. Supervisor One had said the maze would change as soon as they became familiar with the route, but she didn't expect it to happen so fast. She brushed her hand against the wall. It felt solid enough, but a weird sensation made her think it could be organic.

The twisting corridors frustrated her. She screamed.

'I don't know the way. Stop changing on me.'

The music had become just noise. With no lyrics or rhythm to follow, it only dulled her senses. Seeing Ash die and Lilly kill herself still shocked her, but now wasn't the time to lose focus.

She kept going. The corridor shifted to the left so she followed it. Then to the right.

Another dead end.

She turned around to see the corridor had changed again. The first three discs had been easy.

Then someone fired and she panicked.

Anya ran. It didn't matter where. All her tactics had vanished. She didn't even know what direction she was headed in. The noise deafened and distracted her. With each corner she turned she hoped she wouldn't bump into Warren.

The music was so loud it drowned out her screams of frustration. Whatever way she tried led to a dead end.

Then something came to her.

The wall.

Anya touched it again. It was solid as ever, but she felt something shiver beneath it.

Could she go through it?

Anya shoulder-charged the wall and winced from the pain.

Okay. Maybe not through it.

But why not?

She glanced at her Electro Gun. It emitted electricity, and organic matter was vulnerable to its blast.

She fired at the opaque wall; it shimmered before her. She slipped her fingers through it. It felt soft, like gelatin. But it solidified fast and pushed out her fingers.

Anya fired again, but this time she pushed all the way through. A slick feeling on her skin felt like the wall had coated her in its organic matter. But with just a leg and arm still to pass through, the gel suddenly tightened around her. She yelped and yanked both limbs out, then checked herself over.

Anya used this new method to gain access to new sections. She fired again, and again, passing fast through the shimmering wall. She found another black disc and fired at it.

Had anyone else thought to try this?

But the maze trapped her again, with closed walls on all sides. She raised the gun and fired. Nothing. She checked her gun to see it had no charge.

She heard more firing. Six, seven.

She couldn't move.

Eight, nine, ten. Vibrations from the deafening music ran from the floor through her feet.

A siren shrilled and the pounding stopped. The bright walls lowered into gaps in the floor and revealed the positions of the other players to her.

A vibration, different to the ones caused by the music, came up through the floor. She saw another disc in the next corridor. She'd been so close to the fifth. But would it have been enough?

The supervisor motioned them forward. Anya caught her breath; the boys were sweating heavily. She looked up at the scoreboard. They had been in the maze for exactly twenty minutes.

'Dom won that round,' said Supervisor One. 'He found six of the discs in the time allowed.' He turned an icy gaze on Anya. 'But Anya tried something different. Why don't you tell everyone what you did?'

They all looked at her.

'I... shot at the wall. It's organic and I was able to pass through.'

'But you wound up trapped?'

She nodded.

'Anya cheated and the maze trapped her. When she ran out of charge she could no longer progress. How many discs did you find?'

'Four.'

Supervisor One held his chin high. 'The lesson is clear. You can cheat and guarantee a low score, or you can play it fair and find more discs. The latter will take you longer, but it is achievable.'

She hadn't cheated. Her solution had been a strategic one.

'Get some rest,' said the supervisor. 'We'll resume the game in the morning.' He pointed at two doors beneath the screen. 'The door on the left will take you to your new dormitories. The one on the right leads to the dining hall.'

The girls all headed for the dining hall. Anya was relieved to discover food was free again. After eating, she was ready for sleep.

The mixed dorm set up gave her pause.

She waited for the boys to choose a side before claiming the first bed on the opposite side. She would never allow herself to get trapped again.

Sheila protested when she saw Anya had taken the first bed, but June dragged her away to a different bed. Sheila grunted, but seemed happy to take one beside Yasmin. June took the bed beside Anya's.

Jerome walked in and June waved him over.

'Jerome, there's a spare bed over here.'

Anya sneaked a glance at Warren. He was pulling a pair of pajama bottoms from his bag. But then he looked up. Looked over. Looked away.

She pulled her knees up to her chest and rested her chin on them. She would sleep in her clothes tonight.

Jerome dropped his bag on the floor and sat beside June on her bed, facing Anya.

'Are you okay, Anya? You seem a little off.'

She sat up straight. 'I'm fine. I'm just tired. How are you?'

He studied his hands in his lap. 'I'm okay. I guess. It's going to take some time.' June rested her hand on Jerome's.

'I decided something today,' he said.

'What?' said June.

'I'm going to finish this program, for Frank. It's what he would have done for me.'

Frank had wanted to live. He'd told Anya as much, right before he'd touched the gold door.

June squeezed his hand. 'We all finish for Frank and Tahlia.'

'For Frank and Tahlia,' said Anya. 'And Lilly.' She slid her legs from the bed to the floor.

A new conversation between two boys she didn't know caught her attention.

'What was the third floor like?' the first boy asked.

'A little bit weird,' said the second with a shrug. 'There was this maze and a gold door we weren't supposed to open.'

Anya looked away.

'It was killing me not to open it,' said the second boy, unaware he had an audience. 'Jerry had to sit on me so I wouldn't go there.'

Anya hid behind her hair. She should have stopped Frank.

She peeked up at Jerome. He smiled softly and mouthed, 'Not your fault.'

Dom entered the room and sat on the bed opposite hers.

She looked across at him. His hands were clasped together and his forearms were resting on his knees. His gaze shifted slightly to the others. She couldn't gauge his mood. Anger, concern. Guilt?

And then he looked at her. Looked away. Looked at his hands. Looked at a different wall.

'So how did you know to shoot the wall?' said Jerome.

'Uh?'

Her eyes flickered to Dom. His attention was on her again.

'The wall. You said it was organic.'

She shrugged. 'I put my hand on it and it didn't feel like a real wall. I was getting turned around so much it felt like the maze was closing me in.'

'And it did, eventually,' said Jerome.

'Yeah. Wasn't a smart tactic.'

Yasmin and Sheila had moved up a bed, closer to them.

'I heard Supervisor One talking to Supervisor Two,' said Yasmin. 'Something about accelerating the program.' She paused. 'Is it just me or does Supervisor One look different to how he looked on the first floor? It's like he bench-pressed 150 pounds and ran a marathon or something.'

Everyone agreed.

'So Dom has earned the most points,' said Jerome, glancing at him. 'I guess we keep playing until we have a winner. How many rounds, do you think?'

'Until we pass their test,' said Dom.

Anya tried to catch his eye. She hated this new distance between them.

The others listened. Except for Warren, who pretended he wasn't interested.

Yasmin whispered in Sheila's ear. Sheila's wide eyes flicked between Warren and Anya.

Anya's cheeks bloomed red. Yasmin, the traitor.

'I like Anya's idea of blasting the walls,' said Jerome. 'How many blasts do we get per gun?'

'Fourteen discs, so fourteen shots each,' said Dom, leaning back on his hands.

'Can't we split into teams?' said June. 'We can each take turns to blast the wall, then the disc. The supervisor said we could do it any way we liked.'

'There needs to be a winner,' said Yasmin.

'Why do we need a winner?' said Sheila. 'Why can't we all finish on the same score and rotate together?'

Anya pressed down her anger. She didn't want Warren to progress. But she didn't want the others to miss out on rotation.

June sat up straight. 'Okay, that's possible. But there are thirteen of us. How do we split the teams?'

The thought of working alongside Warren sickened Anya.

'Warren's with Sheila and me,' said Yasmin quickly, shooting Warren a look.

Dom frowned at her.

'The girls against the boys?' Jerome suggested.

'No, that won't work,' said Sheila. 'The boys finished higher.'

'We need the girls to split up, so it's even,' said Dom. 'The boys are better at navigating the maze.'

'Dom, you should partner with Anya and June,' said Sheila. Anya stared at her. It wasn't what she had in mind. 'Jerome, you're strong, so you should take one of the teams. You should make it through, no problem. That makes it three teams of three and one of four.'

'Good idea,' said Dom. Anya tried to read him, to work out if he was disappointed not to be teamed up with Sheila. Sheila was still his best chance of rotating. But Anya could be fast, and June was trained in combat, like him. Together they would help him to succeed.

'Okay, the strategy is for all of us to finish on the same score,' said June.

'If you decide to shoot the wall,' said Anya, 'don't hesitate. Push through. It solidifies almost immediately.'

Jerome yawned, an action that set off Anya. But she felt too wired to sleep.

They each climbed into their beds. Anya tucked the sheets around her neck. Dom gave her one last lingering look. She broke eye contact first and turned on her side.

The dorm was too public.

After they rotated, she and Dom needed to talk.

38

The morning began with three short, sharp siren blasts. The overhead lights flicked on. Anya groaned as she got out of bed. It felt like she'd only slept for a couple of hours.

They all gathered in the games room, dressed in their combat gear. The outfit looked right on Dom, June and Sheila, rebels who belonged in a world that Anya knew nothing about. When she finished this program where would her place be?

Supervisor One—or rather his twin—stood before them.

'There's been a change of plan,' he said.

Anya's heart skipped a beat. Did that mean the rebels and Jason were close?

'The Collective will decide who rotates after one more round of this game.'

The rules were becoming more fluid. Something, or someone, had rattled this Collective group.

Anya glanced at Dom. He was staring at the ground, a faint smile on his lips.

'Same rules as this morning,' said the supervisor. 'This time you have fifteen minutes to complete the task.'

The Facility

Five minutes less.

The music started and Anya tagged on after June. Carrying an Electro Gun each, she and June followed Dom inside the maze.

The first corridor turned them left. At the end of a longer section, they found the first disc floating in the air and Dom standing in front of it.

He yelled over the music. 'I'm ahead on points, so you both need to shoot it.'

Anya and June both fired at the disc. Their names glimmered faintly in the air, then disappeared. Anya hoped their strategy to finish on the same points would work.

Shots rang out across different parts of the maze. Anya's team ran along the outer wall until they reached a turn. Together they took a left, then a right, and found a second disc. Again, Anya and June both shot the disc, bringing them closer to Dom's score.

The first discs were easy.

'Which way now?' said Anya.

Dom looked one way, then the other. The maze ran in different directions. He pressed his hand against the wall. 'You're right about it being organic. I can feel the different textures.'

'But as soon as we learn the pattern, the wall changes,' said June.

Anya felt a new vibration, out of sync with the music, shuddering up through her legs.

At first, she thought it might be nothing, but June had also noticed it. 'I felt that.'

Dom stared at Anya. 'What is it? What did you feel?'

Anya shouted next to his ear. 'For the last couple of days, I've been feeling strange vibrations just before rotation.'

He pulled back. 'You think they're linked to rotation?'

'Three on the floor below,' she yelled, holding up three fingers. 'This is the second one I've felt on this floor. I could be wrong.'

'The vibrations are the by-product of some bigger action,' he yelled back. 'The dip in power could be enough to get the rebels past the force field.'

'This can't wait, Dom,' said June. 'You need to let Max know, now.'

Dom hesitated and looked down at his gun. 'You both have twelve shots left and I still have fourteen. I think it's too early to shoot the wall.'

'I agree,' said Anya. 'The maze changed a lot faster when I shot it.'

'Keep going. You two run ahead while I make the call.'

Dom trailed behind June and Anya to relay the message. Anya guessed that June didn't have the same means to communicate.

When he finished he took the lead again.

Another succession of shots sounded around the arena as the other teams found more discs. Anya and her team spent too long finding their third black disc. June shot it to even their scores.

'Okay, that's three,' said Dom. 'But this strategy is too slow.'

The clock showed thirteen of the fifteen minutes had passed.

'We need to get to where the others are,' said Dom. 'We have to finish on the same score.'

They kept moving, but Anya saw the maze was already beginning to change.

'What if we climb up?' said June.

Dom raked his nails down the wall. 'Nothing to hold on to. Plus we might not see the discs from up there.'

They heard someone fire a shot close by.

'That sounded like it was right beside us.' Dom aimed his weapon at the wall. 'I think we should try Anya's way.'

'Move through it fast,' Anya reminded them.

Dom shot the wall. Anya pulled June through the shimmering surface. Dom didn't hesitate to follow. She saw a disc on the other side.

But she also saw Warren.

Anya froze at the sight of him.

Warren looked equally shocked as he stared at the wall they had just passed through. There was no sign of Sheila or Yasmin.

'Where's the rest of your team?' Dom shouted over the music.

'They were slowing me down,' said Warren.

Anya shook at being so close to her attacker.

'We agreed to stick in teams,' said June.

'No. You all agreed without me,' said Warren. 'I was always getting off this floor my own way.'

The thin tether keeping Anya grounded snapped. She lifted her Electro Gun and fired two perfect blasts into Warren's body.

'That's for Tahlia, you *bastard*. And for all the... crappy things...'

Warren convulsed on the ground.

A shocked Dom pushed her gun down. 'What did you do that for?'

She couldn't speak. Anger made her hands shake. She snapped the gun away from him and aimed for her third shot.

This time June pushed down the weapon. 'Save your shots for the discs. He's not worth it.'

Anya directed her rage at the disc instead and fired. Dom and June copied her. That made four discs, so far. Dom had twelve shots remaining and one disc. June had ten. Anya had nine.

'June, it's your turn,' said Dom, pointing at the wall.

Another shot sounded close by. June fired at the wall. The second they passed through it the maze shifted, closing off one of the routes. It forced them to head right, into a small, square dead end.

Anya heard Jerome shout, 'We're here.'

Dom fired at the next wall. They pushed into the next corridor where they found Jerome's team, and the group of four.

'How many have you shot?'

'Four,' said Jerome. 'We're all on seven.'

'Same here.'

'Where are Sheila and Yasmin?'

'I don't know. Warren ditched them.'

Dom called out Sheila's name, but Anya didn't think she'd hear him above the music.

She glanced at the clock. They had less than a minute left.

'We have to do it without them,' said Dom.

He was right. Arcis wasn't a game. It was about sacrifice; saving a life, or even taking one.

The Facility

They raised their guns together and shot the remaining disc that would count as a score. With just ten seconds remaining they had no time left to find another.

The timer ran out and the music stopped, but the thumping in Anya's ears played on. The wall disappeared into grooves in the floor.

She saw Sheila and Yasmin together at one of the discs. Had they shot it in time? Warren was back on his feet. His movements were slow and jerky, but he had managed to find another disc.

They came together slowly. The overhead lights flickered; a sign that rotation was imminent.

The only sure sign so far.

The strange vibrations might be another clue, but unless someone had received Dom's message, it wouldn't matter. Anya ditched all previous negative thoughts about the rebels. Right now, they were her only hope of getting out of Arcis alive.

Supervisor One entered the room looking calm and collected.

The scoreboard drew Anya's attention.

She read the names and cursed.

Not all of them had made it through.

39

Jason vied for space at Charlie Roberts' kitchen table as everyone tucked into pots of meat, fruit and bread. Max was busy looking over the Atomizer and the Disruptor gun. Preston had a screen balanced on one knee and the orb on the table in front of him.

That morning, they had come to realize that the orb was the strongest signal-booster they had. Charlie had kept a record of every flicker of light in Essention, every moment the scanners' blue light cut out mid-scan, every time the guns didn't rotate with the apparent ease he knew they could. Charlie had also charted the dips and peaks of power. Combining it with the data that Jason and Thomas had gathered, they came to a conclusion: the power went down for one minute and eight seconds.

Just enough time to reboot something?

But they still lacked one thing: an early detection system.

His idea to source the frequency code for the force field had been put on hold. With no clue as to where the codes might be, Dom, Sheila and June were on their own.

Jason took a bite of bread roll. He paused mid-chew when he caught the slight stiffening in Preston's shoulders.

Preston hissed for everyone to shut up. Max silenced the room with a wave of his hand.

Charlie stood, frozen, behind Preston.

'It's Pavesi's signature,' said Preston.

Jason heard a succession of flat-sounding beeps. Preston typed in a response and waited. But there was no reply.

Jason's appetite vanished as his adrenaline kicked in. This was it. They were going in.

But then Preston shook his head at Max. 'There are two messages. One was delayed. The second message says they've just announced rotation.'

Max cursed. 'What was the delayed message about?'

'Pavesi says that a succession of vibrations is occurring on each of the upper floors. One a day.' Preston paused and rubbed the back of his neck. 'He also said they were rotating shortly. But that was part of the delayed message. Sorry.'

Charlie and Max appeared fine with it, but Jason was not. His sister's safety was all he cared about.

He stood up fast, knocking his glass of water to the floor. 'So, now we're getting delayed messages? How long do we have to sit here and wait?'

'At least until the next rotation happens,' said Max.

'It's only just happened. We can still go.'

Preston cursed, drawing everyone's attention back to him. 'The power held steady during this rotation. There's no way we could have used it to get back in.'

Jason sat down hard in the chair. 'What does that even mean?'

'It means that whatever they need power for, they're no longer doing it straight after rotation,' said Max. He took the screen from Preston and handed it to Charlie.

'These supposed vibrations correspond with unexplained dips in the power here, here and here,' said Max, jabbing at the screen. 'The dips last for about a minute and they're not very low, but they could be enough to allow us to blast the force field surrounding Arcis.'

Charlie nodded, then handed the screen back to Preston. 'Ask Dominic to inform us as soon as the next vibration happens.'

Jason pushed his food away. 'So Arcis knows we're here and now they're keeping rotation activities to a minimum.' It was the only thing that made sense. The power dips during rotation were too great.

'Possibly,' said Max. 'But they won't come out here to check. Humans are too unclean for them. By now, one of the copies will have found Noah's body.' He couldn't have been more than fifteen. 'They'll think we tried and failed to get someone inside. We all have chips now and Charlie has kept our location up to date. They won't know we've been monitoring the power all along.'

Preston leaned on the table. 'Up until last week, the grid consistently powered down after rotation. Whatever they need to do they'll have to do it again.'

Charlie nodded. 'We'll only have one shot to get inside Arcis. So let's make it our best one. Unless Jason and Preston can come up with a better solution, the power fluctuations are our only way in. Reinforcements will be here soon.'

Preston typed a message on the screen. It translated into a series of beeps that Jason assumed only Dom Pavesi could decipher.

The Facility

Jason's interest in Preston's work waned. Rescuing Anya would have to wait.

40

Nine had made it to the next phase: Anya's group and Jerome's group, plus Yasmin, Sheila and Warren. According to the scoreboard, the last group of four had finished on fewer points.

Seeing Warren hobble to the walkway drew a smile from Anya. Sheila and Yasmin, walking behind him, pinned him with their icy glares.

In the changing room, Supervisor One climbed into the elevator with them. He touched a finger to his ear, as if listening. Then he pressed his palm flat against the panel.

No access cards, no way out. Anya hugged herself. This was now a one-way trip.

The doors opened and the supervisor exited.

Anya stared at the elevator panel with the number seven on it. They had just skipped the sixth. She followed him out. Three people she didn't recognize—two boys and a girl—were waiting in the changing room. Supervisor One seemed distracted by the voice in his ear. He entered the elevator and the doors closed.

'Where did you come from?' said one of the new boys. 'You weren't on the sixth floor.'

'We were on the fifth,' said Anya, still hugging herself. This floor felt colder than the last. 'What's on the sixth?'

'Remember the wolves on the ground floor?' said the second boy. She nodded and shivered. 'We had to look after them, get them anything they wanted.'

She couldn't imagine what demands the wolves might make. 'What was that like?'

'Humiliating. You think you're making progress, but then you end up back on the ground floor.'

'Okay, so what now?' Sheila looked around.

The far door opened and Supervisor Two rushed in. She ignored them, more interested in the voice in her ear than the people in the room.

'I know that, but they're already here,' she said, glancing at the group. 'What do you want them to do first?'

Anya tried to listen in.

'I don't know, I...' The supervisor turned away. 'Yes. I understand, Quintus.'

Anya caught Quintus' voice; it sounded strange, flat and tinny. *This is not protocol, 69-C. The tests must continue. We need the complete data.*

'As you wish.'

The impeccably dressed supervisor without a hair out of place turned around. She cast a critical eye over their appearance. Most of the group was still dressed in combat gear. The smell of fresh sweat lingered in the air.

'Follow me, please.'

They followed her across the walkway to the other side. The outer walls of the room in Tower B were covered in bright white panels, similar to the walls of the fifth-floor maze. Twelve white leather reclining chairs with extendable arms and screens lined one wall, around thirty meters apart from another twelve on the opposite wall. They reminded Anya of dentist chairs.

'Girls' and boys' dorms are together, bathroom, dining hall,' said Supervisor Two, pointing. She showed them the dining hall with its rows of white tables and benches and the familiar food counter on the back wall. Apart from minor variations in the food choices, the dining halls all looked the same.

'Wait here,' the supervisor said. 'We're not ready for you yet.'

Everyone sat down. As soon as the supervisor left, Dom got up and started pacing. Sheila led him away to a corner of the room to talk privately.

It had reverted to how it should be: Dom and Sheila planning their escape without her.

So why did that decision hurt her so much?

She looked around at the others in the room. Jerome was asking the new boys about the robotic wolves, while the new girl was caught in the middle of their conversation looking lost. Warren sat close to Jerome, listening in. Jerome clearly hadn't heard what had happened between Anya and Warren, or how Warren had deceived them all about Tahlia. Seeing Warren act as if everything was normal made Anya want to punch him again.

The idle chatter gave her a headache.

She needed out of this room.

She needed to talk to Dom.

Anya stood up. June shot her a worried look; she had become her protector.

'I'm just going to take a look around.' She picked up her bag. 'I'll be back soon.'

She claimed the first bed in the dorms by placing her backpack beside the locker. She sat on the bed with her back to the wall, legs stretched out. She could do this. She *would* do this, for Dom.

The quiet and calm soothed her enough that she closed her eyes. But when she felt a slight tremor rumble through the wall she opened them, hoping Dom had passed the message to the outside.

The sound of approaching footsteps startled her into a rigid position. The door creaked open and June's face appeared in the crack.

'Is it safe to enter?'

Anya didn't feel like company, but June had been good to her. She nodded.

June sat on the edge of her bed, regarding her quietly.

'I'm fine,' said Anya, even though June hadn't asked her anything.

'I just wanted to check on you.'

Anya relaxed her shoulders and sighed. 'I'm sorry. It's been a crazy twenty-four hours.' She studied June's soft, delicate face, framed by a beautiful veil of pale-blonde hair. There was depth to her light-blue eyes that Anya hadn't noticed before. But something else lived there: strain, worry, sadness.

June looked down at her lap. To Anya's surprise, she was close to tears.

'I'm fine. I just...' She took a deep breath, and looked at her. 'I'm glad you're feeling better.'

'What's going on, June?'

June looked away again. 'I thought I could be strong in here, but seeing how easy it was for Warren to use you like that... It really upset me.' Anya squeezed her hand, but

June shook her head. 'I don't mean what Warren did... Well, I do. It was awful. But... It's something else. It's this place. Arcis. Look how easily they've pitted us against each other. We used to be friends. All of us.'

Anya wasn't sure if that was true. She'd only really been close with Warren on the ground floor. Look how that turned out.

And there was Dom.

'We'll get through this. It will be fine.'

'I came here of my own free will,' said June, her voice rising a little. 'I do what I do because I believe it to be right.' Anya guessed she meant the rebellion. 'What if we don't find what we're looking for? What if this is all for nothing?'

Anya squeezed her hand. It felt good not to be the focus for once. 'We'll get there. Dom can find his mother, I can see Jason again, you... Who did you come for?'

June straightened up. 'My younger sister.'

'Where? When?'

'Five months ago. A couple of months before I came to Arcis. I need to find her, Anya. She's all alone. She's all I have left of my family.'

'What was her name?'

'Carissa.'

Anya liked that name. 'What happened—I mean, on the outside?'

June sighed and leaned back on her hands. 'My uncle told us about this place that Praesidium had built. That they'd been targeting different groups of people according to age. I didn't believe him until they came for my sister. My uncle tried to convince them she was matched, but they said she couldn't be because she was only thirteen. So they took her and brought her here.'

The Facility

Anya stiffened at the word 'matched'. She swallowed, her throat suddenly tight and uncomfortable.

'Why would he lie about her being matched?'

June looked at her, surprised. 'Matching was a tradition invented by the towns. It's what they all said to keep Praesidium away. When the city started giving them medicine they couldn't live without, improving farming methods... It was never as impressive as what Praesidium had, of course. Then there were the school trips to Praesidium's library. Some adults became nervous about the city's true motives. So the townspeople invented the tradition of matching, to keep Praesidium from taking their children.'

'It wasn't a real thing?' Anya whispered, looking for the cameras.

What had Grace and her father known about it?

June shrugged. 'It doesn't matter if Praesidium hears us. They knew the towns were lying about matching. The radiation attack that was supposed to disable the machines worked out well for them. It gave them an excuse to force us from our homes.' She dropped her gaze to her lap. 'Matching was a way to keep us safe. There's a Collective that runs the city, and a leader called Quintus who needs us for something. I don't know what. The girls appear to hold more value than the boys. It's why my sister was taken.'

Anya thought back to that fateful evening, when her parents had been killed, when she'd hidden in a space behind the wall.

'Why not just take us? Why kill our...' She couldn't say it.

'The radiation was our attack on the machines, but Praesidium twisted the situation to get what they wanted without lifting a finger. There are too many people in Essention who still believe Praesidium cares about us.'

The antidote. 'We know why *that* is.'

June nodded. 'But even while on Compliance, we still have our own minds. We enter here believing what we did while we were in the towns. It just makes us less capable of arguing, less able to stand up for ourselves. That's all.'

Anya worried about who might be listening. Quintus, maybe?

But June was right. It didn't matter anymore. They were too far gone. They had to complete the program, or whatever this was supposed to be.

Anya hated how she'd treated her mother. A new purpose drove her now, a new reason to live, and to survive. She would do it for her parents. Because they had tried to protect her from a danger that targeted her because of her age and gender.

Anya had already lost her parents. But June would not lose her sister.

'We'll find her,' Anya said. 'We'll find all of them.'

A second set of footsteps approached outside. Sheila entered the dorm without knocking and closed the door behind her.

Sheila smiled warmly at June, like they were old friends.

June nodded. 'Hey.'

Sheila shifted her gaze to Anya and folded her arms. 'Dom wants to talk to you. He's driving me crazy out there. He thinks you're avoiding him.'

'I was.'

'Well, I've had enough of him.' Sheila scrunched up her face, her voice mocking. '"What's Anya doing, Sheila?

Is she okay, Sheila? Why did she leave? Is she happy, sad, sleepy?" Ugh. Un-avoid him, so I can have some peace.'

Anya grinned. Sheila turned on her heel and left just as June got to her feet.

'Thanks, Anya,' said June. 'I'm sorry for being a mess, with everything.'

Anya wanted to tell her she didn't have to be strong for everyone else. It was okay to fall apart.

'Anytime,' she said.

June slipped out the door, leaving Anya alone on her bed. The hummingbirds pecked at the hole in her already damaged heart. She knew she needed to talk to Dom, but she wasn't sure she wanted to hear what he had to say.

After what felt like too long Dom opened the door.

'Can I come in?'

She wrapped her arms around her legs. 'Okay.'

He stepped inside the room and closed the door behind him. He shoved his hands into his pockets.

'I thought you'd like to know. I passed on your theory.'

About the vibrations.

Anya nodded. 'Good.'

He stayed where he was, staring down at the floor.

'Sheila told me what happened with Warren.'

'She shouldn't have done that. So I guess everyone knows?'

He freed his hands from his pockets and made two fists.

'Not everyone.'

He strode over to her. She pulled her knees up tight as he sat on the edge of the bed.

'Why didn't you tell me?'

'What would you have done if I had?'

'Knocked Warren out, probably.'

Her anger melted away and she smiled. 'I already did that. I didn't need you coming to my rescue.'

Dom grinned. 'I know, I saw.' His liquid-brown eyes were filled with mischief and secrets she desperately wanted to know. But his smile disappeared too fast.

'I can't sit back and watch bad things happen to you.'

'You and Sheila need to reach the ninth floor. I can't be a distraction.'

He smiled. 'If you hadn't noticed, we're doing just fine.'

Anya glanced away for a second, her cheeks heating up, but she forced her eyes back.

'I had. I saw your scores on the fourth floor.'

He scooted closer to her, his brows lifting. 'You think Sheila and I were... together.'

Anya pulled her legs in tighter.

'It's none of my business, Dom. Really.'

She meant it, but the blush made it harder to convince him.

Dom chuckled.

He held out his arm, the one with the chip. 'Here, let me show you what we did.'

'I don't think we need to—'

He silenced her by grabbing her left arm gently so their chips were pressed together. Warmth from his fingertips passed through her skin. Her pulse galloped at the memory his soft lips and hair. But him pulling away from her when she'd touched his scars brought her back to earth.

'If you hold them together like this for a while, it registers as if you've... you know. It's all about proximity.'

She wished Dom had told Lilly and Ash that. But she couldn't be sure Ash wouldn't have tried something anyway.

He kept hold of her and rotated her arm gently, examining the wound.

'Is this still bothering you?' She caught the flash of anger in his eyes.

'No. It's beginning to heal.'

His gaze, softer now, touched on her face, her mouth, her eyes.

Just so you know,' said Anya, 'I don't think *this* counts as a score on this floor.' She flicked her eyes to his arm on hers, trying to lighten the mood.

'I know,' he said, rubbing circles with his thumb. 'It's just... everything has been so rushed in here. I miss talking to you.' He laughed softly. 'I even miss you giving me a hard time.'

Anya lifted a brow. 'I'm fine with picking up where we left off.'

'It's been so tense between us. I just don't want to lose the good stuff.'

Anya smiled. 'Even though we used to drive each other crazy?'

He laughed, shifting closer. 'Actually, that was my favorite part.'

Dom grabbed her legs and pulled her toward him. Anya's breath caught in her throat. He stroked her cheek with his thumb. His touch was light, in contrast to Warren's.

She shivered at the memory.

He pulled back. 'I'm sorry. I shouldn't have presumed—'

Anya brought his hands back to her face. 'No, it's fine. I just... It's nothing.'

Flashes of anger flitted in and out of his eyes. He whispered, 'You're so beautiful, Anya. In more ways than you know.'

She shook her head. 'Sheila is beautiful. I'm ordinary.'

'There are plenty of ordinary girls in this world and you aren't one of them.' He looked away, looked back. "Unique" fits you better.'

'I'd like to be taller,' said Anya, grinning.

He stared at her, unblinking. 'What's wrong with the height you are?'

'The tall girls usually get the boys.'

'Is that so?'

'Sheila always turns heads.'

'Well, she doesn't turn mine. I prefer girls around five foot six with cinnamon-brown hair, beautifully pale skin and dark-blue eyes that I could stare at all day. If you know anyone who fits that description, would you give me a heads-up?'

Anya pushed him playfully and smiled. She inched closer to him. Except for the rapid rise and fall of his chest Dom didn't move. His eyes had a mix of emotions in them: concern, worry, anger, fear.

But then Dom's expression softened and he drew her face to his, until she was close enough to catch his scent: musky with a hint of sweet. She stared at his lips. Strong and certain, like the man before her.

His kiss was so feather soft it melted her bones a little.

In one swift movement Dom pulled her onto his lap. She gasped as her legs slid either side of him.

'Is this okay?' he asked. 'I just wanted to feel you again.'

She almost said no, that it was too intimate. But her arms were already wrapping around him.

She nodded and gazed down at his lips that had parted slightly. He wove his fingers into her hair and pulled her closer. Sweet and hot breath landed on her cheek.

He brushed his lips against hers, gently at first. She felt him tremble, holding back from touching her the way she wanted him to. She shifted slightly in his lap and he gasped. Then his lips parted hers and he tasted her. Tiny sparks of electricity supercharged the air between them. His breathing turned shallower. She pulled back before she lost herself completely.

The way he looked at her—eyes bright and hungry—made her *want* to lose herself, give him anything *he* wanted. No caution, no waiting. No barriers.

No clothes.

Instead, she worried about the cameras she knew were watching.

When Anya shifted back Dom groaned and reached out for her again. She cupped his face and gently tilted it up.

'You're perfect,' she said, examining the slightly crooked curve of his nose.

'I'm not.' Dom's eyes dropped to her throat. 'Not like you.'

She almost laughed. Dom was far from cocky, but how could he not notice how girls looked at him when he entered a room? He had something that went beyond physical beauty. He commanded a presence.

The longer he avoided her gaze, the more she wanted to kiss him. But she made an even bolder move and moved to sit behind him. His eyes followed her, curious at first.

She placed her hands on the outside of his T-shirt.

He tensed.

She tugged up the edges.

He grabbed her hands. His breath quickened.

'Anya. What are you—'

She should have asked first. She kept her hands on his tee.

'Please, let me see.'

'No.'

'Why?'

'Please, Anya. I—'

She stayed still, waiting for him to push her away. To stand up. To leave.

But when his grip loosened and he leaned forward, she pulled up the fabric, to reveal what he was so insistent on hiding from her.

Anya traced her fingers along the edges of the old, ragged white scar shaped like a C that ran from under his armpit to the middle of his back.

She pulled her fingers away, hesitated, then touched him again.

He didn't flinch like before, but she heard him draw in an uncertain breath.

'Does it hurt?' she whispered.

'The opposite,' Dom said. He turned his head to the side. 'I just don't like people seeing it.'

Anya swallowed. 'Sheila says you have more.'

He undid his belt buckle, unbuttoned his combats and inched the waistband down a little.

A straight scar ran from the middle of his back, curving around his left side. It ended just below his waistband.

Anya touched it gently and felt Dom quiver.

'And another one on the front.' He turned around to face her, his tee pulled up to his neck.

A straight line cut across his flat abdomen with a small intersecting cut in the center, heading north.

'What happened?'

'I was a sick child and needed surgery. Lung, kidney, liver. My mother took me to see many doctors. This is the result of many tests and eventual surgery.'

'Is that why you run?'

He nodded. 'I keep in shape because I don't want my loss to ever hinder me.'

'And Sheila? When did she, I mean, how does she know—'

'Sheila and I grew up in Foxrush. I've known her since we were kids. She used to beat up anyone who teased me about the scars.'

Anya wanted to say something reassuring, but her throat tightened with sorrow.

'I wanted to show you before now,' said Dom, his voice raw, 'but I didn't know how you'd react.'

She traced a line of light kisses along the scar on his abdomen. He drew in a sharp breath. She turned him around and kissed his other scars before wrapping her arms around him and pressing her cheek to his bare back.

'Like I said, perfect.'

Dom pulled her arms tighter around his middle.

They stayed like that for a while, with only the sound of their breathing breaking the silence. She closed her eyes, feeling safe. She hadn't felt that way for a long time.

A knock on the door startled Anya. She sat up straight.

Sheila peered in, her hand covering her eyes.

'You'd better be decent in here.'

Anya yanked Dom's T-shirt down and sat innocently on the edge of the bed. Dom moved slower as he buckled his belt.

He winked at Anya. 'No, we're not. Come back later.'

Anya slapped him on the arm and he laughed, grabbing her hand and kissing the back of it.

'As much as I hate to break up this *thing* you've got going on,' said Sheila, 'you're needed next door. The witch is back.'

41

Anya and Dom joined the others in the dining hall. Her new smile and Dom's protective hand around her waist drew knowing looks from June and Sheila.

Warren was also watching. Anya caught his stare—something between anger and regret—and her smile vanished.

In the room with the chairs, Supervisor Two divided them into two groups of six. Dom and Anya waited by two chairs on one side of the room, with Sheila, June, Yasmin and one of the new boys. Jerome and Warren were on the other side.

Anya tensed when Warren got up and headed her way.

'Anya. *Please*. I need to talk to you.'

She recoiled. 'Don't come any closer.'

Dom stepped between them and pressed his hand into Warren's chest.

'What the hell do you think you're doing?'

She'd never heard him sound so angry before.

'Get out of my way, Pavesi. I need to speak—'

'If you take another step toward her, I'll do more than just punch you.'

'Anya, I'm sorry. I just want to explain—'

Her back hit the wall. 'No, Warren. Leave me alone.'

Dom pushed him away. 'You heard her.'

Warren let out a frustrated yell and muttered something under his breath. He stalked back to his chair.

Anya's hands shook hard as Dom led her away from the wall and the first chair. She looked up into his eyes. Flashes of anger flitted in and out of them.

'Are you okay?' he asked.

'I'm fine.'

He stared at her, unblinking. 'No, you're not. You're shaking.'

'Please, Dom. I can't do this right now. I just need to think about something else.'

Dom was blocking her view of Warren. It helped her to calm down. His eyes were hardened and angry. She squeezed his hand and felt him relax.

The supervisor was busy attaching something to the sides of Jerome's head. Anya sat on her chair. Dom sat on the next chair along.

In her row, June had resumed her chat with the boy from the sixth floor. Anya heard Sheila snort with laughter.

She looked down at where Yasmin and Sheila were sitting.

She couldn't remember ever hearing Sheila laugh like that. That fake, nasal whine while she'd pretended to be with Dom was all Anya had known. Anya's eyes flickered to Dom, but he wasn't looking at Sheila. He was watching Anya in amusement.

Anya looked at Sheila again. How had she missed it? Sheila was too much of a goddess for fake *anything*.

Sheila's fear of negotiating with the boys on the fourth floor. Her easy friendship with Yasmin, someone she clearly trusted. Dom was not her type. Never had been.

She grinned at the more relaxed Sheila and decided she preferred this version.

Her eyes returned to a smiling Dom. All she wanted to do was kiss him, but Supervisor Two was on her way over.

With a sigh she settled for holding his hand.

The supervisor eyed their joined hands. Anya let go and sat properly in the chair. The supervisor walked round to the back of Anya's chair and picked up a small, white box that sat on a glass shelf there. She removed three flat metal discs and placed one on either side of Anya's head and one on her wrist, next to her chip.

'What are these for?'

The supervisor set up Dom before explaining.

'The discs act as relays for your thought processes and the power cell in your chip enables us to download your responses. Each of the consoles will present a series of questions or situations you must solve. You must answer honestly. To do otherwise will hurt your chances to progress to the eighth floor. This is a silent test. When you're ready hit the blue button, think about the response and it will appear on screen. Are we clear?'

They both nodded: Dom once, tight.

Her screen powered up and, as the supervisor set up the other participants in her row, the first question popped up.

'Do you consider yourself to be a good person?'

Anya immediately thought of Tahlia and how she'd scuppered her chances to make rotation. But Warren had tricked her. And she had tried to save Frank and Lilly.

She pressed the blue button on the screen, and thought *yes*. Her answer appeared briefly, then vanished as a new question took its place.

'Are you an ambitious person?'

Back on the ground floor she would have said no. But the farther up she traveled, the more she wanted to reach the end. She thought *yes*.

'Do the rebels' actions concern you?'

Yes, at the start. But after nearly three months in the program, she no longer felt that way. What Arcis was doing, what Warren had done—not just to her, but to Tahlia—concerned her more. She hated how expendable their lives were in Arcis, but she trusted Dom, Sheila and June.

She replied *yes*, adding, *I trust Arcis to help keep us safe*.

'How many people do you know on the seventh floor?'

All, except the three who had arrived from the sixth floor. *Nine*.

'How many would you save?'

She answered without hesitation. *Eight*.

'Would you sacrifice your life for theirs?'

It depends.

'If there were only four oxygen masks and five people, how would you decide who gets the masks?'

She frowned. If it came down to it, would she save herself at the expense of someone else's life?

I don't know.

'There are four oxygen masks and they contain only enough oxygen to get one person to safety. Would you give everyone equal amounts of oxygen for a short while, or let one person reach safety? How would you pick that person?'

The question was the same, but asked in a different way.

I would pick one person. The one most likely to succeed.

'Do you value strength over friendship?'

What kind of question was that?

No.

'You said you would sacrifice the weakest to give to the strongest. What if one of the weakest was your friend?'

Tahlia came to mind. Her stomach lurched.

You're taking my answer out of context.

'Explain.'

If I was about to die, I would look to the strongest. If I was safe, I would try to give equally.

'If you were about to die, would you sacrifice your friend?'

It depends.

'On what?'

On the situation. Do I have a chance to live? Do I want to live knowing I've killed someone else? How close am I to that person?

There was a pause before the next question.

'Would you kill another human being if your life depended on it?'

She wanted to hurt Warren for attacking her, and it had felt good to fire a couple of blasts of electricity into his body. But she had done it because she'd known the shots weren't lethal. If Warren had been trying to kill her though...

She answered *yes* and added, *in a defensive context*.

The screen went blank and the questions disappeared. She looked at Dom. He was calm, still answering.

The screen flickered, then a picture appeared.

The scene showed an old man of around eighty and a fifteen-year-old boy standing in a farmers' field. Each carried two baskets brimming with vegetables.

'If you had to choose one of these people to save, whom would you choose?'

It depends.

'Answer the question.'

The boy.

'Why?'

Because the boy has his whole life ahead of him.

'What if both man and boy had an equal life expectancy?'

She studied the scenario more closely. The man and boy carried an equal number of vegetables in their baskets.

Then I would look at what each person did on the farm. The man is more experienced, but the boy may be stronger. I don't have all the facts.

The picture disappeared.

A short film played out on screen.

A crying woman sat between two hospital beds. On one bed was a screaming infant, while on the other a four-year-old child waited, sobbing and terrified. The woman gripped the four-year-old's hand. A doctor walked into the room carrying a syringe.

Anya touched the screen. The scene looked so real it scared her.

The doctor stepped forward, steadied the infant's head and pushed the needle into the soft part of its scalp. The infant began to convulse.

Anya gasped at the murder scene. And the reality of it.

A question popped up. 'In this scenario, would you have saved the infant?'

Tears sprang to her eyes. 'Why would you show me this?' she demanded out loud.

'Answer the question silently. Would you have saved the infant?'

She jabbed the blue button. *Yes.*

'Why does this scene bother you?'

Because it's wrong. It's just an innocent baby.

'What if this baby was genetically compromised and living in constant pain?'

Then let it live out its last remaining days in comfort.

'The baby can't breathe without a ventilator. Its skin is so raw from its condition that it screams every time the mother touches it.'

Anya saw no point in such cruelty. She pressed the button one last time.

I gave you my answer already. Let the baby live.

She pulled the metal circles from her head and wrist and let them drop to the floor.

She ran to the dorm and threw herself on the bed, smashing the pillow over her head. If the purpose of the test was to get a reaction, then it had worked.

A few minutes later, Dom appeared.

He sat down beside her.

'Are you alright?' He plucked the pillow away from her head

Anya sat up, her face wet. 'What's the point of this test?'

'I suppose they want to test our emotional responses. Was it the last question that rattled you?'

'Yes. How could it not? Why would they show us someone killing a baby?'

'I don't know.'

She sat up. 'Did you say the baby should be saved or not?'

Dom looked away.

'The baby is innocent!'

'Did you ask about the mother, or the child with her?'

'No. But that doesn't change anything.'

'Well, I asked.'

Anya relaxed her tense posture. 'What about them?'

'The child has a rare condition too that only the baby can cure. But the baby wasn't going to survive. So the mother sacrificed one child to save the other.'

Her shoulders sagged. What a terrible decision to have to make.

'You didn't wait until the end of the test,' said Dom.

'I couldn't see anything beyond the baby being killed.'

Dom grabbed her hand and whispered, 'We're nearly there, Anya. I don't know why they're asking us these questions, but I need you to pay attention, to see things I might miss.'

Anya nodded. She looked at him, a question in her eyes.

'Who was the man who cut your hair?'

Dom flashed a smile. 'I'll tell you soon, but not in here. It's not safe.' He stood up.

Anya bit her lip.

'There's more?' said Dom, sitting back down.

'I heard you tell him you wanted to save someone on the inside.'

A hint of color brightened his pale-honey cheeks. 'Yeah, I remember.'

'Someone who might help when the time comes?'

Dom nodded.

'I want to be that person. You know. Who helps.'

Dom cupped her face. 'You already are. More than you know. We're almost there. It will be over soon.'

She nodded. She wanted to believe him.

A tremor passed through the bed and she jerked away. Just as Anya touched the wall behind her Dom tapped the communicator chip behind his left ear.

They returned to the test room to find it empty. The others were in the dining area. Sheila, June and Yasmin looked up when they entered.

'You okay, Anya?' said June.

She wished she were strong like June. She'd been forced to dig a little deeper than physical to find that strength.

'Yeah, I'm fine.'

Two of the boys from floor six argued. 'You were supposed to pick the old man.'

'Maybe your version was different from ours.'

'How?'

'For starters, the old man and boy were in a farmer's field,' said the second boy, rolling his eyes.

'Well in our scenario, the *middle-aged* man wore a business suit and the boy was shining his shoes. I picked the man because he contributed to society more than the boy.'

'And in our scenario it was about hard work and manual labor. The boy was physically stronger.'

Anya didn't say it but they were both wrong. She was starting to believe this floor had nothing to do with competition, that Arcis was simply recording their responses.

She checked out the food counters. Dom followed, one hand on her waist.

She smiled up at him. 'I think I can manage to pick out some food on my own without falling apart again.'

Dom returned a crooked grin. 'I know. I was hoping you'd make sure *I* didn't.'

She stared at him, wondering what he'd been through in his life.

She turned back to the food and selected three pancakes, a slice of bacon and an apple. Dom chose eggs and bacon.

Anya slid her tray to the next section, not quite ready to return to her seat. 'You know how you asked me to pay attention to everything?'

Dom nodded, his gaze turning sharp.

'Well, I don't understand the purpose of this floor.'

'What do you mean?'

'In order to rotate, we have to be better than the others. It's what we've been doing since the ground floor, right?' Dom nodded. 'But there are no right or wrong answers here. You heard the boys in there. Two completely different scenarios and several ways to answer.'

She slid her tray along and filled a cup with ice-cold water.

'It's like they're cataloging us, recording our responses to see what we'll do.'

Dom's brows drew forward. 'To elicit emotional reactions, like you said earlier.'

Anya leaned her shoulder against the counter, facing him. 'If I really think about it, that's been the point of all the floors.'

'I don't understand.'

'On the ground floor, we saw the suicides. The first floor, the electric shocks, which the supervisor said were about seeing how well we worked under pressure. The second, you were purposely kept awake.'

'And the third floor, with the gold door?'

Anya shuddered. 'I don't even want to think about that.'

'So, maybe now we've made it this far, there's no need to pit us against each other.'

'Yeah. Or it was never a competition in the first place. Maybe they were just monitoring what we did. What do you know about the Collective?'

Dom shrugged. 'Not much. Max says it controls Praesidium.'

'First the group brings adults into Arcis, then June's thirteen-year-old sister and others like her, then us. All different age groups.'

'Because you think the Collective is cataloging us.'

Anya nodded. 'But if it needed to monitor our actions on each floor, why was I allowed to skip floors?'

Dom's breath hitched. 'Because it brought us together.' He brought his lips to her ear. 'They know there are rebels in the program. Sheila and I were rotated together. The strongest pairing. They must have seen you and me together and rotated you to our floor. Then June.' He pulled back. 'They're selecting us.'

With trembling hands Anya carried her tray back to the table. Dom followed and sat beside her. She stared down at her food. The boys still argued over who had answered correctly.

'What's going on?' said Sheila.

'Later,' said Dom.

Supervisor Two entered the room.

Anya studied her. While the woman looked like the supervisor from the fourth floor, Anya couldn't shake the feeling she was a different person. It was like her eyes were an icier blue or something. Or her raven-black hair, which never changed, was styled differently. She got the same vibe from the male supervisors.

Dom blinked and refocused on the supervisor when she cleared her throat.

'Games commence in one hour. This is your last opportunity to eat. Rotation will occur after the next test.'

Anya looked at Dom in surprise. Another tremor came and went.

Were the rebels already inside Arcis? His hand found hers under the table. She threaded her fingers through his and squeezed.

42

Nightfall approached when Jason, Max, Preston and three soldiers neared Arcis on foot. A thick carpet of grass encircled the entire building, broken by the walkway to the front. To blend in they wore Essention's brown-tunic/black-trouser ensemble. According to Charlie, the scanners operated at 9am, 1pm and 8pm.

Jason and the others stole around to the rear of the complex. Three sides were made of concrete and one of tinted glass. The glass was too dark for Jason to see through it.

Max had said to act normal, which in Essention meant a little vague. But a new fear gripped him at the idea of facing off against a bunch of Copies.

Preston elbowed him. 'At least pretend to belong here. The scanners can detect elevated body heat and heart rate. They can tell if you're not on Compliance.'

'Sorry. I'm just nervous.'

'If this goes wrong, who do you think will get the blame? Me, you and probably Thomas.'

'Yeah. Sorry.'

Thomas had arrived with several others that day, and was now holed up with Charlie. He'd begged to come, but Max had insisted he needed engineers more than an inventor.

Max growled at them. 'Concentrate, you two.' He stopped in what Jason assumed was a blind spot for the scanners.

Preston pulled a screen out of his bag and rested it on top. They would use it to check for another substantial dip in the power.

The Disruptor was hidden in the waistband of Max's trousers. Jason carried the Atomizer. It made him nervous to carry a gun that contained antimatter.

The three soldiers were empty-handed. Max planned to rectify that when they got inside. Their leader pulled out the Disruptor and pointed it at the force field.

Preston hissed with excitement.

'It's Pavesi. He says they're on the seventh floor. I can isolate his and Kouris' signatures easily this close to Arcis. He's at a power-based unit. Probably a screen or terminal.'

Jason hovered over his shoulder. 'Is Anya safe? Ask him. Please.'

Preston typed quickly. He nodded. 'She's safe.'

Relief flooded through him. He lingered by Preston's shoulder. 'I want you to send her a message. Tell her—'

Max growled at him. 'You can tell her yourself, when we're inside.'

Jason watched the power fluctuations on Preston's screen; a wavy line that dipped and peaked along a straight line. Anything below the second line could be enough for the Disruptor to get them inside. The power dropped suddenly. It wasn't by much, but it was enough for Preston to signal Max.

The Facility

Max extended his hand out to the force field. He pulled his hand away slowly instead of snatching it back. He fired the Disruptor at the invisible barrier. Then, he fired again and braced against the shudder of the barrel as it sucked in the energy. He touched the barrier again.

This time his hand passed right through it.

'Close enough. We need to hurry before the force field repairs the weakened area.'

Jason's heart pounded as they stepped through. No alarms sounded. They hadn't been detected—yet. But a man and a woman had stopped outside the force field and were staring at them.

'Act as if you belong here,' said Max.

Max hid his gun and Preston put his screen away.

Jason glanced briefly at the couple. He followed after the others slowly, hoping the couple was too dazed to understand what this was. Just as he reached the entrance, he saw them turn and walk on.

The glass lobby with its gleaming white floor tiles was wider than he'd expected, and far too quiet. There was an elevator on one side, and two doors on the opposite wall.

Preston pulled out his screen and checked the energy levels. 'They're powering back up!'

Max pressed his wrist to the panel next to the elevator. 'We need to get this working.' Jason saw no buttons, no other way to operate it. Max tried to wedge his fingers between the closed doors.

Movement nearby startled them. The colonel ordered everyone into an empty changing room. Jason moved farther inside while Max stayed close to the door, keeping watch. Jason's heart pounded so fiercely, he was sure the others could hear it.

The sound of metal clacking on the smooth tiles set Jason's teeth on edge. Then several voices: one strange and distorted, others low and curious.

Max closed the door quietly.

'We have to get to the elevator opposite. We'll need to distract it.'

'Distract what?' said one of the soldiers.

'That *thing* has the codes for the elevator. Jason, you'll need to use your gun first so I can shoot it.'

Outside, the 'thing' spoke.

'The elevator will take you to the first floor. Your new supervisor will greet you upon arrival.'

Max opened the door just enough to hear the elevator close and the low and curious voices disappear. He grabbed Jason's arm and pulled him outside.

Jason stopped short when he saw a giant, robotic dog—no, *wolf*—with yellow eyes. The machine was covered in a metal exoskeleton.

'I am not detecting your chips in the Arcis system,' said the wolf. 'All visitors must scan their chips.'

Max took a casual step forward. The wolf's eyes snapped to his movement.

'I wonder if you can help us. We're a little lost.'

Max inched to the side, drawing the wolf's eyes to him and away from Jason. Jason carefully removed the Atomizer from his waistband. But then the wolf snapped its gaze back. Jason hid the gun behind his back.

Max moved again and the wolf shifted its attention back to him.

'We've got a delivery for the second floor,' said Max. 'We're from the factory in Southwest.'

'Deliveries are between 8am and 9am only. You must come back then,' it said in a flat voice.

The Facility

The wolf stalked slowly toward Max, leaving its body open to attack.

Jason whipped the Atomizer around to the front and fired a couple of shots. The wolf yowled. A spot in the exoskeleton softened and became paper-thin. Through the weakened, almost translucent exterior, Jason saw sinewy muscles, metal veins and a beating heart. The wolf yowled again and twisted around to examine the damage.

Max pushed him out of the way and fired the stored energy from the Disruptor at the hole in the wolf's side. The gun appeared to shudder in his hand as it absorbed the new power.

The wolf dropped to the floor.

'Hurry. I've only temporarily disabled it. We don't have much time.'

Max yanked on the wolf's paw, straining against the weight of the machine. Jason grabbed a metal leg as the others emerged to help, and together they dragged it over to the elevator.

'The paw contains the command to operate the elevator,' said Max. 'I saw it press it against the plate and open the doors.'

Preston scanned the wolf and checked his screen. 'Energy levels are low, but rising. It won't be out for much longer.'

'Jason, help me.'

Max lifted up the paw while Jason pressed it against the plate.

The door opened.

'Get in.'

Max produced a brushed-metal card from his pocket and touched it to the silver panel inside the elevator.

Jason stared down at the card.

'A gift from Charlie.'
The elevator started to move.

43

Supervisor Two returned to the dining hall an hour later as promised, and they followed her back into the main room for the next test. While the woman reconnected the others, Anya waited with June, Sheila, Yasmin, Dom and a boy she didn't know.

'Problem-solving was never my strength,' said Yasmin, biting the skin around her nail. She looked around, checking for the supervisor.

Sheila patted her hand. 'Just pick the answer that seems right.'

'But there are so many variables.'

'Ignore the variables,' said Sheila. 'There has to be a right or wrong answer.'

But Yasmin was onto something. There were too many variables. Anya had already discovered that delivering a black or white response meant little to the outcome of the tests. All she knew was the tests weren't about competition.

Dom's eyes were on her. 'What are you thinking about?'

She pulled him away from the others. 'How did you answer the question about the rebels?'

'What question?'

'The one about the rebels' actions and if they concerned me?'

Dom shook his head slowly. 'I didn't get that question.'

'So why did I?'

'They want to know what side you're on. They must know I'm not supposed to be here.' He rubbed the back of his neck, looking agitated.

She touched his arm. 'What does it matter to them if you are? You can't escape. You're no threat to them, this far in.'

But he wasn't listening to her.

'Jesus, this is a mistake,' he whispered. 'They know about me, they know about Sheila, June—'

She frowned. 'You're not the threat, Dom. Arcis... the Collective has you where it wants you. It's more concerned about the others. The ones who are coming for us.'

Dom made no reply. His wide eyes said it all.

'Oh, *God*,' said Anya. 'Tell the rebels to abandon their plans. It's a trap. Jason... I couldn't bear it.'

Dom's focus sharpened. 'I'll try, but it might be too late. They might already be here.'

Anya opened her mouth, to say anything that might calm the stormy look in Dom's eyes. But before she could reply, Supervisor Two crossed the room. Anya slid into her chair and dug her fingers into the white leather. The supervisor attached the metal discs as before.

'The test format in this round is the same,' the female supervisor said. 'Answer the questions honestly, as before.'

The Facility

A new feeling of dread washed over her. She glanced at Dom. The intense look on his face frightened her. She knew so little about him, where he came from, what made him laugh.

What if they were too late? What if the others had already been captured?

Dom would send a warning. It would be okay.

The screen flickered to life like an old television.

The first question appeared and Anya almost laughed at the absurdity of it.

'Yellow or red?'

She reminded herself this was a test. For Quintus? She'd heard the supervisor talking to him.

Back to the question. Her bedroom walls at home in Brookfield were painted primrose; Grace's favorite. She pressed the blue button and thought her answer.

Red.

'Do you like quiet or noise?'

The thumping music on the fifth floor came to mind.

Quiet.

'Do you prefer manual labor to intellectual stimulation?'

Her experiences in Arcis had taught her an important truth: physical strength was nothing without a strong mind.

Intellectual stimulation.

Anya couldn't shake the feeling that the question had a deeper meaning to someone. To Quintus.

'Would you rather live in a house or an apartment?'

Brookfield only had bungalows and houses. East Essention had prison-block apartments.

House.

Two faces popped up. Her breath caught in her throat.

One was Jason, the other was Dom.

'Please state your preference.'

She exhaled sharply.

Both.

'Pick one.'

She reminded herself there was no right or wrong answer.

Dom.

'If one had to die, whom would you kill?'

She touched her fingers to her lips to hide her gasp. She had prepared for another shocking scenario, but not one involving people she loved. Dom's gaze was on her. She closed her eyes and swallowed. Was he looking at a similar photo of her and Sheila?

She shook her head, refusing to play into Quintus' hands.

Neither.

'But if you have to kill one...'

I would sacrifice myself.

'That's not an option. You must kill one of these people. Choose one to kill and one to save.'

I won't choose. I would rather die.

'You are under mind control. Whom would you kill?'

Neither. I'd shoot myself in the head. I can't kill someone if I'm dead, can I?

The screen went black. There were no more prompts, no more questions. Dom's screen was still active. He was staring hard at something, his fingers curled deep into the white leather. Anya moved her head to look.

She swallowed back bile when she saw two pictures: one of her and the other of Sheila.

Dom's eyes never left the screen.

The lights flickered overhead and Anya concentrated on the ceiling for a moment. Dom's screen went blank. He'd chosen someone.

Something flickered on Anya's screen: a message.

The female supervisor walked along their row and Anya read the message with a heavy heart.

'We're inside. Stay safe. Jason.'

The message disappeared just as the supervisor stopped beside Anya. She disconnected the discs from Anya's skin.

'The first five people on this side of the room have made it to the next level.'

Everyone in Anya's row except the boy from the sixth floor.

'The rest of you will take the test again.'

Jerome punched his chair. Warren folded his arms.

Anya wanted to tell them—even Warren—that there was no prize at the end of it. It wasn't a competition. They were being cataloged. She had no idea why.

She swung her legs to the side and stood up. Dom's shaken appearance surprised her. She grabbed his hand and smiled at him.

'We're almost out,' she said.

He smiled weakly at her, then looked away.

They'd done enough to progress.

She hoped Jason and the others were okay.

44

The doors had opened too early. This wasn't the ninth floor. If Jason were to hazard a guess, they were somewhere at the midway point. Their group met with no resistance as they stepped out of the elevator and into a changing room.

'Maybe Charlie's card only gave us clearance for the first few floors,' said Jason.

'It did,' said Max. 'But this is the floor I wanted.' He nodded to the gun in Jason's hand. 'We need more weapons.'

Jason looked at the empty-handed soldiers, then at his molded-plastic Atomizer.

'If you see another wolf, aim for the side of the body, near the heart, as before. It will work on the Copies, too.'

'The ones that look like us?'

'Yes,' said Max, with a grim smile.

Jason shivered and glanced at Preston. But he was too busy looking at the screen to notice.

'There,' said Preston suddenly, pointing to a door. 'The energy spikes in the next room.'

The Facility

They followed Max into a room with a large, central black unit and an array of identical blue-veined guns.

'Pavesi said there was an arsenal on the fifth floor, and here it is.'

Jason walked up to one of the recesses. He brushed his fingers lightly over the cold, black surround. He picked up one of the guns and weighed it in comparison to the Atomizer. It was lightweight. A slight vibration ran into his hand, as though the gun was primed for firing.

'Take what you can carry,' said Max to the soldiers. 'They're Electro Guns. They deliver mid-level blasts of electricity. Pavesi and Kouris said they used them only a few days ago.'

Jason's head snapped up. 'Why were they using them? For what purpose?'

A chill ran through his veins as he remembered Anya being hospitalized after her electric shock.

'Some kind of game,' said Max. 'Nothing lethal. Just stings like hell.'

Jason gritted his teeth. He had to keep a cool head, to believe Anya was still in one piece. She was strong. She could handle herself... But she'd been so fragile when he'd left her.

The soldiers carried two guns apiece and tucked two extras into their combat waistbands.

'So what now?' said Jason. 'Do we try the elevator again?'

Max shook his head. 'Charlie's card won't work. The floors higher up run on separate codes, and the ones closest to the ninth floor each have individual encryptions. The Copies could have sole control.'

'So, we're trapped on the fifth floor?'

Max shook his head. 'Preston is going to hack their system and you'll help him. But not here.'

He pointed to another door. 'If we're to access the ninth, we need to do it from the second tower. It will take longer, but it should be a safer route. They'll be expecting us to hit them from the elevator. There's a stairwell at the back that will give us access to some of the floors. After that, we'll have to use a little brute force.'

Preston cursed at something on the screen. 'They've just rotated to the eighth floor. I'm seeing a hefty usage of power.'

'The elevator, now,' growled Max, and took off running.

They followed him back to the changing room.

'If the power's down,' said Max, 'then they're blind.' He pointed to the control panel that called the elevator. 'See if you two can bypass the commands before the system comes back online. We may be able to sneak up a couple of floors.'

Jason took charge of the screen while Preston started to unscrew the panel. 'And if we can't?'

'Then we'll use the stairwell and stay off the grid for as long as possible.'

45

The elevator door opened. The eighth floor. Anya heard music. Not the brain-scrambling nonsense of the fifth floor; something soothing and peaceful. It was a familiar, soft tone.

She allowed herself a small smile. Maybe this floor wouldn't be so bad.

Anya loosened her grip on Dom's hand as she prepared to leave the elevator.

He bent his neck and whispered, 'Don't be drawn in by their lies.'

Anya tightened her grip.

They waited in another changing room; identical to the others except for the music.

What *was* that tune? Soft and melodic. Non-lyrical. Comforting.

It sounded like something her mother used to sing to her when she was a child.

A door opened and Supervisor Two walked in. She looked like the woman from the seventh—thin, sharp, cold eyes—but she wore a gray uniform with a purple collar; not black with gold.

Anya looked more closely. There were other differences: this version's eyes were slightly sharper, the mouth a little thinner.

She loosened her grip again. Dom squeezed her hand as a reminder.

The frantic disorganization of the previous two floors was absent here. It was as if the rebels storming Arcis were no longer a threat. Anya swallowed back tears. Was Jason safe?

The supervisor listened to a command in her ear. From Quintus?

Only five of them waited, and Anya wondered if Jerome was going through the tests again on the seventh floor. She even wondered about Warren. Would they rotate next time round?

Supervisor Two spoke quickly to a voice Anya couldn't hear. 'No more...We have enough... I think that would be wise, Quintus... I have the code. Yes. Okay.'

She stepped past them, entered the elevator and placed her hand on the flat plate beside the control panel. She punched in some numbers. The elevator jerked and went silent. She had locked it in place.

Anya glanced at Dom. He was searching the room for the cameras, something he used to do often on the ground floor.

'Follow me,' said the supervisor. She entered the next room that was some kind of storage area. Stacks of sealed brown-and-white boxes lined the walls. A few were open, but Anya couldn't see what they contained. She thought she smelled powder.

The music stopped as they exited for the walkway. Anya looked down, hoping to catch a glimpse of Jason, to see that he was all right. Her head swam suddenly.

The Facility

Dom grabbed her. 'Slow steps. Are you okay?'

She nodded. 'We're high up.'

He helped her across the walkway, keeping his arm around her.

The music started again as soon as they entered Tower B. Except this time it was louder, more invasive, as if its function was to mask the other sound: crying babies.

Anya glanced at Dom. He looked at her, then back at the room.

Again, the music reminded her of Grace's lullaby.

How could that be?

'I think I know that song,' said Anya.

Dom looked ahead, his jaw tight. 'My mother used to sing it to me. Many mothers in the towns did.'

'Where did they learn it from?'

Dom flashed a dark look at her. 'Where do you think?' His fingers curled deeper into her side.

His mother had come through this place. Had she sung it in here? Had they stolen it from her mind on the last floor?

Anya removed Dom's arm, but kept hold of his hand as she looked around.

Ahead of them was the all-too-familiar hangar-sized room. The walls had been painted bright yellow, like her room in Brookfield. The room was divided in half by a red velvet curtain attached to the ceiling, its ends trailing on the floor. Large ball-shaped lights hung from the ceiling, attached by thick wires, their light diffused through frosted-glass covers. The floor, a white tile, was partially covered by red and yellow rugs which all looked new, their pile still soft and springy.

She caught a strong odor of freshly cut freesias. Her nose tingled at the peppery irritation. But she saw no fresh flowers in the room.

In the center was a room within the room; a square box with transparent walls and a dozen cribs inside.

The crying became more insistent. It was both disturbing and unfamiliar to her. Anya had never been around babies much.

June walked into the sub-room without hesitation. She picked up one of the babies and started to pat its back. Anya wondered if she had helped to raise her younger sister.

Dom let go of Anya's hand and followed June.

Inside he picked up a different baby without pause, and soothed it with a quiet hushing sound. He looked out of place in his black combats and black T-shirt, holding a baby that seemed so small in his arms. Yet, he was a natural.

The female supervisor stood stiffly outside the box, looking in. She focused on June, assessing her clinically.

Anya stepped into her line of sight, keen to draw the supervisor's interest away from the rebels. The supervisor snapped her gaze to her, then away.

Sheila and Yasmin waited with Anya outside the sub-room.

'You will nurture these babies,' said the supervisor, her voice rising to match the volume of the insistent crying. 'We wish to observe you in these surroundings, to see how you interact with these creatures.'

'Creatures?' said Sheila.

'Yes, infants. Children. Choose what name you want. It makes no difference.'

She waved her hand and walked away, as if she couldn't stand being here. She exited through a single door on the back wall.

Sheila and Yasmin glanced at each other, then followed Dom and June inside. Only Anya stayed where she was; rooted to the spot, clasping and unclasping her hands. Maybe she was cold-hearted, like the supervisor.

The cries rose into full-blown screaming that no volume of music could obscure. Anya flicked her gaze to the door Supervisor Two had used to leave. She thought about following her.

But then she caught Dom looking over, full grin, with a baby draped over his right shoulder. He hooked a finger at her with the same hand he used to rub the baby's back.

Anya approached the open side of the transparent cube/day-care center slowly.

Dom put the baby back down and picked up another that screamed for attention. He burped it, and it seemed to settle.

It? He? She? Anya had no idea if they were boys or girls. They all wore white baby grows.

June picked up a different baby and cradled it in her arms, using her little finger as a pacifier.

'I can't believe they've just left them here like this.'

Anya took one step inside and peered into one of the cribs. The baby in it was about three months old. Another, whose crib was larger and taller, was standing up. He or she was around nine months old. Some cribs were just shallow boxes for the babies who didn't seem to move much. Where were the colorful mobiles, the stuffed animals, the books?

'Apart from the crying, they seem to be well looked after,' said Dom. 'This one's just been fed.'

Anya stared at Dom. 'How did you know to do that?'

'My mother used to run a crèche in Foxrush. I picked up the basics.' He gave her a lopsided grin. 'You don't like babies?'

'I don't know what to do with them.'

Her eyes slid to Sheila and Yasmin, who both seemed to be getting the hang of it.

Dom moved to a different cot and picked up another irritated baby. He sniffed the air and his nose wrinkled. A table with a changing mat was pushed up against the wall of the room with a white box full of diapers underneath.

He carried the baby over to the table. June did the same with hers.

With a new diaper in place, June tickled her baby and it laughed. 'They just want to be held.'

Dom placed his back in the cot. He looked at Anya. 'You want to try?'

She stared at the baby as if it were an alien. That earned her a chuckle from Dom. 'Here.' He picked up the baby and cradled it in his arms. 'Hold him like this.'

Him.

She took the boy and held him as if he were a delicate piece of china. The baby began to cry. Dom coughed to disguise his laugh. He took the baby back and put him in the crib.

'Don't worry. You'll get used to it.'

She didn't want to get used to it. She wanted off this floor and to move on to the ninth. Then she wanted go home. Teary eyed, she ran from the room and stopped at the wall.

The Facility

Dom walked up to her. 'Are you okay, Anya?'

'I don't want to be here.'

'Is it the babies?'

Anya shook her head. 'I don't want to be *here*, in Arcis, trapped inside their creepy test, program, whatever this is. I want to get out.'

'We're almost there.'

'Have you forgotten what this place is?'

'No,' said Dom, his voice almost a whisper. 'But it's not the babies' fault they're here. We may be the only people they see today. I wanted to remind them that there is still kindness in the world.'

She lowered her eyes. 'I suppose I didn't think of it like that.'

He lifted her chin. 'Let's just make it through this floor. Then we'll be free.'

'Will they really let us go?'

Dom's eyes dulled for a moment. 'I don't know.'

'Okay, so what happens next?' She couldn't look at him. 'What will happen when we get out of here?'

He inhaled sharply. 'You mean between us? You want to know if this is a one-time thing.'

She nodded.

His lips touched hers gently. 'You have to ask?' Then he pulled her closer, fitting his body to hers.

He parted her lips and kissed her deeper, harder.

Anya's knees buckled. Dom kept her upright. Somewhere deep in her core, her body set itself on fire. She threaded her fingers through his soft, loose curls and pulled him in tighter.

His ragged breathing kept time with his roaming hands that slid down her back, along her hips, and up her arms, to cup her neck.

He moved his lips briefly to her ear.

Every part of her shivered hard.

'Anya,' he said, resting his head against hers. 'I was helping you on the ground floor for purely selfish reasons. This isn't circumstantial, at least not for me.'

She bit her lip, wanting him close.

He held her gaze. 'Unless it is for you?'

'No, it's not. I just... I don't know how to explain how much—' His lips on hers cut her off. The flame smoldered in her core, driving her to bite his lower lip, just for a second. Dom groaned.

She became aware of eyes on them both, watching their moment from inside the cube. Sheila gave a muffled yell, 'Get a room,' quickly followed by June saying, 'I think it's cute.'

Dom held her face and kept the kiss soft. Anya tried to ramp it up, to ignite more within him. His body was rigid with tension, as if he were holding back. He kept the pressure soft and even.

She felt him smile. 'I don't know if you're aware, but we're not alone.'

'I don't care,' she said.

'Well, I'm not going to kiss you like that here, so you can stop trying.' His voice was deep and husky.

She kissed him over and over. 'You already did, and why not?'

Laughter rumbled in his chest. 'Because we're not in some porno film.'

'I thought you were impulsive.'

'I'm trying to change.'

She tried to get him to open up again. His defenses slipped, and his body leaned into hers. She did everything she could to evoke a new response, because it felt like it would end soon and it would never be this good again. Anya kept kissing him, pulling him closer, wanting to remember this moment, how he felt, and every word he said to her.

A deep ache urged her to treat every moment between them as if it were their last.

Dom broke the kiss first. She gripped his T-shirt to keep him close but he was too strong for her.

'I don't know what's going to happen and I've no idea what to expect on the next floor. But I do know one thing. I want you with me.'

'Me, too.'

He flashed a familiar grin.

Remember, Anya. Remember all of it.

A sudden thought tugged her back to reality. She examined the transparent cube, and turned back to Dom.

'Where do you think these babies come from?'

Dom frowned. 'A crèche of some sort. For the supervisors' children?'

'The supervisor was even less interested in the babies than me.'

'What are you thinking?'

'I don't know. Something's bothering me about this floor, and it's not the babies.'

Her gaze settled on the giant, red velvet curtain which split the room in half.

'What's on the other side of this?'

She walked toward it. Dom followed her.

She found a break in the curtain. Dom pulled it back to reveal a frosted-glass partition, and a door.

They opened it and stepped through to another room within a room. Before them was another transparent box with no privacy, but much bigger than the first.

This one was sectioned off into ten separate units. Each section contained a child. The boys were dressed in white tunic separates, the girls in long white dresses with cap sleeves. Their ages ranged from around three to ten years of age.

They were quieter than the babies next door. Each unit had some toys and books while some also had small tables and chairs and coloring books. The youngest played alone with primary-colored shapes and squares. Some of the children sat and read, while others watched them with bright, strange eyes.

The eye color was all wrong. Too vivid.

Dom drew in a sharp breath.

'What are they doing? I mean, why?' He ran a shaky hand across his neck.

Anya circled the box. The children watched her impassively as she searched in vain for a way inside. She came around to the front again.

She found Dom staring at one boy in particular. Dom had gone pale.

The boy sat on the floor with his back to them. He was about four years of age and was hunched over an opened coloring book, clutching a stubby crayon. He colored perfectly within the lines. Then Anya saw what Dom was looking at.

As he leaned into his work, the boy's top had slid up.

And there it was: the same crescent-shaped scar that was on Dom's back.

He'd been sick as a child. That's what he'd told Anya.

Had these children been sick, too? Or experimented on?

'What are they doing here?' Dom tugged at his hair. 'Why does he have—?'

Anya pinned his arms down by his side.

'Maybe they were sick, like you were.' She didn't want to worry him.

But his eyes were wild, unfocused.

'Talk to me!'

Dom snapped his gaze back to her. He grabbed her hand and pulled her back to the side with the younger babies.

'I don't know. I just don't... I need to leave.'

Anya wrapped her arm around his middle, surprised to feel him slipping to the floor.

The lights dipped overhead. At the same time she felt a strong vibration running through the floor.

Without a word, Dom returned to the baby room and busied himself with one of the babies. Anya watched from the outside, as before.

Dom kept his focus on the babies.

She couldn't imagine what it must have been like to lose a lung or a kidney at such a young age.

Dom gripped the baby tight against his chest. He looked pale and unsteady.

The strange eyes of the children next door continued to haunt her. Had they come from Praesidium? Had Quintus ordered them to be here? Were they an extension of the test on the previous floor?

For an hour Anya didn't move from the entrance to the box. She thought about going back to the older children and asking them some questions, but she imagined Quintus watching her every move. She wouldn't give him the satisfaction.

Supervisor Two appeared in her peripheral vision, alarming her.

'Put the babies down,' she said to the others. 'We've learned all we can from your interactions. You're being rotated to the final floor.'

46

Anya should have felt relief, but she stepped into the final elevator feeling numb, as though she were still on Compliance. She gripped Dom's waist so hard she thought he might object. But he was gripping her back just as firm. June, Sheila and Yasmin held hands behind them.

The doors closed. She looked behind her to Sheila, who jerked her head at Dom and gave her a what-the-hell-happened look. Anya shrugged and faced the front again. She couldn't tell Sheila what they had seen.

The elevator jolted slightly, then hummed its way to the final floor: the mushroom cap sitting on top of Arcis. She looked ahead despite Dom's gaze on her. Her heart thudded too loud. She closed her eyes and concentrated on breathing.

In, out. In, out.

Dom's breaths were short and sharp.

This was it. The end.

She would be brave. For Jason. For Dom. For her mother, who had tried to protect her from this moment.

She loosened her grip on Dom. She didn't want to die, or vanish like the others who had gone through Arcis.

She wanted to show Jason she could be brave, as Grace had always believed her to be.

The hummingbirds returned, smacking their tiny wings against her heart; slicing her, making her bleed. She jammed her fingers in to stop them. Dom grabbed her hand, breaking through the pain. She looked up at him. He was staring straight ahead.

Remember this, Anya. Don't be erased from existence. Remember all of it.

The elevator doors opened and they exited into a corridor of partitioned walls made of frosted glass. A soft-yellow backlight gave the glass a welcoming feel to it. The corridor ran in a straight line to a single door at the end. The space soothed the rough edges of Anya's earlier panic.

Her group looked around. Nobody was in a hurry to move on.

June touched the nearest partition. 'What's beyond these walls, do you think?'

'Is this another test?' said Sheila.

Dom shrugged at her.

Anya ran her fingers over the partition to test its organic state, like the ones on the fifth floor. But it felt solid, with no hint of a ripple.

'Participants. Welcome to the ninth floor.'

A voice she recognized cut through their solitude.

Dom's jaw tensed as he searched the ceiling; for the cameras, Anya assumed.

'Continue through the door at the end of the corridor. Don't delay. There isn't much time.'

A powerful tremor—much stronger than anything she'd felt on the lower floors—ran through the floor into Anya's legs. She readjusted her feet to compensate.

'What was that?' said Yasmin.

'That's exactly what I felt on the floors below,' said Anya to June.

Dom took the lead, keeping hold of Anya's hand.

'What's going to happen to us?' said Yasmin. 'I mean, we finish this and then what? We don't go back to Essention. So where *do* we go?'

'Please, Yas,' said Sheila. 'I'm nervous enough as it is.'

But Yasmin was on a roll. 'I can't go back to those gray prison cells in East Essention they call homes. I want to do something with my life. I don't want to be stuck in a pokey town forever, wishing I had nicer things.' She looked up to the ceiling and spoke to Quintus. 'Did you know I wanted to be a doctor? I know Praesidium has a really good program and a medical facility. I'd like to do something worthwhile—'

'Shut up, Yasmin,' said Sheila. 'You don't know what you're asking for.'

Yasmin frowned at her. 'Of course I do. I'm not going to say no to an opportunity if it comes my way, just because you told me a couple of things—'

'Everyone be quiet,' snapped Dom. 'We can talk about this after.'

Anya bit her lip and focused on the only door in front of them. This felt too real, too dangerous. She wished she were still on Compliance, like Yasmin.

Another tremor vibrated through the floor and rattled her teeth.

The door was just twenty meters in front of them, but they walked so slowly it could have been ten times that distance. Dom slowed down, probably running last-minute strategies through his mind.

Then he let go of her hand and opened the door.

Anya took a deep breath.

47

'Congratulations for making it to the ninth floor,' said Quintus. 'Please keep moving. We have no time to waste.'

They stepped farther into the mushroom cap that was the size of the atrium on the ground floor.

Anya saw no windows, only light-gray tiles covering every inch of the area, from floor to rounded ceiling. A large machine sat in the center; an open tunnel with archways divided it into three sections. A different-colored light marked each sectioned archway: white, blue and green. The open tunnel sat on a raised platform and connected to the floor by three steps. Anya followed the curve of the first arch, its edge decorated with inlaid blinking white lights.

They inched closer to the machine, standing shoulder to shoulder now.

'Wow,' said Yasmin.

Sheila inhaled sharply. June was staring at the structure in the center, while Dom looked around. For a way out? For evidence that his mother had been there?

Hurry, Jason.

She wasn't sure how much time they had here before Quintus would make them disappear. Maybe Anya could stall him until help arrived.

Quintus spoke again.

'This is your final test for the Collective ten. It is a test of faith and trust. You must not ask questions of the arches you see before you. You must walk through each of them. After, you will find yourself back in Essention, at the start of your journey.'

'That's bull,' Dom yelled at the ceiling. 'My mother came through here six months ago and never came home. Where did she go? Tell me where she is.'

Yasmin gasped, as if the truth about this place had just hit her.

'You must take a leap of faith, Dominic Pavesi,' said Quintus. 'You are lucky to be part of this exclusive program. Not many are invited up here. You are on the cusp of adulthood, an equally wondrous and dangerous time in your life when feelings are both overwhelming and exciting, but also confusing and scary. You will make the best and the worst decisions of your life. At this age you are impulsive, rash. You seem to love the hardest, but easily betray others at the hint of opportunity. You do not have the confidence to choose your own path, so you let others decide for you. We are fascinated by you. Much more than we were by the others, younger and older, who came through here.'

Hearing Quintus describe their actions reminded Anya of Compliance's control. She'd lacked confidence, she'd let others decide. Her emotions had controlled her.

But Quintus did not account for her learning from her mistakes. And while she'd made some bad decisions on Compliance—listening to Warren, hurting Tahlia to progress and chasing Dom further into Arcis—she'd also learned how to keep her anger in check. But most of all, she'd learned how to trust her instincts.

Right now, they told her to stall, stall, stall.

Dom growled and stepped closer to the machine. Anya touched his arm, stopping him.

'I know all about life,' he said. 'I've experienced far more than your pathetic program can teach me. Tell me what happened to my mother, Mariella Pavesi. You recognize the name. I know you do. You knew my name the minute I stepped inside this place.'

He was shaking. Anya tried to pull him back—confronting the Collective would only accelerate their plans—but he was too strong for her. Too determined.

When she sensed another verbal attack brewing, Anya stepped in front of Dom, facing the machine. He grabbed her waist, but she wriggled free.

'What are these tests for, Quintus?' said Anya. She needed answers, and Quintus was averse to Dom's anger. He seemed to enjoy curiosity most.

Stall, Anya.

'So you know my name?' Quintus sounded surprised. 'The tests prepare you for emerging adulthood. This was explained to you at your induction, Anya Macklin.'

'I was not told my friends would be killed. Tell me why people had to die?'

'Death is a natural part of life. We all must die at some time.'

'Yes, in the real world. But not in a game, or test, or whatever this place is.'

'We have learned all we can from you,' said Quintus. 'It is time for you to step through the machine so that we can extract that knowledge.'

'No!' said Sheila. 'I want to know, too. We've spent months in here while you've watched us complete your idiotic tests.' She stepped forward. 'Tell her what she wants to know. Then tell Dom where his mother is. Tell June where her sister is.'

'It would serve no purpose.' Quintus sounded angry.

'Please,' said Anya, softer. 'I asked you what the tests are for. Is it because you're curious about us?'

She glanced back at Dom. His eyes were wild.

Quintus spoke again; flatter, more neutral. 'Yes, the Collective was curious. Your group was the most resistant in the tests and we wanted to know why. Then I saw your friends breach our defenses and...' A pause. 'You must complete the program now.'

Anya frowned. 'Why are we really here?'

Another pause. 'Why do you need to know?'

'Because I do.'

'Curiosity is a human flaw,' said Quintus.

'Tell her,' said a second voice. 'We need their experiences.'

Quintus paused a third time. 'If I tell you, Anya Macklin, will you walk through the arches?'

'Yes.'

Dom hissed behind her. 'Maybe.'

Quintus laughed; it was a strange and stifled sound.

'The Collective likes you, Dominic Pavesi. That's why we picked you for our hybrid program. Mariella was in this very room, pleading for your life. She told me how brave you were. She also told me that the scars are your weakness, your Achilles heel.' Quintus sounded amused.

'She wanted us to return to you what we stole, in exchange for her life.'

Dom was shaking. 'Where the hell is she?'

'She is not here, Dominic Pavesi.'

Anya kept a calming hand on Dom. 'What is this place, Quintus? What is its purpose?'

'This facility exists so the Collective ten can learn.'

'Learn what?' said Anya, raising her voice. 'What's in it for you?'

'We learn by studying you. Your emotions, your reactions to events, good or bad, your strategies, your mistakes. The purpose of this place, Anya Macklin, is to help us evolve.'

48

The tech inside the dismantled panel looked unfamiliar to Jason. For one, there wasn't a wire in sight. A gelatin-like power source reminded him of the orb scout, but the level of detail here surpassed the orb's simpler design. Jason had no clue where to begin.

While he and Preston poked various elements, the soldiers fanned out with their backs to them, guns ready. Beyond them, Max paced. None of it helped to ease Jason's nerves.

A *clunk-click* occurred higher up in the elevator shaft, causing the whirring of mechanics to stop altogether.

The power in the unit died.

'Crap, they've locked us out,' said Preston.

Jason kicked the panel away from him.

'This isn't over,' said Max grunting. 'Preston, put that panel back exactly as you found it. We'll find another way up.'

He did, and they all followed Max out of the room and through the next.

They stopped at the floating walkway. Jason hesitated before he stepped out and crossed it.

The Facility

On the other side was a room that was larger than expected, with slashes in the floor. It looked like they might contain retractable walls. An inactive screen hung above three doors at the back of the room. A faint smell of sweat lingered in the air. Jason tried not to think about what game Anya had been forced to play here.

And with Electro Guns, no less.

Max strode over to one of the doors under the screen and held it open. Jason followed. He stopped when he heard voices coming from the second room.

'We can't help them yet. We need to keep moving. None of this will end unless we reach the ninth floor.' Max put his hand out. 'Give me your weapon.'

Jason did and Max swapped his Atomizer for the Disruptor. They slipped inside what appeared to be a dormitory. Two dozen plainly dressed beds lined the room, twelve on each side.

Jason looked around not seeing a way out.

Preston continued to monitor the spikes in energy on his screen.

Max walked along the walls, knocking at various points. When he tried the back wall Jason heard the sound change, as though there might be a hollow space behind it.

They gathered around Max, keeping the guns directed toward the door. Jason glanced up to see the ceiling and the wall didn't quite meet.

Max slid the Atomizer into his waistband. 'Help me knock through this.'

Jason and Preston both pushed against the partition. At first it seemed solid, but then it creaked and wobbled as it broke loose from its bindings. The divider came apart at a seam and they created enough of a gap to squeeze through.

The three soldiers were the last to enter the gray-bricked corridor, replacing the partition as neatly as they could.

The corridor ran in both directions. They tried one way, but hit a dead end. The other route, closer to the outer edge of Arcis, brought them to an open stairwell.

Max frowned. 'Proceed with caution. They're expecting us.'

They climbed the stairs. At the eighth floor, a locked door halted their progress.

A small panel shimmered off to the side. It appeared to want a bio signature, like the elevator on the ground floor.

'This is too easy,' said Jason, prising the panel off the wall. He stepping back to let Preston take a look.

Its design was different to that of the elevator panel: for one there were wires. A copper-colored sphere sat inside the unit. Jason struggled to make sense of how everything worked.

Using the screen Preston scanned the tech. 'The wiring I could probably figure out, but I'm not familiar with its safety features.'

Max moved Preston away from the panel. 'We don't have time.' He raised the Atomizer. 'Let's see if this thing does anything.'

Max fired at the exposed panel; the sphere shimmered and its edges softened. Around it, the other components melted or fused into a jagged mass. But then some of the pieces surrounding the sphere began to remold themselves.

Self-repairing tech? He'd never seen anything like it.

'Did you just see—'

The door unlocked.

Max entered the new stairwell with the Atomizer out in front. The soldiers followed. Jason carried the Disruptor in one hand and an Electro Gun in the other.

At the top of the stairs they found an open door.

'I told you this was too easy,' said Jason.

Max pushed the door open with the tip of his gun. He entered the room and froze.

Jason followed, his heart hammering at what awaited them. All he could think of was Anya.

But Anya wasn't there. Someone—or something else was.

The room, longer than it was wide, contained dozens of silver units recessed into the wall. Each section contained a person. Each person looked the same.

On one side of the room, the man he and Anya had first met in the hospital stared out blankly from a recess, alongside six identical men. On the other side, the female from the hospital stood still with seven of her counterparts.

'Are these... Copies?' said Jason.

Max approached the first female in a black tunic. The soldiers shadowed him. Preston barely looked up from his screen.

'Praesidium uses them to run Essention and Arcis,' said Max.

'But what are they copies of?' said Jason. Thomas had told him about the concept of Copies, but being in a room with them... It turned his blood to ice. 'Are they just designed to look like us, or are they actual duplicates of people?'

'They are copies of people who once lived. Genetically similar skin-bags. They use biogel machines to make perfect copies. The biotech—lungs, brains and hearts

—is added after the creation process.' Max touched one. 'I've never seen one up close before.'

A thought made Jason shiver again. 'Are there Copies of us walking around?'

Max shook his head. 'Not likely. They don't use living test subjects. As far as I know they only copy people who are dead.'

'And you're sure? How?'

'I'm not. It's what I've been told.'

Preston was still staring at his screen. 'The energy in this room and the next is off the charts. This must be where they're making the Copies.'

Max turned. 'What did you say?'

Preston looked up and frowned. 'I can't be sure. What else would they need that much power for?'

'They make them in Praesidium,' said Max. 'I'm sure of it. My sources... That would mean they're using these kids...' He trailed off.

A door at the other end of the room swung open. Jason jerked both guns up to chest height. Three identical-looking men stepped into the room brandishing pistols and shotguns. Three others blocked their exit at the stairwell.

'Drop your weapons,' the lead male said. His duplicates kept their guns high.

'Drop yours first,' said Max. 'Then we'll talk.'

'Your guns are useless on this floor,' said the male. 'Try them if you don't believe me.'

Max squeezed the trigger on the Atomizer, but it only clicked. The soldiers flanking Max tried their Electro Guns. They all emitted a flat fizzle. Jason tried both of his weapons, but nothing. Power-neutralizing tech must have been active in the room.

'Place your guns on the floor now,' said the male.

Max complied first, followed by the soldiers, then Jason. Preston put his screen down on the ground even though he wasn't asked to.

'So, what now?' said Max. 'Are you going to kill us?'

The male stared at him. 'The Collective wishes for you to witness the true purpose of Praesidium.'

49

'We designed each of the floors to have a specific purpose,' said Quintus. 'We wanted to observe you in your natural surroundings.'

'Natural?' said Sheila. 'There's nothing natural about what you've done to us.'

Anya needed to keep stalling.

Please be close, Jason.

'What is the exact purpose of each of the floors? I want to understand.'

Dom turned slightly, as if he finally understood her plan.

Quintus paused.

A new voice came through. 'The Collective says to answer her, Quintus. They will not remember anyway.'

Quintus hesitated. 'On the ground floor we wanted to see how you dealt with humiliation by forcing you to clean up after the upper floors.' Anya shuddered, remembering the dead girl and boy. And Lilly and Ash. 'On the first, it was your ability to work under pressure.'

'Why did our friends have to die?'

The Facility

'We hadn't factored in that variable at first, but the participants' reactions to the deaths on the ground floor provided us with some interesting statistics.'

Her body shook. 'That's all we were to your *Collective*? A bunch of statistics?' Dom squeezed her hand. She ignored his attempts to calm her.

Quintus continued, unperturbed by her outburst.

'The second floor tested your altruistic side, to see how willing you were to help others. The third was about problem-solving. We left you without instructions to see if you would figure it out for yourselves.'

Anya was told that she'd skipped the second floor because she'd helped Tahlia. But Frank had also skipped the second floor, a decision that had felt like an afterthought. Just like the decision to leave Jerome and Warren out of this group.

'The fourth pitted the sexes against each other and introduced class structure into a classless society. We found it interesting that many of the suicides came from this floor.'

Anya drew in a shaky breath.

'The fifth was about competition, seeing whether you'd work individually or in teams. The score didn't matter. We wanted to see how you behaved in a predetermined environment. We also noticed some of you had been trained in the use of guns. It was then the Collective realized there were rebels inside Arcis.'

Anya stared ahead of her. She would not give up the identities of her rebel friends, even if the Collective already knew who they were.

'None of you here made it to the sixth, which was designed to see if you still possessed your humility, or if you considered it beneath you to care for our wolves after having progressed so far. We designed the seventh to understand you better. Humans over think their problems. Machines simplify them too much. We wanted to see if your strengths could balance out our weaknesses.'

Anya swayed as she realized what Quintus was saying. Arcis *had* been cataloging them. She opened her mouth to speak, but Sheila beat her to it.

'So, this,' she said slowly, 'was so you could satisfy a sick curiosity about us?'

Sheila had it wrong. This went beyond curiosity.

Anya looked up at the ceiling. 'What was the purpose of the eighth floor?'

'To see how well you cared for infants. Some of you performed better than others.'

'There were other children there with scars like Dom's.' His hand loosened in hers. She tightened her hold on him.

Dom had to know.

'They are part of a different program. Only the younger ones were part of your test.'

'Did you butcher them?' said Anya.

'The Collective has not harmed them. If anything, they are better designs than before. They are also not your concern.' Quintus paused. 'Without sacrifice, we will never know what we can become.'

Dom let go of Anya's hand. 'And what did I sacrifice? What lesson did I learn when you cut me open —'

'Dom...' said Sheila, softly.

'What lesson did *you* need to teach a terrified seven-year-old?' His voice rose in pitch. 'What had I done to deserve your attention?'

'Nothing, Dominic. You were in the right place at the right time.'

'The right *place*?' Dom laughed and ran a hand across his neck. He turned away.

'Dominic's sacrifices were not in vain. Neither were the children's. They gave us the knowledge to better ourselves.'

Dom turned back around, his eyes flashing with anger.

'Anya, you asked what the tunnel was for,' said Quintus. 'When you pass through the first archway, your experiences, your time in Arcis, will be downloaded to our memory banks so our Copies might learn. You have already met a selection of our most recent creations. They have acted as your supervisors during your time here. We created many versions of them, some better than the last, others worse. Each time new participants complete the program we learn something new to perfect the algorithms. The presence of rebels in our program has given us a richer experience. We have learned about hate, revenge, hope, grief and even love.'

'You said there were three parts to the machine,' said June. 'What's the second part for?'

'The second will only sting for a moment.'

Anya swallowed hard.

'The third will take you to a place where you will continue to be useful to us.'

'Useful? How?'

'For whatever we deem necessary, in whatever capacity we need.'

'Why are you telling us all of this?' said Anya. And where the hell was Jason?

Quintus paused, as if he were consulting with one of the Collective.

'Your group was the most interesting. We particularly liked seeing how you, Anya Macklin, changed your mind about the rebels. When you started here, you were convinced they had killed your parents. The Collective wishes to know why you doubted the authenticity of that story.'

'I thought they had, until I met some in real life.'

'What gives credence to those doubts? You bore witness to your parents' murder.' Dom stiffened beside her. She hadn't told him about that. 'You believed it was the rebels. Yet it only took your relationship with Dominic, whom we know to be a rebel, to change your mind.'

Quintus' questions, his curiosity; it all sounded so childlike. 'It wasn't just that,' she said. 'The truth is always there, in among the lies. You just need to read the signs.'

'What signs?'

'It's hard to put into words.' She feared she had said too much.

Quintus's voice was neutral, careful again. 'Yes, it usually is. That's why the first part of the machine is so important. It downloads your experiences, exactly as they happened.'

'Where is my mother?' said Dom.

'She's waiting for you in Essention. That is where the machine will take you.'

'I'm not walking through that thing until you explain—'

The Facility

The door to the rear of the room opened suddenly. Jason appeared and Anya gasped with relief. But then she saw the handgun Supervisor One was pointing at his head.

'Jason!'

'Anya.' He tried to go to her, but the supervisor restrained him. An adult and four others around Jason's age followed, all with guns against their heads. They were dressed in the Essention uniform. The fourth boy, tall and thin with brown hair, clutched a bag to his chest.

'Max!' Sheila called out.

'Dom, Sheila, June. Are you all right?'

'They're forcing us to go through the machine.'

'And you will,' said Quintus.

The Copies moved the new arrivals farther into the room.

'The Collective has learned a thing or two about sacrifice since the program first began,' said Quintus. 'But we learned the most when you answered our questions on the seventh floor.'

Anya's throat tightened. *Don't make me choose...*

'So it is very simple. The longer you wait the more of you will die.'

Anya couldn't bear it. She wouldn't. Nobody else would die. In the test, she had told them she would sacrifice herself.

Anya stepped forward.

Dom yanked her back. 'Anya, what are you doing?'

'We almost had a volunteer there,' said a different voice. 'Perhaps she needs a little encouragement, Quintus?'

A sharp bang sounded and she stumbled back. The boy holding the bag crumpled to the floor.

'Preston!' yelled Jason. He tried to go to him, but the supervisor restrained him.

Blood trickled along the cold, gray tiles. The boy stared blankly at the ceiling.

Another bang. Another body.

Then a third bang. Two of the boy soldiers dropped.

Max, Jason and the third remaining soldier stood stiffly, handguns pressed against their heads.

When the Copy next to Jason shifted slightly, Anya twisted out of Dom's grip.

'Stop, Quintus. I'll go. I volunteer. Please. No more.'

'No. Anya, wait.' Dom stepped forward. 'I'll take her place. Take me.'

'No replacements,' said Quintus.

'Then we'll go together.'

'One at a time.'

Anya stared at the ceiling through blurred vision.

'What will happen to me when I walk through the first archway?'

'You will lose your memory of this place and the people you've met here,' said Quintus.

No.

She glanced back at Dom. 'Everyone?'

'Yes. It will be as it was before you came to this place. You will continue to believe the rebels killed your parents.'

She had to remember, she would try to remember.

'But it wasn't the rebels. It was you.' She said it as much for herself as for her brother. She smiled sadly at Jason.

'I'm sorry I didn't believe you, Jason.'

He wriggled in his captor's grip. 'This isn't the end, Anya.'

She turned to look at Dom one last time. He was a mess. His hand was in his hair, his unflinching gaze on her. She almost changed her mind.

Almost.

'Don't forget me, Dom.'

'No!' His voice was tight with emotion. He went to her and crushed his lips to hers. Their final kiss was fierce, rough and desperate, like they both knew it would be their last.

If Arcis hadn't forced them together, would they have become friends?

She wanted to believe they would.

'I'll find you, Anya,' he said, his voice thick with emotion.

She broke away, unable to look him in the eye and see the pain he was in.

She nodded at June and Sheila. June had her fingers pressed to her lips. Sheila was shaking her head, tears in her eyes. Anya nodded to a shocked Yasmin.

'We'll find your mother together,' she whispered to Dom. 'I promise.' She turned back and stepped toward the machine.

Quintus spoke again. 'This experience will be erased from your memories, but it will make a great addition to ours. The Collective saved you from the rebels. And now you will free us from our imprisonment.'

Anya squeezed her eyes shut. Her galloping pulse was all she heard.

She opened her eyes and climbed the three steps to the first archway and the blinking white lights.

Shaking, she took another step forward.

50

Their voices faded into the background.

Her memories of recent conversations sped up and slowed down, then fell softly away. Visions of beasts with yellow eyes and sharp incisors flashed before her and disappeared.

Jason's birthday. Their arguments.

Her jealousy toward Sheila.

She reached out for all of them, eager to lock them away in her heart and keep them safe. But her fingers only clutched at air.

More memories tore loose from her mind.

Tahlia's pink hair.

Lilly's enthusiasm before Ash.

Warren forcing himself on her.

She shivered and tasted blood in her mouth.

The arch vibrated through her hands and feet. The vibrations seemed like a memory, too, but even that wasn't clear.

She thought she saw Jason to her left with a gun to his head.

Shaking away the distraction, she concentrated on what would soon be no more. The memory of Dom's urgent kisses, the feel of his soft curls. The way he looked at her—soft and tender—when they were alone. The things he said, the way he said them. Every intimate conversation they'd ever had. Every place they'd talked together.

Each memory danced away like a feather caught on the wind.

Her most recent memories of Dom remained strong.

Her heart soared.

I still remember him.

She frowned.

But not how they had met.

Lullabies and screaming babies kept her mind from focusing. She had to remember Dom. June and Sheila, Tahlia, Frank, Jerome. Even Warren.

'Please step forward,' said a voice.

The second archway twinkled with blue. The lights dazzled her as they merged into a single, glowing slash that swept the length of her, twice. It stung a little.

She forgot why she was there.

'Just one more,' said the voice. 'Please step forward.'

Anya stared at her feet, then up at the last archway, the last set of lights: bright green, like grass caught in sunshine. Sparkling like light reflecting on water.

The space in the final archway looked like a mirror. She reached out to touch a face that resembled her own. A sudden bright light forced her eyes closed.

I'm supposed to keep going.

She remembered that much but not why.

An invisible force drew her to the mirror, marking the end of something old and the beginning of something new.

She closed her eyes.

Voices screamed her name. One voice in particular.

Deep, husky, strained.

A strange energy pulled her forward.

One more step.

The mirror.

It hummed with restrained power. Her bones shook.

The power enveloped her, like warm water in a bath, slipping over her skin.

The deep voice yelled, 'Don't forget.'

She took her final step.

51

The brightness faded.

She sensed movement around her. Slowly, everything came into focus.

She was in a partitioned white room with a low ceiling, a white-tiled floor and no obvious door. The place didn't look familiar. She looked down to see she wore a white dress with capped sleeves.

When had she ever worn a dress?

Movement behind startled her and forced her round.

Four others were with her: a tall boy-man with dark hair and dark eyes and three blonde girls; one with wiry hair, another with hair as fine as silk and a third who looked... proportionately accurate.

The beauty of the last girl drew her gaze for the longest. The perfect creature stared at her until she looked away.

The others picked at the fabric of their white clothes.

The male caught her attention next. His eyes were a fascinating shade of trouble. Deep, curious, dangerous. He was the only one more interested in the room than his clothes.

Then his eyes found hers.

His unblinking stare unnerved her, but she held his gaze. Then he turned and touched the perfect creature's arm.

'Sheila.' He said in a soft and deep voice. 'Where the hell are we?'

The perfect creature turned to him. 'I've no idea.'

He stared at Sheila a moment longer, his brow furrowed, his eyes questioning.

A pang of jealousy hit her as she watched the male and Sheila together.

She walked away from them to the other side of the room, looking for a way out.

She pressed her hand to the partitioned walls made of a white, opaque material. Someone behind her startled her.

'I thought about doing that,' said the boy-man.

She spun around to face him.

'I'm Dom. What's your name?'

My name? Deep breath. My name. I know this.

'Anya.'

Dom nodded, watching her as she continued to press her hand to the panels.

'If they can put us in here,' she said, 'there's got to be a way out.'

'Makes sense,' said Dom.

She stole a glance at him.

His eyes pressed into every inch of the walls. He moved to the other side of the room and pushed on each panel.

The others mimicked his actions, and soon they were all feeling their way along the walls. But their efforts revealed nothing.

The Facility

They came together.

'Why are we here?' said Sheila.

'What's the last thing each of you remember?' said Dom.

Everyone's answer was the same: home. Only the town differed.

A noise outside the room caught Anya's attention. One of the panels slid to the side.

A new light stung her eyes. The sun. People dressed in white entered the room. Some wore medical suits and carried green medical kits. One woman, dark-skinned and in her forties, wore the most vivid green dress Anya had ever seen. Long and flowing with capped sleeves. She admired it until her painful eyes began to tear up.

'You must be disorientated,' said the woman in the green dress. 'You've been in here for two days.'

'And where's here?' said Dom, shielding his eyes.

'This is Praesidium.'

He jerked forward. 'I demand to know why you have locked us in this room.'

'Precautions, Mr Pavesi. You, in particular, carry diseases from the outside world. The Collective deemed it necessary to quarantine you for a short while.'

The woman pointed at Anya. 'This one comes with me.'

A man in white grabbed her arm. Dom blocked his attempts to move her.

'Where are you taking her?'

'She has been designated to work alongside me in the library,' said the woman.

Anya fought against the man, but he was too strong. He dragged her outside where her eyes stung worse. The man sat her in the back seat of an open-sided car.

'Sit with her,' he said to the woman in green, and climbed into the front.

The woman slid into the seat beside Anya, and the car moved off. Was it hovering? It felt too smooth to have tires.

Anya pressed her fingers to her eyes to stem the pain. But the tears kept coming.

She blinked a couple of times. The car passed by blurry square and rectangular shapes, blues and greens fluttering in the wind. Flags, perhaps?

Green grass lined the edges of road they were traveling on. White shapes, multicolored shapes. People. Their clothes.

Her memory of visiting Praesidium and the library were vague.

But Brookfield was stronger. *Jason.*

'I need to go home and find my brother. He'll be worried—'

'You *are* home, Anya,' said the woman. 'Please stay still.'

The man turned and handed the woman a silver box. 'She needs time to adjust.'

She opened it and Anya stared at the syringe. 'What's that for? Why am I here?'

'Hush, now,' said the woman, holding her arm steady.

Anya jerked back.

'Hold still. This will only hurt for a moment.'

'Please. I don't want—*Stop.*'

The woman jabbed the syringe into Anya's upper arm; the action release a memory of Dom injecting her in the same way.

'I don't want this.' She trailed off, feeling her eyes grow heavy.

'We're almost there. Just rest now.'

'Why do you placate her like that?' the man asked.

'I need her calm. They're more difficult to manage if they're agitated.'

Anya's tongue thickened. 'What did you give—'

'Something to help you to relax.'

Her eyelids drooped. The world around her slipped away. She closed her eyes for a second.

$$\Omega$$

Anya blinked twice and stared up at a dark ceiling. Around her were shelves stuffed with more books than she'd ever seen.

Praesidium's library.

But the room she was in was dark and cramped, unlike the open, light-filled space she remembered.

The dark-skinned woman hovered over her, smiling.

'Good. You're awake.'

Anya sat up too fast. Her head pounded. 'Who are you? What am I doing—'

'My name is Vanessa Walker. Take it easy. You're disorientated. You've been through quite an ordeal.'

Vanessa sat her up. She was on a bed.

'Take it slowly. It will take a day for you to adjust.'

Anya looked around. There was a desk in one corner with a reading lamp and a door ahead of her.

'Where am I?'

'We're underneath the library. This will be your home for a while.'

'Why? What am I doing here?'

Vanessa took Anya's hands.

'You're here to learn.' She smiled. Looked away. 'Well, that's what the Collective will think, anyway.'

She looked back. Her gaze had hardened. 'You'll start to remember things soon. Things that won't make a lot of sense to you.'

Anya tried to stand up, but Vanessa kept her seated with a firm hand on her shoulder.

'The Collective will only allow you to keep her memories for a short time. You will remember Arcis for as long as needed to observe you in your new surroundings. In a week they will strip every single memory from you and you'll start again. That's what happens with all the new Copies. Every new experience from that point will be your own.'

'Where are the others? From the room— '

'They were taken to other zones in Praesidium.' Vanessa's grip on her shoulder intensified. 'I need you to listen to me, to understand.'

'I don't understand.'

'I need *her* memories to help me find the others, before the Collective erases everything you know.'

'I don't remember anything.'

'You will, soon enough. I need the real Anya's memories from Brookfield.'

'But I'm Anya.'

'No, you're not. You're her Copy.'

Anya stared at Vanessa. 'Who are you?'

'I'm a friend of Grace and Evan Macklin. You're going to help get me out of here.'

52

Carissa opened the thin paperback that Original Vanessa had given to her. She brought the book up to her nose and inhaled.

Musty, slightly old.

She slammed the book closed. The words made perfect sense but the story lacked context. She hid the book in her waistband and frowned at the library. When Vanessa was finished with the newborns she would ask her to explain the story.

The open car passed by. Vanessa and the newborn sat in the back. Except for her white dress, she looked exactly like the original Anya.

If the newborn was here, that meant the real Anya was too. And June.

She tempered her excitement by thinking about something safe: playing with her orb. The Collective didn't need to know everything.

The newborn would remain in Vanessa's custody for the first week. The others who had arrived with her would be reassigned to tasks: guard duty, the nurturing center, training with the Inventor. Except for Dom.

That's what always happened with the newborn Copies.

The Collective were excited about the variation in this group.

Carissa hurried to the footage room in the east wing of the Learning Center, eager to see what had happened to the others in Arcis. She closed the door and stood in front of the large screen split into smaller ones. To her relief they had left it connected. She overheard Vanessa tell the group they'd been in Praesidium for a couple of days.

Truth was they'd only been here less than twenty minutes. Lies eased a newborn Copy in faster. After creation, they were too disorientated to hear the truth.

The machine was visible on one screen, no longer teeming with energy. The front section—the uploader—was dead; the second part—the scanner—offline. The third part contained stores of depleted bioprinter gel used in the process of replicating three-dimensional layers of living cells.

The participants were gone, all copied. All in Praesidium.

But three people had been left behind: injured, not dead. Anya's brother, Jason, was among them.

The machine always needed time to recalibrate, to replenish enough energy to make more gel for the bioprinter. But the Collective had broken rules, told the participants too much to get them into the machine.

A familiar voice came through her cerebral unit.

'173-C, we must dismantle Essention immediately and retrieve the copying equipment from Arcis. Remind the Inventor to seal off the town and cleanse it. The rebels will try to come for the others.'

'Understood, Quintus.'

The Facility

It was standard protocol to cleanse the site with gas, to kill anyone still in Essention. The town had served its purpose.

And that bothered Carissa.

She found the Inventor in the low-lit machine room that he rarely left.

'The Collective wishes to dismantle Essention,' said Carissa.

The Inventor smiled wearily. 'You could have told me that over the communication disc.'

Yes, she could have. But she had one thing to ask: something she didn't want recorded anywhere but in her memories, where she could erase it.

'I want you to delay the order.'

'Delay?' The Inventor lifted both brows. 'The machines are ready to go. We can dismantle the town now —'

'Delay the cleansing by an hour. Tell them the machines are broken.'

'But they're not—'

'Then break one. The people need time to escape Arcis and Essention.'

The Inventor stared at her. Then, he laughed and shook his head.

'It's beginning to make sense to me now.'

Carissa frowned at him. 'What is, Inventor?'

He stood up straight, arms folded, looking more alert than she'd ever seen him.

'Miss, I've been so misled by this place I never even noticed.'

'I don't understand…'

'I've waited a long time for one of you to finally develop a conscience.'

Eliza Green

Ω

Thanks for reading! I hope you enjoyed *The Facility*. Turn the page to read an excerpt of the exciting second book: *The Collective.*

The Collective - 1

Anya

Day One

Anya woke to a gentle humming noise. She sat up too fast, kicking off a deep pounding in her head. The last time she'd had a headache this bad was... never? The pain eased for a moment and her hands sank into a too-soft mattress as she looked around the darkened room. The noise was definitely nearby.

This wasn't Brookfield, nor was it her bedroom. So where was she? Her last movements were but a distant memory. She'd been in Brookfield with her brother, Jason. Both of them had been violently ill, unable to keep anything down. Her parents...

She pressed a fist to her mouth. Both murdered. The illness had followed some kind of explosion in the land beyond Brookfield.

The skin lesions on her arms and face during that time, blotchy and red, would be etched on her mind forever. Her pallid skin had glistened with sweat. Food and water had acted like poison.

Another memory hit her. Two men dressed in white protective suits waited by the door where she and Jason had collapsed. One of them had spoken in an icy tone.

'Don't worry. You're safe now.'

Had the men brought her here?

Anya shook away the last thought, too unclear for

her to say if it was real or a dream.

The humming got louder, sounding more like a song with short breaks than a random occurrence. Her eyes adjusted to the dark. A deep-blue carpet covered the floor and a pair of thick red velvet drapes loosely covered a window.

A sliver of brick peeked out from behind the curtains, and Anya shivered.

She looked around at the walls, adorned with painted landscapes set in gilt-edged picture frames. Nobody in Brookfield could afford this kind of opulence. Castles or mansions didn't exist in her world. So where the hell was she?

On the other side of the room were two white doors with gold handles, set into two facing walls. One door had to be the exit.

Her hands sank further as she shifted position on the squishy bed. The brick wall, coupled with her lack of knowledge as to where she was, sharpened her senses.

She ripped back the covers and glanced down at her clothes. A soft breath escaped her lips. She wasn't naked, but the leggings and camisole weren't hers.

She placed both feet on the floor. The details in the low-lit room opened up to her some more. A large chest of drawers was against one wall, and to its right, a chaise longue. A vanity table and a backless chair with a cream-cushioned seat and ornate edges sat between the drapes and chaise longue.

The drapes reminded her of another room, a large open space split by a similar velvet covering. The sound of crying babies had dominated that space. Was it a real place? A real memory of the towns, or somewhere else?

She walked over to the window and pulled the

The Facility

drapes back, feeling the weight of the fabric in her hand. Her fingertips grazed the brick wall.

The only place she'd been to outside of the towns was Praesidium, to visit the library filled with books, not babies. Anya shook her head to dislodge the memories she began to doubt were even hers.

The humming drew her attention away from the drapes. A chill shot up her spine as she searched for a floor lamp and groped for the switch.

Then she saw it: a chair on the other side of the room. And a blond-haired boy sitting in it.

Anya gripped the flimsy material of the camisole, which she was sure was transparent.

'Who... the hell are you? What are you doing in my room?'

The boy got to his feet and smiled at her.

More of a smirk than a smile.

He walked toward her forcing her to step back. He was a head taller than she was, with messy hair and the greenest eyes she'd ever seen. She tried not to blush as his hot gaze ran over her body.

'I asked you what you're doing here!' She backed up when he got closer.

He held his hands up, eyes sparkling with mischief. 'Relax. I'm supposed to be here. Did you sleep well?'

'Were you here the whole night?'

The boy's smile transformed into a grin. He was dressed in a loose pair of khaki trousers and white T-shirt —clothes that hid a lean body with a hint of muscle.

He nodded at the bed. 'You don't think that bed's just for you, do you?'

Panic swelled inside her. What exactly had happened last night?

Anya's uneasy gaze settled on the boy, stood too close for her to feel in control. 'Where are we? What is this place?' She stepped back.

The blond boy played it smart and stayed put, giving Anya the opportunity to claw back some dominance.

She placed him at around eighteen; a year older than her.

'You're different from the others,' he said. His grin dropped back to a smile.

'Different? What are you talking about?'

'They were more accepting of their fate. You, on the other hand, are feisty. I like feisty. It's a challenge.'

Anya hugged her body tighter. 'I'm not here to challenge you. And I'm not going to do whatever it is you have planned.'

The boy just looked at her.

'Why am I here?' Anya lifted her chin. 'What's your name?'

'Alex.'

'Well, *Alex*. It seems as if there's been some kind of mistake.' Her back hit the door and she groped for the handle. It opened into a large bathroom. 'I'm not supposed to be here.' Alex didn't move as she raced over to the second door.

She tried the handle, but it wouldn't open.

'Oh, you're supposed to be here,' said Alex.

She rattled it again. Nothing. 'You don't even know me. How do you know where I'm supposed to be?'

'I know your name is Anya Macklin. You're from a town called Brookfield and you have one brother, Jason. Your parents were killed recently, by the rebels.'

Anya spun around to face Alex. He stood near the vanity table, arms folded, and with a look that needed to be slapped off his face.

'How do you know all of this?'

'I'm supposed to know everything about you.'

Anya gave a short laugh. 'Yeah? You sound like a stalker.'

'Had I known you'd fight me on this, I'd have woken you up earlier, not let you sleep in. You looked so innocent with your eyes closed. You even snored a little.' Alex cocked his head to the side. 'If I knew there was a beast hidden beneath your vanilla exterior... This will be fun.'

'Stop talking to me like I'm up to speed. What will be fun? Why am I here?'

'Over the next week, you and I will get to know each other very well.'

Anya scowled, but her heart thrummed at the innuendo. 'Whatever you think is going to happen... well, it isn't. I don't even like you.'

Alex laughed. 'That's the beauty of this place. You don't have to like me. But you're attractive, so that helps.'

His gaze made her feel naked. She glanced at the chest of drawers. 'Helps with what? What do you think I'm here for?'

Alex took a step toward her, cutting off her means of escape. She pressed her back up against the locked exit.

He lunged for her and a scream bubbled up into her throat. She prepared to hit him when he grabbed her fist and pulled her into the center of the room. She stumbled a little as he twirled her around.

'Welcome to the Breeder program. You and I are going to have sex, and there's nothing you can do about it.'

Anya yanked her hand from his. 'Sex? In your

dreams.'

'It's not my dream. It's theirs.'

'Who?' When Alex didn't answer, she demanded, louder. 'I said, who?'

'We've been genetically matched to create the perfect child. It will happen whether you want it to or not.'

Alex's insistence stirred a memory of a boy forcing himself on her. Strawberry-blond hair and freckles; nobody she recognized. But it felt real. She would not let Alex intimidate her in the same way.

'I'm not having sex with you, Alex. So you can forget about it.'

'You don't have a choice.'

'Says who?'

The fire in Alex's eyes died a little. 'Says Praesidium.'

Anya's gaze roamed the room. 'Is that where we are? Why is the only window boarded up?'

'We're deep underground. Nothing to look out at. There's no point.'

A short laugh escaped her. 'Breeder program, though? You're joking, right?'

'Nope. It's why I'm here.' Alex stroked her arm. She shivered and jerked away from him. 'You and I are literally perfect for each other.'

The pain in his eyes hit her like a punch to the gut. This was real. Her shallow breaths winded her as her back touched the exit.

'I don't want to be here. I don't want to be part of a Breeder anything.' She locked eyes with Alex. The thought of kissing him, of having sex with a complete stranger, made her feel sick.

Alex followed her to the exit and leaned against it.

The Facility

His mood turned somber. 'Like I said, you don't have a choice.'

Anya hugged her middle. 'So you're going to force yourself on me? Is that how you get girls to like you?'

'Not force.' Alex's cockiness wavered for a moment. 'The program, it's designed to make us fall in love. At the end of the week, you won't have a choice.'

'I always have a choice and so do you.'

His jaw clenched.

Alex's vague answers irritated her. 'So what's this *Breeder* program for, exactly?'

'To create a genetically perfect child. I told you.'

'I am not having a baby. And I won't to be part of some stupid Breeder program that forces me to.'

Alex's tone softened. 'I wish it were that simple. It's not about what you want. It's about what the city needs.'

She couldn't believe she was having this conversation. 'There are other ways to do that. Artificial insemination, test tubes. These days, you don't have to be present for the task.'

'All fine examples. But the Collective is addicted to learning, and it has already learned everything it can from test tubes, from laboratory conditions. Now it's after results. It wants to see what happens when two genetically compatible people fall in love and conceive. It wants to learn how a baby created from love differs from one created in a lab. But what it really needs is the babies. So it can create something new. That's why you're here. You're not the first to be in this room and you won't be the last. The results vary from subject to subject.'

The Collective. She'd never heard of them, yet the name sounded familiar.

'So you're saying the Collective's watching now?'

Alex's gaze lingered on her covered chest. Anya folded her arms higher. 'I'm not here to be part of some pervert's experiment. And falling in love takes longer than a week, you know.'

Alex laughed. 'I'm not a pervert, but thanks.'

'Maybe you are. I haven't decided yet.' She stepped around him and went to the chest of drawers, looking around. 'Are there cameras in the room?'

'Just one.' He followed her and leaned in close to her ear. 'But I've worked out where the blind spots are.'

She tore her ear away from his hot breath. 'You're disgusting. Don't think I'm sneaking off with you so you can do what you like. I told you, I'm nobody's experiment.'

A vague memory of an atrium and a camera blind spot surfaced in her mind. She was standing beside a different boy, one with dark hair.

Alex's eyes darkened. 'Soon you won't have a choice.'

'Yeah? You keep saying that. And I keep telling you it's not going to happen. There will be no conception. I've no interest in touching you. And you won't touch me without my permission.' She opened one of the drawers and let out a breath when she saw a gray hoodie with a zipped front. She put it on and yanked the zip up fully before turning back to Alex.

His smile, sad not cocky, both surprised and disarmed her. 'I like your optimism and I've tried to fight them but when they inject us with Rapture, we won't be able to keep our hands off each other.'

Continue the Breeder Files series

The Collective (Book 2)
The Haven (Book 3)
The Beyond (Book 4)
The Rebels (Book 5) is *The Facility* retold from Dom and Warren's perspective.

Other Eliza Green Books
Genesis Code

A hunter seeking revenge. An alien dying to stop him. Could a government conspiracy put them both six feet under?

Investigator Bill Taggart's wife is missing. He can only find her by confronting the World Government's biggest fear: a dangerous alien species on a distant planet.

When his government sends him on a covert mission to deal with the threat, Bill ends up confronting one alien. He is disturbed that the natives are not what he expected, and may have nothing to do with his wife's disappearance.

Worried he's made a huge mistake, Bill reports back his findings, only for them to be ignored. No closer to finding his wife, the investigator stalls in his progress. But when he stumbles upon secrets that could destroy lives on both worlds, he is shocked into new action.

Caught between two sets of lies, Bill is no longer sure who he can trust. Can he stop chasing ghosts long enough to save humankind from the real enemy?

Get *Genesis Code*

Available in Digital and Paperback from Amazon

www.elizagreenbooks.com/genesis-code

Get a free story when you sign up to my mailing list. Check out **www.elizagreenbooks.com** for more information.

Duality (Standalone)

A delusional man caught between two realities. Two agencies fighting to access his mind. Could one false move trap him in the wrong existence?

Available in Digital and Paperback from Amazon

www.elizagreenbooks.com/duality

Kate Gellar Books

Eliza also writes fantasy under the pen name, Kate Gellar.

The Irish Rogue Series begins with *Magic Destiny*.

Book 1: A mysterious family bloodline. A novice witch without a clue. Can she get on the right side of magic before the underworld claims her?

Available in Digital and Paperback from Amazon

www.elizagreenbooks.com/magic-destiny

Rogue Magic (a free prequel to *Magic Destiny* when you sign up to my mailing list. Check out **www.kategellarbooks.com** for more information)

Word from the Author

Hey reader superstars! Thanks for checking out *The Facility*. It has all the science fiction flavor I love to inject into my books but with an added bonus: Dom and Anya. I absolutely loved writing those two. They were so much fun. And there's plenty more of their story left to tell.

The acknowledgements are all about the praise, so let me start with my sci-fi loving best friend (who prefers to remain nameless like the Copies), for beta reading the first draft of my book. And to John and Madeline for beta reading a later version and helping me to craft a better, sharper story.

Thanks to my editors, Andrew Lowe and Rachel Small, for copy editing and proofreading the earlier versions of my book. Your enthusiasm for my words rocks! I love working with you two. Andrew, I slack off way too much on Slack. Curses for introducing me to that platform.

Special thanks to Kate Tilton, my assistant, for keeping my writing schedule on track and for speeding up my painfully slow decision-making process. I live inside my head way too much. You get in there and shake everything loose.

Thanks to Lori Baird for coming up with the right name for one of my characters: Vanessa Walker. And to Vanessa Deneen and James Blaisdell for suggesting first and last name.

To Douglas F and Mike C for their awesome help in ironing out some of the sciency bits in the book. You guys know your stuff. My jaw literally dropped open a few times.

The cover? Wow. Love this one. Thanks to the team at Deranged Doctor Design.

My launch team? I couldn't do this without you. Seriously. You are helping in such a big way.

And love to you, my readers, whether you're new to my books or an established fan. None of this would happen without you. I feel a crazy desire to please you all.

Reviews! Please leave one if you enjoyed this book. Or if you didn't. It's your opinion. Every one of them counts.

Connect with Eliza Green

You can also find me on:

www.facebook.com/elizagreenbooks
www.instagram.com/elizagreenbooks
Goodreads – search for Eliza Green